Praise for C.K. Stead's short stories

'Elegant clarity.' Robert Gilmore, *Auckland Star*

'. . . unusual and challenging, a clear and welcome step beyond the patient liberal developments of much of our fiction.' Patrick Evans, *New Zealand Listener*

'Enjoyable, urbane, confident, witty and masculine, these stories are a breath of cool air through the female living-room of domestic fiction.' Jane Westaway, *New Zealand Herald*

'Seamless and civilised.' Norman Bilbrough, *New Zealand Books*

'Intellectually bold, emotionally liberal and watchful, technically adroit . . . The buoyancy and boyishness can soar into lyricism: "the old absurd ebullience, the unreasonable sense that life is its own reward."' David Hill, *New Zealand Listener*

'With wit and his customary disregard for what was and is now the fashionable conformity, with attention to illuminating detail and lovely writing, Stead's stories challenge and entertain.' Barbara Wall, *Timaru Herald*

'Suddenly what seemed to be interesting takes flight into the infinite white spaces, the blank page of the imagination, and life becomes art.' James McLean, *The Evening Post*

'Delightful, ingeniously comic, elegant and sensitive . . .' John Mellors, *London Magazine*

'Stead writes the way Torville and Dean skate. He makes it look so easy . . . Very few people can put together such luminous sentences.' Iain Sharp, *Sunday Star-Times.*

C.K. STEAD

THE NAME ON THE DOOR IS NOT MINE

STORIES NEW & SELECTED

ALLEN&UNWIN
SYDNEY·MELBOURNE·AUCKLAND·LONDON

First published in 2016

Copyright © C.K. Stead 2016

Derrida, Jacques. Translated by Gayatri Chakravorty Spivak. Line from *Of Grammatology. Corrected Edition.* on page 13 © 1974, 1976, 1997 The Johns Hopkins University Press. Reprinted with permission of Johns Hopkins University Press.

Eliot, T.S. Lines from 'The Waste Land' on page 28 from *Selected Poems of T.S. Eliot.* Reprinted with permission of Faber and Faber Ltd, 2005.

Perec, Georges. Translated by Andrew Leak. Lines from 'A Man Asleep' on pages 30–1 copyright © 1967 Editions Noel. Translation © 1990 by William Collins Sons & Co., Ltd. American edition published by David R. Godine, Publisher, Inc. Reprinted with permission of the publisher.

Every effort has been made to obtain permission to use copyrighted material in this book.

Allen & Unwin
Level 3, 228 Queen Street
Auckland 1010, New Zealand
Phone: (64 9) 377 3800
Email: info@allenandunwin.com
Web: www.allenandunwin.co.nz

Allen & Unwin
83 Alexander Street
Crows Nest NSW 2065
Australia
Phone: (61 2) 8425 0100
Email: info@allenandunwin.com
Web: www.allenandunwin.com

A catalogue record for this book is available from the National Library of New Zealand

ISBN 978 1 877505 81 2

Cataloguing-in-Publication details are available from the National Library of Australia www.trove.nla.gov.au

ISBN 978 1 760295 36 3

10 9 8 7 6 5 4 3 2 1

MIX
Paper from responsible sources
FSC
www.fsc.org   FSC® C009448

The paper in this book is FSC® certified. FSC® promotes environmentally responsible, socially beneficial and economically viable management of the world's forests.

To O, C and M again:
the olives are almost over
and the future is now.

Contents

Stories in this collection have appeared in *Arete*, the *Kenyon Review*, *Landfall*, *The London Magazine*, *New Writing 6* (British Council), *Sport* and *Griffith Review*. 'Last season's man' won the *Sunday Times/ E.F.G. Private Bank* short story prize for 2010. Earlier versions of several appeared in two collections—*Five for the Symbol*, and *The Blind Blonde with Candles in her Hair*, both long out of print.

A small apartment in the rue Parrot

I

HELEN WHITE WAS SITTING on the grass with her back against a tree just inside the iron gates of the Luxembourg Gardens, eating an ice cream she had bought from the vendor's cart out there on the street, and dreaming of home. Like (she thought) 'Drake was in his hammock and a thousand miles away, slung a'tween the round-shot in Nombre Dios Bay, and dreaming all the time of Plymouth Ho'. Nombre Dios must be Name of God. Funny, she'd never thought of that. When she'd sung it as a child she'd thought it had something to do with number. Nombre Dios. Drake had God's number. But home for her had not been Plymouth Ho and was not at this moment a thousand miles away. It had been in Oxford, where her mother had been a paediatrician at the Radcliffe Infirmary and her father a Fellow of St John's. And now she supposed it must be Norfolk, where the parents lived, semi-retired but still both professionally busy, in a beautiful old mill house with wooden beams inside and white weatherboards out, and the mill stream running by under willows, and with a wood, or perhaps it was a spinney or copse, of poplars at the back. (A spinney of poplars. A copse of poplars. She tried them both for sound and liked them equally.) She had gone to school in Oxford, and then to the university, St Anne's College, and had flourished, she thought—everyone thought—until her mind became over-filled with poems, including one by Edward Thomas called 'Adlestrop'. It was not just the poem that became an obsession but the word. Adlestrop. It represented Englishness, the country rail-stop in late June surrounded by willows in full leaf, with meadows and pasture and hay and a blackbird; and then, as in the Hitchcock movie, the just one bird became all the birds of Oxfordshire and Gloucestershire—a congregation of polluters of silence, which was what birds were if you cared about it, if your ears were sensitive. And if you said the word Adlestrop to yourself too often the birds got more confused and the scene mistier until everything was lost and there was just ADLESTROP, too many syllables fighting for the light—sinister, secretive, dangerous, and perhaps hinting at something you did not want to know, ever . . .

Time to change the subject. So she went in her head to Gerard Manley Hopkins, always a comfort, 'Margaret, are you grieving over golden-grove unleaving?' Gerry Hopkins, the unhappy priest of so long ago, who 'caught this morning morning's minion' and wrote about the cutting down of the Binsey poplars at Oxford ('my aspens dear whose airy cages quelled') which had, since his time, grown again and could be seen on the walk across the port meadow from Southmoor Road to a pub called the Trout . . .

Oxford where she had encountered the philosopher Roger Scruton with his idea that there were two kinds of metaphysics, descriptive and revisionary, and she had tried, in an essay for her tutor at St Anne's, to apply the same distinction to poetry, making Keats the 'descriptive' poet and Blake the 'revisionary'. This was not the . . .ake who was in his hammock and a thousand miles away, but William Blake in his London garden naked with Mrs Blake pretending to be Adam and Eve. Two of them, Mr and Mrs. The Naked Blakes. Aching for Eden, and Blaked.

The ice cream was eaten and she would have liked another but lay on her back listening to the traffic and looking through the trees at the sky, like the sky at Adlestrop, with small white cloudlets, floating. I could be happy there, she thought. It was better to be Keats than Blake, Keats than Shelley, Kelly than Sheets. And when was it she had first encountered that book by Derrida and the sentence that had taken hold of her, demanding that she understand it though she didn't and couldn't, and yet she had wrestled with it? She said it over: 'We are dispossessed of the longed-for presence in the gesture of language by which we attempt to seize it.' Her boyfriend in Oxford had said this was a description of a failed rugby tackle. His name was Hugo and he came to Oxford from Rugby, and played it. He had tried to keep her there, in Oxford, but Derrida had won, had brought her to Paris, though he was already dead, had been dead ten years. In fact on 9 October, only a few months away, it would be a decade exactly. Derrida a decade dead. She'd thought she would be nearer to his mind, the French mind, if she put herself inside the French language, but perhaps she should have taken his Algerian childhood into account and gone there. Would that have helped, nothing would have helped, Derrida was like his name, or a nursery rhyme, something you just had to struggle with and make the best of, like the refrain of a song by Shakespeare, da derri-*da* down dilly, and da derri-*da*.

Thinking this in a kind of silent singalong she drifted asleep for a few minutes and dreamed she was in a room with high sash windows wide open and white curtains billowing in a faint breeze. Beyond was the green of trees and lawns and the mild thwack and knock of tennis. She was dressed all in white and so was Hugo, who was also Professor Max Jackson; and perhaps she and Max had just made love because she was telling him he did not know what it was to feel shame. He said (and now it was definitely Max) this was nonsense everyone knew Shame, Shame was everybody's friend, and she'd had an answer for that, perhaps about degrees of it, but as she woke she couldn't remember what it was, only that it was a good one, unanswerable . . .

What she needed now was to be conscious, in the Gurdjieff sense of consciousness, which included focus, finding her centre. Professor Jackson—Max, as she was allowed to call him—had agreed to come with her to Fontainebleau-Avon, where they would go on a little organised tour to the house and gardens that had been Gurdjieff's Institute for the Harmonious Development of Man. Max had sent her a nice little message in reply to her letter, agreeing to meet her at the Gare de Lyon . . .

No need for shame. She must be mindless, centred; must pass through the gateless gate and walk freely between heaven and earth. She must work towards Zen, towards enlightenment, towards Satori . . .

II

HELEN WAITED IN THE forecourt of the Gare de Lyon, keeping her eye on the clock in its tower, on its beautiful, faintly blue face with the ornate numbering. The train for Fontainebleau-Avon would go at two minutes past the hour. It was twenty minutes to. She was early. The Professor—Max—would be late—or not come at all. He'd said he would come but she was sure—almost sure—he would not. She repeated Zen lessons.

'Watch whatever you say, and whatever you say, practise it.

'Do not regret the past. Look to the future.

'Have the fearless attitude of a hero, and the loving heart of a child.'

She wondered whether she was confusing herself by mixing Gurdjieff with Zen; yet they seemed to go together, not to conflict.

She wondered what the Buddha had meant when he said he saw Nirvana as a nightmare of daytime.

It was ten to the hour, then five to . . . No, Max would not come. She had bought two tickets . . .

She tried to not think, to achieve mindlessness, but her eyes were on the tower, on the blue-faced clock up there, waiting to hear it strike. Would she go without him?

But here he was, beside her, come from the other direction, the wrong, the unexpected one. 'Quick,' she said. 'Downstairs . . .'

He was apologising for being late. And, 'Tickets,' he said.

'I have them,' she said. 'Quickly, Max.'

They boarded the train just as the whistle was blown. They found a double seat and dumped themselves down, panting. 'I'm sorry,' he said again.

She had collapsed halfway over him, holding him by the shoulder. 'Don't be sorry.' And she pecked his cheek as she pulled herself into a sitting position. 'I told myself you'd be late. I knew you'd be dithering right up to the last minute.'

He didn't argue with that, and they sat, recovering, composing themselves. She pointed to the bag at her feet. A baguette stuck out from its top and there were shapes, two bottles, other things . . . 'Picnic,' she said.

He nodded, smiling. 'Nice. I came in such a rush I brought nothing but a newspaper.'

'A newspaper,' she said. 'That's important.'

'In case we need to know what day it is?'

'Yes that kind of thing. And what's going on.'

Several kilometres clicked by. Feeling his warm thigh touching hers, she asked what Max was short for.

'Maxwell,' he said. And sang, 'Maxwelton's braes are bonny where early fa's the dew.'

'Oh, you sing in tune,' she said. 'And a nice—what are you—tenor?'

'When my wife's feeling playful she calls me Maximus.'

'Your wife . . .'

'My ex. My sometime. My sometimes . . .'

'Are you getting a divorce?'

'No, I don't think so. It hasn't been mentioned.'

Helen stared, and he added, 'Not to me. She lives upstairs. I have the ground-floor flat.'

'She's famous,' Helen said.

'Yes I guess. Famous in France.'

'Which is where we are.'

He touched her arm. 'Good point, thank you for reminding me.'

'Famous for Flaubert.'

'As his editor. The Pleiade edition.' He smiled. 'She's the senior professor in our marriage.' It seemed he didn't mind.

'And she calls you Maximus.'

'Sometimes, yes. Playful, you know. Or displeased. Sometimes both.'

'Max, Maxwell, Maximus,' Helen said. 'It's like conjugating a verb.'

She told him about her recent discovery of Zen Buddhism. 'It's my new medication. I'm cutting down on the lithium. More Zen, less lithium.'

He asked was that safe and she said it was. She thought it was.

'Instead of Gurdjieff?'

'Not instead of. In addition to.' And more kilometres clicked by.

He held up his newspaper which had a front-page shot of the

French President in New York. Hollande had been in trouble lately. His current partner, Valérie Trierweiler, had kicked him out and written a book about his infidelity with a French actress.

Helen said, 'I don't like him. I'm on Valérie's side.'

'Trierweiler? She's a very angry woman.'

'He lied to her.'

'About Julie Gayet. Of course he did.'

'Why "Of course"?'

'Because she's a very angry woman.'

'But he'd been unfaithful.'

Max shrugged. 'So he had something to hide.'

He told her that when he was young there had been another socialist President—François Mittérand. France was still testing nuclear bombs in the Pacific. Greenpeace had a ship, the *Rainbow Warrior*—had she heard about that?

'I think maybe . . .' she said. 'They were protesting . . .'

'Yes they were, and French secret agents blew up their ship—sank it in Auckland Harbour. I was a student at the time. I remember hearing the big boom, and then a few minutes later a second one, even bigger. It was late at night. I said to the girl I was in bed with that we were being attacked. I meant it as a joke, but it was true—sort of true. Most of the agents got away but two were caught.'

He told her the story—their conviction for manslaughter and how after that the Mittérand government put economic pressure on New Zealand to release them.

'After a couple of years the New Zealand government agreed they could serve out the rest of their sentence on an island in French Polynesia. As soon as they were there, France said they were unwell and had to be brought home.'

Their train ran on through the outskirts of Paris, past tall suburban houses and little tree-shaded villas, on, out into green countryside. Helen was quiet a while, and then asked, 'Was she nice?' He was unsure what she meant, and she said, 'When the bombs went off—the girl you were in bed with.'

'Oh . . . Yes, she was nice.' And then, 'Very nice.'

'Where is she now?'

'Where indeed, good question. Where do the dead go?'

'She died?' Helen looked at him, frowning, trying to show the concern she felt for him, for his loss.

'Oh, it wasn't a tragedy,' he said. 'I mean it was, but not for me. We'd long since gone our separate ways. She married, had two children, and then she died in her forties. Cancer.'

The train rattled and clacked, rattled and clacked. Helen closed her eyes, listening. 'Did you know,' she said, 'that during the Battle of Waterloo a British soldier told the Duke of Wellington they had Napoleon in their gun-sights, and the Duke said it wasn't proper in war for commanders to be shooting at one another.'

Max laughed. 'No I didn't know that.' After a few seconds he said, 'Someone picked off Lord Nelson. He was a commander.'

'Different rules,' she suggested.

'The Navy, d'you think?'

She told him a story about a young Zen monk called Kitano who studied Chinese calligraphy and poetry, and grew exceptionally skilful at it, until his teacher praised him so highly Kitano thought, if I go on like this I'll be a poet, not a Zen teacher, so he gave up and never wrote another poem.

Max nodded slowly, absorbing this. 'Is that a message for me?'

She said, 'I don't know.' And then, 'Is it?'

Helen had come to his room because she'd found a poem he'd published long ago when he was first in Paris. He said, 'I gave up poetry in favour of being a professor—is that what you mean?'

'Only you can say.'

'Only I can say what?'

'If the cap fits.'

He thought about that and said, 'No it doesn't. The young

monk—his was an act of will . . . A decision . . . A decision to stop writing poems.'

'Decisions are not always conscious, are they?'

His shrug, she thought, was irritable, but he didn't argue.

At the Fontainebleau-Avon station a minibus was waiting to gather those enrolled for the Gurdjieff tour. They drove straight to the building that had housed Gurdjieff's Institute for the Harmonious Development of Man, three storeys and quite grand, in beautiful grounds, now a block of private apartments. Gurdjieff's home, a big wooden house, was next door. This whole complex was where the great man's devotees had come to live under his command, to learn 'wakefulness' rather than the 'sleep' which was, he'd taught, the norm for human lives. They were to become 'conscious', to rid themselves of wasteful and negative emotions, to eschew regret, to shed 'personality', and to make their life's work the creation of a 'soul'. You were not born with a soul, but you could create one. That was the 'work'.

The tour commentary was partly a lesson. They had to imagine it all happening within these walls—the importance placed on very early rising, on chores and menial duties, on preparing meals, drawing water from the well, milking the cow, feeding the hens and finding their eggs; bee-keeping, and especially gardening; and then, in the evening, listening to a talk by the Master which might be on any of his favourite themes— the law of three, the law of seven, the four bodies of man (carnal, natural, spiritual, divine), even 'Beelzebub'; and then would come the thrilling Sufi dancing, and the music.

They were shown the stairs where the writer Katherine Mansfield, one of the Master's better-known devotees, had had the tubercular haemorrhage that killed her. As the group moved on Max hung back at the bottom of the oak-brown stairway with its heavy banister, and Helen waited for him at a discreet distance, thinking she was respecting an observance; but when he turned and hurried to catch up she saw he'd been checking his cell phone.

It was very hot and they walked in the extensive gardens, rested under trees, listened to further accounts of the Institute's way of life; and then they were set free there to roam, to eat and drink whatever they'd brought for refreshment. Helen found a sort of bower in the long grass under the shade of a tree, and opened her bag, taking out two cans of fruit juice, the baguette, which she broke into pieces, ham, cheese, tomatoes.

Max lay in the grass, propped on one elbow. 'What are you thinking?' she asked, hoping it might be about the Zen monk, Kitano, so skilled when young, who stopped being a poet.

'Nothing. Not thinking.' He took a bite of the crusty bread. 'Just enjoying this good bread. I should have brought something.'

'You're here,' she said. 'That's your contribution. Imagine if I'd brought a picnic and you hadn't come.' As she said it, she did imagine him *not* there—a space, an emptiness. It frightened her, because for a moment there was a space, just pressed-down grass and the trunk of a tree, where Max had been. She shivered. Perhaps he had no soul, it had not yet been created, and she had seen its absence. But then who had written that poem she so much admired? Where was the youthful Max's soul hiding? She would make it her project to find it, to bring it out.

When they'd finished eating he sat up and brushed the crumbs away, then settled down again, his head resting on her thigh.

'Maximus,' she said, and giggled.

So they both dozed for a while in the warmth of summer and the scent of grass and flowers, but out of the sun, until the phone in his pocket buzzed him awake. He sat up, looking at it, then stood up. 'I'll have to take this . . . My wife . . .'

As he walked to put a little distance between them she heard him say, '*Ça va?* How are things?' When he spoke next he was out of range. She could pick up only a word here and there.

LOUISE WAS ASKING WHETHER he could do a little bit of research for her. 'There's a passage where Hélène Cixous compares Flaubert's style in *L'Éducation sentimentale* with Clarice Lispector's in I'm not sure what. Possibly *A Breath of Life*. It's a male–female thing of course, and I can't find it in the books I have here.' She thought he might call in at the Sainte- Geneviève for her. 'I'd be so grateful, darling.'

He took a deep breath. He should not have taken the call. 'There's always a queue.'

'Not at this time of year, Max. And I can't get away from here today. The kids are home early.'

'Tomorrow I could do it.'

'Tomorrow I could do it myself. I need it now.'

Only a wife would press like this—or a husband of course. Were they married or not? 'Not sure,' he said. 'I don't think I can . . .'

'Come on, Max. What's the problem? It's only a few blocks away.'

'Not from here it's not.'

'Where are you?'

Unable to think of a better answer, he said, 'Out of town.'

'Really? Out—how far?'

'Fontainebleau-Avon.'

'Why? What on earth are you doing?'

He thought of telling her that he and she now occupied separate apartments and separate beds precisely so that this kind of inquisition, of either party by the other, would not be necessary. But no, that would suggest he had something to hide, something to be ashamed of.

He said, 'I'm learning about Gurdjieff. Did you know Katherine Mansfield couldn't decide whether he looked like a wise man or a carpet seller?'

A pause, and then, 'No, Max. I didn't know that.'

'And then she died. Right here. I've seen the very spot. It's a staircase.'

After a long silence she said, 'So you can't hunt out that quote for me.'

'I'll do my best, Louise. Depends on the trains. But if I can I will. I'll phone you tonight.'

Another silence. He knew he should end this conversation but he didn't want to just cut her off. 'So . . .' he said.

'So are you going to tell me what you're doing?' And then, 'Who you're with?' And then, 'I know I have no right to ask.'

'I don't mind your asking. I only mind the conclusions you'll jump to. I'm with a student.'

Louise was on to it at once. 'The one who writes you letters?'

'*One* letter—yes, that one. And how do you know that?'

'You left it on your table.'

'And you read it.'

'No, Max, you know I wouldn't do that. It was open. I saw her name at the bottom of the page—Helen someone.'

'Of Troy. Yes, that's her.'

'You're a fool, Maximus.'

'She's English—from Oxford. St Anne's. She's had a few problems. She needs help—a sympathetic ear, that's all.'

'At Fontainebleau-Avon?'

'It's the summer vac isn't it? We had a bit of a picnic.'

'What kind of problems?'

'Mental . . .'

'Max . . .'

'I don't mean she's mad . . .' As he said this he remembered she'd said that's exactly what she was: mad; bipolar.

'And you're with this disturbed young woman . . .'

'She's not disturbed . . .'

'Learning about that fraudulent Russian . . .'

'Gurdjieff—was he Russian?'

'Armenian mother. Greek father.'

Oh for god's sake, how did she know *that*? He wouldn't ask. 'I'm sure it sounds odd, Louise . . .'

But there was a click and she was gone.

THEY WERE TAKEN NEXT to the Gurdjieff grave in the local cemetery. It was a large level raised oblong in grass, with a border of flowers and a massive rough-cut stone at either end. There was a small stone seat where you could think about the man in the ground under you, and his philosophy and what he meant when he said 'I cannot die.'

The guide explained that you could spread a cloth on the grave and it would absorb something of the *kaife* that would come up through the ground from his body—the emanation of his great spirit.

Helen told Max that devotees would sometimes bring cloths ornately woven in bright colours for this purpose; and one or two of their group now did have rather superior-looking pieces of coloured silk which they laid out reverently. Helen had only a fine, beautifully laundered and ironed cotton handkerchief, which she spread on the grass.

'They could have buried a horse in there,' Max said, looking at the size of the grave. 'Even lying on its side.'

While Helen listened to the guide, Max wandered about among the graves. Only a few metres away from Gurdjieff he found Katherine Mansfield. The inscription said 'Katherine Mansfield / Wife of John Middleton Murry'. It didn't mention that she was a writer.

There were a few delays on the line and the journey back to the Gare de Lyon took more than an hour. It was too late for a visit to the Sainte-Geneviève library. Max's sunburned face was hot. His head throbbed faintly. He wanted to lie down again and go to sleep. He felt he'd been foolish, and yet he argued with himself. Why had it been foolish to go on this expedition? As he'd said to Louise—it was summer wasn't it? Vacation time? The sun was shining, the flowers were out, the countryside was lovely. What harm had been done?—unless it was harm to his wife's French bourgeois sense of propriety; to the necessary grandeur of the professorial role. Yes, that was it, undoubtedly.

Louise had unsettled him, but when Helen told him she lived in the rue Parrot, just a short walk from the station, and suggested he should come in and have a cup of tea—or even a bowl of pasta if he felt like staying a while—he said, very properly, even primly, tea would be nice.

The apartment, five floors up in a rickety lift, was very small, long and narrow like a railway carriage, with two windows on one side, a divan-bed on the other against the wall, a small table and two chairs at the far end, an alcove kitchen at the other, and a cubicle *douche et WC*. 'Dinky', she called it, and it was, especially with her decorations, which he was invited to admire—a modest couple of book shelves, sea shells, a single Roman tile, a Japanese glass paperweight, a framed photo of a mill house and mill stream with trailing willows, and one of what appeared to be an English country rail-stop with the word ADLESTROP.

There was no space for easy chairs, and hardly room to pass one another between the windows and the divan, which, though placed longwise, was quite broad. In fact, with its bright orange cotton cover, the divan (where he imagined she slept) dominated the room and made everything else subsidiary. The windows, pushed open, looked out on the Mansard roof, ending in the rainwater guttering, and beyond that, five storeys down, was the rue Parrot.

Helen pushed him into a sitting position on the divan, took three steps into the kitchen to fill the kettle and switch it on, and three steps back to dump herself down beside him. She's very vigorous, he thought.

'Come on,' she said. 'Relax. You're tense. Look at you.' And then, laughing, 'Relax, Max! *Relax!*'

Her hands were on his face. 'Close your eyes. That's right.' She ran fingers delicately over his eyes and up into his hair; then down over his ears to neck and shoulders.

'Lie face down,' she said. 'Let me give you a massage.'

He allowed himself to be pushed forward on to his face. She lifted his lower legs up on to the divan, pulled his shirt up from under his belt and began to massage his back.

The kettle whistled and she paused long enough to turn it off.

Now she climbed on to the divan with him, knelt beside him, then straddled him, and applied strong hands, strong fingers, to his back, to every inch of it, to his neck and up into his scalp.

'I like this,' he said, surrendering.

'Of course you do. Everybody does.'

Helen's hands moved up to the back of his neck again. 'This is beautiful,' she said. 'You're relaxing now. I can feel it here. And here.'

He drifted, and for a brief time slept, then woke feeling her no longer massaging but lying half over him, her limbs loose. Perhaps she too was asleep. Yes, she was sleeping—he could tell by the even, just-audible sound of her breathing, with a small whistle at the end of each breath. He could feel her breasts against his back and wondered why he hadn't noticed them. They felt quite large. They must be the broad kind, not pointy.

He was thinking in a rather uncertain way of the Gurdjieff doctrine that ordinary lives were a 'sleep' and that 'wakefulness' had to be worked for, worked *at*. And then of Shakespeare's 'sleep that knits up the ravelled sleeve of care'—which merged into what were really just words—misty, mysterious, meaningless . . .

Then he really did sleep.

THAT NIGHT MAX WALKED all the way back to the 5th arrondissement. A light rain was falling, but he pressed on. He was happy. Summer was making strategic advances through streets and gardens, and Paris was bright and loud, busy and pleased to be Paris—'Nobody's dream but your own' as he had written in that long-ago poem that had brought Helen as a visitor to his room —but everyone's dream too.

III

AUTUMN ARRIVED ON TIME, and the two trees in the courtyard Max Jackson looked out on turned quite a showman's orange-yellow or yellow-gold, depending on what the light was doing—and it was all, as any photographer would tell you, a collaboration with the light. Still at this date, the first day of November and a Saturday, there were, among the leaves, a few pallid green survivors, brave rather than bravura and soon to die. It was a collaboration too, quite as significantly, with the wind, which came and went, or refused to come, sending down (or not) showers of orange-yellow gold over his small garden and over the paved (he would have called it cobbled—they were lumpy enough underfoot, though not true cobbles) courtyard, the protected enclosure that had all the secret charm of Paris as it had appeared to him, and had captured him, in the uncertainty of his youth. There was, erratically, sunshine too, but it was the first sun of autumn rather than the last of summer, with little of summer left in it, hardly a hint, only a memory. It was the sun of the northern hemisphere November, a shadow of its former self.

As he watched from his window the casual gardener employed by the Syndic was sweeping leaves from the paved area with a broom, but he was armed also with a noisy blower (no modern gardener is without one) with which he would soon blow leaves out of the garden beds and hedges. But here in this sheltered courtyard his blower was the worst of winds. Out in the boulevards, where the real wind blew, the fall was more advanced, and the leaves, most often plain brown, were showering down and clattering along the pavements faster than the men in their sweeping machines could keep ahead of them. The trees in the Luxembourg Gardens had lost their summer shapes and the reflecting pool of the Medici Fountain was so cluttered it reflected nothing but its own failure.

Sitting there in the window embrasure Max was invaded by a particular memory of his early days in Paris. He had been there perhaps a year, much of which had been spent hunting for street names and managing maps, often in wind and rain, getting lost, finding his way, congratulating himself for having done well or cursing himself for failure. This particular day it was autumn, November like today, fine but cold, and already the drunks and homeless ones were lying down over the pavement grilles to warm themselves in the air coming up from the Metro; and, as Max was walking towards the river in the morning sun, he found himself wondering what had changed, what was the different (and wonderful) feel about this day? It was then he recognised that he was walking freely, not checking constantly where he was, because he knew and didn't need even to think about it. Paris, or this part of it, had become his city, and he was its inhabitant. And just then, as he was crossing the Pont Sully from left to right bank, he looked downriver and there was Notre Dame in full morning sun, with its twin towers, its iron spire and flying buttresses, looking like the great ship of souls sailing towards him up the river. It took him by surprise and he was faint with the beauty of it, and of the city, and had to stop and lean on the balustrade and stare. He tried to think of a French poem to suit the moment, knowing there must be many, but could only bring to mind Apollinaire's 'The Mirabeau Bridge', which didn't match the place and the time. So he quoted to himself T.S. Eliot's lines about the Thames and they seemed to fit perfectly because the trees over the Seine were also shedding their tent of leaves:

The River's tent is broken. The last fingers of leaf
Clutch and sink into the wet bank. The wind
Crosses the brown land unheard. The nymphs are departed.

He was, that day, already in love with Louise, who was resisting him with a sort of French—or perhaps it was just female—ambiguity and cunning. The problem, insofar as she was willing or able to make it clear, was his foreignness, his 'Britishness'. It made no difference to tell her he was not British, he was a New Zealander. And when he tried to explain the differences, their complexities and declensions, she said he was being needlessly subtle and essentially boring—and he thought so too.

'One day you will want to go back there,' she said. 'Or to Britain.'

'Only if you were with me,' he'd said. It was a commitment.

The gardener had gone now, taking his portable wind with him, and Max moved to sit outdoors in the courtyard as if to encourage the sun, as if to tell it not to be faint-hearted or sorry for itself: there was honour in old age. Like a true Frenchman he took *Le Monde* to read out there. Today it was featuring the tortures the ISIS militants had inflicted on their Western captives before releasing those for whom the governments of Spain and France had (though denying it) paid a ransom, and beheading one by one, and by hand, the two Americans and two British whose governments had announced that no blood money would change hands.

In the section on the arts and culture he read that Patrick Modiano, France's new Nobel laureate, was unknown and unread in his own country. Was this true? Surely no longer. The bookshops now were full of his work, displayed with their red banners announcing a Nobel Prize-winner. Louise, who had read most of them, thought the award spoke for intelligibility against the old Nouvelle Vague novelists and their apologists. Enough of Claude Simon (who had received France's last Nobel for Literature). Enough of Alain Robbe-Grillet, and Roland Barthes, and long live the clarity, limpidity, transparency for which French literature had always been celebrated. Louise saw it as an indirect vote for her hero, Flaubert, whom these 'New Wave' novelists and critics had disparaged.

Max moved on to the 'economy and enterprise' pages, where a philosopher, Pierre Zaoui, drew subtle distinctions not only between a *crisis* and a *catastrophe* in the money world but between two kinds of *catastrophe*—the 1929 jumping-out-of-windows kind in which even wealthy families lost everything, and the less serious kind in which life went on for the rich, whose loss was a reduction of their wealth, not an end to it. In support of all this, Machiavelli was quoted, and also Nietzsche. This piece, it seemed to Max, was not so much high finance as highbrow finance, a kind of brain-straining and heartless entertainment: 'Money' for *Le Mondeans*.

The wind was really blowing now, even here in the shelter of the courtyard, making it difficult to keep the paper together, and Max moved indoors. He should be thinking about the *Habilitation* jury he was to be part of at the Sorbonne, and the presentation on the subject of British Commonwealth poetry by the candidate they were to examine; but, standing at the window again, he allowed his mind to drift back to the comfort of that long-ago November when his epiphany on a bridge over the Seine had made him feel for a moment that he had become a Parisian, a true *flâneur*, and that his times of trouble were over. It was the mood in which he had written that long-ago poem Helen White had discovered in an old literary journal, and which had brought her to his office door to tell him how marvellous it was, how magical and mysterious, urging him to become the poet he had once been, and write more. Where was she now? There had been that day with her, and its strange ending of massage and pasta in her little apartment in the rue Parrot. Recently she had written him a small note in somewhat crazed handwriting, telling him she had shifted to be nearer the university and giving him her new address in the rue Mouffetard—a message to which, warned off by Louise, he had not responded. But he thought of her.

IV

HELEN TOOK THE METRO from Cardinal Lemoine to Sèvres Babylone, changed and took the line north towards Porte de la Chapelle, changed at Saint-Lazare, and went two stops to the place de Clichy. She had been reading a novel by Georges Perec about a young man, a student in Paris, who decides to drop out of everything—the university, exams, friends, ambition, work, play—in effect to go to sleep, to stop living. It fascinated her because it was the reverse of what Gurdjieff advocated—that you must work hard, making a continuous effort to be awake, to be aware of every passing moment, and thus to create a soul. It was the story of willed depression—the deliberate welcoming of what sometimes enveloped her even while she tried to fight it off. It was an account, a fiction, of a young man working not to create a soul but to be rid of one.

In the end he fails to achieve what he's aiming for, the ultimate indifference. His project has been a kind of egotism, a wish to be special, especially blighted, cursed, cast out, reviled. He is none of these things, and he tells himself, at last, to stop talking to himself like a man in a dream. 'You are not the nameless master of the world, the one on whom history has lost its grip, the one who no longer feels the rain falling.'

The book ends with this awakening, which comes to him on a rainy day in the place de Clichy, and that was why Helen, with what she recognised was a dogged literalness, was going there today, when the rain was falling.

She stood on a corner in the rain, enjoying the sound of its myriad small feet on her umbrella, its coldness when it found its way on to her right arm, and the feeling that now and then it was putting fine jewels in her hair, while she tried to think herself into the state of mind of Perec's student, coming back into the world after a long self-imposed absence: waking to the discomforts and pleasures of existence, as if for a long moment they had gone away.

And what came to her first, sharp and clear, at this moment at the busy intersection of avenue de Clichy and boulevard des Batignolles, was the fantasy that she might be pregnant, and that she did not know for sure whether she would want it to be the Professor's child or Hugo's. The idea of the pregnancy did not distress her, but she was bothered by the question, which of them, Max or Hugo, should it belong to: either or neither—or both? She could not think of an answer to this; but she knew she could think of ways of writing about it in the book she was calling (though she had now left that address) *A small apartment in the rue Parrot*.

And now the rain fell less like a fine mist, more heavy and persistent, the cars splashed through puddles, the air grew colder, and she went back down into the Metro, to its warm dry air, and the smell of rubber on metal that always reminded her of the excitement of being in Paris for the first time.

'It was the best of times, it was the worst of times'

THE LORIKEETS ON THE RAIL wake me. I'm aware of them before I wake properly. They begin quietly as if they're making small talk and waiting patiently. I suppose they get noisier as they become hungry and quarrelsome, but it's hard not to believe they're slowly lifting the decibel level in order to get me up.

I roll out on to the carpet. That's a start. I'm grateful to the lorikeets. I don't like to sleep late, but when I'm alone . . .

And that hits me hard this morning. Consciousness—coming to it. Memory. She. They. I don't want to think about it. The purpose is what counts. Give it a capital. The Purpose. It consists of piles of typed sheets on the big table, scribbled all over with corrections and tidied on either side of the portable. Drafts. Redrafts and revisions. Everyone used to tell me I ought to buy a word processor. Now no one tells me that, or anything. I see no one. I came here to be alone. I have the lorikeets.

I go to the balcony. They shift to left and right along the rail, making room for me. I think I can distinguish the boss pair—the couple who claim proprietary rights. The rest vary in number—anything from three to ten. This morning there are six altogether. Five. Seven.

Down there, eight floors down, is a school. The early arrivers are there, running about in plastic raincoats, in and out of the shelter, with little bags on their backs. I don't want to think about them either. What is a passable way of saying that 'something tears at your heartstrings'?

Beyond the school are Simmons Point, Mort Bay, Ballast Point, Long Nose Point. Across the water a huge tanker has been tucked into Gore Cove. It seems to fill it. It must have been brought in during the night, or in the early hours of the morning.

I go through to the kitchen and do bread and honey for the lorikeets. They like brown sugar too, but Mrs Shrimpton, the old lady I met at the bus stop, told me if I filled them up every day on that stuff I might ruin their health. I thought at first it was only like giving them nectar. But watching them take it from the rail I noticed their short stubby tongues. They're not equipped for getting into flowers. I don't know about these things—I'm an amateur—but I want to treat them right. They're my companions—they and the magpies that come to the balcony at the front. The old lady said they needed seed as well as sugar, so I devised the bread and honey diet. They like it. They stand on one leg, hold the piece in one claw and nibble at it. Sometimes one holds a piece while another nibbles. If you reach out to touch them they don't fly away in fright. They give you a hefty peck. Bugger off, I'm eating. No gratitude to the provider. But they will climb on to my open hand and eat off my palm. It's a nice feeling. And they're beautiful. Those extravagant colours—blue and green and orange and gold. On which drunken day of the Creation were they so splashed and daubed?

I came here to work. To work and to forget. To work is to forget—etc. Bullshit—but partly true. I'm writing a novel which is set partly in Auckland and partly in Los Angeles. For reasons which are not clear to me (and that may be a way of saying for no reason at all except the wish itself) I felt I had to write it in some place which was neither. Neither Los Angeles nor Auckland. So I came here. I live with these birds in the foreground, and long views (two directions) of Sydney Harbour and the Sydney skyline, while in my head I fight my daily battles, live and die and rise again, in Auckland and LA. They have become places of the mind. That's how it has to be.

Everyone is tired, I am told, of the novel about the novelist writing the novel. Was it invented by the French Existentialists? I think I read somewhere that it was. (But what about Laurence Sterne and the *Sentimental Journey?*) In any case, I'm not tired of it. I've written one and would write another if I thought it safe. Since it's not safe, I'm defusing that impulse with these notes. The novel is about Auckland and Los Angeles. It is not about the writer in Sydney who is writing it. These pages are about him.

His name is Simon Dexter. He is forty years old. Forty-two. He has brown hair and good teeth except for one that was punched out in a game of rugby. In its place is a tooth on a bridge. He is the father of two, a boy and a girl. No more about that. The Purpose (it has to be said again) is all that matters. Everything else (and I mean everything—the world and all its wonders) is either irrelevant or it's material for fiction. There must be no third parties. No life but this one—the life that goes down on the page.

My breakfast is muesli and fruit followed by bacon on toast. And coffee. As I get older the start of the day gets more miraculous. It's as if I wake young again. It doesn't last, but there's that hour, or those few hours, when everything is jumping out of its skin. And because the brightness fades from the air, because it's not normal, it seems more marvellous than it did when one wasn't aware there was another, duller, more ordinary world underneath. And here I wake not only to the lorikeets and the bays I see looking west from my bedroom, but also to this view I have in front of me as I sit on a stool at the kitchen bench-table, spooning my muesli blindly because my eyes are taken up with this eastern down-harbour dazzle, the grand ugliness of the coathanger, the skyward mock-Manhattan off to the right of the picture, the ferries coming and going, the water-taxis, the orange-topped police launch, the black-and-white tugboats, the latest container ship in from Montevideo or Liverpool or the Gulf tying up across the water at Pyrmont. And just beyond the downward curve of the Bridge, one fin, two if I stand, of the Opera House.

I have the sliding glass doors open to the balcony at the front. From out there comes a whirl of wing and the strange pedestrian sound of my two magpies as they flat-foot up and down the rail or around the rim of the iron table. I take them cheese and some small pieces of meat. (Again I've been advised by Mrs Shrimpton.) They eat while I watch from an armchair, finishing my coffee and glancing (trying not to let my interest be roused by anything) at the front page of the morning paper. Unlike the lorikeets, the magpies are silent before they've been fed. It's only when they've finished that they do me a few cadenzas. It's my favourite bird-call. I close my eyes and see the green and brown river-flats of the Manawatu, which must have been where I first heard it; or the veranda of a hotel in a small northern New South Wales town. A fanning of feathers again and they're gone. I feel I've been thanked. Even rewarded.

This morning I've promised to call on Clarry. Clarry Shrimpton. He's the husband of the old lady I met at the bus stop. They live down near the ferry wharf in one of those typical terrace houses that have an upstairs veranda with an ornate iron railing. Like a lot of those houses, theirs has been spoiled by having the upstairs veranda built in. But it's unusual in that the railings remain, giving a strange baroque texture to the front face of the house.

I have mixed feelings about these visits. I'm not sure how I got myself committed to them, or why I haven't found an excuse to stop. I don't like them and yet I'm glad of them. Maybe in a way I do like them, but my expectation that I won't makes me feel as if they're an imposition. The fact is, Clarry is ill—very ill. There's been talk of chemotherapy. He says he won't have it—it makes your hair fall out. 'What hair?' she asks, and they change the subject.

Clarry has a single bed in the veranda room from which he can look out and down the street to the wharf. He keeps a watch by his bed—his wrist is too thin to wear it any more—and checks the ferries against a timetable. This morning he looks worse—thinner, his skin a strange brown colour—but he's sitting up, in good spirits. He has some money and some bets he wants me to place for him at the TAB.

They've had news their daughter in England is coming home. 'About time,' Clarry says. 'I dunno how she can stand them.'

'Them' is the Poms. Clarry hates Poms. But he hates Americans more. He hasn't anything good to say about New Zealanders either ('present company excepted, of course'). They come over here and live on the dole. Bondi's full of them. Bludgers. New Zealanders are like West Australians, Tasmanians and Queenslanders—bloody hicks.

On my last visit, when Clarry was complaining about the Chinese taking over everything (he'd looked out and seen a Chinese bus driver down by the wharf), I asked him whether there was any national group he admired. He said the Krauts had made bloody fine enemies. You could shoot a Kraut with respect.

Today he reminds me of the fireworks. He doesn't ask directly.

He just says his daughter might be out in time to see them. I tell him again he's welcome to come and watch from my apartment. I don't see how it will be possible unless he improves—and I dread the thought of it—but I've said he can come, and I'll stick to that.

THE FIRST TIME I MET Mrs Shrimpton (she hasn't invited me to call her Zoe) it was raining. I hadn't been long in Balmain and I'd always taken the ferry into town. But now a ferry had just left, it was wet, and I was wondering whether it might be quicker to take a bus. There was one standing down by the wharf. Its door was closed and the driver was sitting inside smoking. I tapped on the doors. He pressed a button and they opened. I asked whether this bus went into town. 'Ten minutes,' he said. 'Over there'— pointing to the other side of the street. And the doors whanged together, almost trapping me by the nose.

'They won't let you in until it's time.' That was Mrs Shrimpton. She was standing well back from the bus doors as if to signal she knew the rules. Rain was falling steadily. She had a bent black umbrella and she wore a raincoat. Also a piece of plastic tied over her hat, which was a kind of skewered beret in blue.

'It's terrible weather,' I said.

'Well, it can happen in this country too,' she said. She'd picked I was a stranger. 'It has to rain, doesn't it. Where would we be without water? So long as you've got a roof over your head you've got nothing to complain about.'

I nodded.

'That's what I say,' she added.

I don't recall exactly how it was I allowed myself to be drawn into conversation with this person I might, in a more confident and happy state of mind, have dismissed as a piece of living history best forgotten. Somehow we got on to the subject of my bird visitors. She gave me advice about feeding them. From that (by now the bus had unclenched its doors and we were riding together into town) we moved to a discussion of the apartment I referred to as mine but which has really been lent to me by a couple who are travelling abroad. It was probably then the first hint was dropped about Clarry and the fireworks. She told me her husband had missed the tall ships. She explained it was the Bicentennial year (I knew) and that a re-enactment of the First Fleet had sailed into the harbour (I knew that too). But there were also the tall ships. They had come from all over the world as a tribute to Australia. Clarry Shrimpton had been too ill to walk up to one of the headlands or coves for a good look. She was hoping someone might offer a pozzy from which he could get a look at the fireworks that were scheduled for next month on the harbour. He'd read about them in the paper. He wanted to see the fireworks very much. Clarry Shrimpton loved fireworks.

IT IS INDEED THE Bicentennial year. You might think that's a good time to be in Sydney. For many people—especially Australians—no doubt it is. But for a writer trying to keep himself alive and well in two cities-of-the-mind called Auckland and Los Angeles, the Bicentennial is just a distraction. A nuisance. It's also (why not be honest?) a thundering bore. I've never known a country so bloated with self-regard.

The couple who own my apartment—old friends from long ago when I lived and worked in New South Wales—were here for the Australia Day celebrations and then left on their travels. They send me postcards. They like Singapore. It's clean, the shopping is wonderful. They're impressed by the Moscow Underground. They think it superior even to the Paris Metro. They find Dublin dirty (the Liffey, they tell me, is *brown*) but they love the Irish countryside and the western coast. But of course nothing matches dear old Sydney.

I become a misanthrope. The sheer effort of keeping my thoughts away from what I left behind (an average broken marriage) induces a kind of arthritis of the mind. Only there are those early hours of the day when I feel myself to be open and available to the world and so I'm able to work. After that the doors close. By evening there's only TV and alcohol to ward off despair.

What I find hardest to take is the school down there, eight floors down, as darkness closes in. Most of the mothers or fathers have come for their kids, but there are a few left with a distracted and irritable minder. The children play more frantically. I try to ignore them. Even from so far below I hear the voices coming up. I hear the minder shouting, 'Come down off that roof.' I go to the west balcony and look down. There they are, the last few, in their bright clothes, their bags on their backs, ready to go—running in and out of the lights, shouting in that hectic way kids do when they're at the end of a long day and anxious.

Today, while we were talking about the Bicentennial, Clarry said, 'Course, you know—I'm descended from a convict.'

'You talk a lot of rubbish,' Zoe Shrimpton said. She was bringing us tea and scones—she'd knocked up a batch, and there was jam as well. As she put down the tray she said to me in a loud whisper, 'It's the drugs.'

'What do you know about it?' he said.

'Come to that,' she said, 'we're all descended from the apes. According to Darwin.'

'Well, if you went up to Darwin you'd think so,' Clarry said. He let out a whinnying laugh.

After she'd gone he said, 'There's a lot she doesn't know. My grandmother saw the welts on his back. Thick as your finger.'

I'VE COME UP TO the Cross for a change of scene. Auckland and Los Angeles haven't been treating me well. I remember the

Cross from my first time in Sydney, years ago. It seemed like a first taste of Europe. I remember sitting out drinking coffee on the balcony of a hotel and feeling I was already there. Now I can't find that balcony or that hotel. I walk past the strip joints and the whores in miniskirts. I think seriously about going with one. They all look blotchy-faced or knocked about in some way—but that's not the problem. It isn't morality either, or conscience, or concern about the exploitation of women. It's fear. It used to be fear of VD. Now it's fear of AIDS. They say it's safe with a condom, but is it? And I'm not sure my machinery would work any more with one of those things.

It's Clarry who set me off on this train of thought. He has a way of craning his skinny neck to look around at me, making sure his missus, as he calls her, isn't coming. Then he reaches under his bed, pulls out his money tin and his race books, and tells me what to put on for him at the TAB. Or, if it's not racing, he comes out with some 'men's talk' that's not meant for her ears.

Today he asked how old I was. I told him thirty-nine.

'Thirty-nine eh. And who're you rooting?'

I told him I wasn't rooting anyone. 'I'm separated. Getting divorced, Clarry.' And I added, imitating his digger lingo, 'I'm on me lonesome.'

He nodded. 'So who're you rooting then?'

I felt like telling him he can be an irritating shit, but I think he knows that and he doesn't care. He has nothing to lose.

'You know how I know I've got it bad?' He pointed between his legs. 'Because the big fella won't stand up any more.'

'Give it time,' I said.

He closed his eyes and seemed to doze. I sat in the battered old basket chair by his bed hearing magpies somewhere out there. I closed my eyes too and saw green and brown river-flats. I might even have dozed for a moment. I was woken by Clarry's voice. 'It's like this,' he was saying. 'A man's programmed to root. All the rest's bullshit. You root, you're happy. You don't root, you're not.'

'What about love?' I said.

'Love's nice,' he said. 'But it's not necessary. Rooting's necessary.'

It made me think of a line of a poem by W.H. Auden: 'Thousands have lived without love, not one without water.'

I said, 'Some people would say it's the other way round.'

'Some people say all kinds of things,' Clarry said.

It wasn't that Clarry had provided me with a new philosophy, or a piece of essential wisdom. It has, really, more to do with what I'm calling the Purpose. I've come to think Clarry is dying and that I'm draining the last life out of him and using it in my novel. It doesn't matter if that's codswallop. If it works, if it keeps me going, that's all that matters. But I've started to interpret what he says to me as if he were some kind of oracle uttering obscure instructions from inside a deep cave. The cave is death. What is it telling me? That I can't create life unless I'm in some way immersed in it? What he calls rooting—I've hardly thought about it. Now he has made me conscious of it—conscious of a need.

So here I am at the Cross. It was a stupid idea to think I could pay some money and buy my way back into life again. But I sit out of doors under an umbrella near the Alamein fountain and drink what they call here a 'flat white'. I'm in a mood of gentle despair I know to be dangerous—like lying on a very comfortable bed for a moment when what you need to do is to get up and get going.

I take the route to the TAB. I go down to Simmons Point and then along the foreshore into Mort Bay where the tugboats are tied up. Then up a street of ugly new townhouses and on up to Balmain shops. I don't go to the TAB to put Clarry's bets on. I go to find out the results, when I've missed the race commentary on the radio, and to get the odds. I don't put any of Clarry's money on the TAB. I keep it and pay TAB odds when he wins. I've become his secret bookie. He doesn't know. I don't know what he would think if he did.

It happened by accident. I forgot to put a bet on for him and the horse won. I thought it might distress him, so I pretended I'd placed the bet and I paid him the TAB odds. Then it occurred to me I could be a gambling man too just by betting against his bet. Some days he wins and I lose; other days I'm the winner. The amounts are never large. I think I'm ahead. I suppose the bookie usually is.

Today I came back from the TAB via the school. I stood outside the gates and looked into the yard. There's an open area with a broad, sloping roof over it and benches underneath. There's one little girl who seems always to wear big baggy shorts and to have her hair held back from her face with a clip. She reminds me so much of my Emma at that age I suppose I always stare. Today I stood at the gate looking in. I ought to have known it would cause alarm. A woman came out and asked me what I wanted. I told her I was lost in thought. She didn't look reassured.

I came back here feeling as if I'd been beaten all over with sticks. But then straight away I sat down at the typewriter and I must have run through three pages with hardly a pause. It was the afternoon, when I don't usually write, and I finished those pages feeling I know exactly where I will take the story tomorrow.

So I cooked myself a meal, opened a bottle of wine and felt it hadn't been a bad day. Now I'm sitting out on the balcony looking at the harbour by night. To say it's a beautiful sight is a ridiculous understatement. If it's true, as Zoe Shrimpton says, that there's to be a fireworks display on the harbour, this will be the place to be. But could Clarry be brought here? I don't see how.

I think again about his advice to me. Did he really say all that about 'rooting'? Or did I dream it in that dozy moment by his bed? I know it's normal enough to feel slightly deranged when you find yourself suddenly living alone after years of family life.

The thought might bother me more if it weren't for the fact of those three pages written this afternoon.

Down on the water a paddle steamer is going past Pyrmont towards the Bridge. I take the binoculars from the living room and pick out the illuminated sign on its side: SYDNEY RIVERBOAT. Then I range over the city picking out the signs in lights—QANTAS, ESSO, ROYAL INSURANCE, HILTON, MARTINS, all in red; IBM, ARTHUR YOUNG, GOLD FIELD in white; CITIBANK in blue. On the North Shore ZURICH, MN and AGL are in blue; PHILIPS is blue-green; SHARP and CIC are red; FP is white in a circle, and NCR white on red. LEGAL & GENERAL has a red-and-green umbrella over it. One of the tallest buildings overlooking the Quay has a sign of 1788–1988. Electric stars and spangles shower from it down the face of the building.

The phone rings. It's Caroline, calling from Auckland. It's late there—past midnight—and her speech is slurred. 'Have you been drinking?' I ask.

She wants to know what business that is of mine.

'You're in charge of my kids,' I remind her.

'Too right I am. And it's going to stay that way.'

'Is that what you rang to tell me?'

'Jesus, Simon, why are you such a bastard?'

'Why are you such a bitch?'

She hangs up on me. I phone her, but she doesn't answer.

IT HAS RAINED FOR three days. The lorikeets come in the morning but after they've been fed they don't leave. They huddle, quarrelling, bedraggled, on the balcony rail. They move to the balcony below, or to the building next door, but for most of the morning they stay close. They're a distraction. I find myself getting up to give them more brown sugar or bread and honey.

Then I recognise that I got up because I was stuck for a word or a phrase. It's only another version of straightening the pictures or making yourself a cup of coffee.

But the lorikeets don't stay all day. Late in the morning they begin to disappear. It's hard to imagine what mental processes prompt them into action. I watched one that had spent most of the morning on the rail. Suddenly it was in flight, out over Simmons Point towards Goat Island. It reached the island in just a few seconds but it didn't stop there. It flew straight on over and I lost sight of it, heading like a little green-and-gold rocket towards Waverton or Wollstonecraft.

As the rain clouds go over, bits of the city disappear. The Australia Tower and the tallest buildings come and go. Occasionally the bridge, straight in front of me there down the harbour, vanishes in cloud. But even when everything is clear and sharp, the rain goes on falling. It varies between heavy and very heavy. It never stops. Today I went to a play at the Belvoir Street Theatre. I don't have a raincoat here, but I found a blue-and-white golf umbrella big enough to camp under. I took the bus into the Town Hall and set off on foot. I should have known that rain, like everything else in Australia, has to be on a grand scale. It poured through the shop verandas wherever there was a weak point or a hole. It thundered on the umbrella, seeped through, and ran down the handle and into my sleeve. It turned the side streets into rivers. I kept looking out for a taxi but the few I saw had the engaged sign up. Going up Elizabeth Street, sheltering as far as possible under verandas, I was soaked by a car steered by its happy-faced driver through the metre-wide flow of gutter water so everyone on the pavement was caught in the jet from its wheels.

The play was *Capricornia* from the novel by Xavier Herbert. The young hero grows up in Melbourne believing he's descended from a Japanese princess. When he returns, against advice, to Port Zodiac, he discovers he's what's known there as a 'yellerfeller'—half Aboriginal—and despised for it. That's the part of himself he has to learn to accept, and to make others accept. In the end he has to make a journey into the Outback to be reconnected with his tribe. He talks to an old Aboriginal woman. He tells her he hasn't any knowledge of the bush and how to survive there. She tells him not to worry. She gets lost in the bush too. 'Buy yourself a compass,' she says.

This morning when I went to my typewriter I was invaded by a terrible panic. I was sitting there thinking about those two cities-of-the-mind—the Auckland and Los Angeles of my novel—and I thought, 'Supposing no one believes in them.' It was like the brown sugar I put out on the balcony rail in the rain. My two cities lost their shape, sagged, sank down, spread out and were slowly washed away. In the end there was nothing but the wet black hard surface of the rail. I couldn't write a word. I didn't believe in them myself.

But I had nothing else to turn to. There were thirteen hundred miles of ocean between me and the wife who used to be 'my' wife, and the children who used to be 'my' children, and the house that used to be mine. This was not my apartment, my city, my country. I was here on the eighth floor of nowhere, and feeling so dislocated, so edgy, so precarious, it frightened me.

I couldn't write so I must walk. I trust in the action of walking, believe in its efficacy. It's something I can do, and here in Balmain all the water's edges, all the points and coves and bays which were once messy and jammed with nautical debris, are gradually being turned into parks and walkways. I walked around a big circuit of foreshore and finished back at Darling Street Wharf. It didn't seem enough and there was a ferry coming in so I took it and got off at Long Nose Point. I walked back along Louisa Street and through Balmain shops where I stopped for a flat white. It was there I remembered Clarry. I'd been neglecting him. I hadn't visited him since the rain began.

I found him much worse. You think a person like that can't lose any more weight—that there's no more to lose—but it isn't so. Today Clarry looked like a skeleton with skin. His head was a death's head. The dark pigmentation seemed to be spreading, as if he'd been baked over a fire. The wrinkles and folds were huge and dark. But the eyes weren't lifeless. The life still burned in them.

He couldn't reach down for his tin. I had to get it for him. The radio murmured from his bedside table while he fumbled and counted. Then he told me: there's a horse called Clanridden. He wanted me to put a hundred on its nose.

I hesitated. What would Zoe think? Wasn't a hundred a bit steep? I also thought about my own role as secret bookie. Did I want to bet whatever the odds were against his bet? I asked him was it an outsider. He told me not to worry my head about that. When I pressed him for an answer he said Clanridden wouldn't be a favourite but it ought to be. It was a dead cert.

I didn't know what to make of that, but I took his money.

He asked me about the fireworks. He said he'd been pretty crook since the rain started. Then he dropped off to sleep, his mouth open, a thin trickle of saliva running out at the corner. He snored faintly. He smelled bad.

I went out to the kitchen where Zoe was making tea. I asked her when the fireworks were happening. She didn't say anything, just kept her back to me, clattering the tea caddy. It came to me that there were no fireworks. They might have been something she'd invented for Clarry to look forward to.

When I stuck my head around the door again he was awake. 'Clanridden,' he said. 'A hundred.'

'Clanridden,' I repeated. And I gave him the thumbs-up.

When I got back here to the apartment I went straight to the typewriter. Auckland and Los Angeles swept back into my mind, dream-cities, fresh and clear and shining. I felt confident; and I felt I could see exactly how the novel is going to end.

I got up and stretched and walked out on to the balcony. The weather seemed to be clearing. Everything was clean except the harbour, which had turned brown with the floodwaters that had sluiced down into it.

Then I remembered the race. I'd meant to go up to the TAB and put Clarry's bet on for him. I didn't want to play bookie if he was going to bet in hundreds, but it was too late now. There was only time to turn on the commentary. Clanridden won by a nose.

I owe Clarry four hundred and fifty dollars. I think, 'I can't afford it.' Then I think, 'Of course you can.' Then I reflect on the 'I' and the 'you' in that exchange. And then I think, 'Four hundred and fifty bucks—it's a small price for the last life of Clarry.'

This morning the weather is clear, the sky blue, and there's a long brilliant track of glittering light stretching away down the harbour to the bridge. The white faces of the terrace houses directly below look washed, and it's as if there are more trees among them; there seems (though it's an illusion) so much more green than when I last looked. The lorikeets bring their blue heads and gold-flecked breasts and green wings to the bedroom balcony but they don't stay longer than it takes to eat what I put out for them. On the front balcony the black of the magpies is blacker, the white whiter. And down on the water three magpie tugboats are dragging that tanker away from Gore Cove and out towards the open sea. As it goes under the bridge its highest point seems only a few feet below the centre span.

In the mail comes another card from my friends, owners of this apartment. They talk of returning. On the other hand, spring has arrived in London parks and gardens, so they're not sure.

From home comes a copy of the *Listener*'s issue for the Bicentennial. It says New Zealand soldiers envied the vigour and style of their Australian cousins. Just a few days ago, on Anzac

Saturday, the *Sydney Morning Herald* said the New Zealanders were the elite on Gallipoli because they combined the discipline of the British with the dash of the Aussies. How is it that we can be so civil to one another? It's so unusual it makes me uneasy.

Yesterday I met Clarry's daughter, Alice. She's very brisk and contralto, stylish, with faintly blue-tinted spectacles and a young businesswoman's no-nonsense approach to traditional male pieties. She told me I wasn't to take any more bets for Clarry. That put me straight into my aggression mode. I told her I would do Clarry any favour he asked that it was in my power to do. She smiled as if to signal that her bullshit detector was in good working order and turned away. I had my instructions.

But Clarry didn't want to talk about racing. He held my hand and from time to time slipped into sleep, and maybe it was a coma. But in between there was something he wanted to say.

'I know where I'm going,' he said. 'No worries, boy.'

'Good on you, mate,' I said.

'Yeah, but . . .' He licked his lips. 'What about getting there?'

'What about it, Clarry?'

He frowned and screwed up his eyes. 'I might get lost.'

I wasn't sure how to respond to that. I just said the first thing that came into my head. 'Don't worry about it. Buy yourself a compass.'

His face was blank for a moment. Then the creases and wrinkles arranged themselves into something that could only be a grin. A kind of cackle ground its way out of his throat. Next moment he was unconscious again.

I put a roll of notes—four hundred and fifty dollars—into the tin under his bed.

THE DAY CLARRY DIED the lorikeets didn't come to the rail. Nature thought them too garish and warned them off. Or was it just that I slept late? The magpies came as usual, in their best black and white.

I'd finished the novel—or anyway a draft of it. Whatever kind of mess it was, it now had a beginning, a middle and an end.

Alice Shrimpton and I were getting on better, in the spirit of Anzac. She let me help with some of the arrangements for the funeral. Zoe sat helpless and desolate, as if she'd never allowed the thought of Clarry's death even a toe in the door.

And that night there were fireworks. I don't know what the occasion was—maybe the Queen's visit to open Expo 88. They seemed to come from somewhere beyond the bridge and Bennelong Point, and they didn't last much more than twenty minutes. But for that short time the whole harbour and the western sky were brilliant with eruptions and showers of fiery light.

I paced about with all the lights off—up and down the living room, in and out through the doors to the balcony. I was thinking of Caroline and the kids. More than once I began to dial home and then changed my mind and hung up. I set out and walked for almost an hour, around the foreshore and back along Darling Street. When I got back to my eighth floor and my double-locked door, the phone was ringing. I fumbled with keys, dropped them, put the wrong key in the lock and had trouble getting it out. By the time I got inside it was too late—the ringing had stopped. I dialled New Zealand.

'Were you calling me?' I asked.

'Calling you?'

'My phone was ringing—I thought it must be you.'

She was silent a moment. 'Does it ring so seldom?'

'No. Yes. Well—it doesn't ring all that often. I'd been thinking of ringing you. I suppose that's why I thought . . .'

'That was nice.'

'What was?'

'That you were—you know—thinking of . . .'

'Of ringing. Oh yes. I was.' Silence. 'So, anyway, it wasn't you.'

'No.'

'Well then. I'd better go.'

'What's the weather like over there?'

'It's been the wettest April since—I don't know. Since the First Fleet probably. What about Auckland?'

'We've had the driest since 1066.'

'Good on you.'

'What about the novel?'

'Finished. Well—a draft, anyway.'

'Finished! Congratulations. Is it good?'

'God knows. Probably not.'

'You must be feeling great.'

'I feel awful actually.'

The conversation ambled on like that for quite a long time. There was a kind of embarrassment about being so nice to one another. It would have been easy to slip back into terms of endearment.

I DON'T USUALLY WEEP at funerals. They have a strange effect on me. The closer the relative the more I go inside myself, hidden. Out there is a puppet, dry-eyed, going through the motions.

I didn't weep at Clarry's but I had to fight it. There was a lump in the throat and tears in the eyes. I don't record it with satisfaction. What was Clarry to me? The tears would have been for myself.

But sitting there in the unfamiliar church I had a thought. It was Clarry who sent me off on that wild goose chase to Kings Cross. But it was Zoe who gave me advice about how to feed the birds. There are more ways than one to skin a cat, and more than one to keep a man who's alone sane and in touch with the common life.

This morning I met Alice Shrimpton in a coffee bar just up from Circular Quay. It turns out she works for Amstrad, and she signed me up to buy a word processor. I've had to go into overdraft, but I think there's a royalty cheque due any day; and Alice is right when she says it will save me not just days but weeks of work now that I'm at the stage of slogging through my novel and making revisions.

The weather remains good though the nights are cool. I miss old Clarry. Zoe potters through her daily routines. She seems stunned. The lorikeets and magpies are here every morning. As I gaze out at it now, Sydney has begun to look not ordinary exactly but just like one more beautiful place. The world is full of them. I think of inviting Alice to come with me to my favourite Greek restaurant, but I'm still a little nervous of those faintly blue-tinted spectacles.

'And still the sun shines'

'On va, on vient; il fera jour demain.'

. . . *I made a dive for the door and got it open but it was too late for the brake. The Fiat tilted, tipped, skidded sideways, the door flew back, knocking me flat and when I scrambled up again the car was careering down the slope into darkness, rolling, sliding, doors flying open and flying off, windows smashing, metal shrieking and showering sparks off stone. Peering into the night, trying to follow it, I thought I saw it bounce upright on a little road down there, fall beyond it, roll again, crash upside down where the road doubled back on itself, and then everything was brilliantly lit up as it burst into flame.*

I don't know what effect it had on the others. For a while I just stared at the flames flicking higher and higher, lighting up the road and the hill slope and the pines. I wanted to get away from it, to disown it.

The gendarmes would come. They would question us. I would have to give my name—and for a moment I had to be sure I knew what it was. That blow on the head from the door . . . 'My name is Miller. Rod Miller.' I said it aloud. 'Age thirty-two, divorced, and in France because . . .'

Because I thought I was a writer, and wanted to prove I was. Could I say that? And would they want to know?

The flames were brilliant, the pines beautiful. Somewhere down there, away down, beyond Garavan, the sea stretched out far and burnished under the stars. I felt a sense of loss, of losses . . .

1. Buying a car

IT WAS LONG AGO—not so very long, perhaps, but before the world was invaded by cell phones and caught in the web of the Web; when intercontinental flights were not uncommon but not quite commonplace; when the Wall was up, and Vietnam was still raging, and South Africa was still an apartheid state.

It was a town in the South of France, the Côte d'Azur, later than Scott Fitzgerald's novel *Tender is the Night* and Cyril Connolly's *The Rock Pool*, but before the sad demise of Grace Kelly, the Hollywood star who had become Princess Grace of Monaco. West along the coast at Mougins, Picasso was still alive, painting and making pottery; and east was Ezra Pound, but silent, no longer writing poetry; and in Paris Georges Pompidou was President of France. But all three, the painter, the poet and the politician, would die in the next year or two. The movie *The French Connection*, which linked Marseilles and New York and drugs, had just won an Oscar, and the Don McLean song about 'Miss American Pie' was top of the charts. So it was a time, you could say, when literary novels told sad stories about alcoholism, and popular songs had words that could be remembered and tunes you couldn't forget. Who that was alive then can't still sing about driving the Chevvy to the levee when the levee was dry, and the good old boys drinking whiskey and rye? Some time ago, yes—long enough to be looked back on with a certain nostalgia.

I remember the first time I walked up into the hills behind the town and down to the village of Garavan. I hadn't bought a car yet. I was looking for an apartment and there was one offering at Garavan. I'd walked there around the waterfront a couple of times. I had a tourist map and it showed you could walk partway up into the hills behind the town and down to the waterfront again on the other side of a ridge. But tourist maps don't give you much idea of ups and downs. It was a steep climb. I found myself up by the cemetery behind the *ancienne ville*—the medieval town—and next minute I was looking down over the Baie de Garavan. It was mid-winter, late afternoon of a clear sunny day, and there it all was, laid out, a large part of what was to be my scene. Below and to the right there were the yellow walls and orange tiles of the old town. Further down, right away down, almost as if it was under my feet, the waterfront road and the new (as they were then) swimming beaches and breakwater—beautiful pieces of public works, empty and waiting for summer. Along the waterfront road, following east towards Italy—that was the village, or perhaps it was a suburb, of Garavan. The railway followed the same direction as the road, but a contour higher. Then further up ran the boulevard de Garavan—the road I was standing on; and higher still the terraced hill slopes rose more and more sharply at the same time pressing in towards the sea until, just beyond the frontier post dividing France and Italy, the rock faces, orange and pink and grey in the changing light, hung directly over it. Beyond again, eastward, it all stretched away, dwindling into the fading afternoon—Ventimiglia, Bordighera, San Remo: another country, a different story.

The Garavan apartment was too big for me and I settled a day or so later for a small bungalow villa, shared with the landlady, who kept the nicest two rooms for herself. It was back in town, up a hill conveniently placed and looking out over *centre-ville* and the sea.

The Garavan apartment I passed on to my compatriots Clifton and Katy Scarf, who arrived in town a week or so after I did with their three small children. Clifton had a year's leave from his university and, through a connection with the University of Nice, had got permission to spend part of it on the Riviera instead of in Paris. He'd brought the family with him, all the way from New Zealand by sea, which was cheaper in those days. It was January. They'd spent a day in Paris cracking ice on puddles and then taken the night train south, and next morning they were having breakfast outdoors at a café near the station. I had done the same journey. You leave Paris sometimes up to its ears in fog, sleet, rain, anything winter can throw at you, and in the morning when the sun comes up you're already racing along the Mediterranean coast, catching sight of green palms, white villas, red rocks, yellow mimosa, blue bays. Colours!—almost candy colours. But that impression can be misleading.

After their hot chocolate and croissants by the station Clifton phoned the Agence Bienvenue and Ernst Bergen came for them wearing one of his immaculate suits and driving his Lamborghini Miura. Bergen was the international Dutchman, but not genial like most of his country-men and -women, managing (as the Dutch seem to do so effortlessly) three or four languages with ease, buying, selling, letting real estate, and then, as if the profits weren't enough, sitting all summer, when he wasn't out attending to his properties, behind the bullet-proof glass of his *Change*, swapping deutschmarks, francs, lire, sterling—any of the pre-euro currencies, so long as the customer accepted his rates. I don't suppose much of that part of his business survived the advent of the euro, which on the other hand would have done no harm to the real-estate side. Bergen had an American wife, Peggy, and two small children somewhere up in the hills, and in his office one inscrutable local woman who might have been his mistress. There were a few signs of strain. He could never meet your eye, even in shadow and wearing tinted glasses. Sometimes late in the afternoons when business wasn't brisk he sat outside on a canvas chair on the pavement, drinking. He became subtly insolent then, with what seemed to me a suppressed displeasure, as if he disliked everyone, and his work, and his life. It was boredom, I decided. Like so many people who were affluent and had found a way to what they considered success in life, he was profoundly bored.

Bergen had made a mistake that day—or his office girl had given him the wrong information. He thought I had taken the Garavan apartment and the bungalow-villa was vacant. There was a ring at the gate and I went down and there he was, his car loaded with the Scarf family, the children bouncing around (no seat belts in those days) and making him nervous. He was offering them the place I had taken.

I invited them all up and we sorted out the confusion. That was my first meeting with the Scarfs as a family, though I had known Clifton at home in New Zealand—not well, but we'd belonged, briefly, to the same tennis club in Auckland and had friends in common. I asked him about his academic career and though he responded with due modesty it was clear he was having success. He was on sabbatical leave and more than one suggestion had been made to him that he might like to apply for posts in England and America. I asked was he thinking of doing this and he said no he wasn't—rather fiercely, as if I'd been suggesting he do something improper or dishonest.

We sat on the terrace drinking kirs, Katy saying she hadn't slept much on the train and looking gorgeous, while the kids played, skidding on the shiny floors. As they were leaving I reminded Bergen about the Garavan apartment. It was a bit shabby, just about right if you were going to have three kids hurtling about in there, and it was big. He drove them there and I heard a day or so later they had taken it.

SHORTLY AFTER THAT the rain started. Not just a few passing showers. Real rain. It went on for days. The spiky plants shone, the feathery ones drooped with it. The sea lost its blue enamelled look. The English colonels and German businessmen and Parisian Jews wintering in the south disappeared from the waterfront. So did the band. I didn't mind. The South of France has its seasons, and the winter one is not the most appealing. Turning out on the promenade on a good day in January or February when the sun brings all the visitors out was in those days like taking a stroll in an outsize geriatric ward. Just one street inland was a normal French town going about its winter business. One street inland was the rue Saint Michel, and it was there, while I was trying to buy myself a car, that I met Katy Scarf in pouring rain hurrying along under a transparent umbrella, with a square of red silk over her black hair. The pavement was so narrow there you had to step into the street to let people pass; and the street was so narrow, when you stepped into it you were holding up the crawling cars.

Katy and I ran into one another. She said hullo and we both stepped into the roadway.

'We're holding up the traffic,' she said, and we stepped back again.

Now we were holding up the pedestrians. I steered her into a doorway. 'Do you speak French?' I asked.

'Oh yes,' she said. And then, 'Well—a little.'

'You don't know what a luggage rack's called, do you?'

'A . . . which?'

'On a car. A luggage rack.'

'Oh yes I think I do. A luggage rack. It's a . . .' She thought a moment. 'It's *une galerie de bagages.*'

I was pleased with that, and so was she. It sounded right. '*Brava,*' I said.

I had been looking for a house called *L'Atrium.* I'd been up and down the rue St Michel three or four times asking shopkeepers, but either they didn't understand me or they hadn't heard of it. It was the home of an architect whose name was given as M. Hirondelle—which seemed improbable: Mr Swallow. But maybe, if you thought of it as Mr Martin, not improbable at all. These had been my thoughts as I'd hunted, but I did not share them with the lovely Mrs Scarf—only explained that M. Hirondelle was offering a Fiat Dino for sale and I'd decided I wanted it. I'd seen it parked in a big garage off the avenue Edouard VII where a young man explained that its owner left it there because he had a weak heart and couldn't drive any more. He'd written Hirondelle's name and address on a piece of paper and now I was standing in a doorway just across the street from a little square, La Place aux Herbes, paved of course, with not a 'herbe' in sight, listening to the soothing sound of the rain and thinking of Katy Scarf, who had just left me there—thinking of her black hair under red silk and great drops skidding over the transparent plastic of her umbrella; and saying over the new fragment of French she'd given me, 'galerie de bagages'. And then, as if it swam up hazily through that film of wet plastic, I saw it, L'Atrium in ornate, shallowly carved lettering in pale-yellow stone.

A stone passageway curved up from the street and opened on to a cobbled path with buildings rising on either side. A flight of stone steps led into a garden hung with leafless vines, brown-black in the rain. The last leaves still floated in the blue-tiled lily pool, drained but filling with rainwater. Two or three large trees grew up the face of the building enclosing the garden on two sides. All the shutters were closed. In the angle formed by the two wings of this building there was an entrance and a stairway. I climbed the stairs, stopping at each of three landings to look at the names on the doors, and then to look out on the garden with its brown vines and blue pool and unswept paths.

At the top landing there was just one door and the name

Hirondelle. I rang, and in a moment an elderly lady answered. Mrs Swallow (or Martin), I assumed. I told her I'd come about the Fiat. Her face was contorted for a moment by some strange convulsion, but it passed. '*Entrez, Monsieur,*' she said. '*Laissez votre parapluie là-bas, s'il vous plaît.*'

I put my umbrella down where she pointed, wiped my feet and went in.

I DIDN'T SEE M. HIRONDELLE that first morning—he was unwell and still in bed—and I had to call twice more before the business of buying the car was settled. I remember the last visit (I had gone to hand over the money, which he wanted in cash) he told me a story—something that had happened to him during World War II. I'm not sure why he told it; not sure where it happened either. It was in one of the mountain villages—possibly Gorbio—but I'm not certain of that. Anyway, Hirondelle was an officer and he'd retreated with his men into a village in the mountains. They sat out of doors in the little square eating and drinking and cracking jokes while away down towards the coast where the sea glittered in the sun they could see puffs of dust rising off the roads and that meant an Italian column was coming after them.

They took their time and enjoyed the food and the wine, and some time during the early afternoon the first shells whistled in and the battle started. One thing he remembered especially was that when he thought about it afterwards he was sure (and yet couldn't be sure) that the cicadas had stopped before the first shell exploded. There was a minute's complete silence, and then the first bang—followed by the screaming of one of his men who had been wounded. It wasn't a mortal wound, he said. In fact he thought the fuss had more to do with fright than pain. But now at last they had a real enemy and were engaged in shooting and being shot at. So much of the war had been waiting, and he was excited it was possible for it to become real.

In the course of that afternoon Hirondelle got separated from his men among olive trees on the slopes below the village. There seemed to be nobody about and then, somewhere in front of him among the trees, there was an Italian soldier who for the moment seemed equally lost, and unaware he'd been seen. Hirondelle took rapid aim and fired, and was astonished (he was no sniper, he assured me) to see the enemy soldier reel back, dropping his rifle, and stagger away. Alarmed at what he'd done, never having shot a man before, Hirondelle followed, more in the spirit of wanting to help, or at least take a prisoner, than of wanting to 'finish him off'. They came to a little valley, like a small interruption in the predominant downward slope, with a couple of whitewashed farm cottages deserted on either side of a stream. The Italian was getting weaker. He crossed a small bridge and slumped against a wall in the sun. There was a curved wayside shrine like an up-ended bath tub with a painted Madonna inside against a blue background. The Italian dragged himself to the shrine, dragged himself up to sit inside it in the shade. He didn't move again, but slumped back and sideways, held by the shrine. Hirondelle waited. The sound of gunfire was still audible, but there was less of it and receding. It was possible to hear the stream running below the road. Hirondelle approached, watching for the least movement. There was none. The Italian was dead.

Because he stopped at that point and was silent I asked, 'What did you do?'

'What did I do?' he repeated. And then, in a tone heavy with irony, 'Like Jesus, I wept.'

IT WAS THE MORNING of the day I was to call on Hirondelle that I met Javine. I went into a café near the Casino. It was almost empty but a young woman was standing with her hands on top of the jukebox, nodding to the song that came from it. It might even have been 'Miss American Pie'. She was singing along, and I joined in. When it stopped she looked up and smiled. I invited her to come and sit with me.

She brought her cup of coffee to my table. She didn't speak a lot of English and I wasn't fluent—in fact I struggled—in French, but we made our way. She told me she had lived her whole life in the town (she pulled a face). Her parents had a small farm up in the hills but she had a room in her uncle's house down near the fishing port. One day soon she was going to go and find herself a job in Paris. In the meantime she was doing courses at the University of Nice along the coast.

I asked her why she wasn't there today and she shrugged. The boredom, you know. Now and then one had to give oneself a holiday.

She put a coin in the machine and chose another song, Italian this time, '*Estate senza te*'—Summer without you. It's one I remember because she liked it so much, and soon so did I. When I knew her better I bought her one of those small LPs of it, a '45'. The singer's name was Christophe, and soon I could sing the refrain, which asked where someone had gone and what would the singer do if she didn't come back. There was something sorry-for-itself about those lyrics, and it's hard for me now to see quite why it was to mean so much to us; why it should have become, as the cliché was, and is, 'our song'.

Javine was a small neat girl with pale-olive skin and very dark eyes so you expected black hair but it was light brown, almost chestnut but paler, the colour of lager. She was slow, graceful, somehow withdrawn behind eyes that looked at you very directly, smiling. Everything was hidden but nothing was absent.

We parted in the street outside the Casino. The billboard was advertising Walt Disney's *The Aristocats*, which had become of course *Les Aristochats*. I told her I was probably going to buy a car that afternoon and asked her whether she would like to come for a drive.

When she looked up to answer she hesitated a moment, smiling, her mouth closed, her eyes full of intelligence, so that I felt, without knowing what it was I wanted to hide, that I was giving myself away.

I got to *L'Atrium* at the appointed hour. The sky had cleared and the sun struck down among the heavy brown stems of the vines and lit up the grey stones of the old wall that enclosed the garden.

Madame Hirondelle showed me in and left me alone with her husband. He was sitting stiffly in his chair, carefully dressed and brushed. He excused himself from standing as he held out his hand. His breathing was heavy and his hand was weak.

But after a general conversation, including the war anecdote, he came abruptly to the point. 'The price is eight thousand francs, Monsieur Miller. That is less than the car is worth. My wife is not satisfied but that is my price. You see I can't get downstairs to drive— there is no lift—and she does not drive. I am an architect, Monsieur, and I designed this building when I was young and fit—an athlete, but an aesthete first. It had to be beautiful. Functional yes, but beauty came first.'

'It is,' I said. 'Very beautiful. And the garden . . . Yes, magnificent.'

'Yes, I think so. Thank you. But now, you see . . . If I went down those stairs I would not get up again.' He smiled. 'The artist trapped inside his design—isn't it so?' And then, 'The price is right for you?'

I said it was right if the car was as good as it looked.

'You won't be disappointed,' he said. 'The young man from the garage has brought it over. He's waiting in the carpark beside the market. Perhaps you would like to go down to him . . .'

I stood up to go.

'My wife believes you are some kind of artist,' he said. 'Is she right?'

I shook my head. 'Not yet, anyway.'

He smiled. 'If Madame believes you are an artist, that's that. That is what you are.'

'I'm glad to hear it,' I said.

It was a time when drivers still spoke enthusiastically of the *corniches*, though even then the autoroute was replacing them in importance: *grande*, *moyenne* and *basse* (high, middle and low) *corniches*—the three famous and romantic coast roads of the Côte d'Azur. I imagined Hirondelle as a young man, the aesthete-architect-athlete, wearing a long scarf, driving with the hood down and the wind in his hair, young Madame beside him holding down a hat.

He said, 'I hope for you it will be a lucky purchase.'

'Thank you, Monsieur, I'm sure it will.'

Twenty minutes later I was driving up to Cap Martin, the *garagiste* beside me. Up there on the heights I stopped and looked back at the town.

'*Elle marche comme un rêve, n'est-ce pas?*' he said.

'Like a dream,' I agreed. But I would have to get used to driving on the right.

JUST BEYOND GARAVAN THERE were still the frontier and customs posts where a passport, or at the very least a *carte d'identité*, was needed. You went through the French border guards, crossed a white line marking the bed of a stream that ran under the road, and forward to the Italian guards. Clifton Scarf's kids used to get him to stop the car on the line so that Mummy and Dad in the front were in Italy and the kids in France. Or they would get out and stand astride it, one foot in either country. Later, of course, when the euro arrived and Western Europe's borders became notional, that whole set-up would be abandoned and the buildings that housed it left more or less to rot or be ransacked. Now, as I write, all at once it's back in use again, with France trying to stem the flood of people coming across the sea from North Africa and the Middle East through Italy—cars being searched, refugees walking along the railway lines, or living on the rocks in makeshift camps just over there on the Italian side, waiting for a chance to make the breakthrough or for liberal voices to win the argument. So Europe, the magnet, changes—and nothing changes: *plus ça change plus c'est la même chose.* Some cynic said recently that the only people who still believe in the ideal of European collectivity that established the EU are the refugees risking their lives by crossing the Mediterranean in small boats.

But in those days the barrier was still the passage from one country to another, France to Italy; and the moment I crossed that line I seemed to feel it like a sudden alteration in the weather. There was more poverty, more colour, more style. Life in Italy was more primitive, more civilised, less bourgeois, more extreme. There was a government and democratic elections (I remember a banner VOTA COMMUNISTA stretched across the roadway); but there were also the Church and the Mafia. And there was the currency—the absurd *lire* in such huge multiples, thousands, hundreds of thousands, just for small purchases, as if everyone, even the poorest, was a millionaire.

As the Fiat gathered speed Javine's hair blew across my face. The cliffs dropped to rocky blue bays, the hill slopes rose in terraces or lifted abruptly to bald bluffs. Neither mountains of rock nor empty canyons had been allowed to present themselves as obstacles. Kilometre-long tunnels succeeded one another, and between the tunnels immense flyovers. Our path was direct, fast, mountains to the left, sea to the right, Genoa ahead. And beyond Genoa . . . I couldn't find a word for what lay beyond, except the literal one, that it was 'Tuscany'—or better still, 'Liguria'. It was (I would have said in my naïve enthusiasm) a sense of space, freedom, movement, colour and light; as if you were about to take off into something like the Infinite, knowing its blue filmy walls would be done out with frescos of the gardens of Paradise.

All in the mind? 'Subjective'? Unreal? Yes, perhaps—if you say so. But in those days, a still young and newly liberated New Zealander with so much to learn, I would have said with that brilliant old culture-snob Cyril Connolly, 'I am for the intricacy of Europe, the discrete and many-folded strata of the Old World . . . the world of ideas.'

Coming back into town that evening I stopped at a rest area, and Javine and I climbed down a path below the *autostrada* into a gully wooded with pines. It was quiet except for the call of birds and the occasional whoosh of cars above. We held on to one another, steadying ourselves as we made our way down over the uneven ground. Javine stopped and leaned back against the trunk of a tree. Her head was back, her hair spreading against the rough bark, catching in it. She was wearing a leather jacket and the leather creaked faintly as she moved. I was aware of the curve of her breast just there under the flap of her jacket, and the shape of her jeans tight over thighs and crotch—and I kissed her. It was a very nice mouth to kiss; an enthusiastic recipient; a satisfactory and satisfying first kiss; a memorable thank-you-to-the-stars moment.

I was older by a dozen or so years but we were both young. I had trained as a journalist and, like every second person in the trade then (or so it seemed to me), I thought that 'one day' I would 'write something serious', meaning a novel. An unmarried great-uncle, almost certainly gay but never out of the closet, had recently died and left me an amount of money, encouraging me to see it as my chance to become 'a real writer'. I knew it might equally be an opportunity to prove that I was no such thing, if by 'real writer' was meant a serious novelist. I was a journalist—and why not? It was a job to be taken seriously, needing talent and ambition and application. In fact it was to be my future. But for the moment I thought I was gathering material and preparing myself to write fiction. So everything, including Javine, including the kiss, might be 'material'.

It's true I had been married and divorced—another learning experience. My learning had been mostly by mistakes. I'd thought in very conventional terms of marriage and children. *She* (her name was Deirdre) had thought, in a way still somewhat advanced for the time, of marriage and a career—kids could be thought about maybe later. So we set off on different feet and never saw eye to eye until it was too late. It was as if we were competitors rather than allies. We quarrelled, seriously, and she left me—that about sums it up. I was angry and resentful, and then regretful, understanding only when it had all gone too far and was beyond compromise. In the end Deirdre would have both, the kids and the career, which was as it should be—but not with me. When I left her behind, I left my country as well, which was one of the reasons why I enjoyed finding the Scarf family, fellow New Zealanders, in the same town.

As for the other half of the kiss—I suspect that Javine too was a bit behind the times, and that she thought of herself as a character out of Colette: the new, the modern, Claudine. I don't know for sure that she had read much Colette, though I did see a copy of *Le Blé en herbe*, and one or two others, among her books.

So let me give this encounter some literary colour and suggest you imagine a Colette-gal and a Hemingway-guy kissing rather nicely, and rather well, under those pines through which even at this present moment—I mean *now, as I write*—real refugees may be escaping across the border; and then you will understand, perhaps, that in the end I stayed a journalist, and even became proud of it, and successful, only to live into this present time when newspapers are vanishing into the internet and even books as solid objects are in doubt.

So even in the era of 'Miss American Pie', Javine and I were probably a bit behind the times—but as that song in the movie *Casablanca* has it, 'a kiss is still a kiss', and never out of date, and we enjoyed it knowing there would be more.

. . . It was Clifton got us moving. He knew a way down. The light from the burning car made it easier. I took Peggy by the hand and we slid down together, following him, braking with our heels. Fabrice followed with Katy.

We gathered ourselves together on a grassy shelf. There was still no sound of anyone coming after us up on the autoroute. The Fiat was burning fiercely. It wouldn't be easy to get past it on that narrow road but there was a track straight down the hillside—we could get down there.

We got as far as the wooden platform before the sound of the first klaxon reached us. We all stopped.

'That's coming up from Garavan,' Fabrice said. 'It must be the CRS. They have a barracks down there.'

We all stood listening, uncertain what to do.

'We've got to move fast,' Fabrice said. 'We've got to get away from that car. Then Rod only has to go into the gendarmerie tomorrow and report that it's been stolen and we're safe. We can forget the whole thing.'

I wondered what my insurance would cover, but said nothing.

'There's a telpher,' Clifton said.

The cage was parked at a platform among pine branches. We decided to try it. Fabrice was first in, then Peggy and Clifton. There wasn't room for a fourth. Clifton moved to come out but I shut the door on them.

'Hurry. And send it back.'

Fabrice pulled a lever, an electric motor started, the cable slipped over well-oiled rollers, the cage swung away—out and down through a gap cleared for it among the pines.

Katy and I huddled together on the platform, listening, watching the Fiat burn. She shuddered. 'We might all have gone down with it.' I knew what she was thinking—what would have become of her children? Who would have looked after them?

The CRS truck was grinding on up the hill, its klaxon sounding, its orange light flashing among the pines of Les Colombières. The cable had stopped buzzing. Now it started again and the cage was climbing back to us.

Up on the autoroute another klaxon wailed and another orange light flashed on the concrete rim protecting the tunnel entrance. Two men in Italian police uniform came to the edge and looked down. The CRS truck was just turning on to the stretch of road that would bring it to the burning Fiat.

The cage arrived. Katy got in. Down the road the truck had stopped. One man got out, then another, with fire extinguishers and set about dousing the flames. I got into the cage, clanged the door shut, pulled the lever. The pine branches brushed over its windows. We plunged away down the hill slope and lost sight of everything up there but the glare of flames and the flashing orange of the police lights . . .

2. The storm

THE STORM BLEW UP one evening not long after the lemon festival. An American warship had anchored off the Baie de Garavan. The town was full of sailors and Fabrice Laurent decided that as Chief of Tourism for the region he should do something to entertain the captain and the first officer. So he got together the little group of us in the town who were fluent in English and congenial together—which at that time meant Fabrice himself, Katy and Clifton Scarf, the Dutchman Ernst Bergen from the Agence Bienvenue and his American wife, Peggy, and me. We took the two naval officers to a restaurant called *La Belle Escale* down by the fishing port, close to the steps that zigzagged up from the waterfront to the old town and the Square of the Churches. In those days it was the town's best restaurant, run by Italians and specialising in seafood, and we ran through the fish courses, choosing this or that among *soupe de poissons, moules marinières, loup de mer, bouillabaisse, paella* and so on. The paella was their best dish, but their senior cook, who was Spanish, insisted on calling it *arroz à la Valenciana*, giving full force to the 'c' as 'th'—*Valenthiana*. It was quite distinct from paella, he insisted, though it seemed the same to me—same ingredients: rice base, with saffron (though perhaps the *soupçon* of red peppers gave it a Spanish tang); and then all the usual kai moana—the white fish, mussels, scampi, prawns, and what we New Zealanders would call pipis.

The captain talked about Jacques Cousteau and the marine laboratories at Marseilles and Monte Carlo. Katy and I shared a corner of the table. When it came to the choice of wines, Fabrice asked the officers, 'Which would you prefer—Virgin's water or the tears of Christ?' It was his joke of course, but there was certainly *Lacrimae Christi* on the table.

I asked Katy why Clifton was so determined to resist the offers of jobs outside New Zealand. Her answer was complicated. Partly what she said was that Clifton was temperamentally conservative, at least in the sense that once he'd made a decision it was almost impossible to shift him. So he was committed to our homeland, and to his university, and that was that. But I suspect that she was also and equally committed, and I detected a defensive tone, that same note of defiance I'd heard from Clifton—as if merely by asking the question I was proposing, or supporting, something improper, a disloyalty.

It grew late and the restaurant emptied out. Our waiter came with a tray of brandy glasses and a bottle of cognac. '*Le patron* sends his compliments,' he announced, 'to the American Navy.'

We raised our glasses to the proprietor, who was at a table across the room, having a late supper with his mother and his wife. They raised their glasses in return and we exchanged compliments.

When it came time to go I found it hard to get out of my chair. I was heavy with the tears of Christ. We scrambled for our coats and the staff lined up to see us off. We shook hands down the line. There was a plump waitress who had urged me to eat my scampi with my fingers. 'When one is in France,' she'd said, 'one must eat like a marquis.' In an excess of I don't know what I kissed her on both cheeks.

The proprietor opened the door for us. He had to wrestle with it. I'd been half conscious of a roar, like the noise of heavy traffic. A big wind had come up. Across the street the canary palms were tossing violently. The masts of the little fishing boats were dancing up and down, swishing left and right, crossing one another against the night sky. The sea was beginning to surge against the breakwater. Out in the bay I could just make out the hulking shape of the warship, leaning, hauling on its anchor chain.

The captain came out behind me. He looked about him, suddenly alert, asking was it an onshore wind.

I made some kind of drunken non-answer and was knocked into the gutter by a sudden gust. The Scarfs stood over me, deciding I couldn't be safely left to drive myself home. So I allowed myself to be helped into their car and driven to Garavan. The wind seemed to be rising every minute. In the lovely garden of the Scarfs' apartment palms and cacti were flicking and snapping, the bigger trees groaning. There was a continuous rush and roar through the olive grove that ran along one side of the building.

Clifton bundled the babysitter into the car and drove her off home. In the kitchen I tried unsuccessfully to kiss Katy. 'Here, drink this,' she said, offering me black coffee. It was a very dark brew and I could only drink it by disguising it with milk and sugar.

She pointed me to the bathroom, and when I returned she had spread a sleeping bag out for me on a divan-bed in the sitting room. I lay down, fell asleep at once, and when I next woke all the lights were out, the wind outside was howling through the olives, and I was sober.

I slept again but later was woken by a crash and a roar. I staggered out and along the tiled corridor towards the noise. Something had burst open in the wind. A shutter was banging violently. In the half-light I could see sheets of paper blowing from an open folder. Up and round the ceiling they went and past me along the corridor. A child's truck moved towards me over the parterre. I turned into the big room at the end of the corridor. Windows had blown open and Katy was wrestling with shutters. I could see her silhouetted against the steel-grey half-light that was steady until wiped out by a white flash of lightning, followed only seconds later by a thunder crack that seemed to come from directly overhead. The wind poured through the gap, over and around her in a continuous on-rushing flood, while out beyond I could see the olive trees with their massive trunks and groaning boughs and tossing heads. Now Clifton moved into the square of light. It seemed strange that they were talking to one another while they battled with natural forces. It was as if the blowing in of the shutters had come in the midst of a conversation which wasn't to be interrupted—so Clifton went on with it, panting, while they fought to get the windows in and the shutters back in place. He was telling her (shouting above the noise of the storm) that Shelley had drowned in a sudden violent Mediterranean storm like this one, and that when they'd recovered the body his friends had made a pyre and burned it on the beach.

All this while the wind rushed through and past them.

'Byron was there,' he panted.

'Byron. Heavens!'

They seemed to have the shutters locked in place now. They hadn't noticed me, and I turned away and went back to my bed, thinking *Shelley? Byron?* What a weird couple they were.

IN THE MORNING the wind was still blowing. The bay was a strange agitated blue, so pale it was almost white, but with long patches of dirty brown where mud had been stirred up. The warship was still anchored, leaning, pulling slowly on its chain. Now and then you could see spray caught by the wind and driven in a great shower as a wave broke over its side. Clouds of spray flew from the far side of the breakwater too. Fabrice phoned to say the promenade for a kilometre on either side of the Casino was covered in debris and waves were still breaking over it.

The Scarf kids wanted to go out of doors. Katy bundled them up in coats and boots and they went out into the olive grove. Little Hermi was blown over and had to be brought in crying. By the time she was pacified and ready to go out again the other two wanted to come in. Hermi couldn't be out there alone and there was a quarrel about whether they were to be in or out.

Katy had said I was to stay for lunch. I thought I should be making myself useful so I went for a walk with young Luke. The wind had dropped a little. In the garden were broken branches scattered over the beds and paths; fronds hung head-down from palm trees, flicking as if alive but expiring. The mimosa looked shaken to pieces and the ground around was scattered with gold.

Luke led me out into the avenue Blasco Ibanez. Enormous trees that might have been some kind of fig towered over it. There was a high yellow plaster wall, riddled with bullet holes, and now and then, beyond it, I caught sight of a wall or upper window of the villa it enclosed, also peppered and torn by gunfire. The garden was derelict and the storm had made it look more wrecked than ever. We pushed our way through long grass and fallen branches, the trees still swaying and groaning overhead, until we came to what looked like a shrine. Steps went up to an ornamental pool surrounded by small marble columns. In the centre at the top of the steps a plinth was surmounted by a bust of Cervantes. Behind him, around the pool, hundreds of tiles set in a low wall depicted scenes from *Don Quixote*. In calm weather, Luke explained, the novelist and the scenes were reflected in the water.

'I come through here on my way home from school,' he said. He was getting on for nine years old.

'It must be nice in good weather,' I said.

'It's kind of creepy, like a graveyard.' And then he added, 'I like it.'

When we got back indoors they were watching television—something about the inauguration of a monument, I think, to President de Gaulle—speeches, bands, military parades and fly-pasts, and President Pompidou wringing the Gallic rhetoric out of himself. It went on for some time, while the kids sat staring at it. I wondered how much French they knew, how much they understood. Pompidou came on again. Five-year-old Arlene's big brown eyes were fixed on him as he delivered his speech. Suddenly she jumped from her chair and struck a dramatic pose.

'And there was a scream from the crowd,' she shouted, 'as Pumpy-do went *farting* down the street.'

IT WAS LATE AFTERNOON when I left. The wind had dropped further and rain had begun to fall. I walked to Javine's place along the waterfront but she wasn't there so I picked up my car and drove home. I tried to read the *Nice Matin* but couldn't concentrate. I turned the most comfortable chair towards the windows. It was almost dark out there, rain driving against the glass. Faintly, at the other end of the house, I heard my landlady coughing and tried to imagine I was somehow living inside a poem by Rimbaud or Verlaine—one of those French poets who make a landlady's cough the signal of world's end.

Then I remembered Fabrice Laurent's invitation to meet him at the Casino at Monte Carlo. There was to be some playing at the tables and then a party somewhere nearby. Soon I was driving along the lower coast road, through rain that was falling now in bewildering exhilarating sheets. On the road rising through Carnolès, posters torn from hoardings hung in huge strips, soaked, too heavy for the failing wind to lift. The roads were almost empty.

At the Casino there were only a few people in the gaming rooms. Fabrice hadn't arrived. At the table I chose there were only two others, a middle-aged Frenchwoman and a desperate-looking young Italian with an aristocratic face betting with handfuls of the big square chips and losing. I'd brought all the cash I had in my apartment, enough to keep me for two months, perhaps three, and I didn't mean to lose it. I experimented for a while without success and then I settled on one number, increasing my betting on it when it didn't come up. I thought that I was being careful; that logic, or probability, or something equally infallible (like the Pope) dictated that if I stuck to one number it had to come up before my money ran out. It didn't; and it wasn't long before I was down to my last few chips.

I was betting one chip at a time now and feeling hopeless. I couldn't change—if I did, that number was sure to have its turn. But as I went to put one of my few remaining chips down a hand clasped over my wrist. It was Fabrice. He must have been watching.

'Logic doesn't apply,' he said. 'Try something more modest.'

I hesitated. '*Faîtes vos jeux*,' the croupier called.

'If your number comes up, I'll pay you what you would have won,' Fabrice said. 'Now put it somewhere else.'

The wheel was already spinning. I dropped my chip on black. It came up and I left it there. It came up again.

'That's it,' Fabrice said. 'Now let yourself float. Relax. Throw them around—but modestly. Forget the single numbers.'

I did. Soon I was laying chips all over the table, randomly, but it didn't feel random. It felt as if I was concentrating, aware and yet not aware of what I was doing. I felt inspired. Dimly in the back of my mind was the thought of Dostoyevski, who might have played at this very table. I was conscious of Fabrice standing behind me, a figure with horns and a tail, silent as I stuffed chips into my pocket. At last the number I'd first backed came up. I wasn't on it and I didn't need to be. My pockets were bulging.

But that number confused me. I didn't know where to lay my bets. 'I've lost it,' I said.

'Then stop,' he said.

I began to count my winnings. Fabrice waited while I took them to the *caisse* and exchanged them for banknotes. As we walked out into the main foyer I tried to make him take five hundred francs.

'Oh, my dear chap, no,' he said, waving it away. 'Buy me a drink one day. Invite me to dinner.'

Through the glass doors the illuminated gardens shone brilliantly, the wet grass pure emerald, the flower beds impossible splotches of colour, and the leaves in the trees looking as if they'd been modelled in wax.

I CLIMBED INTO THE FIAT and followed Fabrice's car up and down the winding narrow streets of the town until we came to a building that was circular and must have gone up at least forty floors. Inside we took the elevator to floor twenty-four. It was a big expensive apartment and there were a lot of people there, most of them, Fabrice told me, from the film studios at Nice where François Truffaut was working on a movie that was to be called *La Nuit Américaine*.

Fabrice faded into the group. I didn't have a lot to drink before it started mixing with my drinking of the night before. I was still affected by the tears of Christ. There was a girl called Giselle and she wanted to talk to me because, she said, we were both colonials. She'd been brought up in Morocco. Her parents were French, her mother a doctor, her father an army officer. Her father had been killed in the Algerian war and after that the mother drank too much and (Giselle said, possibly only for dramatic effect) became a whore. When she was seventeen Giselle married an American soldier and moved with him to the States where the marriage soon broke up. Giselle's next man was a German diplomat in Washington. Now she had run away from him and come to France where she'd scored work for herself as a sort of clean-up girl and coffee-maker on the Nice movie set.

'That must be fun,' I said.

Yes, she was enjoying herself, but there had been a disappointment. Truffaut had asked her to be filmed as herself, the clean-up girl and coffee-maker, walking into a room. The movie was about a movie director making a movie, and this room was his temporary office. On the wall there was a small lithograph Truffaut had bought at a show somewhere along the coast while the filming was going on. It was called 'Satyricon' and it was by Jean Cocteau and his pupil Raymond Moretti. Each of the artists had done a part of it, and you could see their two different styles quite clearly. It was very bright and full of action, and Truffaut liked it so much he wanted it to appear in his movie—so he had her walk into the room and for a moment the lithograph appeared behind her. This was very exciting, she said, because it meant she would also appear in the movie. But then when he saw the rushes he cut the scene so that the lithograph appeared but not Giselle.

'So not a movie star after all,' I said.

'Not yet,' she said. 'But he likes the look of me—I can tell. I'm working on it. Maybe he'll put me in somewhere else.'

She'd always thought of herself as French but this was the first time she'd set foot on French soil and after a couple of months she'd decided she didn't belong. France was too bourgeois. The women didn't like her and she didn't like the men—except Truffaut of course, who was gorgeous. After the Truffaut movie, she said, 'If he doesn't want to employ me any longer I'm thinking about going to Spain. Spain might be better, d'you think?'

All I knew about Spain at that time was what I'd read in long-ago Hemingway novels. It sounded pretty good there. 'Bull fights,' I said. 'And wine-skins, and Flamenco dancing.'

There was a movie director there she had her eye on, but he was some kind of secret Leftist and she thought the Franco regime might be about to move against him.

'What about Italy?' I suggested. 'Fellini?'

'Ah oui, *La Dolce Vita*,' she said. 'But he's tied up with Giulietta.'

'Giulietta?'

'Masina. You know—*La Strada*? *Nights of Caberia*? *Juliet of the Spirits*?' She thought Fellini was married to her, and that, it seemed, ruled him out. Evidently she was planning on a close relationship, and didn't fancy tangling with Giulietta Masina. I wondered about this, and thought it was amusing and absurd. But then I remembered it was said that T.S. Eliot's second wife had told her school teacher that she was going to marry him; and that she had got herself first into the post of his secretary, and then, after some years, into his bed. So why not? These days it's called 'aspiration' and said to be a Tory virtue.

She wanted to know whether I felt about England as she felt about France.

I began to answer but made the mistake of closing my eyes. Behind them I was still semi-conscious but I couldn't raise the lids. 'I see,' I said to myself silently, solemnly. 'You've been drinking without noticing. Quenching your thirst. When will you learn, Buster?'

The voices went on around me and I seemed to be on the floor. Someone, Giselle perhaps, put a pillow under my head. Later I half woke feeling myself carried, put down on a bed, my shoes taken off. It was a good bed, and a nice sensation. My limbs were heavy.

When I woke again a long time had gone by. It was daylight and I could feel the weather had cleared. I could hear Fabrice talking to someone in French. He walked softly up to where I was lying. 'Pretty boy,' he said, and I thought he bent over the bed and kissed me.

I shuddered awake. He wasn't there. I heard a door shut. The apartment seemed to be empty. Everything was clean and tidy, no glasses, no dirty ashtrays. A sliding glass door was open on to the terrace. The rain had gone, the sky was clearing and the tiles were almost dry.

Giselle came in from the terrace. 'So the big gambler is awake.' She spoke English in an accent that was both French and North American.

I wanted to know where the crowd had gone. 'The crowd?' She laughed, tapping her head as if to suggest I'd only imagined it. 'Gone. Vanished. *Pfut!*'

When she turned her back I checked my wallet. It was still there, still stuffed with all those lovely banknotes.

I tried to smooth the creases out of my clothes. Giselle brought me a cup of milky coffee and a banana, and I took them out on the terrace and walked up and down among the potted shrubs and vines, fruit trees in tubs, ferns and flowers in troughs and hanging from baskets. All the time the sky was clearing, becoming blue and bluer, and the sea with it. The wind had gone, the rain had gone, and now invisible dusters were polishing everything—sky, sea, the city-principality, the surrounding hills and headlands. Minute by minute they came up brighter, especially that cobalt sea—deeper and more extraordinary in its blueness.

Giselle was standing at the edge of the terrace, looking down. I noticed a bee on a flower—two bees. 'They work their way up thirty floors,' she said, 'going from one terrace to the next, like making their way up a mountain.'

As I drove along the coast road that morning I was thinking about those bees, and Giselle, and about Katy Scarf and the tears of Christ, and about Javine. I felt good. The storm was over. I had some money. I had new friends, a new car. It was spring, I was in the South of France and I was making 'a new start'. Who could say I would not one day be able to introduce myself as a writer. I tried it out: 'Rod Miller—I'm a writer.'

Strange, but I couldn't imagine that. It didn't ring true. I was glad I hadn't tried it with Giselle.

. . . Katy and I clinging to one another in the swinging iron cage that swished down through the pines with the light of the burning car fading up there. And I was trying to put it all together in my sore head, the long day that had begun on Fabrice Laurent's terrace and was ending in flames. We'd had lunch at Fabrice's villa. In the afternoon we'd sailed with sinister and power-packed Carlo. He had returned us to the town and sailed on down the coast to prepare a party at his friends' villa. I'd gone home and changed and found Javine waiting for me. We quarrelled and she ran away, crying, down the steep street under the pepper trees.

Then had come the drive over the border and down the coast, and at the villa somewhere near Bordighera where the party was to be held Bergen's Lamborghini was parked in the entrance, blocking our way into the courtyard. So I'd had to turn the Fiat around, backing and filling in the small space, and drive back up the narrow stony road until I found a place wide enough to park.

The party was in two very big rooms opening on to an enormous balcony-terrace that hung out over a rock-enclosed bay where Carlo's yacht was anchored, decked out with coloured pennants, and with a set of pontoons running out to it from a shingle beach lit by oil-burning flambeaux.

I was dancing with Katy, saying, 'Parlez-vous jig-jig, Madame,' when the knocking started, a very loud and insistent banging on the burly gates that were shut on the courtyard. We were dancing to that dreamy Christophe song,

'Estate senza te'—Summer without you. The knocking got louder, people were running this way and that, and Clifton, who had put away a lot of the party-giver's beautiful wine, threw back his head and howled, 'Wake drunken with thy knocking, I would thou couldst.'

'Duncan,' I corrected. 'Wake Duncan . . .'

Fabrice was pale and trembling. 'It's a raid,' he said. 'Must be a raid.' And he shouted down to Carlo, who was already casting off down there, to wait for him—'Merde-shit-you-asshole-cunt, wait for me.'

But the yacht was moving. And then from the bay entrance a searchlight flicked on and swept the water. A launch was out there, waiting. No escape!

At the gate they were still hammering, shouting 'Polizia' and telling us to open up. It was then I remembered Ernst's car had blocked us at the gates of the villa. I asked Fabrice was there another way out, and told him I'd parked five hundred metres along the road.

'Mon-Dieu-Jesus-Christ-and-Santa Maria,' he said. 'There's a track up from the beach.'

So we stumbled after him, Katy and Clifton and Peggy and I, down the iron spiral to the beach, over the shingle and pebbles, up the track among rocks on to the dark road, while at the villa the police were just breaking into the courtyard, and out in the bay Carlo's yacht was being boarded . . .

3. French polish and the Spanish cow

JAVINE HAD A ROOM and the use of kitchen and bathroom in her uncle's house close to the port—still a fishing port in those days, catching real fish and bringing them in direct to the market and the restaurants. When I'd got to know her well she used to leave her key on a leather thong under the stairs so I could let myself in if she wasn't there. I used to call on my way from the market in the mornings and leave her fruit and bread; or if I had nothing to leave I made a 'sculpture' of what was there—fruit, bottles, books, pens, candlesticks. It was my call sign.

Her family farm was so small it was hard to see how they made a living from it. It was in the foothills behind the town. The house was below the road. A piece of land that couldn't have been more than an acre ran down from the house to a stream, and a corresponding slope, only slightly larger, went up the other side. It was all more or less contained in a hairpin bend of the road, and the stream disappeared into a culvert underneath. But those slopes caught the sun and were protected from the worst of the wind.

It was all beautifully terraced, down to the stream and up to the road on the far side, all supported by ancient stone walls, and every inch planted in vegetables. There were olives, cherry trees, plum trees along the boundary, and against the stone walls that rose up to become the parapet at the road's edge there were espaliered apple trees. All around the house were vines, and on the terrace directly below was the poultry shed.

They weren't a peasant family. They had modest bourgeois pretensions. Javine's father was a hearty, vigorous sort of man who took your hand warmly at every meeting. In the summer he rented a strip of one of the man-made swimming beaches, and hired out deckchairs, beach umbrellas and paddle boats, sold ice cream and drinks and gave swimming lessons. Madame Rive did what she called 'supplementary laundering' at the height of the season when the established laundries couldn't cope. Javine's older brother helped on the farm and also worked as a stonemason, doing a kind of mosaic work that was traditional in the villages. I once saw him at work with a team that was tiling a public section of the olive grove that was called *le parc du Pian* near the Scarfs' apartment. They were wearing hats made of paper folded in triangles, as you do to make a paper boat. I don't know what purpose they served but it seemed to be a kind of uniform. Each man (they were all men) had his paper hat, a plain baguette for lunch, and a plastic bottle of red wine.

Javine was described in the family as the clever one. She was what I thought of (perhaps unfairly—I was no expert) as a typical French young woman. She could look at you with big expressionless eyes, pools of innocence, and with a mouth almost petulantly neutral. But somewhere at the corners of the mouth, and around the eyes, were faint lines of irony which made you feel it might be a mask that could come off—and then what?

When I had known her a while she issued a kind of warning. She'd come to the door to see me off. The vines that climbed around the door and up to the balcony of her room were just breaking into bud. It was one of those velvety nights you read about in the guidebooks. Down at the port the lights were glittering on the water, the fishing boats were bobbing gently up and down at their moorings, knocking lightly against one another and apologising as people do in a crowd, while the big light flashed from the bastion. I turned to say goodnight and she held on to me, brushing the hair back from my face, hooking it behind my ears. My hair was rather long in those days. It was the fashion.

'I want to tell you,' she said, speaking in French, 'I'm in love with you so you must . . .' And she hesitated.

This, I felt, was a Colette moment, a Claudine moment, and I played my part. 'So I must . . .?'

'You must,' she said in French; and then in English, ''old on to your 'at.'

Well I hoped so. I wanted to be 'swept off my feet', *bouleversé*, knocked flat, wrung out. I wanted the plangent note of Christophe's 'Summer without you' to cut deep—to wound with sweet pain. It was happening—and yet it wasn't. There was, I discovered, something maddeningly tenacious about my affections, and consequently about what 'falling in love' meant. It was a trick not easily done nor, once achieved, easily repeated or repudiated.

Are such matters different now? It may be they are, when sex is so effortlessly available and casual (I do not speak disapprovingly, but as an observer) that you can read about couples being 'fuck buddies'—partners who are friends-who-fuck but with no significant emotional engagement or deep attachment. I think I would have liked that, but it didn't figure when I was young; or if it did it was not publicly acknowledged—had not entered the common parlance of 'relationships'. The truth is I had been in love with Deirdre, and she still inhabited my dreams—not my day-dreams, but my night ones, which were more potent and not under my own control. The regret I'd felt at losing her would not entirely leave me, and in weak moments I yearned for her.

So yes, I was ready to 'old on to my 'at; I can even say I was 'opeful—but I was not sure it would 'appen.

But on the other hand, would it be possible to argue that Javine and I, far from being behind the times, were ahead of them; that, without knowing it, we were 'fuck buddies' already?

When I give this matter further thought I have to remember there was also my more than slight obsession with Katy Scarf, who was, you might say, the wife-and-mother I'd imagined my own wife was going to be. So there was the part of me that would have liked to be Clifton, married to Katy and the father of their three lovely kids; and there was the other part that wanted to be 'a real writer'. It had all come up while my divorce was in the air. My gay great-uncle, Desmond, who told me he would have been a writer himself 'if things had gone differently', was pleased I'd trained as a journalist. But he wanted more for me, and from me—'better' he would have said—and we talked about it during his protracted dying. He was an admirer of Somerset Maugham and even encouraged the idea of a stint for me in the South of France. It was not that Maugham had written much about the region, but he had lived there; and it was clear that Great-uncle Desmond wanted me to believe that he had himself visited the famous Villa la Mauresque, Maugham's home for many years, and that the visit was a secret because of the wicked things he had got up to there. So he would hint, and then deny it in a tone that seemed to wink. He told me Maugham had called the French Riviera 'a sunny place for shady people'—and he told me this in a way that gave the impression Maugham had said it to him in person.

He recommended Cyril Connolly's book—not the novel, *The Rock Pool*, which he said should have been called *The Rock Bottom*, because that was where its narrator ended up, but one called *Enemies of Promise* about the things that can stand in the way of genius producing the great works of art it is capable of; and one such sombre obstacle was what Connolly called 'the pram in the hall'. Marriage and small children stood between the writer (thought of as male) and his work. In my uncle's naïve but touching equation, you must understand, I was the one whose 'work of genius' might be obstructed by the pram.

So Great-uncle Desmond, though he didn't encourage our divorce, didn't stand in its way either; and even provided in his will for me to have the means by which it might be seen as a release and an opportunity.

I'VE DESCRIBED MY first view of the Baie de Garavan from above the town cemetery. I have two recollections of that scene, each probably made up of a number of different occasions but quite distinct. Both are fine-weather recollections, but one is winter, the other summer. In the winter view the sky is cloudless, the sea is blue and calm, the horizon is a clear line. The colours of the rocks rising up from the frontier posts are clear and sharp. Everything has a hard edge. And straight down there, directly below where I'm standing, the two man-made beaches that run for almost a kilometre from the old port to the port of Garavan stand out empty and bright, their stone breakwaters forming a yellow-brown T-shape against the blue sea.

In the summer recollection the sun no longer picks out colours and sharpens edges. Distinctions are blurred by its force. Every line is hazy. Colours and forms seem to melt and run into one another. Where sea stops and sky begins is uncertain. The sky is neither quite clear nor cloudy; it's a burning haze. And down there the beaches are a mass of colour and movement, with rank on rank of brilliant parasols in matching groups, like football teams, and under and among them so many human bodies the sand colour is almost extinguished. The sea is disturbed and discoloured with human bodies too, and it only begins to clear and look blue beyond the breakwater.

It was up there before the storm that I had my first conversation with Fabrice, when he invited me to join him at the Casino. I'd stopped the Fiat and was admiring the view when he pulled up behind me. 'So you bought the old guy's car,' he called. He got out and came over. 'Looks good,' he said, though the tone did not suggest *very* good. He was fluent in English, which he spoke like an American, as if he'd learned it partly by watching movies. 'Yeah, that's a real nice automobile.'

We shook hands and stood looking down at those empty beaches in the winter sun. I noticed the bullet holes in the walls directly below us—great gashes ripped through the outer plaster, narrowing to neat black holes. I pointed them out to my companion. 'You had your share of the war here,' I said.

He pulled one of those pouting French faces. 'That was our Fascisti friends from along the coast. They waited, of course, until France had fallen to the Germans, then they came to claim the town.'

We were side by side now, our hands on the railing. 'This is a good view,' he said. 'I bring visitors here when I want to impress them. But you can have too much of a good thing. We must not let you get bored.'

'I'm not bored,' I said. I was wondering how to deal with the fact that his left hand was moving over my right. But he just squeezed my fingers lightly and moved away.

We walked back to the parked cars. His was a heavy black official-looking Mercedes. 'Can you remember a date,' he said—and gave the invitation to meet him at the Monte Carlo tables and to come afterwards to a party.

He got into his car. The window was still down and he stared out at me, standing there looking uncertain, wondering had he really squeezed my hand and what I should make of it. He shook his head slightly and laughed. 'Does life trouble you so much, *mon ami*? Here . . .'

He pushed a couple of big printed tickets into my hand. 'Take that nice girl to the Nice Opera House,' he said. The tickets were to an event celebrating the eightieth birthday of the composer Darius Milhaud, who would be present to see some of his own works performed.

'*That* nice girl?' As he drove away I was left wondering how much he knew already about my new life—and more to the point, *how* he knew it.

AFTER THE STORM spring arrived. It didn't march in obviously as it does in the north, a big festival of green. There had been green all winter, and colour too, but now there was more of both. Snow vanished from the mountain peaks you could see from the town. Buds appeared on grape vines and opened into small pale-green leaves and grew into larger darker-green leaves—so fast around Javine's balcony you could almost watch it happen. And the flowers that had bloomed through the winter were replaced by others. My landlady's last supplies of mimosa had blown away in the storm. All along the coast spring was like a changing of the toy-soldier palace guard at Monte Carlo. One set of flowers marched off and another, even prettier, took their place.

But up in the mountains it was more like spring in the north. Driving up into the villages, and beyond towards the receding snow, you noticed blossoms on the fruit trees, primroses, daffodils and violets in the woods, oaks and beeches bursting with new leaf, and on the higher slopes that had been dull green or bronze all winter, brilliant splotches of alpine flowers.

I think it was only at this time I began to notice the frogs in the Scarfs' garden. Maybe they'd been there all winter. But with the longer days and milder nights Katy began to leave the windows open on to the balcony, and after the sun was down you heard the frogs, first one, then three, and soon there was a chorus. And at the same time, over the heads of the date and canary palms, among the cacti, in the spaces between the olives and especially around the huge cigar-shaped silhouettes of cypresses, bats would be soundlessly flickering like big frantic butterflies against the fading light.

I remember Clifton taking little Hermi out one evening to listen to the first frog. Hermi was almost three and just beginning to notice that some words she knew were French and some English. Maybe she was confused too by Clifton's habit of referring to the French as 'Frogs'. She wanted him to speak to the frog that was croaking from the garden.

'Erk, erk,' Clifton said.

The frog replied.

'Erk, erk,' Clifton repeated.

A few seconds' silence, and then the frog again.

'What does he say?' Hermi asked.

'He says it's time small girls were in bed,' Clifton said.

Hermi frowned. She pushed her face between the balusters and shouted, 'Erk, erk.'

'What did *you* say?' Clifton asked.

She looked pleased with herself. 'I telled him froggy shut up.'

WITH SPRING EVERYTHING SEEMED to change. Javine for example. I can place exactly the moment I began to feel I was getting out of my depth and that, even though it was what I thought I wanted, it might not turn out to be a happy experience. I arranged to meet her one afternoon and at the appointed time she wasn't there. I walked down to Judlin's photography shop and exchanged a word with the beautiful blonde assistant and then back to the corner where we were to meet but still she wasn't there. I strolled along to the paper shop where there was another beautiful blonde. I bought a paper and asked her why the town was full of beautiful blondes. Weren't fair heads supposed to be rare in this region? '*Ah oui, Monsieur, bien sûr*,' she agreed—very rare. All of those others came out of a bottle.

I went back to my corner to wait. Another twenty minutes passed. And then I saw her outside a café. The tables had been put out of doors in the sun and she was sitting with a young man. I'd met him before. His name was Raoul and he was a student. So had she forgotten our arrangement to meet—or was it just that Raoul's good looks took precedence? I didn't plan to ask.

I went over and joined them at their table. I shook Raoul's hand and kissed Javine's cheeks—the regulation mwa-mwa and back again for the southern third. I knew my feelings shouldn't be obvious and hid them behind the English newspaper I'd bought.

Javine responded with a shrug and went back into a rapid exchange with Raoul. Hiding behind my paper I wasn't able to follow more than a little of it, and that made me angry as I suppose it was meant to. A feeling of rebellion against the language rose in me. Like little Hermi I wanted to tell them, 'Froggy, shut up!'

Late that evening, when Raoul was gone and the tensions had been resolved in the usual way, I explained all this.

'Oh, *mon pauvre bébé*,' she said, stroking my brow (I was lying with my head in her lap and my feet on her balustrade among the unfolding vine leaves), 'but you speak our language so beautifully.'

And then, perhaps because this was such an exaggeration: 'You make it sound so *exotique*.'

'I speak it,' I said, using a phrase the French use of one who can't manage their wretched tongue, *'comme une vache Espagnole'*—like a Spanish cow.

'I wish I could speak English like that Spanish cow,' she said.

It was a good example of what I was coming to think of as 'French polish'. No reply was possible.

I HAD BEEN READING Jung since I arrived in the town, and because of that was recording my dreams in a notebook kept at my bedside. The idea was, I suppose, that this would help me as 'a writer' and possibly provide me with ideas. I was finding that the more I recorded them the more spectacular they became, as if the dreaming function was pleased to be taken seriously, and responded with gratitude. I flick through the notes I kept, which I still have, and wonder whether I elaborated, or even fabricated, in writing them down. Sometimes they were of the architect Hirondelle, whom in the notes I called (keeping up the joke shared with Katy) 'Mr Martin'. I dreamed of him following the Italian soldier he'd shot, down into that little valley. Or, still in the uniform of an infantry officer, he would step into the lift that should have been included in his design of *L'Atrium*. The lift was the shrine in which the soldier had died—and then (according to the notes) up it went against a cobalt sea and opal sky, and when it stopped it was the Virgin who stepped out to be welcomed by Giselle among the flowers and bees thirty floors above the streets of Monte Carlo.

Once I visited Gorbio, one of the mountain villages—not in a dream but with the Scarf family. Luke had explored it before, and took me along the first terrace below the parapet to a rock where, on his earlier visit, he'd seen a red adder sunning itself.

There was no adder this time so he took me further up into the village, through the winding cobbled streets too steep and narrow for cars, and into a public square hardly bigger than a large room. In the centre was an oak, bursting into new leaf; three old peasant women dressed in black sat talking on a bench; and there was a small marble plaque let into the wall of one of the cottages. It said that in this square, on a June night in 1944, a resistance fighter (and it gave his name) had been *fusillé* by the Germans.

For a moment I stood there imagining it, pointing the plaque out to Luke. 'Oh yeah, he got shot,' Luke said; and he went into a boyish pantomime of the execution, falling to the ground, gurgling and dying.

After that the Gorbio square figured in my dreams. It was like a stage set. Fabrice was there, interchangeable with (sometimes indistinguishable from, as if they were the same person) 'Mr Martin', one or the other shooting or being shot under an immense oak and a big golden moon. There was a strange self-mocking but nonetheless dark atmosphere about all this, as if some part of my mind was trying to scare another part which was refusing to take it entirely seriously. So I was tied to a post while the architect in his officer's uniform stamped up and down, looking impatiently at his watch and smacking his leg with a swagger stick, and the executioner, unmasking himself, was Fabrice. 'How beautiful death is,' he said—'*Comme la mort est belle*'—coming towards me and kissing me.

I wrote it all down, hoping something might come of it. Nothing did, of course—or not until now. After two years in the South of France I would go back to journalism, in London first, then as a foreign correspondent, foreign editor—the usual upwardly mobile path, finishing once again, and quite sufficiently grandly, in London. There was to be another marriage of course, and after two children and many years together another divorce, which was really no more than a mutual and almost-amiable severance. She liked London, I had had enough of it. When I retired it was not back to New Zealand but to Spain, where I live now and run a small wine business that keeps me busy and in contact with people. My children—even the one who has chosen to marry a New Zealander and live there—visit me from time to time.

The ghost of Great-uncle Desmond also visits, nudges me sometimes in the night, reminds me of those terminal conversations when he was on the way out. He may even be overseeing these pages as I write.

. . . All the way to the frontier Fabrice keeping up a continuous rambling lament in three languages. We weren't going to make it. Carlo was no baby. He was big time. They didn't turn out the civil guard for a few ounces of hash. When we got to bed that night it would be behind bars on a plank. They wouldn't worry whether they were going to get a conviction against us. They would put us in the cold store. It would cost Fabrice his job—or, at the very least, more than he could afford in the form of a bribe. And what about Carlo the shit? He'd pulled up his anchor and made a run for it. That was an Italian for you. It didn't matter what flag they marched under—red, black or tricolour—they were all yellow.

The headlights picked up red flowers and grey-green cacti flashing by among the rocks—an agave, an aloe, a Barbary fig, a pistachio tree.

Up to the autostrada we went, to get us away from the coast road, the obvious route for runaways, and at the toll booth, while I paid out silly numbers of lire and shouted 'Grazie! Ciao!' a phone rang, and as we pulled away Katy looking back saw someone running, waving. I put my foot down and they didn't come after us—but they didn't need to, there was no way off. They would phone through to the next booth ten kilometres on the French side and there the gendarmes would be waiting.

And that was when Fabrice emerged out of his monologue with a bright idea. On the autoroute where it comes out of the tunnel on the mountain slope above Garavan we would double back on our tracks—bounce the Fiat over the median strip (there was no steel barrier in those days) so we were still on the autoroute but pointing back into Italy. And then we would pull up on the shoulder. Fabrice and Clifton, Katy and Peggy would get out and scramble down the slope to the little road that ran up there close to the autoroute, and down on foot all the way to Garavan, and I would drive back solo and unnoticed into Italy and then return by the coast road, a quiet Kiwi tourist rambling back late after a night of innocent fun.

So it was agreed, and coming out of that tunnel, one or two hundred metres from the exit, I chose my place and swung hard. There was nothing else in sight up there and the Fiat bumped and scraped up and over the centre on to the other ribbon of autoroute. I pulled over on to the gravelled shoulder—too far over. We had all got out and were looking over and picking out where they could make their way down when the Fiat started to slide, to skid, to kick and fly . . .

That was when I made my dive for the door and got knocked down by it, painfully. I picked myself up, holding my bruised head, to see the car bouncing down there, rolling, and finally crashing and bursting into flames on the lower road . . .

4. The quarrel

THE GULLS THAT HAD come ashore with the storm and had filled the town with their insistent cries were gone back to sea, or the seafront, and the soundscape was full of swallows again, that elongated twitter as mad and mysterious as the fact that they never landed until it was time to nest, but slept on the wing, and spent their lives in the air, hunting and twittering. What was the use of the twitter if they were only up there to hunt? I still hear it as one of the memory markers of that year—like the faint drains smell of French towns of that period, mixed always with the perfumes of the coast; and the roar of powerful cars, ostentatious, self-assertive, emerging late at night from Italy; or the parallel baby-noisiness of motor-scooters ridden by school kids and students who liked to remove their silencers for greater effect. And then there were the weekend weddings with their barrage of car horns.

There was swimming too, another marker. I swam a lot, sometimes with the Scarf family, sometimes alone—seldom with Javine who seemed to regard it as a Northern fetish, something done by Germans and Swedes so astonished to find water they could get into without pain, and so health-crazed, they came all this way only to get wet. But it was not like the sea-swimming I had done in New Zealand—the water was so clear, and with a pervasive blueness, as if the colour was not just of the surface, and the sky, and the sky reflected on the surface, but was of the water itself, a kind of dye. And then there was the deeper blue when you swam out far enough and couldn't see the bottom—dark, 'navy blue', the colour of oceans. It wasn't always calm clear and blue like that—there were days of wind, of overcast skies and cloudy-brown shallows, and even (as I've recorded) of storms— but more often than not 'the Med' matched the brochures and brought the crowds.

Now it was a Saturday and the wedding-horns were blaring. I was sitting at my table, writing. Wasn't I? Something didn't seem right. A suspicion hovered that I wasn't writing at all but sleeping. Sleeping and dreaming. I checked. There was the pale flecked wood of the table top. There was the pen in my hand. There was the lined notebook open before me, the pen travelling neatly over it, the black ink-marks travelling from left to right, then down a line and again from left to right, steadily. There was the blue portable Olivetti, open on the table, a pile of books beside it with red and blue dust-covers. And out there to my left beyond the yellow curtains was the terrace, the heads of palm trees peering over the parapet, the southern light glittering on the sea beyond the town. And—yes, my pen still moved over the page, steadily over, left to right and down, left to right and down.

I was writing about Javine. That was my subject, was it? Was *she?* Javine? I was making love to her on the terrace of Fabrice's house below the boulevard de Garavan. The terrace seemed to hang high and absolute over the sea off which that southern light struck more than ever dazzlingly.

Javine's head moved from side to side, at first slowly, then faster. '*Je . . . Je . . . J'a . . .*' she said, and it came to me as a surprise that her language, even at this moment, should be French—her head thrust sideways now, staring into the great blindness of sun-struck sea, her mouth open.

'*J'arrive,*' was what she said. '*J'arr-iive!*'

Was I inventing? 'Javine—*J'arrive*'— it was the verbal echo that bothered me, made me uncertain, made me doubt the dream.

From somewhere above I seemed to hear Fabrice saying, 'If you don't believe what you write, who else will believe it?'

And then I was falling from the terrace and was jolted awake. I was sitting at my table as in the dream. There was no pen in my hand. The notebook was open but the page was blank. The typewriter was on the floor. Outside, a cloud had drifted across the sun.

I MET KATY SCARF sometimes in the mornings at the market and we would have coffee together in the Place aux Herbes. I was now, in a mood of self-analysis and squaring up to being 'a writer', which seemed to call for self-knowledge, considering seriously my obsession with Katy. Wasn't she, I asked myself, the lovely full-time mum I'd wanted the wife I'd divorced to be? Wasn't there a part of me that wanted to *be* Clifton, with this wife, with these children?

If the sun was shining Katy and I had our coffee out of doors. The two older Scarf kids had started school, but Hermi was always with Katy. Hermi could be bribed into good behaviour with chewing gum. I handed her a stick as Katy and I sat down, and she wandered away across the square, addressing remarks in English, with just the odd experimental word or phrase of French, to anyone who looked her way. When the gum lost its flavour she returned, handed the chewed piece to Katy and hung on to her mother's knees, looking sideways at me and threatening to break up the conversation. I slipped her another stick and off she went again; but the intervals got shorter until the time came when she accepted the stick but didn't move. At that point our talk was over for the day.

Katy knew well enough how much I liked her. She didn't seem to mind but she didn't encourage me either. She let me tell her about my failed marriage. She probably guessed that with her good looks and her three charming and beautiful children she filled the role I had blindly assigned to Deirdre. She treated me warmly, like a real and welcome friend, but at the same time just faintly mocking. I was someone she was confident she could manage.

Once when I was visiting the Scarfs at their apartment Clifton was in the dining room getting the kids up to the table and Katy called me to the kitchen to help her carry in the meal. She handed me a covered dish and in a moment of I don't know what—confidence, or more likely it was just experiment—I put my hand over her wrist and stared into her eyes with a look that was probably meant to be challenging and soulful.

'Take it,' she said. 'It's hot.'

I took it but I didn't get my fingers around the oven cloth. The dish was very hot. I dropped it and it broke.

I crouched down to gather the potatoes off the tiled parterre. 'Sorry,' I said. 'Sorry sorry sorry-damn-and-fuck.'

She crouched beside me with a new dish. 'No harm done,' she said, helping me gather them up.

As we stood again I said, 'Apologies, Katy. Wrong time, wrong place.'

She was smiling and looked amused. 'And wrong person,' she added.

The weather was getting warmer and I called once at their apartment on a Saturday afternoon. The door was open and from the sitting room I could hear a strange murmuring and scuffling, and sometimes a squeak or squeal that had to be Hermi.

I knocked and called, 'Can I come in?' No one answered and I called 'Hullo?' and 'Anyone home?', walking towards a noise that I thought might be someone sweeping the floor. When I got to the door I saw all five Scarfs on the floor. They were rolling about, little Hermi chirping with pleasure, Clifton and Luke emitting low tiger-growls, Katy lying on her back, her eyes closed, alternately smiling and wincing, the middle child, Arlene, climbing on to Clifton's back and falling off.

It looked like their own private circus and, not wanting to embarrass them, I withdrew before they'd seen me.

A few days later having coffee with Katy I told her what I'd come upon. 'Why did you go away?' she said. 'You should have joined in.'

BUT THEY HAD THEIR troubles too. It was one morning at the Place aux Herbes that I heard about the quarrel. The same afternoon I met Clifton at the *bar tabac* and he gave me his version of what had happened. It involved Peggy, Ernst Bergen's American wife. I owed her a visit and of course wanted to hear what she would say about it—so in the end I had the story from all sides. I was still thinking of myself as a writer, and that it was my job to understand and represent—that's how I would have put it to myself. It was an excuse for what a less pretentious person would call curiosity and gossip.

This, then, briefly, is what it was all about. Ernst Bergen (as I've mentioned) drove a Lamborghini. Like a lot of rich men, he was generous to himself and mean with his wife. He had the best car in town, which he parked within sight of the Agence Bienvenue, and Peggy had no car at all. He was always promising to buy her one but would never actually sign the cheque or hand over the cash. Peggy wouldn't have cared what kind of car so long as it did what cars are supposed to do—moved forward and carried loads; but Ernst thought, or pretended to think, that his wife's car ought to be a good one. He talked about brands while Peggy dreamed of a *voiture d'occasion* at 2000 francs. Meanwhile Ernst who (she told everyone) was growing a paunch and needed exercise, never walked. Even in such a compact town, he insisted on being seen everywhere in the big L.

Peggy's revenge was simple. Three mornings a week she togged herself up in protective clothing, put on a woollen cap and immense goggles, and drove a little power cycle to the market. To see her roaring home with strings of onions and bags of potatoes balanced on either side of that machine made you think again about the pioneering spirit. It perhaps shocked the town, or Ernst said it did, but still he didn't buy her a car.

Just occasionally, when there had been a row between them about it, Ernst would let her have the Lamborghini. On those days she drove him to his office and then took the car across the border to the market at Ventimiglia. It was on one of those days that she passed Clifton walking from his apartment to the Villa Maria Serena, down by the frontier posts, where the town provided him with a small office. Peggy stopped and offered him a lift. He accepted, and that was the start of the trouble.

Young Luke had set off early for school that morning and taken a big detour down to the Garavan port to take note of the latest fast cars parked there. Back on the promenade and heading for school he saw Bergen's Lamborghini coming towards him. To Luke it was the most beautiful piece of machinery in France. Of course he was surprised to see his dad riding in it, and that was the first thing he mentioned when he went home for lunch.

Now it just happened that Katy had offered to drive Clifton to Maria Serena that morning and he had said no because he wasn't getting enough exercise. Katy agreed it was a good thing to walk, but when she stood out on their balcony she'd seen a black cloud out beyond the port, down the coast towards San Remo, growing and approaching. She'd insisted Luke put on his raincoat because he was making that detour to the port. And Clifton should let her take him. It might be one of those quick drenching squalls and if he got caught in it he would be working all morning in wet clothes.

Clifton asked couldn't she let him make up his own mind whether to walk or go by car? To which she replied she only had his wellbeing in mind; that it suited her fine not to have to drive him; and that he was welcome to inflict colds on himself if he could manage it without making the whole family suffer with him when it happened.

Clifton stamped out slamming the door, the black cloud dispersed somewhere out at sea, the sun came out along the promenade and so did Peggy Bergen in her husband's Lamborghini. As Clifton told it afterwards he accepted the offer of a lift only because it would have seemed unfriendly to explain that, for the sake of his health, he preferred to walk—which Katy countered by saying he hadn't minded explaining the same point to her. And as for Peggy, she was sure Clifton had been glad to get in with her, and that he hadn't minded at all when a sudden turn to avoid a double-parked car had thrown them cosily together.

That was where part of the trouble lay. Peggy was bored and she was stirring the pot. It had started the first time she met the Scarfs, the night of the storm when we had entertained the American Navy at the *Belle Escale*. Peggy liked Clifton and didn't hide it. I'm not sure what he felt apart from being flattered.

So now Katy was angry. But like most rows this one soon lost sight of its first cause.

MY INTEREST IN THE Scarfs' quarrel wasn't just at the level of gossip. They had become part of my inner life, or so I told myself. That evening I had some idea I should maybe visit and stay late because that would prevent them from quarrelling. I even thought I might make myself unpleasant—get drunk, argue with Clifton, or with them both—so they would feel united against me. I hadn't worked that out exactly either. I just set out thinking I would call on them and see what developed.

But I was intercepted in the darkness of their garden. There was an old painter, I knew him only as Aristide, who lived in the apartment next to theirs. He spoke no English, but Clifton had long halting conversations with him about the theory of art. Aristide was a sort of uncle to the children. He'd been a pastry cook before retiring to be a painter, and he liked to make cakes and pastries for the family.

Aristide was just coming out into the garden as I arrived. He saw me in the light over the gate and stopped me. 'You'd better not visit them,' he said in French. 'They won't want to be interrupted.'

I didn't know what to say to that, or what it meant or implied. He tapped me importantly on the shoulder with two fingers. 'Please,' he said. 'This way.'

It was like being led to your seat in a theatre, quietly, discreetly, after the performance had begun. From the garden you looked up to the Scarfs' front balcony. But the olive grove was on higher ground, more or less level with their floor. Every room in their apartment had a balcony looking towards the olives across a narrow concrete canyon that let light and air down into the concierge's basement quarters. So if the shutters weren't closed you could look from the grove into any of their rooms.

There was no more than a faint flush of light in the western sky when Aristide led me through the gate and up the slope among the trees.

I asked where he was taking me.

He hushed me and led me on. Opposite the side-windows of the Scarfs' sitting room he stopped. 'Here we are,' he murmured. '*Bonsoir, Madame.*'

'*Bonsoir, Messieurs.*'

I peered in the twilight and made out the figure of Madame Hugo, concierge of the apartment block. She was sitting on a camp stool and knitting.

Aristide introduced us and she shook my hand rather grandly. 'Make yourself comfortable,' she said, pointing to a log on which Aristide was already settling himself. She spoke in a hoarse whisper, as the painter had done.

In the sitting room the shutters were open. I could see Clifton looking at a newspaper as if he was trying to read it but couldn't settle to any particular item. He was holding it awkwardly, at arm's length, turning the pages over, dropping them and picking them up again. Katy was running her hand along a shelf of books, taking one down, glancing at it and returning it, taking another. The television was on. I couldn't see it but its bluish light flickered in the room and I could just hear the voices and sound effects of one of those interminable ORTF dramas about life in occupied France that were still in fashion even though the war was more than twenty-five years in the past.

This was a strange, unexpected, awkward situation in which to find myself. 'Do you mean to watch them?' I asked.

'Well as to that,' Madame Hugo husked at me, 'it is my habit to sit up here in the evenings, especially in the warmer weather. Le parc du Pian is public land, Monsieur. In any case I hear most of what they say to one another down in my quarters, especially when voices are raised. It echoes down that well there. What difference does it make if I watch? It's like radio or television. For my part I prefer to see the faces. Have no fear, Monsieur. They are a strong family—not Catholic, it's true, but a family. You understand? It will resolve itself, I assure you.'

There were footsteps, the sound of a dog snuffling and panting in the grass. A middle-aged couple were walking their spaniel. Madame Hugo greeted them. They exchanged whispered *bonsoirs* with her and Aristide. I was introduced as a friend of the Scarfs.

'Ah!' They shook my hand. 'And how is it going?'

'I was just explaining,' Madame Hugo said. 'In my opinion it is not serious. These things need time. They have to be allowed to run their course.'

'Let's hope you are right,' the man said.

'And which one do you blame?' the woman asked.

Madame Hugo spread her hands, puffing herself up. 'Who am I to blame either one?' she asked grandly. 'Do I blame the wind when it breaks the trees?'

Ah yes, they thought that was pretty wise, and there was much nodding of heads and murmuring of assent, interrupted by a small crash and the tinkle of falling glass. Whether we had missed an angry exchange, or Clifton's nerve had just broken out of the protracted silence, it appeared he had suddenly punched his fist through one of the small squares of glass in the french doors opening on to the balcony.

Madame Hugo clucked disapprovingly.

Katy had come over to him and was looking at his hand, dabbing it with a handkerchief. They were half out on the balcony and I could hear their voices.

'You're a chump,' she said. 'You'll have the old crow after us now.'

I hoped 'the old crow' had not heard, or didn't understand.

'Sorry,' Clifton said. And then, smiling at her: 'In case of emergency, break the glass.'

As they withdrew indoors I whispered a translation.

'Bravo,' Aristide said. 'That's the spirit!'

Madame Hugo was still clucking. 'That's the spirit yes. But he will have to pay for the glass.'

. . . And it had been the afternoon after sailing with Carlo and before his party that I arrived home to find Javine waiting, sitting in a deckchair on the terrace. I hadn't expected her. She usually spent Sunday with her parents on the little farm, and as soon as I saw her I knew trouble was coming. She was not pleased with me.

She asked, frowning, where I had been.

I began to tell her I'd been to lunch at Fabrice's, and out on Carlo's yacht, and that I hadn't expected to see her because it was Sunday . . .

But she cut across me. She didn't mean today. She'd hardly seen me all week.

I was confused. It was true we hadn't seen much of one another, but I thought it was I who hadn't been able to find her.

'I want to spend the evening with you,' she said. 'The night.'

'Sure,' I said. 'That's great. Carlo's putting on a party. It's some kind of celebration. Down the coast near Bordighera—at a friend's villa. I'm taking the Scarfs in my car. Come with us.'

She seemed checked by that, as if it was not what she'd expected. 'I don't like the Scarfs,' she said. 'They're boring. People who talk about their kids . . .'

'But there's a party. Carlo's . . .'

'Carlo's a drug dealer.'

'You don't know that.'

'Everybody knows it. And I don't want a party. I want you. It's time we sorted out a few things.'

I groaned—wrong of me, but this 'sorting things out' was a conversation I was wanting to avoid. It would have to come, but why tonight?

She stamped her foot on the tiles. Didn't she have any rights? Why should she be treated as a plaything, taken up and used when it suited me, dropped when it didn't? A wife might put up with that but a wife had no choice. A mistress might have no rights but at least she had free will. Why should she let herself be treated as a prostitute—an unpaid prostitute . . .

'If you'd prefer to be paid,' I said. (Wrong again—ridiculously wrong. Culpable.)

'Oh, I'd prefer to be loved,' she said, beginning to weep. And she ran away down the street under the pepper trees. I went to the edge of the terrace and called to her to come back, that I was sorry . . .

But she took no notice and I didn't run after her, which I knew I was meant to do. It was in the script. She was right and I was wrong, and that was in the script too, probably, but I was still young and morally lazy. I was on some kind of a roll. There was a party, Carlo's (was he a drug dealer?—I didn't know, or care) and I was going to be there with Katy and Clifton, and Javine was running away from me, down the hill.

It was to be my day for watching things running away downhill.

5. The crash

STOCKHAUSEN'S *GESANG DER JÜNGLINGE* in the beautiful Salle Garnier at Monte Carlo. Chopped children's voices and gobbled electronics, clicks, bumps, wails (and whales), trills, all stereophonically directed under a green light, growing steadily brighter, bathing the auditorium. Everyone's flashback. The young in one another's arms, birds in the trees. The old subdued or outraged.

I was thinking of the skins of tomatoes, how durable they are. Boiled, grilled or fried, pickled, thrown out with the rubbish, eaten raw or cooked and excreted twenty-four hours later, a tomato skin remains what it was—a tomato skin. Indestructible. So I was thinking if you could grow them big enough, outsize tomatoes, tomatoes big as houses (small houses), you could manufacture tents of them. I imagined them in camping grounds, tomato-coloured tents . . . The lights were changing all the time, red was slowly swelling alongside the green. The tomatoes were ripening, the children's voices gargling and garbling, and all at once clear as day I had gone back to my first morning in the room with the balcony, only the earliest signs of buds showing on the grape stems beyond the french windows. I was lying naked in the big bed, just awake, and Javine beside me was running her hands over her thighs and telling me she was a good Catholic.

'So you'll have to confess,' I said.

'I don't think so,' she said. And then, 'Maybe a prayer of thanks.'

'Not to the Virgin.'

'No just to—Him, *tu sais?*'

'Just to 'eem,' I mimicked. 'That might be blasphemy.'

'Ah, so you are a theologian now, *mon ami?*'

JAVINE HAD WARNED ME I would have to hold on to my hat, but I knew now that wouldn't be enough. I needed to hold on to my heart as well.

That key hanging on the nail under the stairs—to me it seemed like the key to Javine herself. I used to go there in the middle of the day when she was away and sit in her chair or lie on her bed, read her books, and sometimes her diary, and play her records. There was a special scent there, composed partly of cosmetics, but also of woman, one woman, Javine. Now and then, in the years since, I have seemed to encounter that scent again. Scent is such a powerful reminder—you can be pulled up sharp by it, riven with nostalgia that borders on regret.

There were three floors to her uncle's house and they were divided into small apartments so the entrance and the stairway belonged to all the tenants. Javine's rooms were on the middle floor and the balcony opened off her bedroom. The bedroom was not large but she had jammed into it a double bed, and a wardrobe with full-length mirror. Over the bed were prints of Picasso's drawings of a naked satyr-like male and a girl, reclining together in the same kind of room, with a balcony somewhere at the edge of the picture and light coming from the sea. Hanging down from hooks in the ceiling there were always three or four dresses, linen or silk, with patterns of tightly interwoven leaves and flowers and long-feathered birds. They swayed up there on hangers, and to put them up or get them down she used a pole with an iron hook of the kind used for sash windows. The wardrobe was hung too with silk scarves that fluttered like an excited crowd at every movement of breeze from the sea.

Her dining room and kitchen were one room, long and narrow with unsealed brick walls which she had persuaded her student friend Raoul to help her plaster white. She'd put a desk in there with a yellow lamp hanging low over it. Against the white-plastered brick there was a crucifix, rough-cast in heavy black iron.

Javine's uncle was one of those Frenchmen who never seem quite drunk or sober but remain permanently stewed somewhere in between. She had told him that I was teaching her English. I don't suppose he believed it but he accepted the bottles of wine I brought him from time to time and made no objection, and no report to Javine's mother, his sister.

Now and then Javine arranged to come home from college after midday and we would make a lunch of things you could buy from the local patisserie—make lunch and make love. After that we would take a siesta together, the windows open, the shutters almost closed, just the odd glint and flash of sun off water darting light here and there on the ceiling.

Those were our best times together—and I remember once looking into her eyes and telling her I was in love with her. I meant it at that moment, and felt it, and was surprised when she laughed and said in English, 'Oh, we are such *actors*, you and I.'

It came as if in inverted commas—as if she was quoting something. I didn't know what it was, who was being quoted, but I had to recognise that it was true. I was sincere, and yet I was acting.

So I had to hold on to my heart. I was half in love with Javine, as Keats was 'half in love with easeful Death'. But it was also with the Côte d'Azur, that region Colette calls 'meretricious' and Great-uncle Desmond said was 'heaven'—and how could they, the place and the person, Javine and the 'warm South', ever be separated?

I AM TO HAVE COFFEE with Captain (I will call him) Dupont of the town gendarmerie under the colonnades across the square from the town hall. The captain's approach is puzzling— 'unofficial' is how he describes it, a meeting on 'neutral territory', 'an exchange of views'. And he insists on using English, I suspect because he is proud of being able to use it and wants to impress me. So the opening exchange goes something like this:

'Ze car you 'ave reported volée, Monsieur Meellaire . . . We 'ave retrouved it. I am afraid it is . . . 'ow you say?'

'Damaged?'

'Oui. Bad dom-age. Quite 'opeless.'

'Wrecked.'

'Oui, yes, as you say, wreckered.'

I am trying to look surprised and shocked. I ask has he any idea who stole it but at this point he orders the coffee. The waitress appears to be a favourite of his and their exchange of witticisms and compliments is so rapid I can only smile, as if I understand it all. If he is lame in English, in French he appears to be an acrobat. At last the coffee is brought and we go back to the subject of my car. There are a few questions he wants to ask and I tell him to fire away.

'Fire . . .?'

'*Posez vos questions, Monsieur.*'

He wants to know what I did on the day it disappeared—and when my answers reveal next-to-nothing (I was reading, listening to the radio, going to the market) he asks about the evening.

'In the evening,' I tell him, 'I got drunk.'

'*Tout seul?*' he asks. 'Alone?'

With what is an attempt at Gallic sententiousness I say in French that when one is drunk one is always alone, isn't it so?

He bows his head, it seems approvingly. But a few moments later, having sipped his coffee and paid my observation the respect of this thoughtful silence, he comes suddenly nearer to the point. I have not been—just for example—at a lunch party given by Monsieur Fabrice Laurent, the town's Director of Tourism? Or out on a yacht?

My problem is that I don't know what the others might have told him, so I resort to that bang on the head. I don't think I did any of these things, Monsieur, but since I fell down drunk and banged my head on the stones, I am suffering lapses of memory.

I don't think he believes this—or indeed anything I say. But I also have the impression that lies are quite acceptable. It's not the truth he is seeking; just a tidy story that will cover the facts of the case. I'm sure Carlo has a long arm and plenty of money for bribes.

I ask Captain Dupont where my car was found.

He tells me it was below the autoroute directly above Garavan. It wasn't identified at once. His colleagues were puzzled because it crashed and burned but the driver wasn't found, dead or alive.

'If you steal a car and crash it, you run away,' I suggest.

He looks at me for a moment. 'Monsieur Meellaire, would you tell me, 'ave you assisted at a party zat eve-ning?'

'Une par-tie?' I am mimicking him now and must stop.

'*Oui, Monsieur*, down ze ghost?'

My puzzlement is not faked, but now he makes it clear what he means. 'Near Bordighera.' He means down the coast.

'I'm sorry, Monsieur. This bang on the 'ead . . . On the head . . .' And I shake it.

'No memory?'

'None.'

'A night of lost memories, Monsieur.' (And he is smiling.) 'You are not alone.'

I look at him squarely, frankly. 'Captain Dupont, are you accusing me of anything? Do you intend to lay charges?'

His smile is broader now, as if he is applauding my acting. He picks up the printed ticket and waves the question away. 'Monsieur, zis 'as been most 'elpfool.'

CAPTAIN DUPONT HAD MENTIONED that I had bought my car from the old architect, Hirondelle, whom, it seemed, he knew, and that gave me a twinge of guilt because I'd promised I would call on him and his wife and let them know how the car, which they had been fond of, was performing. I'd never been back. It would be too bad if they should hear of the crash from the police.

When I got away from my interview I went hunting for Katy. I wanted to call on 'Mr and Mrs Martin', as she and I called them—but not alone. I found her in the market with little Hermi and she agreed to come with me.

We each took one of Hermi's hands and led her along the rue St Michel, hoisting her high when the pavement ahead was clear, making swooping noises to accompany her squeals of pleasure. This was where Katy, her black hair shining under the plastic of her transparent umbrella, had told me the French for 'luggage rack' was *une galerie de bagages*. We turned into the stone passageway, up the stone steps, through the gateway into the walled garden. I had seen it first under a downpour. Now it was full of sunshine. The yellow walls of the building soaked it up. The pool with its pale-blue tiles threw light up to the great vine leaves that absorbed it into their richness of green. Everything was in leaf or in flower. The shutters were open wide. Sounds of a woman singing, a child crying, the clatter of plates, the crack of a mat being shaken came from the apartments.

We climbed the stairs slowly, waiting for Hermi, who stopped often to look at things close to the ground and wouldn't be hurried or carried. At each landing I stopped and looked down. The sun struck down on the leaves and through them, making a chequered pattern on the paths and beds.

At the top I rang the bell. There was only a moment's pause before Madame Hirondelle opened the door. She was wearing a strange brown hat that made her head look bird-like. Her face suffered the momentary convulsion my presence seemed always to inflict on it and then settled into an intensity I couldn't interpret.

'Monsieur Meell-aire,' she said. 'How kind of you. Please come in. You want to see my husband. And this must be your wife, and little one. Come in, please. Come in, *ma petite*. How very kind. This is a sad time. My husband is in here. This way, 'sieur, 'dame, if you please.'

Tears had begun to roll down her cheeks. She hustled us in, crying and talking at once so there was no chance to find the words for a reply. We were led into the sitting room. On the table there was a coffin half buried in flowers. In the coffin lay the architect.

'Look at him,' the old woman mourned. 'Doesn't he look fine? Ah, Monsieur, didn't I tell you he would not walk down those stairs again? Tomorrow he will pass through his garden but he will not see it.' Her grief increased. The brown hat nodded over her brow. She uncovered the dead man's hands. 'Look at his beautiful hands,' she said, stroking them, rubbing them as if to warm them. 'They were always beautiful—and so delicate, so gentle.'

I was struck dumb. Katy wept. Little Hermi's bell-like voice chimed, 'Want to see. Want to see.'

Katy picked her up, and Hermi stared. 'Why is he on the table?'

'Well you see,' Katy said, 'the poor man died.'

'Was he old?'

'Yes, he was very old.'

'Is that his bed?'

'It's a coffin, darling.'

'What's a coffin?'

'Oh god . . .' She looked at me.

'It's a sort of box,' I said, 'for dead people.'

'Will he get up soon? Does he have a cough?'

'No he won't get up,' Katy said. 'Because he's dead.'

Madame Hirondelle smiled through her tears, patting Hermi's cheek. 'She asks questions.'

Katy nodded. 'The usual questions, Madame.'

'It was kind of you to come. Don't weep, Madame. You are very kind, but it had to be.' There was a suppressed sob, a pause, and then to me, 'The car, Monsieur. It goes well for you?'

'Very well, thank you, Madame.' And I added, remembering what the young *garagiste* had said all that long time ago, '*Elle marche comme un rêve*'—it goes like a dream.

. . . The villa to which the telpher belonged was silent and dark. Katy and I lurched as the cage jolted to a stop. We let ourselves out. The others were waiting, whispering in the dark. The flames up there had been extinguished, or were hidden by the thickness of the pines.

We clambered over a low stone wall and found the track down to Garavan. I was beginning to sober up, with the dull-witted sobriety of someone badly in need of sleep. I said it had been an eventful day. I must have thought it was all over.

We stood in a circle under the umbrella pines by the Garavan station, holding on to one another, tottering. There was nothing to say except goodnight. We would talk about it when we met again. They were sorry about the car, but there would be insurance, and at least we'd escaped the raid—all of us except Ernst, who was back there with the Lamborghini. We went our different ways in the darkness—the Scarfs to their apartment, Peggy and Fabrice down to the port where his car was parked, and as for me—I decided to go at once to Javine. I felt guilty about her, and wanted to make peace.

There was just the faintest glimmer of morning light as I walked along the broad new promenade towards the old town. The sea hissed on the gravel of the new beaches. My pace got faster. I could see a light in Javine's uncle's house. I crossed the street and went in, looked for the key under the stairs but it wasn't there. I tried to take the stairs quietly, two at a time.

Her door wasn't locked. One lamp was on in the sitting room. I put a hand on the table to steady myself. There was a chess board set up, and a game had been half played and abandoned. I tried to assess the state of play, and moved knight to queen 4. Then I walked into the bedroom.

The shutters were open. Colourless in the pewter light Javine's dresses swayed from their hooks in the ceiling. Her crowd of scarves stirred. I stood at the bottom of the bed and looked at her. She was asleep. So was her student friend Raoul, lying beside her. She faced the wall. He faced her back, one arm lightly over her shoulder. I remember noticing how their profiles seemed to match.

6. The departure

THE TAXI PULLED UP by the carpark and out came one two three, four Scarfs followed and hustled by Clifton with camera. 'Hurry now, everybody,' he said, looking at his watch, trying to get them to stand still against the background of the fish stalls outside the market. I went over and took the camera out of his hand. 'Join the group,' I said, and I got three or four shots of the whole family.

Then Clifton took one of me with Katy and the kids. Katy took one of me with Clifton. They promised to send me prints. It was before the days of digitals and emails and we were all still using old-fashioned film. It was all done in a hurry, but I still have the prints, which are very bright and clear. Those kids are married now, with children of their own, making the beautiful Katy (hard to imagine!) a grandma. Clifton was soon to be a full professor, and the last word I had of them he had become a vice-chancellor.

They were on their way to the station. They'd sold their car, someone had secured an apartment for them in Paris, they were leaving in just a few minutes. I embraced them all, singly and together, and we made promises (which have not been kept) that we would meet again. They jammed themselves back into the taxi, all shouting and waving and throwing kisses as it pulled away—and that was it. They were gone.

I closed my eyes against the glare of the sun. Though it was afternoon, the market long since closed, the stalls and pavements hosed down and scrubbed, still the smell of fresh fish and vegetables hung in the air. Half drowsing in the warmth of the wall I heard footsteps behind me, and felt a hand come down lightly on my shoulder. I opened my eyes, turning to see who it was. '*Ah, mon cher*,' said Fabrice, 'are these tears? You are so indelibly Anglo-Saxon. But never mind. That is life. People come and they go, and still the sun shines, *n'est-ce pas*? This evening, *mon ami*, you must come and have a drink with me and I will take you to a little place . . .'

True love

IT WAS A LONG time ago—many years—that my friend of that time, Mike Deniston, phoned to say he needed to see me. He needed help—it was urgent. There were no jokes, no obscenities, none of his usual stuff.

I said, 'Come around here.'

He said, 'No. Down at the boat.'

Since leaving school I'd gone in with my father as a fisherman. We took turns, or fished together, and shared the profits. Mum was gone already, a victim of what was called 'medical misadventure' or 'a slip of the knife'; my two sisters, both a lot older (I was 'the afterthought') had married and left home. So it was just the two of us working together, keeping the boat in the water and the nets in use. But Dad was getting lazy, complaining about his back and his hips, letting himself off when the weather turned against us—and that suited me. I was twenty-one and already I could feel myself taking over, becoming the boss.

Mike's tone suggested a crisis. I knew that voice well. We'd been at school together. He'd left as soon as he turned fifteen, the legal leaving age then, to be an apprentice builder. I'd passed School Cert and stayed on to the end of my sixth-form year, then became Dad's partner.

It wasn't a big boat, but fishing was good if you knew what you were doing and where to put your nets. We fished out in the Hauraki Gulf and north, up the coast. There were good days and bad days; there was fine weather and rotten weather; but I was out on the sea, which I loved, and there was for me a primitive hunting thing. I liked the chase, the excitement of a big haul; and I was making good money.

I agreed a time with Mike and waited down at the boat, which was tied up in what's now called Viaduct Harbour. He came in the small builder's truck he drove for his boss. There was a tarpaulin tied down over the tray: it was yellow, and wet from a recent shower that made the colour shine.

As Mike slammed the cab shut and walked over to the quay I noticed how he looked around, taking note of who was there, what was going on. There was a lot of activity, plenty of people about. He climbed down to the deck and said, 'Can we go inside?'

'Inside' was a small cabin full of lines, nets, ropes, vats, gutting knives, and a bench on either side. We sat opposite one another, knees angled left and right.

'I need your help,' he said, and took out his tobacco tin and began to roll a cigarette.

'Yes,' I said. 'OK.'

He offered me the tin and I rolled one. He lit his. It was thin, finely made—he had delicate hands. He took a drag and said, 'I've killed Rose.'

'Oh Jesus,' I said.

I must have believed him at once. I didn't say, 'You're joking' or 'What do you mean you've killed her?' I just said 'Oh Jesus.'

He said, 'You've got to help me get rid of the body, Ken.'

I asked how he'd killed her and he said it was an accident. That was all he said about it—all he wanted, or was willing, to say.

I said, 'You're sure she's dead?' and he said yes he was sure.

Now I have to tell you about Mike and Rose. Rose was a nice middle-class young woman, engaged to a rich youth (sufficiently well off, anyway, for us to think of him as rich) who was slightly built, sensitive-looking, a bit of an intellectual. These days you might call him a geek. Mike on the other hand was a big strong good-looking rugby guy, a flanker who was big but fast—faster on his feet than with his tongue, but not stupid. Sometimes Mike's silences could be more effective than my fast talk. He had 'presence'. People were impressed. When he left school the headmaster told him it was a pity he was quitting because there was a future for him in which he might have been captain of the first fifteen and a prefect.

Mike said nothing to that; just took the reference he'd come for and left. He went on playing club rugby, and even made it into the Junior All Blacks. This was a fact that featured in the papers during his trial. There were vague stirrings of sympathy for him, especially when it was suggested his obsession with Rose had got in the way of his chances of representing New Zealand.

I'm not sure where he first met Rose. He would have been twenty-one, so no longer a green teenager; but he fell in love with her, head over heels. If that sounds like a cliché, that's what it was—the size of it, the scale of his obsession. He was smitten, enraptured, besotted. He walked up and down in the darkest hours outside her house. He sent her flowers, cards, followed her, intercepted her in the street.

These days it might be classed as stalking. Then it was just a rather bad case of 'love'. He'd declared himself within a week or two of their first meeting. She was flattered, then irritated, finally anxious. He went too far too fast; she was engaged to the rich boy, 'in love' with him she said, and told Mike to forget her.

I got news of all of this over many weeks—progress reports, the ups and downs of it—because soon Mike began to see signs that she was softening. She would let him walk with her to the tram, chat to her when he contrived to be in the same public place. Once, walking with her in the street at night, she let him put an arm around her waist; even, for just a moment, let her head rest on his shoulder.

'I'm winning,' he told me, even though that encounter had ended badly, with her weeping and begging him to please leave her alone. Her tears had moved him and he'd promised not to bother her any more—but that was a promise he knew he could not keep. He didn't phone or write but he still waited in the shadows when he knew she would be coming home from the tram stop, and sometimes patrolled outside her house in the hours after midnight. So there was another encounter, another argument, shouting, threats, tears and a first kiss.

Soon the boyfriend was drawn in and gave warnings, made threats of unspecified consequences if Mike didn't lay off. Even that seemed an advance. Mike couldn't just be laughed at and waved away. He gained in confidence, and the boyfriend shrank, blustered, began to look weak and ineffectual.

Inch by inch Mike made inroads. He became the wedge, forcing himself into the life of this young woman, who was handsome enough, well-shaped, well set up, with good features, nice legs, commendable breasts, a nice voice and a lively personality, but hardly a great beauty. She just happened to be the measure of Mike's dream. Six months after his first telling me about her, her engagement had been broken and she and Mike were lovers.

He was like a man who'd been visited by the Holy Ghost and entrusted with the secrets of the universe—quieter, more serious, more inward, with an exalted glow. Even so, I could see it wasn't plain sailing with Rose. There were good times but there was turbulence too. She was still in two minds, remembering the intellectual boyfriend, missing his talk, his jokes and clever ideas, feeling sorry for him and asking Mike to allow her time to 'sort things out'. Maybe the difference was sex—in Mike's favour because I can't think he had the advantage in much else. But who knows? These dynamics of attraction are always mysterious.

And then he killed her.

I only know as much as emerged during the trial. She had received lethal blows to the head—not just one blow, but three or four. I imagine a huge row, Rose saying she was leaving him, Mike losing his temper—perhaps one of those events where, once the first blow is struck, the striker finds himself unable to stop. But I'm only guessing. And then, it seems, while he was still standing there trying to comprehend what he'd done there was a knock at the door. It was a friendly neighbour, a woman who said she thought she'd heard someone calling for help.

Mike told her Rose was unwell and had vomited. He was going to call a doctor or take her to the hospital. And then he did something daring. He said, 'Would you like to come in and speak to her?'

The woman hesitated but then said no, not if Rose was unwell. Perhaps she'd call tomorrow.

What did he have in mind? What would he have done if she'd said yes? Would he have killed her too? That was a question that was left hanging at the trial, suggesting he was an extremely dangerous man.

And now he wanted my help getting rid of 'the body'— all there was left of his dream girl. I went out on the deck to straighten up, to stretch, to breathe. The smells of fish and of the salty harbour were clean and fresh. There was a pleasant whiff of smoke from the Devonport ferry, just then chugging out and hooting. Mike followed me and we stood side by side looking over at the truck with its yellow tarpaulin. I said, 'Mike, if you mean she's in there, we can't load a body into the boat.'

'Not here,' he said. 'You take the boat around to the wharf at Maraetai, I drive, and we do it there.'

I told him dumping a body in the sea never works. 'Even if you anchor it to something, they always come loose and wash up somewhere.'

It was strange, 'surreal'. I was talking as if he'd presented me with a practical problem and I wanted to help.

He said he wanted her 'buried at sea'. He thought that was what she would want. We would take her body a long way offshore; and he had some concrete to keep it on the sea floor.

'Will you do it?' he said. And when I took my eyes away from his and looked down to my shoes he said, 'Please, Ken.'

I said OK, I'd do it; but as I steered my boat out into the harbour that afternoon, past Devonport, on down that coastline, with Rangitoto and Waiheke Island away to the left, my mind began to clear, and I knew I couldn't. Heading into the wind, which was coming up from the north-east and would soon bring rain, I made that decision. How could he expect me—really, seriously—to do that? It would make me a party to whatever he'd done. I was so relieved to be free of this responsibility a sort of hilarity briefly took hold of me and I sang a song of those times:

Girl of my dreams, I love you

Honest I do . . .

At Maraetai he was waiting on the wharf. I tied up and climbed the steps. There was no one about and it was getting dark—perfect for what we were there to do. I could see the truck, which he'd brought as close as possible to the wharf. We would not have far to carry Rose's body . . .

He came up to me on the wharf and I said, 'Mike.' I think I even grabbed his wrist.

'What?'

'I can't do this.'

He didn't say anything. He stepped back, found a rail or

bollard and sat. I could still see his face in the half-light. I felt bad. 'Sorry, mate,' I said.

He rolled a cigarette and handed me the tin. My fingers were cold and blunt but I rolled one, crouching there, and we smoked in silence. The rain was coming now, feathery showers, and the wind getting up, whipping them along. When the cigs were finished he stood up. I wanted to tell him why I couldn't help, but he knew why. I wanted to say he would be better to admit what he'd done, explain how it had happened, and take the consequences, but he must have known that too.

'You sure?' he said.

'Quite sure.' And then, again, 'Sorry.'

Another long silence. 'All right,' he said. 'You know nothing—I've told you nothing. This didn't happen.'

I said, 'Yes of course.' There was no handshake—no need for it. He turned and walked back down the wharf, got into the truck and drove off up the hill. The yellow tarpaulin was caught for just a moment in the light of a street lamp—my last sight of Rose.

Heading back to Auckland Harbour that evening in the rain and with the wind behind me I felt I'd failed him but also that I'd had no choice.

The next day, or it might have been the day after, was a Saturday and we were to go together, Dad and I with Mike, to watch Auckland play Otago at Eden Park for the Ranfurly Shield. It was a time when Auckland seemed invincible and held the Shield for I think it was four years through more than twenty challenges. I didn't expect to see Mike, but he came, and we went by tram and then on foot. Nothing was said about Rose; and not much about anything else. We had some beers and sat on the terraces.

Rugby in those days was going through a static phase: there were too many scrums and lineouts and, compared to the professional era, scores tended to be low. It was often grim grinding muddy rain-soaked stuff, and you had to wait, shivering, for those moments when the back line got it out, fast and without a fumble or a forward pass, to a speedster on the wing who scored in the corner; or for a big man on the scale of Don ('the Boot') Clarke to put it between the posts from fifty-five yards. This was a good match and our team won; but I remember little about it except that I was sitting silent between my silent Dad and my silent former school-mate who had killed his beloved Rose and asked me to help him dispose of her body. On the way home we bought fish and chips.

Days passed and I didn't see Mike and heard nothing about Rose. Then there was an item in the paper that she was missing and 'fears were held for her safety'. Her little blue Morris Minor had been found abandoned on a street in Hamilton. It was said she'd been ill and was thought to have gone there to visit family, but no one in that town had seen her. Her bank account was untouched.

The police visited me and I had my first intimation that it wasn't going to go well for Mike. They were suspicious by now, and perhaps already believed he'd killed her. There was the evidence of the neighbour who thought she'd heard a cry for help. Mike had not taken Rose to a doctor or a hospital. He told them she'd been ill but recovered quickly. He said the neighbour's impression that there was blood on his sleeve was wrong. The last he'd seen of Rose was when she'd set off in her car to visit relatives in Hamilton.

It was true she had an uncle, aunt and cousins in that town, but they hadn't seen her recently, nor heard from her.

I said I had nothing to tell them except how much Mike loved Rose. 'He wouldn't have killed her,' I said. 'He loved her too much.' They were the dangerous ones, the detective said—the 'madly in love' ones. They were often killers.

The cops went away for a while, then came back with more questions. They'd talked to the boyfriend, who said he thought

Mike was dangerous and that Rose had been frightened of him. What did I think?

They knew I had a boat.

Soon they were suggesting there'd been a murder, that I had helped get rid of the body and possibly driven the car to Hamilton and left it there. They began to threaten. They cited the case of George Cecil Horry, convicted of murder even though the body had never been found. They had a witness in Hamilton who would say she'd seen someone, a stranger to the district who fitted my description, same age, height and hair colour, 'acting suspiciously' in the same street and around the same time the car was found. They would put forward their version of the murder. I would be part of their story and the jury would believe them. I would be convicted as an accessory at least, possibly as one of two murderers.

There were two of them of course, one bullying and threatening, the other begging me to be sensible and save myself. The fact that I'd seen the movies they had seen and knew they were playing 'good cop, bad cop' didn't make it any easier to remain silent.

I talked to Dad, told him what had happened, and he panicked. 'Tell them the truth or I will.' He got me a lawyer and soon there was an agreement reached with the police. I had, after all, refused to help the killer, even though he was an old friend. If I would tell them what I knew, make a statement and give evidence at the trial, it was unlikely I would be charged with a crime.

Mike was already under arrest when what was left of poor Rose floated up towards the surface of the Waikato River, close to the Fairfield Bridge. It was only a mile or two from where the car had been abandoned. Mike pleaded not guilty. I gave my evidence, which turned out to be crucial because he'd said to me 'I've killed Rose'—the one and only time he ever admitted it. That, together with the neighbour's evidence, the boyfriend's, and police and pathology reports, was enough. Mike said nothing throughout the trial. He'd said to me, 'It was an accident,' and his lawyer wanted to know what kind of accident so he could make a case for a verdict of manslaughter—but Mike wouldn't help. He seemed to have set his face against everything and everyone, as if we were all interfering in something that was private, belonging only to himself and Rose. The fact that he hadn't called emergency services, that he'd wanted me to help him get rid of the body, that he'd got rid of it himself—all that went against him. His lawyer made what he could of very little, and the jury didn't take long to return a verdict. He got a life sentence. Hanging had been abolished by then, and non-parole periods were not as severe as they've since become. There was a good chance if he behaved himself he would be out in ten or twelve years. I got on with my life.

Over the next decade I married, had two children, discovered books and took courses. I was still a fisherman, but my life followed a pattern like rugby itself—it grew more interesting, faster paced, more wide ranging and professional in every way. Once I wrote a Christmas letter to Mike and offered to visit, but there was no reply. I supposed he bore a grudge—that wouldn't be surprising. On the other hand he might have recognised by now that I hadn't had much choice, and that he could never have got away with his crime. But I had no way of knowing how he thought about me.

Just occasionally I would have reason to drive past the grim grey stone walls of Mt Eden prison, built in Victorian times like a warning to the world, with conspicuous black iron bars and battlements, and I would imagine him in there, bored, cold probably, restless, longing for action and for love. Now and then there was an escape, and I would hope it was Mike, and imagine hiding him, helping him get away, even though I knew it would be better if he sat tight and planned for life after an authorised release. I was going to write saying I could offer him work when he was freed, but the idea made my wife nervous and she was against it. 'In any case,' she said, 'you don't know what his parole conditions will be.' Twice I sent him books I thought might interest him. I got no acknowledgement.

Ten years passed, twelve. As someone involved in his conviction I had certain rights to information. I was told he'd taken up painting in prison and had even been coached by one of our best-known painters, who used to make prison visits and spoke highly of his talent. This didn't surprise me. At school Mike had always been awful at English, hopeless at maths, but brilliant in the art room.

Otherwise his prison behaviour was described as 'normal'. He'd been a reasonably docile inmate, not a trouble-maker, but his release had been delayed because he was still refusing to acknowledge responsibility for Rose's death. That made the parole board fearful he might act violently again. There was some anxiety in particular because he'd suggested in one interview that the person who had given the most damning evidence against him might have been the real killer. It was probably the kind of black joke he was capable of, but it hardly served him well if he hoped for release.

The authorities didn't give it any credence, but they felt it had to be reported to the police and investigated. The police came and talked to me about it. They were apologetic. For the moment Mike would remain behind bars.

In the end, after about sixteen years, he was released, but because of the board's anxieties the parole conditions were strict. His father was now a widower and had retired back to where he came from, a small town on the east coast of the South Island under the shadow of the Southern Alps. It was a beautiful remote dreamy place, with seabirds, seal colonies, whales offshore and high cliffs looking over stony beaches that roared as the waves rolled in and rattled like laughter as they sucked back. Mike was required to live with his father, report twice a week to the local police, and not go further than thirty miles north or south of the town without permission. Thirty miles either way got you nowhere. There was no other town to visit, nowhere to go. The gossip was that he had settled into this new life, accepting its limitations, and getting on with his painting, which had become an obsession, his only *raison d'être*. It was reported in the papers he was preparing a show for a small gallery down there.

And then, after just a couple of years of freedom, with the show ready to go up on the walls, he went missing. His father's car, which Mike drove, was found half submerged at the bottom of one of those cliffs. The doors were wide open, big waves washing through. There was a hunt for a body. None was found; but the seas there are so wild at times it could have been swept out on currents that surge around the peninsula, in which case it would never be recovered.

There were some who believed he must have faked his own death, and the police were said to be 'keeping an open mind'. The police mind was still 'open' seven years later when the court officially declared him dead. And that was when his father, his sole heir and by now a very old man, arranged for the planned show of the paintings to go ahead. It was called *True Love*, Mike's own title, and I felt I had to see it.

I flew down for the show and stayed overnight. It had received a lot of media attention, but by the time I got there the interest had subsided. I spent an hour of one afternoon with those paintings, but there were still a lot of people coming to see them so I returned next morning when it was quieter. There were thirty-seven (the magic number) all of Rose—'Rose 1', 'Rose 2', 'Rose 3', all the way to 37—Rose from many angles, in every part of the house, wearing anything from evening clothes to jeans to nothing at all, and with the full range of expressions from reflective inwardness to eager animation. He must have kept perfect (together, I suppose, with a few photographs) his recollection not only of her face and form but of that crummy little house on the edge of Grafton Gully where she had briefly lived with him and where he'd killed her.

The attention Mike had given to the backgrounds was almost as intense and particular as the attention to Rose herself. It was as if the place, scheduled at the time for demolition, and long since vanished under the motorway that now sweeps down the gully towards the port, had been his *paradiso*. Everything looked marvellous, not because the objects—chairs, tables and rugs, mugs, plates and vases, the black phone on the wall with its circle of numbers, the bath on its shell-shaped feet, the WC with its chain and china handle, the untidy bedroom with its ancient chest of drawers, its unmade bed on which flowery dresses and a guitar lay casually dropped—were all beautiful, elegant, finely crafted, but because they were real, and of their time, which meant (because that was what was fashionable then) *before* their time. This was the house, 'a 1960s hippie house' I would have said, as I remembered it; or rather, as the paintings brought it back to me. It was Rose's style—the flowery ankle-length dresses, the long hair, the smell of incense and the talk of Hermann Hesse and Kahlil Gibran. And in each painting, awake, asleep, reclining, walking, reading, cooking, turning away, looking back, looking out, taking a bath, there was the face or the figure of Rose—authentic, irreplaceable, admired and adored.

At first viewing they were wonderful; but on the second visit I began to have misgivings, and to react in ways that were contradictory. Being 'taken back' in time, by sights or sounds, or (often with surprising intensity) by a smell, can be exhilarating; and these paintings 'took me back'—so keenly! But I began to ask myself what was missing—and the answer was nothing, and everything! There was no weapon, no blood, no dead body.

There was no truck with the yellow tarp. There was no Mike either, smoking roll-your-owns—no guilty party, and no guilt. It was like the silence he had maintained all these years, which had left us all imagining such a range of scenarios but not knowing what had happened. There was only the house, and Rose. All the rest was gone, replaced by what: art? illusion? the poetry of fact?

The last painting was called 'Rose 37' but in this one she was absent. It was that kitchen. There was a back door, a short step down into a tiny yard with a patch of grass and a washing line, and beyond that the green wilderness of Grafton Gully, full of a tangled mix of native and exotic trees, flowering vines and creepers. In that final picture the door is open wide. You can see the old gas stove, the sink bench with a draining board and gas califont, a pewter-looking kettle and a china teapot, an ironing board, a rail with hand- and tea-towels. The door so open to the wilderness seems to say that someone has just stepped outside and, like Captain Oates, 'may be gone some time'. It is Rose, absent at last, gone for good.

The paintings were a statement—they said something. I'd told the police Mike loved Rose and would not have killed her, and that was what he was saying, through these pictures, which seemed to me beautiful because they were so real. ·

They were a story, not true because radically incomplete, but creating their own reality.

I listened to a distinguished chap talking about them to an intelligent-looking younger woman. 'They can't have been done in prison,' he told her. 'Too detailed. Must have been done down here, since his release.'

'What about memory?' I asked, poking my nose in—but he didn't seem to mind. Just shook his head and said again, full of confidence, 'Too detailed. He's one of these hyper-realists who have to work from a model and a scene.'

As they drifted away from me I heard her ask were they any good, did he think?

The chap laughed. It was a civilised chortle, not a guffaw. 'He had talent all right. No doubt about it. But he was uneducated.'

I thought of asking whether I could buy one, but there was no one to ask. These two were just visitors and for the moment there was no one at the desk. And when I thought about it I didn't want that either. Whichever one I chose would really need all the rest; and I could imagine getting used to it, and then being troubled by a sense of all that it left unsaid.

There was a book in which visitors could make comments. 'Lovely,' someone had written. 'That's all very well,' said the next, 'but think what he did to her!' A third declared that the killer had 'paid the price for his crime'. A fourth added '*If* he was the killer!!'

The knowledgeable older chap and the young woman just signed their names and were leaving when she ducked back and scribbled, 'Most interesting. Thanks!'

Now the room was empty. I took up the biro. I felt disturbed by these reminders—and troubled that I couldn't think of anything that seemed right or appropriate to put in the book.

'Nice work, Mike,' I wrote; and then, just in case he, or his ghost, was hiding somewhere, watching me: 'Sorry I couldn't help.'

Sex in
America

THIS IS THE MOMENT when he relaxes. He thinks he may
only have learned it recently—learned it consciously—and even
now it doesn't always happen. It's when all the anxiety goes, and
all the effort. He is no longer worrying whether he is pleasing
her, whether she wants more or less, slower or faster, where
they are going, when they will arrive. All of that deliberateness
collapses and dissolves into this sense of the pleasure of it, body
and mind that have become one, bathed in it, irradiated. There
is nothing else he wants in the world, only this moment when he
can stop like a rower resting on his oars, gliding between banks,
listening, looking.

He is now that part—exclusively has become—'it'. Hooked in
hard. Locked by her at base. Anchored. That's where his sense of
himself is clearest. No boundary: himself as part of her; herself
as part of him.

But no—not exclusively. Not quite. Isn't he also two eyes turning sideways to see the nameless couple on the big hotel bed in the big hotel mirror—recognising the self that is not-self, the voyeur taking private note of it, remembering.

He meets her eyes in the mirror, half answers her half-smile, her eyes looking, then rolling back as he moves slowly down and out, up and in, back into the lock.

She is small and perfect, laid out there on the sheets, one neat leg thrown wide and hanging off the bed. He likes that image which makes him look so large, over her, in her.

If they were talking about this moment rather than living it—if they should talk about it afterwards—he might say to her, naïve, laid open and made innocent by the pleasure of it, that he wonders whether fucking is like this for many, or most, or few. Why should there be so many shadows over the landscape, so many storms, so much violence? Why is the human world not full of benign and stupid sex-junkies, high and happy on their drug?

But they have not talked in that way; not in words; only in the language of skin and hair, textures, moistures, groans and sighs.

When, two days ago, he was woken in her apartment by her climbing over him, getting out of the bed, trying not to wake him, saying, '*Reste, mon ami. Bouge pas*'—because she had to go to work while he, the visitor, did not—he was not able to remember her name. While she was in the shower he scrabbled through her pocketbook to find it; and then didn't at once recognise it—Catherine Demas—because she pronounces it in French: to his Anglo-ear, 'Cutreen'.

'Cutreen.' He said it, lying there in her bed, the first morning after the first night, a cable car clanking by on the hill—trying to live it as if he, who has never been to Paris except in his mind, were Henry Miller, and she some magic woman from *Quiet Days in Clichy*.

That first night there was more of the anxiety, the effort, the need to prove something (this was, in his brother Greg's phrase, *sex in America!*); less of the pleasure. Or rather, the pleasure was in the excitement—because it was happening to him; because he was doing it, and well.

She has thrown her head sideways and is shuddering—once, a moment later a second time. These shudders are what she told him last night were her 'leetle comings'. 'Ze beeg one' she likes to save up, hold off . . .

He responds to something, moves as she seems to require, and wonders how this can be, how it works, that already, like long-established dancing partners, some intuitive monitor in each feels what it makes the other feel—and responds.

But there is separateness too. He recognises it as he recalls, sees behind closed eyes, the sea lions among the wharf piles in the harbour at Monterey, lolling back in the green water, barking for scraps, and the huge pelican birds looking down at them— some part of his consciousness going randomly off on a track of its own, indifferent, different, and then puzzling at itself.

It is as if the mind were a series of shut doors any one of which he can choose to open and look into—or may choose to open itself. Here are the sea lions. Here is the beautiful monastery on the hill. Here are the shade-trees, some species of pine, and the white sands at Carmel; or the barren slopes of Big Sur about which Miller wrote what might be his only boring book.

And here, behind this door (she twists on him and it springs open of its own accord, slamming the others shut) are simply colours— greens and purples and plum-reds, strong, heavy, dark . . .

And there are thoughts. Thoughts about thought, about thinking, about not-thinking. Thoughts about images. About time . . .

'Timeless' is the word that comes to him. And then a phrase— 'No yesterday. No tomorrow'—at once rejected (she has turned on her side like a swimmer, resting, and he adjusts the angle, slows the pace) because it belongs not to reality but to Hollywood. There *is* before; there *will be* after. Yesterday was the day of the Berkeley campus, and Fisherman's Wharf, and the deer in the garden at Wildcat Canyon Road. Tomorrow will be whatever comes to fill the blank space that represents it. Today is now— this body-surfing, this skin-skimming, this cave-craving.

So why, in the midst of it, should he receive at precisely this moment, like a brief urgent interruption at once cut off, a sensation as if he were hearing screams and breaking glass? Is it one of those mind-doors marked, 'Future: Enter at your own Risk'?

A few weeks back in a bar in Los Angeles he met a scientist, Austrian originally, now American. Otto Bergman. Theoretical physicist, his subject Time. Otto talked about relativity. About (for example) how old you would be if you set off at age twenty and went through space and returned after one hundred earth-years. Tried to explain that, no, you would not be one hundred and twenty—then gave up and told it another way. (Or was it an unrelated anecdote?) Once when he was a child in Vienna, lying in the dark drifting towards sleep, he was jerked into full waking by the sound of the large single electric light fitting that hung in the centre of his bedroom crashing to the floor. He yelled in fright. His mother rushed in, turned on the light switch, and the light fitting crashed to the floor . . .

He leans back and without withdrawing puts one hand down where the curls of her pubic hair lightly brush his fingers and palm. Pleasure: the desire not to be other than this, and here, and now. Or rather, the absence of the desire to be other. The loss of ego in the discovery of self: 'Is it' (the question comes, he thinks, from *Moby Dick*) 'I, God, or who, that lifts this arm?'

On the dressing table, under and reflected in the mirror, is the Manual. Why did he bring it on this journey? Glossy. Plastic. Hard and bright. Not those in-the-head velvety colours of sex. The pages perforated and slipped into place over multiple wire hinges so its company information can be brought always up to date. Quick-fire, easy to use, for hard-pressed physician-subscribers.

In that little back room of the gallery where she showed him the Mirós two days ago, she asked was he a travelling salesman. It was the Manual—hated object—that prompted the question . . .

She is making strange sounds now, in the throat and between the lips—murmuring, twittering—in French, Esperanto, Desperato, Ecstatica. Her fingers going (so to speak) to the keyboard, going at it, scripting it, all action, the eye of her storm making precarious his control, her tongue forced suddenly, big and unmoving into his mouth. He does what he can with it, sucking on it hard as on a great lozenge . . .

HE CAME (HE TOLD HER in the little room among the Mirós) from a far country away to the south, down under the earth's curve, Ireland's matching state, you might say (some of his forebears were Irish)—much rain, many sheep and cows and no serpents. Travelled then, in his early twenties, to its nearest neighbour, notable for arid spaces, more sheep and many serpents. Then, after some years, came here to America, and had still not, despite his best efforts in that neighbouring southern vastness, and more recently here in the Land of the Free and the Home of the Brave, seen a living snake—not until this day. The day of the snake. The day of the Mirós. The day of (he would forget her name, and find it on a card in her pocketbook while she sang in the shower her comic-gravel Piaf imitation, '*Je ne rrrregrrette rrrrien . . .*')
Catherine. Cutreen.

He had scored (it was a long story) a green card, scored a job working out of LA, and so rode in his company car the highways of the West Coast states—California, Oregon, Washington—and even inland through desert and canyon and mountain country, Arizona, New Mexico, Utah, Nevada, signing on medical men, supplying those who were already subscribers with the latest updates, collecting their annual subscriptions. He was no salesman, liking best the desert routes where there was least business, the strange, down-at-heel, off-the-main-highway motels, the red rocks, the more-than-mansize cacti holed by nesting birds, the coolness of morning in desert towns like Phoenix, their gardens under sprinklers in the clear dry early light.

The land of wasted water that couldn't last but was lovely while it did.

And then there was Yosemite. Long ago and far away, as a child in that innocent dismal-distant home-place, listening to rain on the iron roof and seeing it fall on the green garden while registering also the intolerable melancholy of a bird that called itself (which was why the Maori called it) *riroriro*, he had read in *National Geographic* about Yosemite, looked at pictures of its steep rock faces, its redwoods, its cabins under them by rushing water; had read, imagined, hunted there in his head, sat around campfires; had played it out to the hilt until the invented stories lost, by dint of repetition, not their charm but their power to remove, and so had been set aside in favour of stronger drugs. Set aside and forgotten.

So he came home to Yosemite as to a previous life. He didn't tire of driving through it. Whenever possible, even when it took him some distance out of his way, that was the route he chose.

The deserts too, and even the Grand Canyon, were landscapes out of a Western-addicted childhood. These were the territories where he had learned to ride and to shoot. Driving through them now, the Manual-man with the accent some thought was Boston, others (closer) identified as Crocodile Dundee's, he made unscheduled stops, wandered off the road among those cacti that looked like set-props left when the movie-making came to an end, turning stones over with his toe (public notices and the local lore warned against it), seeking sight of what was still denied. Scorpions, spiders, lizards, fungi—yes; but a snake—never!

Was there upon him some spell, some reverse curse, the luck of the Irish which was the blessing of St Patrick, determining that where others saw serpents, and even sometimes died of their bite, he should see none?

Or not (he explained to her, his eyes sometimes on one or another of the Mirós, sometimes on her perfect upper lip) until this morning, the morning of this visit. He was to come up by air from LA, take the shuttle flight, a break from his work, his endless driving on the roads. He had a room booked in a hotel. He was to see *Parsifal*—that was his purpose, the one which circumstance, or more precisely *she*, would forestall—at the San Francisco Opera House. Ticket by courtesy of a satisfied customer, a lonely Las Vegas medic, lover of opera, fanatic of Wagner, who enjoyed talking to this bringer-of-the-Manual, and looked forward to his next visit (now it would be an embarrassment—or could he read up Wagner in a library and pretend?) when they could discuss the music, the drama of the king's wound, the king's bath, the holy spear, the magic chalice and the sexual charms of (could he have said she was called?) 'Kundry'!

So he was walking that morning down Pearl in Santa Monica to Lincoln Boulevard where the bus ran that would go all the way to the airport. In no hurry. Knowing it was early, and that the planes flew on the hour . . .

And there it was. Right there. Moving. Rippling along in the gutter, keeping pace with him. Bronze back, yellow sides, beady eye, flickering tongue. Not much more than a half-metre in length. Not happy to be where it was, nor to have him watching it—and when it came to a car access it turned and made its way up from the roadway, slipping, hesitating, seeming to find the smooth concrete uncongenial, unhelpful to its means of locomotion. So he had time to take out his camera and photograph it—once, twice, a third time—before it reached the front garden of the house and slithered quickly away among low shrubs at the side of the drive.

SHE TALKS CONSTANTLY of Paris, plans to return there, is glad that he knows some French, can read it, even speak it a little, however haltingly; that he seems to understand her francophone jokes, her little obscenities; that Paris is high on the list of sacred places he plans to set foot in before (and that will be soon) he reaches thirty—the age when, for some reason no more explicable than why Cinderella should have to cut and run at midnight, he sees his *wanderjahre* coming to an end with a return to that green dark under-region of rain and cows.

Naked, they sprawl in her bed, on the rug beside it, on the divan in her sitting room; or sit in kimonos (she has one from a past lover that fits him) at the table in her kitchen, drinking coffee, eating fruit yoghurt and croissants, looking out over the rooftops towards the bay where the morning fog is lifting, while much of her talk is of Paris, or of the means to get back there.

Yes France is home. Yes she can return at any time. But she plans to go with money, enough to open her own little gallery in Paris. Otherwise it will have to be the provinces, Aix-en-Provence perhaps, or her home town of Dijon, and though that could be good it is not what she wants.

She tells him about the little Paris street she lived in when she was a student. The gravelled square at one end with the big church and the fountain and the two cafés with tables out on the pavements. The two bookshops, three picture galleries, the *épicerie*. The *boulangerie* on the corner halfway up the cobbled street, where once (once only) she let the baker fuck her in return for a *gâteau*, *très grand*, sculptural, for her boyfriend's birthday, and came home with puffs and handprints of flour on her quickly lifted skirt. And at the end of the street the palace and the fountains, and the extensive gardens so full of statuary you kept coming on some famous head or torso or figure you hadn't seen before, peering out of a clump of bushes or crouching among them, just when you thought you knew them all.

Then, embarrassed at having talked so much and with such enthusiasm, she asks him again to talk about *his* home. He tells her instead about Santa Monica, his apartment there not far from the sea—one long white room with kitchen and bathroom off—and how he has furnished it: at one end his 'office', a white-topped desk on white-enamelled steel legs, a small black computer (company issue, for his records), three black shelves for books and CDs, red plastic trays for paper, a white phone, white scanner/copier and printer, and black office chair. On the wall above the desk a pink-faced electric clock that advertises piston rings; and along the outer wall under a window, the red futon on which he sleeps.

'That,' he explains, 'is the working and sleeping end'; and when she frowns at this conjunction he explains that if she should visit LA, *when* she visits, the futon will be opened out to make a double bed, and everything on the desk will be shut down, the machines switched off.

At the other end is his kitchen-eating-living space, with small dining table and chairs, divan with florid cushions, and two chairs in dark red canvas, DIRECTOR in black on the back of one, SCRIPT EDITOR on the other. This is the end where he eats, sits, watches television and (very seldom) entertains.

Out there, through the windows, is his sandy back garden, watered daily, his small patch of lawn, with a lemon tree, and bougainvillea over the high enclosing fence.

And (turning to the left past the windows) the long blank wall on which he imagined the Miró . . .

Ah the Miró. 'Miroir de l'homme, II'. Her eyes light up. 'You will buy it. You will buy it, *mon amour. Il faut, absolument.* You must.'

She pushes him to the floor, and as he crawls away she throws a leg over, bestrides him, rides him around the room, tightening her knees on his naked flanks, asking can he feel what she calls, mixing French and English, her 'levers' kissing his back.

Suddenly he tips her sideways on to the rug and falls on her, pinning her down. 'What was it like with the baker?'

HIS PLANE LEFT LATE. There had been an hour, more than an hour, while it waited, fully loaded in the Los Angeles sun, for word that a backlog of planes stacked to come in through fog at San Francisco had reduced sufficiently for this one, heading there, to be cleared for take-off.

When, after the delay and an hour's flight, they got there, the fog had lifted. He took the bus into town, checked in at his hotel, the Holiday Inn at the City Centre, made sure that he knew the route to the Opera House, then headed for Union Square.

He was strolling, looking for somewhere to sit down, drink coffee, read a newspaper, when the painting (if that was what it was) took his eye. It was in the window of a small art dealer close to the square. There was a vivid central column, just off-vertical, rising as if from two mounds and ending in a sky containing streaks and puffs of bright colour that might have been fireworks or fantastic clouds. He did not know what kind of art work it was, what technique it exemplified, only that its strange mixture of billowing unbounded colour and fine hard dark ink-lines excited him, and that he imagined it (not 'seriously', not thinking of himself as a person who 'buys works of art') hanging on that emptiness of white wall which had seemed, the better he made his apartment look, the more to demand that it be adorned with something bright and bold.

He looked at the work, enjoyed, moved on, returned, noticed

a detail: around the base of the colour-column a small serpent curled, its eye black, its forked tongue flame-red as if the mouth were filled with fire.

It was not the name, Miró, which he now saw at the bottom corner beside the date, 1970, but the serpent—that fortuitous conjunction with what he had seen only a few hours before in Santa Monica—which made him step into the gallery, guessing he must look as he felt, tentative . . .

There, however, to be greeted reassuringly by a young woman—strong French accent, small neat good looks, a manner that mixed neutral practicality and unobtrusive charm.

The Miró, she told him, was one of a series. Number 66 of 250. The technique, aqua-tint and dry-point. As for the form (she was talking as she removed it from the window)—phallic obviously, wasn't it so?

And he saw now that the central column ended in a kind of arrowhead, while the two mounds it rose from might have been symbolic testes.

'Maybe about the Fall,' she suggested. 'It's called "Miroir de l'homme par les bêtes, II". The beasts as a mirror of man.'

She took him into a small back room, closed the door and hung the picture under perfect lighting. It was very pretty, decorative, bright, with a lot of lines and what might have been pairs of eyes—he liked it. It didn't matter, and he didn't say, but he couldn't see any beasts.

She brought out other Mirós to place beside it for comparison; showed him documents of authentication which came from a dealer in New York; opened books on Miró and showed how 'Miroir de l'homme, II' was characteristic of the artist's last phase; talked about recent Miró prices in London and Paris, and suggested they were higher there; told him she had a client whose way of financing his summer holiday in Europe was to buy a minor work by a major Modernist here on the West Coast, and sell it in London, Paris or Madrid.

'Signed and dated,' she said at intervals.

Somewhere in all of this a price was mentioned, $4750, though she thought her employer, the owner of the gallery, might consider a lower offer, this was not unreasonable.

In some part of his mind he was trying to disentangle his interest in the painting from his interest in the woman. Before this moment he would have said he did not have $4750 to spend on a work of art. Not even one thousand. But why not? He was employed, and saving. He would have spent that much—more— on a car, and only did not because the company supplied one. This might even be a profitable investment, if the Frenchwoman was to be believed . . .

It was late afternoon. When they emerged from the small room, the gallery was closed, the staff had gone. He said he would now have to go away and think seriously.

'Ah, *mon ami*,' she said, shaking her head. 'Thinking is not so good as doing. In this art business you must strike . . . What do you say in English? While the iron is . . .'

While it was hot, he struck. He asked her to let him take her to a restaurant where they could continue to talk about it. He was surprised when she accepted; and there was even a moment of regret about *Parsifal*.

That night and the next he spent at her apartment. The third, because she had a woman friend coming through town to whom she had promised a bed for the night, they went to his hotel. The day after that he was to return to LA.

THE STORM (HIS AND HERS) is passing, passes, is passed. The big hard lozenge has been removed from his mouth. They roll apart, holding hands, legs (his left, her right) still interlocked, murmuring, staring up at the ceiling which is dimly lit by a single bedside lamp. They drift into sleep.

Later they half wake, pull covers over one another, rearrange legs and arms, switch off the lamp, kiss as sexlessly as sister and brother, and sleep again.

After how long—one hour? three?—he is dreaming of *Parsifal*, the opera he has not seen, when the characters' singing changes, becomes shrieking, screaming. Something is shattering. Now it is a scene in the movie of *Doctor Zhivago* when a sheet of ice that has filled the open door of a railway wagon is smashed. No, not ice. Glass. And the voices, yelling. Calling for help . . .

'*Cheri.*' She is speaking into his ear—he can feel her hair against his cheek. '*Réveille-toi.* Wake, darling.'

She shakes him gently. He can hear sirens now. 'Something is happening.'

'Some-sing?' he murmurs, imitating her.

They are on the eighth floor and their room is in darkness, but light comes in from outside. Naked, they go to the window.

There is a fire in the next-door hotel, the San Franciscan. It seems to be on the floor exactly opposite theirs, and the one above. Elevators are not working and fire has cut access by the stairs, trapping those in the two top floors who have not already escaped. Corridors are filling with smoke. People are shouting down into the street, some unfurling useless ropes of knotted sheets. In a room directly opposite a man, very calm, very orderly, goes to the window and looks down, goes to the door and looks out into the smoke-filled corridor, picks up the phone and speaks, sorts things in his room, returns to the window and looks down where two ladder trucks have arrived.

The ladders ascend. Soon rows of dark huddled figures are climbing out, helped by firefighters. Some people have to be encouraged, almost forced, but the line keeps moving. There is less noise now as they clamber down the eight or nine floors to the street. Other firefighters wearing masks are up there with hoses. Some appear to have the job of breaking every window on the two top floors. Panes, smashed out, crash down to a street now full of police cars, fire trucks, ambulances, and a small late-night crowd held back behind a police line. There are shouts of encouragement, cheers, flashlights.

He stands behind her at the window and feels her begin to push back against him, moving from side to side. He looks down. She is leaning forward, legs apart, arms forward, propping against the sill. The vaguely diffused light from the night city gleams on the perfect white curve of her buttocks. She turns her head to look at him. She is like some lovely animal. 'Do it, *mon vieux,*' she says. He thinks of Miró—the beasts as a mirror of man.

He tries, spreading his feet wide, bending at the knees, but his legs are too long. He can't quite get in under, and up.

On the floor there are two books of the San Francisco telephone directory. She moves them into place and stands on them. 'Now,' she says. 'Do it.'

He does. Flames are licking out through the smashed window of what was the orderly man's room. He sees fire through the wild aureole of her hair. The smell of smoke has begun to reach into their room. Shouts come up from the street, where the whirling lights of the fire trucks spiral round and round. Glass continues to crash down. Men dressed as for a space-walk can be seen moving from room to room, in and out of patches of light.

Someone still left on the top floor yells for help, and the spacemen turn and look at one another and lumber off in the direction of the cry.

'Harder,' she says. 'Harder!'

He drives up into her with more force, grunting, thighs slapping upward against buttocks and the back of her legs. She is lifted with the force of each thrust.

'*Harder,*' she says.

NEXT MORNING THEY HAD room-service bring them an early breakfast. He had the television on without the sound, looking at images of the fire next door, when she said, '*Mon cher*, today you must confirm.'

'Confirm?'

'The purchase, darling. The Miró.'

'Ze pur-chase, duh-leeeng.'

She cuffed his head—and he was himself aware that imitating (and exaggerating) her accent was less amusing each time it was repeated. 'I'm serious,' she said. 'You must sign the paper. Put down a deposit.'

He rolled over and looked at her. 'I can't buy the Miró.'

'Why not? You like it. You want it.'

'I don't have the money.'

'I don't believe you.'

'Well, let's say I have it but I need it.' He saw her expression and decided to make it clear. 'I mustn't accumulate . . . *things*. That's all. I'm on the road, honey.'

'You could make a profit.'

'If I sold. But would I? I don't know the market, the dealers . . . Look, I've thought about it, carefully. The Miró's lovely. But not for me. Not this time.' In case there should be doubt he added, 'That's final, Catherine. It has to be.'

It was as if she had been shot out of the bed by the release of a spring. Naked, her face set hard in an expression he had not seen before, she fumbled to put on her bra. 'So it was all a lie.'

'What was?'

She didn't reply—she was too angry—and he asked again: 'What was a lie?'

'All this.' She waved a hand at the bed that was like a battlefield. 'All this fucking me . . .'

Silence, until he said, in a voice that sounded strained and weak, 'You mean you fucked me so I would . . .'

She was not listening. She had found her underpants. Now she dragged her skirt over them. The face was still hard, but there were tears. 'You are not a man of honour.'

'A man of . . . *Jesus!* Did you think I was the baker? Did you fuck me for a *cake*?'

Silence. She had dragged her shirt on and was tucking it in, roughly so there were creases and lumps. She went to the mirror to look at her tears and touch them with her finger.

'What do you get for making a sale, Catherine? A commission? Ten per cent?'

No answer.

'Is that what you're worth? Ten per cent of four seven five zero? Four hundred and seventy-five bucks? For three days of heavy sex? What's that? One five eight a night? Is that how I'm supposed . . .'

That was off the top of his head. He would check later on a pad and be surprised to find his heat-of-the-moment arithmetic was good.

He got out of bed, his movements expressing indignation, displaying it. In his travel bag he found his chequebook. He went to the table and wrote her the cheque—held it out to her. 'Take it.'

She was standing looking down at it. He did not think of it as the payment of a debt—did not really expect that she would accept it. It was a way of making clear to her . . .

She took it, read the figures, folded it, and tucked it into her pocketbook.

HE HAD A WINDOW SEAT. Down there the arid landscape of Southern California rolled and lifted away towards the mountains, with here and there startling green patches where irrigation water had been pumped in from the north. Through the windows on the opposite side he caught the broad glare of afternoon sunlight striking off the ocean. They had just begun the long descent into Los Angeles.

His tray table was down and there was a postcard lying on it. He had addressed it, and written 'Dear Greg'.

Greg was the brother who had sent a card saying all was well, life was boring, the government was going to fall, and 'tell me about *sex in America!*'

He remembered now what she'd said when he asked, 'What was it like with the baker?'

The baker, she said, was nice. But he was—not old, but not a young man cither, and they had done it standing up in the back of the shop. When it was over he had slumped to the floor and removed his tall white baker's hat. She had never seen him without it. He was bald, and there were beads of sweat shining on his brow.

'He was very nice,' she said. 'Very *sympathique*, that baker. But I would never let him do it to me again. I was afraid I might kill him.'

In small neat spider-letters he wrote on the card, 'Have just spent three beautiful nights with a lovely French mercenary. Won't see her again. Thought I was after (your phrase) *sex in America*. Feel now as if I'm in love. Can you explain that, little brother?'

Anxiety

I'D HAD A SUCCESSFUL trip to several South American countries and was boarding a Lan Air flight back to Auckland from Santiago, flying Economy as I always do, but reflecting that if my company, Preston Products, went on like this, bringing in new overseas orders, I would soon be able to think about an upgrade to Business. The time hadn't arrived when we would be instructed to switch our electronic gadgets to flight mode, or off, and I was catching up with a few messages. There were several old ones from Mahinarangi Marsden, signed Lucy Matariki, the name she'd recently taken. I regretted the change. Maori words very often have several meanings, sometimes quite distinct, and Mahinarangi could mean (or in my free translation I might read it as) 'gift of the sky'. But equally I could see it as 'maker of songs'—and among her many talents that's what she was. I liked both versions, and the sense that I did not have to choose: she could be both.

But I had to admire the cleverness of her reasons. Matariki, she had explained, was that little star cluster, the Pleiades, and its appearance in the night sky of mid-June marked the beginning of the Maori new year—the shortest day, the exact equivalent of St Lucy's Day in the northern hemisphere. It was the dark point after which (though the days might sometimes get colder) everything would slowly improve—days would get longer, nights shorter. 'If winter comes can spring be far behind' was what it meant. So the new name, Lucy Matariki, was combining her Maori and her Pakeha heritages. But she cast a slightly grim light—or darkness—over this change when she told me there was always, in her mind and in her life, a doubt about whether the light would really return. So I would rather have been able to think of her as the gift of the sky and maker of songs than as our Maori St Lucy, the blind girl (as she was in the northern hemisphere mythology) representing mid-winter's day.

Mahina (as everyone still called her) had been our most useful IT person—very eccentric, often unsettling in the office, with great swings between what I, in my layman's shorthand, called her manic and depressive phases. She once told me she had been officially designated as 'somewhat bi-polar'—and we had both laughed at that word 'somewhat'. There were times when I had to warn her to ease off, quieten down, even take a day or two off work, because she was unsettling the staff. I sometimes grumbled and even thought of being rid of her. But she was a constant source of entertainment. And finally, and I suppose most importantly from an employer's point of view, her work was always good. She could do things with computers which none of the rest of us in our little company was capable of. She was our mad, indispensable Mahina.

She was a frightful sentimentalist, so full of the milk of human kindness, and the honey as well, I had to protest and tease her about it. But I was careful too, aware that she was precarious. I treated her gently and with respect. In fact I'm afraid I rather prided myself on being 'good with her', able to handle her, manage her, get the best out of her—and though there was an element of delusion in this, it can't have been entirely wrong or I'm sure she would not have stayed with us as long as she did.

I believe I was the employer who lasted (who endured her, others would have said) longest. In the end she left, not to go to a rival firm offering more money for the same work, but to an organisation that helped people with (as they were described) 'mental issues'—people like Mahina herself who'd had a period of hospitalisation and treatment and were out in the community again. They were such lovely people she said, hearts of gold every one; and she insisted on taking me to their office to meet them. It struck me as a scene out of Dickens. Just a normal office, but in which the jolly ones were jollier and noisier, the glum ones glummer and more withdrawn—normality, you could call it, but with a very broad brush. And it was clear they all loved Mahina, and she was happy there.

But the emails between us continued after she left, sometimes brief and infrequent, others (at least from her end) copious. Why did I keep it up—or allow her to? It was in part an addiction I suppose, because her messages could be very clever and original, and she got something out of me that no one else could. It was also a feeling of friendship and responsibility. So though I saw her seldom now, I thought I could have told anyone who wanted to know—a doctor, for example—pretty exactly how her inner landscape was looking from one day to the next.

Lately that landscape had been dark. She'd told me she was full of fears which had caused her to move some of the furniture in her bedroom against a door that opened on to a deck overlooking the garden. She said, too, that she suspected someone might be trying to poison her so she was being careful about what she ate.

I suggested she might want to report to the psychiatric ward that had treated her before, to receive some therapy and drugs.

But she wouldn't do that. She said the rooms there were bugged and the bugs were bugged in turn by *beings from outer space*—she sent it like that, in italics. She told me these things in a way that made it clear they were jokes. But I knew by now there was a part of her mind that believed them—that's why she was scared. It was a question of which part of the brain was in charge at any one moment. If I'd known people she trusted out of her past I might have alerted them. I knew she'd been married and divorced, but to whom, and what their relations were now, I had no idea.

She told me she was hearing voices too; and that one she called the Bad Voice was sinister, and *sometimes threatening*. This was where I persuaded myself I'd been useful. I adopted the calm, reasonable, unsurprised tone of the practical man. 'Use my name, Mahina,' I told her. 'Tell the Bad Voice that Peter Preston says *it should go away*'—my italic matching hers.

That had been my last message, sent in fact from Medellín in Colombia, once the murder capital of the world and still a dangerous city, where my focus had been on staying close to our small party, taking care not to be robbed, or kidnapped for ransom, and where the trauma hospital had a sign in Spanish which meant, 'We never close'. Paranoia seemed hardly possible in Medellín: any threat or danger might be real, and every fear reasonable. That, I suppose, might have been part of the reason for my taking Mahina's anxieties less seriously than I would have at home: I was in a state of anxiety myself.

But at this moment, waiting to taxi out for take-off at Santiago, there was nothing new from her. I skimmed other messages, then turned my attention to my fellow travellers and recognised the anxiety of a woman across the aisle from me. She might have been trying for some minutes to catch my eye. Could I just stand up, she asked me, and see if there were two engines on the wing on our side or just one. I stood up and could see only one. I thought probably there was a second, out of sight forward of and below the window—though there are plenty of these wide-bodied jetliners now that have only one on each wing. But since I could see she was anxious, and that it was important to her, I confirmed there were two out there on our side. 'And no doubt two on the other,' I joked.

'Oh yes, thank you,' she said. 'I'm such a bad traveller.' She was very handsome, of indeterminate age, plus or minus forty, a real-estate agent in California, she told me, formerly married to a man from Transylvania—'And please,' she added, 'don't make the usual joke.'

I assured her I wouldn't, though it's probable that only a hesitation about how to frame it ('Madame Nosferatu, I presume?' or perhaps 'Countess Dracula?') had prevented me.

'It's like names,' I said. 'You can't make a joke about a person's name that they haven't heard before a dozen times.'

I foresaw a lot of chatter as we crossed the vast unbroken reaches of the South Pacific, and took out the book, a thick thriller, behind which I planned a protective retreat.

My attention however was now drawn to a woman in late middle age who was telling a steward of uncommon Latin American good looks that she was somewhat breathless and would he bring her a glass of water so she could take her pills? He was back in a moment, leaning over her, attentive, producing such an effect that I felt it must be a game he liked playing, inducing in an older woman the illusion that he might be the devoted son she didn't have—or even the young lover, the man of her secret dreams. She was breathless now indeed, with the thrill of it. He exercised a practised, and even cynical, talent, full of charm and subtlety, while her husband sat stone-faced beside her, ignoring the pantomime which he had no doubt seen before, but seldom, I'm sure, played by such an artist.

But it went on just too long. Now she was truly agitated, and complained of a pain in her chest. The steward's smile faded, he seemed to drift away from her, and a moment later was back with his senior, a commanding female who bent over asking questions I couldn't hear, which the traveller, though still panting delicately, dismissed. She was fine, quite recovered. It had been just a momentary thing . . .

But it was too late. The mention of chest pain had been a mistake. Combined with breathlessness, and pills, it could not be ignored.

'She's quite all right,' her husband said, gruff, frowning, displeased. 'She gets angina—that's all. I assure you, there's nothing wrong with my wife.'

But already the call had gone over the intercom for a doctor— and soon two appeared, an Australian woman and a younger New Zealand man. They bent over the now unhappy centre of attention, one taking her pulse, the other questioning. After a few minutes they moved away, nearer to my seat, to talk out of earshot. I pretended to be absorbed in my book.

The Australian didn't believe there was anything seriously wrong. The New Zealander wasn't so sure. Probably not; but did they want to be responsible if they were five thousand miles out over the ocean, with nowhere for a landing, and the old girl's heart . . .

So it went back and forth, and in the end they agreed they should play safe.

They returned to her and explained that in the interests of her health and the welfare of all they'd decided she should have tests. There were very good hospitals in Santiago that would check her over and she would soon be on her way again.

This was no part of the poor woman's plan and she protested. She was soon in tears, insisting she was quite well, pleading. The senior cabin staff, then the captain, finally two security guards were brought in to reason with her. When she flatly refused to budge she was told her luggage had already been removed from the hold. A wheelchair was brought and she was taken weeping away, followed by her husband, whose rage was silent but unmistakeable. He was white with it.

It had all taken time and our departure had been delayed. In the final minutes before we began to taxi out for take-off I checked my laptop again. There was a new message from Mahina. It read:

'I told the Bad Voice that Peter Preston said it should go away. The Bad Voice said "I *am* Peter Preston."'

She'd signed it 'Matariki'.

A fitting tribute

To Barry Humphries

I DON'T ASK YOU to believe me when I say I knew Julian Harp but I ask you to give me a hearing because in every detail the story I am going to tell is gospel true. I've tried to tell it before. After Julian's flight I even got a reporter along to the house and he wrote me up as 'just another hysterical young woman claiming to have known the National Hero'. That was a year ago or more and I haven't mentioned Julian Harp since.

What reason can a person have for telling a story that she knows won't be believed? I have two: a cross-grained magistrate and a statue. You might have heard about the case in Auckland in which a woman, a shopkeeper in court for trading without a licence, happened to say in evidence that Julian Harp had once come into her shop and bought one of those periscopes short people use for seeing over the heads of a crowd. The magistrate asked her to please keep calm and stick to the truth. Then he called for a psychiatrist's report because he said she was obviously a born liar. Next day, which happened to be the anniversary of Julian's flight, he sentenced her to a month in jail and the *Herald* published an editorial saying no one knew Julian Harp. Julian Harp knew no one. A privileged few watched his moment of glory; but he died as he had lived, a Man Alone . . .

Of course if the woman hadn't mentioned Julian Harp she might have got away with a fine. But she insisted she remembered his name because he asked her to keep the periscope aside until he had money to pay for it. And she said he wore his hair down around his shoulders. That was unthinkable.

When I read about that case I knew what no one else could know, that the woman was telling the truth. But it was the statue that really persuaded me it was time I tried to write down the facts. I was walking in the Domain pushing my baby Christopher in his pram. Some workmen were digging on the slope among those trees between the main gates and the pavilion and what pulled me up was that they were working right on the spot where Julian first got the idea for his wings. Then a truck arrived with a winch and a great slab of polished granite and in no time all the workmen were round it swearing at one another and pulling and pushing at the chains until the stone was lowered into the hole. I thought why do they want a great ugly slab of graveyard stone there of all places? I didn't know I had asked it aloud, but one of the workmen turned and said it was for the new statue. The statue was to go on top of it. What new statue? The statue of Julian Harp of course. The one donated by the Bank of New Zealand. *The statue of Julian Harp!* You can imagine how I felt. I sat down on a bench and took Christopher out of his pram and rocked him backwards and forward and thought how extraordinary! Miraculous! That after all the arguments in the newspapers about a site, not to mention the wrangling about whether the statue should be modern or old-fashioned, they had at last landed it by accident plonk on the spot where Julian thought of his solution to the problem of engineless flight.

I sat there rocking my baby while he held on to my nose with one hand and hit me around the head with the other, and all the time I was thinking, I might even have been saying it aloud, what have I got to lose? I must tell someone. If they laugh at me, too bad. At least I will have tried. And besides, I owe it to Christopher to let everyone know the solemn truth that he is the son of Julian Harp. By the time I had wheeled the pram back through the Domain I was ready to start by telling Vega but when I saw her there in the kitchen cutting up beans for dinner and looking all straggly and cross I knew I oughtn't to tell anyone until I had the whole story sorted out in my head and perhaps written down.

I should explain before I go any further that Vega is a sort of awful necessity in my life. Before Christopher was born I had to give up work and I didn't know how I was going to pay the rent. I wanted to stay on in the house I lived in with Julian, because although everyone says he is dead no one knows for certain that he is. I wasn't planning to sit around expecting him, but I had to keep in mind that if he did come back the house would be the only place he would know to look for me. The house and Gomeo's coffee bar. So when someone advertised in the *Auckland Star* that she was a respectable middle-aged clerk wanting board, I took her in; and now there are the three of us, Christopher and Vega and me, sharing the little two-storeyed wooden house with three rooms upstairs and two down that sits a yard from the footpath in Kendall Road on the eastern edge of the Domain. Vega isn't a great companion or anything. She hasn't much to say—except in her sleep; and then although she goes on for hours at a time it isn't in English or any other language. But when I was ready to start work again at Gomeo's I discovered I had been lucky to find her. I needed someone in the house at night to watch over Christopher, and when I mentioned it to Vega she said in her flat voice I could stop worrying about it because hadn't I noticed she never went out at night. She was afraid of the dark! Then she told me she was named after a star we don't often see in the southern hemisphere, and she made a noise that sounded like a laugh and said had I ever heard of a star going out at night.

All the time I was feeding Christopher that evening after seeing the workmen in the Domain I kept thinking about the statue and how wrong it would be if no one ever knew that Julian had a son. So when Christopher was asleep and I was helping Vega serve the dinner I asked her whether she thought Julian Harp might have had a family. She said no. I asked her what she thought would happen if someone claimed to be the mother of Julian's child. She said she didn't know, but she did know there was a good deal too much money being spent on a statue that made him look like nothing she'd ever seen and that kind of sculpture was a pretty disgusting way to honour a man who had given his life. I said but leaving aside the statue what would she think if a girl in Auckland claimed to be the mother of his child? Vega said she thought some of the little minxes had claimed that already, out for all they could get, but she didn't think Julian Harp would have been the marrying kind. She said she imagined him like Lawrence of Arabia, married to an idea. When I said I hadn't mentioned marriage but only paternity she said there was no need to be obscene.

I gave up at that and I didn't have time to think about Julian for the rest of the evening until it was quite late and something happened at the coffee bar that made me remember my first meeting with him. I was bending over one of the tables when Gomeo came out of the kitchen and put his hand on my buttocks and said in a sort of stage whisper you could hear all over the shop that tonight he'd gotta have me or that's the end. The sack. Finish. I said nothing and went to wipe down another table but he followed me and said in the same whisper well was it yes or no. So I swung round and said no, no, no—and each time I said it I pushed the wet cloth in his face until he backed all the way into the kitchen. By now the people in the shop were waiting to hear me get the sack but Gomeo only said one day I would really make him mad and my God that would be the finish of us both.

You might wonder why that should remind me of Julian. It's because Gomeo threatens to sack me and for the same reason nearly every time there's a full moon, and it was after one of his more spectacular performances I first talked to Julian. Julian was in the shop and like everyone else he took it all seriously and thought I had lost my job. So when I had finished pushing Gomeo back into the kitchen where he belongs Julian asked could he help me find a new job and he said he would even be willing to hit Gomeo for me if I thought it would help. I had to explain that Gomeo isn't quite one hundred per cent and he doesn't mean what he says. But you have to pretend he means it and fight him off. If you just laughed at him, or if you said yes you'd like to go to bed with him, you would be out on the pavement in five minutes because Gomeo only wants the big drama, nothing real. I explained all this to Julian and he looked relieved but then he said he was sorry because now there wasn't any excuse to invite me to his bedsitter after I had finished work. When I looked at his face I could see he meant just what he said so I asked him did he have to have an excuse.

And thinking of Julian's face reminds me I ought to say something about his appearance because reading about him in the papers will have given you a wrong picture of him. It's well known there's only one photograph of Julian, the one taken by a schoolgirl with a box camera just before he took off. His face is slightly obscured by the crash helmet he's just going to put on and the camera hasn't been properly focused. So all the local Annigonis have got to work and done what they call impressions of him and I can tell you quite honestly the more praise the picture gets the less it looks like Julian. They all dress him up in tidy clothes and cut his hair short and some of them have even put him in a suit and tie and stuck his hair down with Brylcreem. Well if it's important to you that your local hero should look like a young army officer I'm sorry but the fact is when I first knew Julian he was one of the most disreputable-looking men I had seen. His clothes never seemed to fit or match and he never went near a barber. Every now and then he would reach round to the back and sides of his head and snip off bits of hair with a pair of scissors but that was all. I think he had given up shaving altogether at the time but he didn't have the kind of growth to make a beard so he was what you might call halfway between clean-shaven and bearded. He wore a rather tattered raincoat done right up to the neck, and at midnight when I finished work and he took me to a teen club under the street where you could twist and stomp he kept it on and buttoned up until I began to wonder whether he had a shirt underneath.

I hadn't turned eighteen then but I was older than most of the others in the teen club and Julian was probably twenty-two or -three so I felt embarrassed especially because Julian looked such a clown. When we arrived we sat at a table and didn't dance until one of the kids called out Hey Jesus can't you dance? and several others laughed and jeered. Julian laughed too and clapped in a spastic kind of way and looked all round like a maniac as if he couldn't see who they were jeering at and then he got up without me and drifted backwards into the middle of the dancers and began to jerk and twist and stamp and roll in time to the music. Julian could certainly dance and in no time they had all stopped and made a circle round him clapping and shouting and urging him on until the sweat was pouring off him. He had to break out of the circle and make his way back to our table waving one hand behind him while they all shouted for more.

After that we drank coffee and danced and talked but you couldn't have much of a conversation above the noise of the electric guitars and when we came out at 2 a.m. I felt wide awake and not very keen to go back to my bedsitter. Julian said I should come to his and I went. We walked up Greys Avenue under the trees and then between two buildings and through an alley that came out at the back of the house where Julian had a room. I followed him up a narrow outside stairway right to the top of the building and through French doors off a creaky veranda. He threw up a sash window and we sat getting our breath back looking out over a cluster of old wooden houses like the one we were in and the new modern buildings beyond and the harbour and the bridge. Julian said the nice thing about coming back to Auckland after being away was the old wooden houses. I had thought that was what people coming back complained about, a town where nothing looked solid, but Julian said it was as if people lived in lanterns. He liked the harbour too and the bridge and everything he looked at and I found that unusual because the people who came into Gomeo's were for ever arguing about which buildings in Auckland were any good and which were not and nobody was ever enthusiastic about anything, least of all those like Julian who had been away overseas.

Julian said he liked living right in the busy part of the city and he liked to be up high. He had worked as a window cleaner on the AMP building in Sydney and as a waiter in the Penn Top of the Statler Hilton in New York. And before coming back to Auckland he had driven a glass elevator that ran up and down the face of a hotel at the top of Nob Hill in San Francisco looking out over the harbour and the Golden Gate Bridge and the bay. He said that was the best job he had ever had and he was willing to make a career of it but they made the elevator automatic to save the expense of an operator. Julian offered to run it for nothing and live off whatever tips he could get from sightseers, and when the hotel managers refused he still spent hours of every day going up and down as a member of the public until it was decided he was making a nuisance of himself and he was told not to come into the building again. A week or so later when he tried to slip in wearing dark glasses someone called the police and Julian decided it was time to leave San Francisco.

We sat without any light drinking and talking or Julian talking and me listening and I remember being surprised when I noticed the wine bottle was half empty and I could see the colour of the heavy velvet cloth it stood on was not black but dark red. It had got light and still I didn't feel tired. Julian said he would make us some breakfast and while he cut bread and toasted it I had a chance to look around his things, and especially at a big old desk that had taken my eye. It was halfway down the room facing one wall and it was covered with a strange collection of letters, newspaper clippings, stationery, bottles of ink of all different colours and makes, every kind of pen from a quill to a Parker, and three typewriters. Pinned to the wall above the desk there was a huge chart, but before I could begin to read it Julian saw me looking at it and called me over to help him make the breakfast.

I got to know that chart well later on because it was the nerve centre of what Julian called his Subvert the Press Campaign. On it were the names and addresses of all the people Julian had invented to write letters to the editor, then a series of numbers which showed the colour of ink each one used, the type of notepaper, and the kind of pen—or t1, t2, t3 if one of the typewriters was used—then examples of their scripts and signatures and details about their opinions and prejudices. Each name had stars beside it to show the number of letters published, and the letters themselves hung in bulldog clips at the end of each horizontal section. It had come to Julian that a newspaper really prefers letters signed with pseudonyms because it can pick and choose among them and print the opinions it likes but within reason it has to print all the signed letters that come in. So the idea of his Subvert the Press Campaign was very very gradually to introduce a whole new group of letter writers who all signed their names. They had to be all different types and live in different parts of town so the paper wouldn't suspect what was going on; but as Julian explained to me later, once he had established his group he could concentrate them suddenly on one issue and create a controversy. He called them his Secret Weapon because he said only a small group of people reads the editorials but everyone reads the correspondence columns.

But when it was put to the test and Julian decided to bring the government down (I think it was over the cancellation of the Lyttelton scaffolding factory and the issue of extra import licences) the Secret Weapon misfired. He sent letter after letter, not only to the *Herald* and the *Star* but all over the country and soon there was a raging controversy. But he wrote his letters in a sort of daze, almost as if voices were telling him what to write, and what each letter said seemed to depend on the person supposed to be writing it instead of depending on what Julian himself really wanted to say. In the end his letter writers said as many different things as it was possible to say about the cancellation of the contract and when Parliament assembled for the special debate not only the Opposition members but the Government ones as well were armed with clippings of letters Julian had written. That was a great disappointment for Julian. He lost faith in his Secret Weapon and when I tried to get him going again he said what was the use of secretly taking over the correspondence column of a newspaper if when you succeeded it looked exactly the same as it looked before.

But it wasn't until I knew Julian well that he let me into the secret of his letters. That first morning he called me away to help with the breakfast before I had got more than a quick glance over the desk and when I thought about the chart afterwards all I could guess was that he might be the ringleader of a secret society of anarchists, or even a criminal.

We sat at the big sash window eating breakfast and watching the sun hitting off the water on to the white weatherboards and listening to pop songs and the ads on 1ZB. Julian sang some of the hits and we did some twisting and while the ads were on we finished off the wine. Julian told me the Seraphs were his favourite pop singers and that was weeks before anyone else was talking about them or voting them on to the Top Twenty. I often thought about that when Julian got to be famous and the Seraphs were at the top of the Hit Parade with 'Harp's in Heaven Now'. And when the NZBC banned the song because they said it wasn't a fitting tribute to the national hero I felt like writing some letters to the editor myself.

It must have been eleven o'clock before I left to go home that morning and I left in a bad temper partly because I hadn't had any sleep I suppose but partly because Julian had stretched out on his divan and gone to sleep and left me to find my own way out. He hadn't said goodbye or anything about seeing me again and when I thought about it I didn't even know his second name and he didn't know mine.

I slept all that afternoon and had a ravioli at Gomeo's before starting work and I spent a miserable evening watching out for Julian to come in. It wasn't that I had any romantic feelings about him, the sort I might have had in those days about one of those good-looking boys in elastic-sided boots and tapered trousers. But I had a picture fixed in my head of Julian with his straggly hair and mottled blue eyes going up and up in that glass elevator like a saint on a cloud, and I kept looking for him to come into Gomeo's as if it would be almost a relief to see just the ordinary Julian instead of the Julian in my head.

He didn't come of course because he was busy writing his letters to the newspapers, but I wasn't to know that. The next day was

Sunday and I spent the afternoon wandering around the lower slopes of the Domain among the trees—in fact it must have been somewhere near where they've built the Interdenominational Harp Memorial Chapel. I was feeling angry with Julian and I started to think I might get back at him by ringing the police and telling them he was a dangerous communist. I probably would have done it too but I didn't know his address exactly and I only knew his Christian name.

I still go for walks down there, with Christopher in the pram, and sometimes I sit inside the chapel and look out at the trees through all that tinted glass. People who come into Gomeo's say it's bad architecture but I like it whatever kind of architecture it is and sometimes I think I can get some idea in there of how Julian felt in the glass elevator. I've had a special interest in the chapel right from the start because Vega belongs to the Open Pentecostal Baptists and her church contributed a lot of money to the building. She told me about all the fighting that went on at first and how the Anglicans tried to get the Catholics in because of the Ecumenical thing. She said they nearly succeeded but then a Catholic priest testified to having seen Julian cross himself shortly before he put on his wings and the Catholics decided to put up a memorial of their own. Vega said it was nonsense, Julian Harp couldn't have been a Catholic and I agreed with her because I know he wasn't anything except that he used to call himself a High Church Agnostic and an occasional Zen Buddy. Of course Vega was really pleased to have the Catholics out of the scheme and so were a lot of other people even though it meant raising a lot more money. Vega said it was better raising extra money than having the Catholics smelling out the place with incense.

It must have been nearly a week went by before Julian came into Gomeo's again and when I saw what a scraggy-looking thing he was I wondered why I had given him a second thought. I ignored him quite successfully for half an hour but when he asked me to come to his bedsitter after I finished work I went and the next night he came to mine and before long it seemed uneconomical paying two rents. We more or less agreed we would take a flat together but weeks passed and Julian did nothing about it. By now he had told me about his Subvert the Press Campaign and I knew how busy he was so I decided to find us a flat myself and surprise him with it. I answered probably twenty ads before I got one in Herne Bay at a good rent with a fridge and the bathroom shared with only one other couple. I paid a week's rent in advance and when Julian came into Gomeo's and asked for a spaghetti I brought him a clean plate with the key on it wrapped in a note giving the address of the flat and saying if Mr Julian Harp would go to the above address he would find his new home and in the fridge a special shrimp salad all for him. I watched him from behind the espresso machine. Instead of looking pleased he frowned and screwed up the note and called me over and said he wanted a spaghetti. I didn't know what to do so I brought him what he asked for and he ate it and went out. When I finished work I went to his bedsitter to explain about the flat. He wouldn't even go with me to look at it because he said anywhere you had to take a bus to get to was the suburbs and he wasn't going to live in the suburbs.

I decided I wouldn't have anything more to do with him. I knew he was friendly with a Rarotongan girl who was a stripper in a place in Karangahape Road and I thought he was possibly just amusing himself with me while she did a three-month sentence she had got for obscene exposure. A few days later when he came into Gomeo's and said he had found a flat in Grafton for us I brought him a plate of spaghetti he hadn't asked for and when I finished work I went out by the back door of the shop and left him waiting for me at the front. The next evening and the next I refused even to talk to him. I was quite determined.

But then he stopped coming to Gomeo's and began to send me letters, not letters from him but from his people who wrote to the newspapers. Every letter looked different from the one before and told me something different. Some told me Julian Harp ought be hanged or flogged and I was right to have nothing to do with him. Others said he was basically good but he needed my help if he was going to be reformed. One said there was nothing wrong with him, it was only his mind that was disordered. One told me in strictest confidence that J. Harp was too good for this world and would shortly depart for another. They were really quite funny in a way that made it silly to stay angry about the flat, so when he had run through his whole list of letter writers I went round to his place and knocked and when he came to the door I said I had come to sing the Candy Roll Blues with him. It wasn't long after that we took the little two-storeyed house in Kendall Road, the one I'm in now with Christopher and Vega.

The first few months we spent there Julian wasn't easy to live with. He liked the house well enough and especially the look of it from outside. He used to cross the street sometimes early in the morning and sit on a little canvas stool and stare at the house. He said if you looked long enough you would see all the dead people who had once lived there going about doing the things they had always done. But I soon discovered he was missing the view he had from his bedsitter of the city and the harbour, and if I woke and he wasn't down in the street he was most likely getting the view from the steps in front of the museum. I used to walk up there often to call him for breakfast or lunch and I would find him standing on the steps above the cenotaph staring down at the ships and the cranes or more often straight out across the water beyond the North Shore and the gulf and Rangitoto.

We had lots of arguments during those first couple of months. I used to lose my temper and walk up and down the kitchen shouting every mean thing I could think of until I ran out of breath and if

I was still angry I would throw things at him. Julian couldn't talk nearly as fast but he didn't waste words like I did, every one was barbed, so we came out pretty nearly even. But Julian caused most of the fights and I used to make him admit that. It was because he didn't have anything better to do. His Subvert the Press Campaign had ended in a way he hadn't meant it should and now there didn't seem to be anything especially needing to be done. He took a job for a while as an orderly in the hospital because the money he had brought back from America was beginning to run out but when they put him on duty in the morgue he left because he said he didn't like seeing the soles of people's feet.

It was Anzac Day the year before his flight that Julian first thought of making himself a set of wings. In the morning there were the usual parades, and the servicemen and bands marched up Kendall Road on their way to the cenotaph. Julian wasn't patriotic. He couldn't remember any more about the war than I can. But he liked crowds and noise so he tied our tablecloth to the broom handle and waved it out of the upstairs window over the marchers until a man with shiny black shoes and a lot of medals on a square suit stopped and shouted what did he think he was up to waving a red flag over the Anzac parade. Julian said it wasn't a red flag it was a tablecloth and that made the man angrier. He shouted and shook his fist and a crowd gathered. When the Governor-general's car arrived on its way to the cenotaph it was held up at the corner. By this time Julian was making a speech from the window. He was leaning out so far I could only see the bottom half of him and I couldn't hear much of what he was saying but I did hear him shout:

> *Shoot if you must this old grey head*
> *But spare my tablecloth she said.*

Then the police arrived and began clearing a path for the

Governor-general's Rolls and I persuaded Julian to come in and close the window.

By now he was in a mood for Anzac celebrations and we followed the crowd up to the cenotaph and listened to the speeches and sang the hymns. After the service we wandered about in the Domain. Julian kept chanting El Alamein, Minqar Qaim, Tobruk, Cassino and all the other places the Governor-general had talked about in his speech until I got sick of hearing them and I turned up my transistor to drown him out. He wandered away from me across the football fields and kept frightening a flock of seagulls into the air every time they came down. When he came back to where I was sitting he was quiet and rather solemn. We walked on and it was then we came to the place where the workmen are putting in the statue and right on that spot Julian stopped and stared in front of him and began slowly waving one arm up and down at his side. I asked him what was the matter and he said quick come and have a look at this and he ran down the slope and lay flat on his stomach on one of those park benches that have no backs and began flapping his arms. When I got down to the bench he asked me did his arms look anything like a bird's wings. I said no but when he asked me why I couldn't think of the answer. Then he turned over on his back and began flapping his arms again and asked me did they look anything like a bird's wings now. At first I said no but when I looked properly I had to admit they did. His forearms were moving up and down almost parallel with his body and the part of his arms from the shoulders to the elbows stayed out at right angles from him. So I said yes they did look more like a bird's wings now because a bird's wings bent forward to the elbows and then back along the body and that was why his arms hadn't looked like wings when he lay on his stomach. As soon as I said that he jumped up and kissed me on both cheeks and said I was a bright girl, I had seen the point, he would have to fly upside down.

It wasn't long before I began to notice sketches of wings lying about the house and soon there were little models in balsa wood and paper. One of the things that annoys me every time I read about Julian's flight is that it's not treated as a proper scientific achievement. People talk as if he flew by magic or just willed himself to stay in the air. They seem to think if no one in human history, not even Leonardo da Vinci, could make wings that would carry a man, Julian Harp can't have been human or his flight must have been a miracle. And now Vega tells me there's a new sect called the Harpists and they believe Julian wasn't a man but an angel sent down as a sign that God has chosen New Zealand for the Second Coming. I've even wondered whether Vega doesn't half believe what the Harpists say and it won't surprise me at all if she leaves the Open Pentecostals and joins them.

Gradually I learned a lot about the wings because designing them and building the six or seven sets he did before he got what he wanted spread over all that winter and most of the following summer, and once Julian had admitted what he was doing he was willing to explain all the stages to me. I don't suppose I understood properly very much of what he told me because I haven't a scientific sort of brain but I do remember the number 1.17 which has something to do with the amount of extra energy you needed to get a heavier weight into the air. And also .75 which I think proved that animals as big as man could fly if they used their energy properly but animals that weighed more than 350 pounds, like cows and horses, couldn't, not even in theory. But the main thing I remember, because Julian said it so often, is that everyone who had tried to fly, including Leonardo da Vinci, had made problems instead of solving them by adding unnecessarily to the weight they had to get into the air. The solution to the problem Julian used to say was not to build yourself a machine. It was simply to make yourself wings and use them like a bird.

But you could only do that by making your arm approximate to the structure of a bird's wing—that was what he said—and that meant flying upside down. Once you imagined yourself flying upside down it became obvious your legs were no longer legs but the bird's tail, and that meant the gap between the legs had to be filled in by a triangle of fabric. In theory your legs ought then to grow out of the middle of your back, about where your kidneys are, and that of course was one of Julian's biggest problems— how he was to take off lying flat on his back.

But his first problem and it was the one that nearly made him give up the whole project was finding the right materials for the framework. He must have experimented with twenty different kinds of wood and I was for ever cleaning up shavings off the floor, but they were all either too brittle or too heavy or too inflexible. Then I think he got interested in a composition that was used to make frames for people's glasses but you would have needed to be a millionaire to pay for it in large amounts. It was the same with half a dozen other materials, they were light enough and strong enough but too expensive.

By the middle of that winter Julian was ready to give up and go to work. It was certainly difficult the two of us living off what I earned at Gomeo's and paying the rent but Julian was so happy working on his wings even when he was in despair about them I said he must keep going at least until he had given his theory a proper trial. It was about this time he decided nothing but the most expensive materials would do and he wasted weeks thinking up schemes to make money instead of thinking how to make his wings.

It must have been early June or July he hit on a solution. He had gone to Sir Robert Kerridge's office, the millionaire who has a big new building in Queen Street, and offered to take off from the building as a publicity stunt if Kerridge Odeon would put up the money for making the wings, but he hadn't got very far because the typists and clerks mistook him for a student and he was shown out of the building without seeing Sir Robert. It had begun to rain heavily and Julian had no coat and no bus fare and he walked all the way back to Kendall Road that day with nothing to keep him dry but a battered old umbrella with a broken catch and a matchstick wedged in it to keep it open. When he got home he couldn't get the match out and he had to leave the umbrella outside in our little concrete yard. He was standing at the kitchen window staring out and I didn't ask him about his idea of taking off from the Kerridge building because I could see it hadn't been a success when suddenly the match must have come out and the umbrella sprang shut so fast it took off and landed on the other side of our six-foot paling fence. I could see Julian was very angry by now because he walked slowly into the neighbour's yard and back with the umbrella and slowly into the shed and out again with the axe and quite deliberately with the rain pouring down on his back he chopped the umbrella to pieces. I went into the other room to give him time to cool off, and when I came back ten minutes or so later he was sitting quite still on one of our kitchen chairs with the water running off him into pools on the floor and held up in front of him between the thumb and the forefinger of his right hand was a single steel strut from the framework of the umbrella. He seemed to be smiling at it and talking to it and even I could see what a perfect answer it was, light, thin, strong, flexible, with even an extra strut hinged to the main one.

Julian was impatient now to get on but he needed a lot of umbrellas because his wings were to be large and working by trial and error a lot of struts would be wasted. We couldn't afford to buy umbrellas and in two days searching around rubbish tips he found only three, all of them damaged by rust. The next morning he was gone when I woke and when I walked up to the museum steps where he was standing staring out across the harbour he said we would have to steal every umbrella we could lay our hands on. So that afternoon and every afternoon it rained during the next few weeks I left Julian at home working and I went to some place like the post office or the museum or the art gallery and came away with somebody's umbrella. It was easy enough when Julian wanted women's umbrellas but when he wanted the heavier struts I always felt nervous walking away with a man's. Occasionally there were umbrellas left at Gomeo's in the evenings and I took these home as well. Soon the spare room upstairs, the one Vega sleeps in now, was crammed with all kinds and I got expert at following a person carrying the particular make Julian needed and waiting until a chance came to steal it. I still have a special feeling about umbrellas and sometimes even now I steal one just because it reminds me of how exciting it was when Julian was getting near to finishing his final set of wings. I even stole one at the Town Hall on the night of the National Orchestra concert when that poet read the ode the government commissioned him to write about Julian and the orchestra played a piece called 'Tone Poem: J . . . H . . .' by a local composer.

I should mention that all the time this was going on Julian was in strict training for his flight. I used to tell him he was overdoing it and that he didn't need to train so hard, because to be honest I always felt embarrassed in the afternoons sitting on the bank watching him panting around the Domain track in sandshoes and baggy white shorts while Halberg and Snell and all those other Auckland Olympic champions went flying past him. But Julian insisted that success didn't only depend on making a set of wings that would work. It depended on having enough stamina left to keep using them after the first big effort of getting into the air. The flight he said would be like running a mile straight after a 220-yard sprint and that was what he used to do during his track training. He had put himself on a modified Lydiard schedule and apart from the sharpening-up work on the track he kept up a steady fifty miles' jogging a week. There were also special arm exercises for strength and coordination and he spent at least ten minutes morning and evening lying flat on his back on the ironing board flapping his arms and holding a ten-ounce sinker in each hand. Julian was no athlete but he was determined and after six months in training he began to get the scrawny haggard look Lydiard world champions get when they reach a peak. It wasn't any surprise to me when he timed himself over the half mile and found he was running within a second of the New Zealand women's record.

By now the framework for the final set of wings was built and ready to be covered with fabric and there were only a few struts still to be welded into the back and leg supports. Julian had bought a periscope too and attached it to the crash helmet so he could hold his position steady, flat on his back, and still see ahead in the direction of his flight. Everything seemed to be accounted for except there was still no answer to the problem of how he was to take off lying on his back. He needed a run to get started but he could hardly run backwards and jump into the air. He considered jumping off something but that seemed unnecessarily dangerous and besides he thought it would be important to hold his horizontal position right from the start and that meant a smooth take-off not a wild jump.

I suppose I won't be believed when I say this but if it hadn't been for an idea that came to me one morning while I was watching Julian lying on his back flapping on the ironing board he would probably have had to risk jumping off a building. It came to me right out of the blue that if the ironing board had wheels and Julian was wearing his wings he would shoot along the ground faster and faster until he took off and left the ironing board behind. I don't think I realised what a good idea it was until I said it aloud and Julian stopped flapping and stared at me for I don't know how many seconds with his arms out wide still holding the ten-ounce sinkers and then he said very loudly my god why didn't I think of that. The next moment he was gone, clattering up the stairs, and then he was down again kissing me and saying I was the brightest little bugger this side of Bethlehem and for the rest of the day he got nothing done or nothing that had anything to do with his flight. Of course Julian dropped the idea of actually putting wheels on the ironing board and the take-off vehicle he did use is the only publicly owned relic of his flight. I find it strange when I go to the museum sometimes and see a group of people standing behind a velvet cord staring at it and reading a notice saying this tubular-steel chromium-plated folding vehicle on six-inch wheels was constructed by the late Julian Harp and used during the commencement of his historic flight. It puzzles me why no one ever says good heavens that's one of those things undertakers use to wheel coffins on, because that's what it is. Julian had seen undertakers using them—church trucks they call them—when he was working in the hospital morgue, and when I suggested putting wheels on the ironing board he immediately thought how much better a church truck would be. I don't know where he got the one he used but I think he must have raided the morgue or an undertaker's chapel at night because one morning I came down to breakfast and there it was gleaming in the middle of the kitchen like a Christmas present.

If I am going to tell the whole story of the flight and tell it truthfully I might as well come straight out with it and say Julian didn't get any help or encouragement from the organisers of that day's gymkhana. It makes me very angry the way it's always written about as if the whole programme was built around Julian's flight, and the way everyone who was there, Vega for example, talks as if she went only to see that part of the programme and even tells you she had a feeling Julian Harp would succeed. Up in the museum under glass that's supposed to be protected by the most efficient burglar-alarm system in the southern hemisphere they show you the form Julian had to fill in when he asked the gymkhana organisers to put him on the programme. They don't tell you he had to call on them six or seven times before he got them to agree. Even then I don't think he would have succeeded if he hadn't revived two of his letter writers and had them send letters to the *Herald*, one saying he had seen an albatross flying in the Domain and another, a woman, saying she didn't think it was an albatross, it looked remarkably like a man.

Then you find there's a lot of fuss made by some people about the fact the Governor-general was there and how wonderful it is that the Queen's representative went in person to see Julian Harp try his wings. The truth is the Governor-general was there because the gymkhana was sponsored jointly by the fundraising committees of the Blind Institute and the Crippled Children's Society and he agreed as their patron to present the prizes for the main event of the day. And in case like everyone else I talk to you have forgotten what the main event was and allowed yourself to think it was Julian Harp's flight, let me just add that it was an attempt on the unofficial world record for the 1000 yards on grass. In fact Julian had to sit around while the Mayor made his speech, a pole-sitting contest was officially started, twelve teams of marching girls representing all the grades competed, the brass and Highland bands held their march-past, and the police motorcycle division put on a display of trick riding. And when he did try to begin his event at the time given on the programme he was stopped because the long jump was in progress.

Of course now it's different. It's different partly because Julian succeeded, partly because he's supposed to be dead and everyone likes a dead hero better than a live one, but mostly because he made us famous overseas, and when all those reporters came pouring into the country panting to know about the man who had succeeded where men throughout history had failed—that was what they said—everyone began to pretend New Zealand had been behind him on the day. People started to talk about him in the same breath as Snell and Hillary and Don Clarke, and then in no time he was up with Lord Rutherford and Katherine Mansfield and now he seems to be ahead of them and there's a sort of religious feeling starts up every time his name is mentioned.

There's nothing to get heated about, I know, but when I hear the Prime Minister (Our Beloved Leader, Julian used to call him) on the radio urging the youth of the nation to aim high like Harp I can't help remembering Julian so nervous that morning about appearing in public he even cleaned his shoes and with me just as nervous the only person there to give him any help or encouragement. And then when we got to the Domain Julian was told he couldn't have an assistant with him because the field was already too cluttered with officials and sportsmen, so there he was crouching down in front of the pavilion with his shiny coffin carrier and his scarlet wings for hour after hour waiting his turn while I sat on the far bank knowing there wasn't a thing more I could do for him. We were nervous partly because he hadn't given the wings a full test and partly because he had tested them enough to know they would carry him. They couldn't be tested in broad daylight and remain a secret, so Julian had to be satisfied with a trial late one night. I remember it almost as clearly as the day of the flight, Julian's church truck speeding across the grass getting faster and faster until I could just see the wings, black they looked in the dark, lift him clear of it. Each time he was airborne he let himself drop back on to the truck because he didn't trust his vision through the periscope at night and he was afraid of colliding with overhead wires. But there was enough for us both to know what he could do and to put me in a terrible state of nerves that afternoon watching the marching girls and the bands and waiting for Julian to get his chance.

Everyone knows what happened when that chance came. I don't think many people saw him climb on to his truck and lie down and the few around me who were watching were saying look at this madman, he thinks he's a Yuri Gagarin. But by the time the little truck and the scarlet wings were shooting full speed across the grass everyone was looking, and when somebody shouted over the loud speakers look at the wheels and the whole crowd saw the truck was rolling free there was a tremendous cheer. There was a gasp when he cleared the trees at the far end of the ground and then as he veered away towards the museum with those scarlet wings beating and beating perfectly evenly something got into the crowd and it forgot all about the athletic events and surged over the track and up the slope through the grove of trees by the cricket scoreboard, then down into the hollow of the playing fields and up again towards the museum. I would have followed Julian of course but I didn't have to make up my mind to follow. I was one of the crowd now and I was swept along with it running and tripping with my eyes all the time on Julian like a vision of a heavenly angel rising on those wings made out of hundreds of stolen bits and pieces. He rose a little higher with each stroke of his wings and even when he seemed to try for a moment to come down and almost went into a spin I didn't understand what was happening. I didn't think about whether he intended to go on climbing like that I was so completely absorbed in the look of it, the wings opening and the sunlight striking through the fabric showing the pattern of the struts, and then closing and lifting the tiny figure of Julian another wing-beat up and out and away from us. I had stopped with the crowd on the slopes in front of the museum and Julian must have crossed the harbour and crossed the North Shore between Mt Victoria and North Head and got well out over the Hauraki Gulf towards Rangitoto before it came to me and it came quite calmly as if someone outside me was explaining to me that I was seeing the last of him. I don't know any more than anyone else whether it was a fault in the wings or whether flying put Julian into some kind of trance he couldn't break or whether he just had somewhere to go, but it seemed as you watched him that once he began to climb there was no way to go but higher and further until his energy was used up. I stood there with everyone else watching him get smaller and smaller until we were only catching flashes of colour and losing them again and finally there was nothing to see and we all went on standing there for I don't know how long, until teatime anyway.

After that I was ill and I lay in a bed in hospital for ten days without saying a word seeing Julian's wings opening and closing above me until I was sick of the sight of them and all through the day hearing people talking about him and reading bits out of the newspapers about him. By the time I began to feel better he was famous and I remember when a doctor came to see me and explained I was pregnant and asked who the father was I said Julian Harp and I heard him say to the sister she needs rest and quiet. Soon I learned to say nothing about Julian. He belongs to the public and the public makes what it likes of him. But if you ever came out of a building and found your umbrella missing you might like to believe my story because it may mean you contributed a strut to the wings that carried him aloft.

Marriage
Americano

IT WAS EVIDENT THAT the young couple crossing the crowded park were uncomfortable. It was not merely the sultry heat of August that troubled them, but uncertainty about where they were, and perhaps anxiety about what they were embarking on. They stopped every few yards to look at a piece of paper which the young man held, and then to turn this way and that, looking beyond the square to the streets that bordered it.

'I'm sure this is wrong,' Paula said. 'The Avenue of Rodriguez is over *there*.'

Peter shrugged irritably. They turned and walked back in the direction they had come and, at a junction, struck off along a new path.

Paula was tall, with a strong, handsome face. There was something fresh and healthy in her appearance and in her movements, suggesting the countryside, not the city.

'Yes, this is better,' she said. 'I'm sure this is right.'

Peter did not argue. He did not trust her sense of direction, but his own had already failed them and he did not want to be wrong a second time. He kept looking at the park benches, hoping to find one unoccupied on which they could rest; but when one with space for them came into view he did not, after all, suggest they stop. There was a black man occupying one corner of it, and his appearance was so depressing Peter preferred to walk on in the heat. The man was ill. He held himself upright with difficulty. His face was drawn and his teeth chattered. In sympathy, Peter was assailed by a feeling of the same lassitude. How he must long to lie down! But where? If he'd had a better place to go he would not have been here in the square. He could not lie on the grass, as you could, for example, in London parks. Even to step on it was forbidden. If he lay down on the seat someone would come and demand he make room. If he lay on the path one of those gum-chewing, baton-twirling cops would take him in. After nightfall, if he could last out the day, he would be tolerated lying in certain doorways and on certain steps. In the meantime he must hold himself upright, shivering, wedged in his corner of the seat.

They were past him now. Dust and paper blew about their feet. Paula had not noticed the black man. She was still turning her head this way and that, as if steering a ship through narrow straits. Peter wanted to tell her what he had seen, but instead he said, 'If we had to get married, why, for God's sake, in America?'

'Look,' she said. 'There. Didn't I tell you?'

They stopped and surveyed the street they had come to. Peter looked again at the piece of paper. 'That means it's away down there to the left. It doesn't look like the right area for a clinic.'

The state laws required a VD test before marriage. They had slept together in five or six different countries across the world, but if they were to make it legal here they must first prove themselves clean.

Ten minutes later they had found the building. They stood for some moments staring at it, then at the newspaper clipping advertising a 'Blood Test Clinic', then at one another. They had expected something of soaring steel and glass in which rubber-soled technicians in dazzling white pushed trolleys of stainless instruments through swinging doors. The building they stood before was of grimy brick, looking more than anything like a warehouse. Among the signs around its doors was one that signified the 'clinic' was on the second floor.

Paula said, 'I don't suppose it can do us any harm.' They went in and found the stairs.

The clinic, they were told, was run by Dr Swartz, and they were shown at once into his office. He half stood as they came in, supporting himself against his desk and sinking back as they sat down. He smiled, but his eyes were vague, as if he had difficulty focusing on anything.

'So you're going to get married,' he said. 'That's a big step. A great big wonderful step.'

Peter was looking about the room. It was in complete disorder, papers, folders, books, bottles, racks of test-tubes, slides, instruments, towels—everything taken up and dropped at random.

'You make a fine couple,' Dr Swartz was saying. 'It gives me real pleasure to help such a fine young couple. I don't mind telling you I get some weird ones. I don't always encourage a marriage. For example, I had a pair in a day or so back. He was six foot three if he was an inch. She came up to about *here*. About the size of an average ten-year-old. I took her aside. I said, "Have you thought about what you're doing? You've been down on the farm, haven't you? Seen the horses . . .?"'

Paula had turned her head away and was staring through the open window. Peter was certain she would soon begin to laugh. 'Couldn't we get on with it?' she said.

Dr Swartz took two forms from the top drawer of his desk.

'First the lady,' he said. 'Full name?'

Paula told him.

'Would you spell them please?'

She spelled them.

Each new question on the form Dr Swartz read slowly, articulating every word distinctly, breathing heavily, stopping from time to time to mop his brow with Kleenex tissues which he dropped on the floor.

He also repeated each word of her answers as he wrote them down. Even 'Yes' and 'No' seemed to present problems of articulation, lengthened out into their separate letters as they were painfully copied on to the form.

When Paula's form was completed the whole business began again with Peter. Peter had been going to suggest that he might fill in his own form; but he had sunk into a stupor and was now enjoying the comfort even of this uncomfortable chair. He did not wish any longer to hurry.

'Now begins the clinical bit,' Dr Swartz said.

He lumbered up from his chair and made his way around the desk to where Peter sat. 'Remove your jacket please.'

Peter removed it. The doctor unbuttoned a shirt cuff and began to roll the sleeve up Peter's arm. For a moment he stared at the bare flesh, as if uncertain of what to do with it. Then he turned away to search among the papers on his desk.

'Here it is,' he said. He took hold of Peter's arm with his left hand. In his right he held an old-fashioned blade razor. Paula could see that he intended only to shave a few tufts of hair from where the sample was to be taken; but Peter, seeing the blade brought up close to his arm, had turned white. His mouth was half-open in protest but no sound came from it.

'Hold on to him, doctor,' Paula said. 'I think he might faint.'

Half an hour later, when they were again crossing the square, Peter remembered the black man, and looked for him. He was still there, still alone on his seat, drawn up stiffly into one corner. The moment he relaxes, Peter thought, he'll fall right down. That will be the end of him.

They were past him before Peter stopped. He felt for his wallet and drew out a single dollar. 'What are you doing?' Paula said.

He walked back and held out the note. The black man shook his head slightly, sucked air in through clenched teeth, and looked away. Then he changed his mind. He reached out, took the dollar, and pushed it into his pocket. His eyes, when they met Peter's, expressed neither gratitude nor resentment. He was past caring. There was nothing in them but despair.

Paula stood watching. She said nothing when Peter returned to her. They continued together along the path. Peter ground his teeth, embarrassed by his own folly. What was a dollar to a dying man? Either you took him in or you left him alone.

SOME DAYS LATER they presented themselves at the courthouse. They were asked to wait in a crowded room in which a single electric fan whirred overhead without seeming to disturb the air. To Peter every face in the room appeared vacant, hopeless. An official came and went, calling names, directing people this way and that.

When their turn came they were shown to a door marked 'Judge Whittaker'. The official knocked and guided them in, closing the door behind them.

Judge Whittaker, sitting behind his desk, looked up at them. 'What's the hurry?' he shouted.

Neither of them could find a reply.

'The law of this state says you register and wait three days.'

'We've done that,' Peter said.

The judge looked down at his papers. 'You're Heinz and Dibble?'

They told him they were not.

'*Donaghy!*'

It was a moment before Peter recognised that this was a name and not an oath.

Donaghy appeared at the door. 'This is not Heinz and Dibble,' the judge shouted.

Donaghy muttered apologies and hustled them into another room. 'Wait here,' he said. 'I'll be back.'

When Donaghy returned he was wearing his jacket and carrying a black book. A typist followed him, and a black porter with a broom.

'I'm going to marry you now,' he said. 'These here are the witnesses.'

They stood side by side, facing him. Peter felt Paula's shoulder begin to shake. He kept his eyes on Donaghy. Paula covered her face. She was giggling soundlessly.

Donaghy took out a large handkerchief. 'That's right, Miss,' he said. 'You go right ahead and cry. This is a pretty big moment in a girl's life.'

She took the handkerchief and plunged her face into it, converting her laughter into plausible sobs.

The ceremony was over and they were heading back to their rented apartment when they found themselves once again on the edge of the square. It was not crowded at this hour, and they went in and sat down on one of the benches. In the intervening days Peter had forgotten about the black man. Now that sick despairing face came back into his mind. He felt the horror of death. He imagined the body naked under a sheet, the face hardened, the eyes open. He imagined it lying unattended in the middle of an empty room, full of light and the reflections of light, silent except for the clanking of trolleys, and the clatter of instruments falling into metal dishes, that echoed now and then from rooms and corridors nearby. He imagined two men in green coats entering the room, taking up the body on its litter and sliding it, head first, into a refrigerated chamber until only the pink soles of the feet, and the big toes tied together with a strip of cloth, were visible. Above and below those feet were other pairs of feet, and on either side of the door which now closed on them were other doors.

As if to save himself from his own fantasy Peter reached out and put his hand on Paula's knee. She laid her hand over his. He looked at her. She was still close to laughter. 'That was a pretty big moment in a girl's life,' she said.

He smiled. 'I suppose we're now legally qualified to commit adultery.'

'Don't let's start at once,' she said.

He looked across the square at the brilliant skyline of the central city. Above the hum of traffic he recognised the lazy chopping of a helicopter. He searched for it in the hot sky, and caught sight of it for just a moment before it sidled away and disappeared behind a shimmering tower of glass on the edge of the square.

Determined things to Destiny

SHORTLY AFTER MY SIXTY-THIRD birthday I stood on—
and in—a machine outside the New Life Superstore in the
Doubleday Grand National Shopping Mall somewhere, I am no
longer sure exactly where, in the United States. I was travelling,
as ageing academics do, talking, as they do, about my subject,
literature at large, poetry in particular. I put in the required coins,
and the machine, telling me first to stand straight, then eyeing me
with a red beam, printed out my height and weight, in metrics
and in the older measures. That these facts came together with
a print-out of the date and time, even to the hour and minute,
gave what might be the most precisely recorded moment of my
biography, should anyone care to write it—and I hasten to affirm
that, to this late date, there has not been the least reason why
anyone should.

What it told me was:

Weight—79.4 kg / 175 lb
Height—1.84 m / 6 ft

Below there was a line showing the 'Ideal Weight (depending on Constitution)' for a male of that height:

Light	Medium	Heavy
76.8 kg / 169 lb	80.3 kg / 177 lb	85.2 kg / 188 lb

It looks almost perfect; at the very least satisfactory. For a six-foot male (which is to say tall in the 1950s, medium-tall in the new century) of 'light' constitution, I was a little overweight, about what you would expect for one of my age who walks a lot, doesn't pant going up hills and can still (briefly—say for a few hundred yards, or even metres) run like an imitation of the runner he once was.

These are the facts. But the truth is not quite (and when is it ever?) caught by them; and it was this hidden discrepancy that set me thinking about Claudia Strange. It was in those late 1950 years, when I was tall rather than (as now) medium-tall, that I knew Claudia as a friend. That was in England where we had each come, she from the United States, I from New Zealand, as post-graduate students—both on scholarships.

'Friend' is exactly right, as in 'just good friends'—meaning 'only' and 'no more than'. I would have liked more; but Claudia had a preference, a predilection, even (it doesn't seem too much to say) a passion for men who were, on the New Life Superstore machine's simple scale, 'Heavy'. Not 'Heavy' in the sense of fat. Claudia's men had to be big; they had to bulk large; but it had to be hard bulk. It was as if she wanted to be crushed by an excess of maleness.

Other things were important. Brain was important. Personality, wit, sensibility, imagination, social skills. A man who wanted to interest her had to have them all. She had no wish to be dominated, oppressed, extinguished. It was only that if a man was to arouse her romantic side and her sexual passion (and we were at an age when the two are only distinguished with difficulty), these excellent personal and social qualities had to be amply housed. They had to inhabit a large strong frame.

Which is why the New Life Superstore's print-out made me think of her. Most of my life I have been a string bean—a *strong* string bean, ego demands I should add. I was athletic, healthy, a very large eater—but thin, gaunt, almost (I am trying to see myself as she would have seen me) emaciated. At fifteen I was already six foot and weighed in for school boxing at under 150 pounds. Thirty years later my height and weight were the same. I was a fat person's dream of success. But (and such is the nature of human perversity) for most of my adult life I yearned, as I put it to my family, to 'achieve fatness'.

I achieved it, or achieved it by my own poor standard of bulk, only in my fifties, by which time Claudia Strange was long dead, and (I think it's not too much to say) famous.

There's a scene I remember very clearly which I think catches something about the arcane nature of our friendship. Claudia was visiting me in London where I had gone to do research in the British Museum, and we were walking in a long narrow park which (at least in my recollection of it) runs north from Kensington High Street somewhere west of the narrow lane where I occupied a bedsit. It was a time when nannies could still be seen about that area in large numbers, walking their charges in prams and pushchairs; and by my observation they divided into two distinct types—the round-hatted uniformed professional English kind, hard-faced relics of what was even then a past age, who gathered at the Round Pond in Kensington Gardens; and the stylish young au pairs, mostly French, sometimes Swedish, who were to be seen in this little park close to what had become my home.

In those days I had women-friends, any number of them. Even my foolish and self-mocking obsession with Claudia Strange didn't prevent that; and there was one of these French nannies who had taken my fancy and who seemed, though I hadn't yet spoken to her, to be encouraging the interest I let her seé she aroused. On this particular day I took Claudia with me so she could see and comment on the young Frenchwoman; also, perhaps, so the young Frenchwoman could see me with a nice-looking American girl.

It was part of what seems, when I look back on it, an elaborate game Claudia and I played. I wanted to arouse her jealousy; and I even believe I did arouse it—or, if it wasn't jealousy, it was at least possessiveness. She would say to me, looking at some young woman I pointed out in a library or at a party, 'Yes, she's perfect, Mark. Go for it.' But I always felt she did it knowing that that was not what I really wanted. And my tardiness, my failure to go into action as long as she was there to entertain me, pleased her, reinforcing the confidence it gave her to know that I was in love with her. Claudia didn't want me; but nor was she quite ready or willing to give me up.

But on this particular day the young French nanny never appeared. We found a park bench and sat waiting for her, watching others of her kind, giving them marks out of ten, making literary jokes and weak puns. And at some point in this aimless verbal tennis which we both loved to play I used the word 'skinny'. Perhaps I said, touching the old wound, that of course this Frenchwoman wouldn't want me as a lover; like Claudia she would find me too skinny.

Her reaction was strange. I don't think it was that she had never heard the word— though I do remember she told me that in America it would be much more common to say scrawny. But the way I had said it delighted her because, she told me, I had 'screwed up my nose!' She got me to say it again—and again.

Over and over I had to screw up my nose and say it: 'Skinny.'

Was she mocking me? I don't think so. It was almost as if, just for a moment, she was in love with me. What is certainly true is that from that moment on I could usually please Claudia, catch her attention, make her laugh, win her back from a displeasure or a sulk, almost (even if only for a moment) make her love me, simply by reminding her that I was 'skinny'.

Claudia, I should explain, was a scientist, a Harvard graduate in physics who had come to England to do a post-graduate degree at Cambridge. But she had been one of those brilliant, and rare, students who shine almost equally at arts and sciences and have difficulty choosing between them. She had loved studying literature, and still liked to read good books and talk about them. She found most of her fellow science students unappealing. The men, she said, were too narrow—either ignorant of the arts or interested (the mathematicians, usually) only in classical music. As for the women (and there were very few in science in those days)—she dismissed them as an unstylish lot, with big legs and no make-up, whose idea of a good time was singing 'Green grow the rushes, oh', or 'No more double-bunking' around a fire in a tramping club hut. 'Weedy' for the men, 'dowdy' for the women—those were her words, and that was her summing-up of her colleagues. It's not surprising that some of them spoke slightingly of her after her death.

Claudia and I got to know one another first by correspondence, and that, as I will explain, was unfortunate. She kept a journal—highly literate, clever, witty, brisk and unbridled—the entries accompanied by excellent black-and-white sketches; and it was a small section of this journal, just a few pages dealing with her journey by sea from New York to London, that appeared in a universities literary magazine edited by the young (as yet unknown) Ian Hamilton to which I contributed a poem. I was struck by what she had written. It leapt off the page, slightly breathless, the words and impressions spilling out and tripping over one another, but vivid, lucid, spontaneous, full of energy and colour. The notes on contributors mentioned her college, and on an impulse, a quite untypical one, I wrote to tell her how much I had enjoyed her contribution.

Back by return post came a letter. I have it here on my desk as I write. 'Very bad form of me,' it begins, 'not giving you a moment to catch your breath, but I'm firing a note straight back to tell you what an immense kick it gave me that someone, a contemporary and student of literature (and a poet to boot—a real one!) should not only like my journal extract, but like it enough to find words for why, words quite wise and carefully weighed, and should even be generous enough to put pen to paper and stamp to envelope . . .'

So it rattled on. That was Claudia's way. She told me about herself, where she came from, what she was doing in Cambridge. She wrote warmly about my poem. I was charmed, as I had been by the journal, and wrote back. It was still an age of letter writing. Our correspondence continued for seven or eight weeks before our first meeting, and in that time more than a dozen letters went back and forth.

By now I was truly interested in her, keen (as she was) that we should meet. We had exchanged photographs and I could see she was at the very least pretty, perhaps beautiful. She, I suppose, could see that I had eyes, nose, mouth, teeth, hair, all in reasonable condition and in the right relation one to another.

As for our minds, these had already met on the page and liked one another, even when there were differences of opinion. So now we could get on and like one another in reality. Neither of us could know, of course, what other lovers, potential or actual, already existed. In my case there were a few, none of them very serious. In hers, since she was an attractive and clever young woman at the University of Cambridge, where men outnumbered women ten to one, my potential competitors were an army. But since Claudia responded as positively to my letters as I did to hers, the omens were propitious, and disappointment lay in wait for us both.

That autumn I bought my first car. It was a second-hand Morris Minor, round and blue and already run off its feet but very dependable. It cost me £250. I looked out at it parked in the mist under a street lamp in the lane outside my bedsit, half pleased, half alarmed at what I'd done. I had no licence to drive, and no immediate prospect of getting one. This had something to do with the Suez Crisis. The queue of new car-owners waiting to be tested was long, and meanwhile I was supposed to drive only with a licence-holder beside me.

One afternoon, on an impulse, I removed the large red 'L' from my front and back bumpers and set off, unlicensed and unaccompanied, for Cambridge. First there was the problem of getting out of London—nothing like as difficult as it is now, but for a learner driver a nightmare nonetheless. There was no M11 in those days, and I can see, looking at a road map which might be the one I used all that long time ago, that once clear of the outskirts of the city I must have ambled north through Harlow, Bishop's Stortford and Great Chesterford.

I remember there was a part of the journey when the charm of rural England swept over me—a charm which, for one of my colonial background and education, was always powerful. It was the 'season of mists and mellow fruitfulness', and so much of what I saw had literary echoes, as if the showering orange woods, the discreet streams and hills, the cropped fields and thatched villages had come into existence as illustrations of famous books and poems rather than the other way about. And this excitement merged with the pleasure of being free of claustrophobic London, and with the prospect of meeting the young American woman whose letters and photograph had taken such a grip on my imagination.

But as I drove the autumn mist got thicker and, near Cambridge, while the afternoon closed down towards dark, became fog. British fogs in those days (it was before the Clean Air Act, or before it had begun to have an effect) were unimaginably thick, and by the time I reached the outskirts of the town I was stopping every few hundred yards and walking up the road in the weak beams of the Morris's headlights so I could be sure what was out there ahead of me.

Somehow I found Claudia's college, and the house nearby where she lived with other American and Commonwealth students who, like her, were already graduates. Inquiring for her there I was directed to a nearby pub. When I walked in I recognised her almost at once, sitting at a table with a group of young women and one or two men. She was dressed in a way which I remember seemed, though I'm no longer sure why, distinctly American. She was wearing a neat brown jacket with a matching skirt (I think she would have called it a 'costume') and a yellow shirt. Her hair, thick and golden-brown, was quite long and softly wavy. Her eyes were blue and keen. She wore bright lipstick which, when she laughed, framed two perfect rows of strong, white, evenly spaced teeth. There was a general look of being well groomed. She had submitted (as the poet Yeats would have said) 'to the discipline of the looking-glass'. And there was in her manner the impression of one eager to please, or to make an impression.

Claudia saw me staring at her, failed to recognise me, and when she looked a second time and my eyes were still on her, gave me the kind of glare a confident woman gives to a stranger whose attentions are unwelcome.

Hungry and thirsty after my difficult drive, I bought a pint and a pie and sat at a table near the door, where I could keep her in my sights without staring.

Half an hour later she got up to leave. As she passed I tugged at her sleeve. 'I'm sorry if I seemed to stare,' I told her. 'I didn't want to interrupt your conversation. You don't recognise me?'

I had stood up to greet her. She took the hand I held out to her, holding it absent-mindedly while she looked hard at me—at my eyes, my face, my hair, my thin shoulders and narrow waist.

'You're not . . . *Mark*?'

I expected this recognition would be followed by one of those broad smiles I had seen her unleashing at her companions around the table. Instead there was a frown. Her mouth closed tight. Her eyes flashed. I'm not even sure she didn't stamp her foot. What did I mean by coming unannounced? I should have let her know, not just burst in on her life like this. She was completely unprepared. It was bad form. It was . . .

I said I was sorry. I was already backing away from her, taking my coat from the chair where I had thrown it, making for the door. In part what I felt was guilt. Because there wasn't time to reflect, I behaved as if I had indeed done wrong. But already there was another part of me thinking this was very strange behaviour; that it was . . . *mad*, wasn't it?

I hesitated at the door and looked back, but she wasn't coming after me or signalling me to stop. Her eyes were on me still, her expression unrelenting. I found my way to my car, got in and drove out of Cambridge, without any certainty about whether I was heading north or south. The fog persisted and soon brought me to a halt. I was lost. I didn't want to pay the cost of accommodation, so I spent the night in the car, curled up and shivering under my overcoat on the back seat. I would have said I didn't sleep at all, only dozed, but in the morning I was woken by a tapping on the window. I wound it down. The fog now was on the inside of the glass. Out there it had cleared. A policeman was peering in at me.

Of course, I thought. He was going to ask to see my licence, discover I was only a learner. I began to prepare my defence.

I was not, when apprehended ('May it please Your Honour'), actually *driving* . . .

'I'm sorry, sir,' he said (in those days if you owned a car you were 'sir'). 'I just wanted to be sure you weren't dead.'

I confirmed that I wasn't, and climbed out. 'It didn't seem safe to drive last night,' I explained.

He was already back astride his bicycle. 'Very wise, I'd say, sir. Nasty bit of fog we 'ad last night.' And he wobbled away, stopping briefly to adjust the clips that held his trousers tight at the ankles before disappearing down the road.

My limbs were stiff. I was hungry, unshaven. I was also, by now, angry, and I remained angry all of that morning as I made my way back into London. That, I told myself, was the end of Claudia Strange. Damn her! What a bitch! There would be no more cosy letters. She could die, for all I cared . . . And so on.

But I think even while inwardly I raged, I knew (and I suppose it added to my rage) that by behaving in that uncivil way she had not really wiped out the fascination she held for me. She might even have added to it. Seeing her sitting with friends around a table, watching her talking, leaning forward, making an impression on them, I'd felt—or believed I had—her intelligence, her wit, the force of her personality. Her outburst had not changed that. Her anger with me had been inexplicable and outrageous. But it was as if she had proved herself. She was not just clever (in those benighted days women who got to a major university had to be clever); she was also complex, intense, mysterious and unpredictable. To wipe her from my consciousness was not going to be easy.

My recollection is that when I got back to London there was already a letter from her, waiting for me. I don't see how that could have been possible. But certainly the letter, which I still have, was written that same night of our encounter, and reached me almost at once. She was, she said, 'truly sorry'. She sent me 'huge and abject apologies'. I had taken her by surprise, but that, she acknowledged, was no excuse. She wasn't able to explain her behaviour. She was like that (she went on)—'badly behaved, given to rages'. Her middle names were 'Sturm' and 'Drang'.

'Life keeps taking me by surprise, and I don't act well. It's like when someone comes into a room and you don't hear them and you get a fright and jump—and maybe shout angrily—do you do that?' And then she gave up explanations. 'Oh God, dearest Mark, what can I say to you to make amends? I squirm. I grovel. I die. Forgive me!'

Dearest Mark? This was new.

Almost at once I could feel my determination not to see her again dissolving. It wasn't masochism—I had no appetite for being knocked about by a strong woman. It was more like simple curiosity; fascination; *attraction*.

I tried not to write back, but it lasted no more than three or four days—and if I am honest I might have to say it lasted only two. Soon we were exchanging letters as if nothing had happened—except that she now addressed me as 'ever fixèd Mark', knowing I would recognise that it came from Shakespeare's sonnet about 'the marriage of true minds'. She came down to London. We sat staring at one another across a table in a Lyons teashop while she explained to me in a voice that quivered with intensity that she valued me, that she wanted us to be friends ('for life' was what she said), but that we could not be lovers—that was something I must accept and must not argue with. It could not be explained because it was, she said, inexplicable. Simply, it was so.

I wondered whether she was telling me she was a lesbian—and argued with myself about it. I didn't think it was so—but that was because I didn't want it to be, wasn't it? And yet my instinct said firmly no.

Later, when we knew one another well (and by this time the game of describing myself as 'skinny' had been discovered) she tried to explain why there had been that outburst at our first meeting. She was a great letter writer, and liked to exchange at least brief notes with her friends, even sometimes with men she saw every day in the lab. On paper, she said, people revealed the way their minds worked—something that wasn't always so clear when their physical presence dominated your consciousness. And by this measure I had been 'simply perfect'. There was never a word, or a phrase, or an image that gave her the kind of sinking feeling, the sense of crushing disappointment, that sooner or later came with every other person she had ever known. But this had led her to build up a physical image of me that was wrong.

Trying to soften her explanation a little she assured me that it was nothing to do with 'good looks'. I had 'a nice, friendly, intelligent face'. What it had to do with was *size*.

She had built up in her head an image of me as a large man— what I suppose would be called these days a hulk—and this had been so powerful, my bean-pole frame had presented itself to her as if it belonged to an imposter. It was as if I, the faultless letter writer, had, after all, made a *mistake*. Of course she had no choice but to accept that the image before her and not the one in her head belonged to the man who had written my letters; but at that first moment of shock and, I suppose, disappointment (though she didn't use the word), it had made her angry.

So we were to be friends, not lovers; and for a time I developed a private life in which there was always a girlfriend, as they were called in those days, but also a friend—and it was the friend I was in love with. It wasn't long before I was loving Claudia with an absurd devotion, all the more painful because of my growing conviction, never confirmed by her and therefore never held by me with certainty, that there were times, moments, when she loved me almost as much.

Much has been written about Claudia's private life, and though I have my own opinions, and my own small but significant areas of knowledge, it is not my intention either to add to or to subtract from what has been said on that subject. In the one biography I'm aware of, I am hardly mentioned; in another, not of her but of Jack Gibbs, I am confused and conflated with a young man, an American she befriended on the liner from New York to London. So if the question whether Claudia and I were ever lovers should be asked I am content, since no simple answer would be adequate, to leave it unanswered—a matter of semantics rather than one of biology. We held hands in teashops. We kissed our greetings and farewells. There were times when we shared a bed—chastely, as she intended, but not (how shall I put it?) absolutely, or infallibly, or entirely. Let it be left there; because the important, or significant, truth is that we were never lovers in the wholehearted, full-blooded, full-bodied sense; and that was because she did not want us to be.

Yet I am sure it would have happened. We were approaching it; we were almost there, when Jack Gibbs appeared on the scene.

CLAUDIA AND I WERE born ten days apart in the same year, but on either side of the line dividing Librans from Scorpios. I, whose professional life was to be devoted to works of the imagination, scorned the idea that our fates were ruled by the stars; she, the scientist, talked as if she considered it a hypothesis as reasonable as any other. Its efficacy, she suggested once, might be said to be demonstrated by our respective temperaments. I, the Libran, was the balanced person, mild-mannered, reasonable, equable— the 'ever fixèd Mark'. She, the Scorpio, was the one who carried a gun in what she called her pocketbook. She could, she claimed, kill someone she saw as a deadly enemy, or even 'just anyone—if I was angry enough'. The scorpion was deadly, capable even of stinging itself to death.

I thought her saying she carried a gun was only an image, a

metaphor, part of the joke, but I was wrong. It was during a secret holiday we took together to Paris (the biography, relying on the letters she wrote home to her sister, says she went alone) that I discovered she meant it literally. We had taken separate rooms but were lying together on a bed in one of them, recovering from a day's sightseeing, waiting to go out for our evening meal. Claudia was reading tourist material, planning what we would do the next day, when I read out to her our horoscopes in a newspaper. I don't remember quite how the conversation went from there; only that she joked again about being a dangerous Scorpio; and then playfully, but taking me utterly by surprise, she pulled out the small handgun and pointed it at my temple. 'Would you die for love, Mark?' she asked. 'Of course you wouldn't. You're a Libran.'

I leapt off the bed, tripping in the narrow space between bed and window, and falling to the floor. 'It's OK,' she said, putting it away. 'Don't panic. There's a safety catch.'

Still on my knees I asked why on earth she kept such a thing. She said, 'Because I dislike it that my life's ruled by fear.'

I'd had such a fright I said no more for the moment, but that evening, when we stopped on a wide wooden footbridge over the Seine to look upriver at the floodlit walls and spires of Notre Dame, I suggested she should throw the gun away. 'Do it now,' I said. 'Get rid of it. Drop it into the river.'

We were leaning on the rail, and she took it out, turned it over in her hand and held it over the water. For a moment I thought she meant to do it; but then she put it back in her bag and walked on.

The anger I'd felt at being frightened, and which I had suppressed, burst out now. 'For God's sake,' I barked at the back of her head. 'You don't need that thing. It's insane. It's probably illegal. Throw it away.'

But to seem to command Claudia was always a mistake. She turned to face me. Who did I think I was? Did I think I had the right to tell her what to do, how to live her life?

And who did she think *she* was, I responded, carrying an illegal weapon, threatening people?

As we crossed the remainder of the bridge I kept on at her. She fell into a grim silence, and then suddenly, as we went down the steps to the street, she turned. 'Find yourself a nice sane safe girl, Mark. Get on with your nice safe boring literary life, and let me get on with mine.' And she walked away from me, fast, disappearing down a narrow crowded street.

I let her go. Then I regretted it, and went looking for her around the streets where we'd intended to choose a restaurant. When I couldn't find her, I returned to our hotel. She wasn't there. Worried now, I walked all the way back to the 7th and wandered the streets again. It must have been nearly midnight before I stumbled into a café and ordered something very ordinary, a pizza, or a *croque-monsieur*—not at all the gourmet feast we'd been planning to have together.

That night I left the door of my room unlocked and at two or three in the morning she came in and sat on the edge of my bed. She talked happily about where she'd been, what she'd seen and done; about the Frenchman, a photographer, met in a bar, who had taken her in a taxi to see his studio somewhere near Montmartre. They had eaten couscous in a local restaurant and drunk a bottle of wine, and she had smoked one of his Gauloises, which had made her feel sick. I must have felt it all deeply, because I remember it as if I had been there.

There was no reference to our quarrel. It was as though it had never happened. I was baffled, helpless, angry with her, jealous of the photographer, suspicious about what might have happened, yet unwilling to show any of this because I was afraid of losing her again. I asked myself was I simply weak, and answered (a good Libran's balanced assessment) that I was not inherently so, but that my position with her rendered me helpless. Claudia was weird, even 'possibly, at times' (I sidled up to the word, afraid to face it) *deranged*—and I was in love with her.

While she talked she removed her outer garments and, in pants and bra, climbed into bed beside me. I thought perhaps she wanted to make love to me as an act of contrition, but I wasn't sure. I felt helpless, almost afraid of her, and I made no move towards her side of the bed.

I was wide awake now, and we went on talking. I had been remembering her saying that she carried a gun because she disliked it that her life was ruled by fear, and I asked what she'd meant, what she was afraid of.

'Of dying,' she said. And then, after a moment, 'Not just of dying. Other things too. Everything. Nothing. Myself.'

She told me how at the age of fourteen or fifteen she had been troubled and depressed by thoughts of infinity—for example that our whole cosmos might be only a molecule in the knee of a giant who was himself as insignificant in his universe as we are in ours; and that conversely, there might be a whole minute universe locked away in a single atom. Infinity of space and time were horrifying enough. But infinity of scale had seemed to her the final horror. Thoughts of this kind, she said, had turned her towards science. But science hadn't really helped. Most scientists shut their minds to everything but what was (I remember her phrase) 'proximate and measurable'. And those who went beyond—the theoretical physicists—were beyond her scope. She'd come to the conclusion that there was no escape from her own thought processes—'brain storms', she called them. 'I just have to suffer them.'

'So you resort to astrology,' I said.

She reached over in the bed, feeling for me in the dark, finding my neck and running her fingers up into my hair. 'You don't understand me at all, do you, Mark?'

IT WAS JACK GIBBS who rescued me from Claudia, and I did not (and I suppose still do not, though I should) thank him for it. He was the hulk of her dreams—six foot three, handsome, broad-shouldered, strongly built, articulate, a top scientist, a 'two cultures' man, well-read and with wide intellectual interests. He was four or five years her senior, had graduated from Cambridge, done post-graduate research in America at MIT, and was now back on his home turf, appointed to a senior position in the laboratory where she was working towards her doctorate.

I thought of him as Antony to her Cleopatra, and I used to comfort myself with lines from that play, saying to myself that I should not lament my loss,

> But let determined things to Destiny
> Hold unbewailed their way.

Jack eclipsed me. He eclipsed everyone in Claudia's firmament. She went for him, went at him, and told me all about it, not out of malice or to make me unhappy, but blindly, because she needed to tell someone, and that need made her unaware of, or perhaps even indifferent to, the pain it gave me. I found her fierce focus on him, her sense of purpose, terrifying; and I remember joking about it, telling her that it put me in mind of an example, under the heading 'Figures of Speech' in my fifth-form English grammar book, illustrating the pun: 'Three strong girls went for a tramp. The tramp died.'

But Jack Gibbs was not going to die. He was the first to recognise in Claudia Strange not just a competent scientist but a brilliant one. Perhaps for him, at least during those first few years of their association, she fulfilled a dream almost as much as he fulfilled one for her.

Jack, now Professor Sir Jack Gibbs, has had a hugely successful career—how could it be otherwise for a scientist who won a Nobel

Prize while still in his thirties? Yet it is Claudia whose biography has been written as if Jack was someone who figured in it, and not as a mentor but as a kind of demon. He used her, it has been said. Her work and not his own was crucial to the discoveries that earned him his prizes and his fame.

I am no scientist and don't pretend to understand anything of the intricacies of their work together; but on the face of it, and little as I care about Jack, I should say at once that those attacks seem unfair. If Jack used Claudia it was because she wanted to be used, and was grateful for it. He was the one who recognised her real potential and employed it towards ends beyond the mere attainment of a PhD. And, furthermore, we know how important her contribution was only because Jack took the trouble to acknowledge it.

Some considerable time after her death (and that, remember, happened long ago, around the time of the assassination of President Kennedy) Jack wrote a long magazine article recounting how he and Claudia had spent weeks together going over the theoretical implications of his experimental work. Without her brilliant and penetrating analysis, he acknowledged, it would have taken him much longer, many years possibly, to arrive at conclusions which in the meantime others might have reached before him. And in a note specifically on his Nobel Prize (it may have been the text of an acceptance speech) he wrote, 'I accept this prize humbly, on behalf of my team and my university, and most particularly I accept it on behalf of the late Dr Claudia Strange. Her work as much as my own earned this reward.'

But the more Jack Gibbs acknowledged her share in his success, the more the acknowledgement was taken as proof of a debt amounting to theft, and as a cover-up of its real extent. At best it was seen by Claudia's advocates as an admission of guilt, at worst as a forestalling of his critics—dust thrown in their eyes. It was said that he had made use of her during those first years of marriage and then, once his great breakthrough was made, had simply abandoned her in favour of another woman—one who was no use to him as a scientist, but who would be compliant and easy-going at home.

These decades have not been fortunate for a man in his position. Jack Gibbs has his glory—his professorial chair, his Nobel Prize, his knighthood—but over it all has fallen the terrible shadow of the Wronged Woman. It is the shadow of Claudia Strange.

JACK APPEARED IN CLAUDIA'S life soon after our return from Paris and at a time when I was sure we were about to become lovers. From that moment on everything changed between us. There were fewer letters. We met seldom now, and when we did I had to listen to stories about Jack—his brilliance, his kindness, his good looks, even his *size*! He was now her supervisor (she had contrived to put herself into his charge almost at once) and her lover (that followed as the night the day), the new star in her heavens, the new principle governing her universe . . .

I exaggerate, do I? Only a little, if at all. Of course I was hurt to see myself fading from her consciousness like the thin, frail wisp of a vanishing comet. But I don't misrepresent her mood of that time. She seemed inspired, a muse of the laboratory, a poet of mathematical calculus; and so totally focused on Jack and on his work it doesn't surprise me that in time he would come to feel it was her thinking as much as his own that carried him over the final obstacles.

She invited me to their wedding in Cambridge, and I think five years must have passed after that (for me) painful occasion before I heard anything more than the most commonplace scraps of news about them—that they were in America; that they were working together, making important discoveries; that they had one child, a son—and so on.

Then they returned to Cambridge and the news became harder, and darker. Soon it was generally known that their marriage was on the rocks and they had separated. Claudia had custody of their little son, Michael, but Jack, who was now living with another woman, took him two or three times a week when Claudia came to London where she had her own small flat and a part-time teaching post in one of the colleges of London University.

I heard all of this from former Cambridge friends, and I remember noticing that whenever her name was mentioned there was a moment when I felt as if I were short of breath. I did nothing. But I waited in hope and fear—hope that she might get in touch with me, fear of how it would affect me if she did.

Finally there was a meeting, just one, at which nothing happened, and everything happened; and soon afterwards she was dead.

The biography traces in detail her final two weeks of life during a vacation when she could choose to be either in Cambridge or in London. It describes how she became depressed, couldn't stand her London flat, moved in with this friend, then that friend; how she went back to Cambridge to be with little Michael, but two days later returned him to his father and came down to London again. They quote her friends' descriptions of her—distraught, confused, rambling (and sometimes ranting) about Jack's infidelity; taking pills by the handful to make herself sleep and then, on waking, more pills to combat her depression.

The last few days are accounted for almost hour by hour; but there is a brief hiatus which the biographer has not been able to fill. One day Claudia made a phone call from a friend's house, after which she seemed more cheerful. She dressed carefully in what the friend called 'a nice dress', did her hair, put on make-up, and vanished for most of the afternoon. When she returned she was silent, shut in on herself. She gathered up her things, saying she was returning to Cambridge, but that is not where she went. Next morning she was found dead in her Paddington flat.

I have never visited Claudia's grave but I'm told it's not unlike Katherine Mansfield's in that it names her as Claudia Maria Strange, but then as wife to Jackson Francis Gibbs, from whom she was already estranged. He has defended this on the grounds that they were not divorced, and that he still hoped for a reconciliation. But the more famous Jack became the more he was attacked as a thief of intellectual property, and virtually a wife-murderer. I met him once in the late 1970s when this onslaught was at its height and getting maximum publicity in the newspapers. He was bitter, of course; but more than anything, he was bewildered.

Jack, some have said, has been too polite to speak in his own defence—the perfect gentleman. That is partly true, I suppose, but I wonder whether he has really had any choice. To defend himself would have involved saying things against Claudia, complaining about her extravagances and outrages (the occasion, for example, when she burned some of his most important research notes), and that would have been, in effect, to conduct their private quarrels over again in the public arena at a time when she could not speak for herself. It would have been said that he wished to deny her her posthumous fame (which of course he did not), and would only have put further weapons into the hands of his enemies. He would not have been able to deny that, while Claudia had loved him passionately and faithfully, he had left her for another woman. And as for his being a scientist who had used, and profited by, his wife's intellectual brilliance, that was a matter for which he had himself frankly provided the evidence.

So while her case has been made by others, ever more extravagantly (and they are extravagances for which Claudia cannot be blamed, and which she would certainly have deplored), Jack, almost of necessity, has held his tongue.

THE CALL I HAD HOPED FOR and dreaded came at one of those wonderful winter moments when the day, for hours unrelentingly grey, had all at once begun to release a brilliant shower of snow. One wants to say that things are like other things—a sky like lead, or pewter, and the snow falling out of it like confetti, or the petals of white roses. But if you grew up, as I did, in a place where snow never falls, then perhaps you recognise more clearly its uniqueness. That kind of sky is like nothing but itself; and snow falls only like the falling of snow. For the phone to ring at just that moment, for the voice to be the only one that had always caused a momentary shortness of breath—these were circumstances that seemed to promise to a thirty-year-old academic, weary of London and faintly homesick, new life, adventure, escape.

She said, in her imperious way, that she wanted to visit me at home—now, at once—and though the prospect made me nervous I said of course she must come. By the time she reached my flat (in the same lane, but larger than the original bedsit) I had been out for fresh coffee and biscuits, and pâté, cheese and good bread in case she stayed for lunch. I have a vivid memory of our conversation, she sitting on the floor on an Indian rug with her knees up, I on the edge of my chair. It was hardly a conversation at all, more a monologue, a catalogue of woes and wrongs, to which I contributed appropriate exclamations of surprise and sympathy.

She talked about the woman for whom Jack had left her. 'It's not her fault,' Claudia said. 'I know that, but I hate her.' Claudia was, she assured me, burning in the hell of jealousy. 'This is where I feel it,' she went on, and she grasped her crotch with both hands—'*Here.*'

There was no doubt what she wanted, and it would be a feeble euphemism to say she wanted me to make love to her. She wanted me to fuck her; and not for her pleasure, nor for mine. At that moment I did not exist except as an instrument of revenge against Jack Gibbs.

It would perhaps earn me a few poor marks for good conduct if I wrote now that I was too high-minded to let her engage in an act which, when it was over, would have left her no happier, no nearer a solution to her problem. But I don't think that thought, though a good and worthy one in retrospect, occurred to me. In the simple physical sense I had always wanted her, and still wanted her. Why then, if at last she had a use for me, should I not have a use for her? That thought would have been uppermost but for something else—a small practical impediment.

It was something so trivial, so much a matter of chance, it belongs only to the category of the absurd. The snow which had so brilliantly showered down just before her phone call had stopped, and there was even a slight break in the unrelenting grey of the sky. Not full sunlight but new light was on Claudia's head, and the glint of it in her brown hair reminded me that the heavy curtains, and the gauze ones which protected my domestic interior from eyes in the windows directly across the lane, had just that morning been removed by my landlady. They were to be dry cleaned and would be returned, she promised, before nightfall.

So mixed with, even dominating, what might be presented as a profound moral dilemma, an occasion of high drama, one of the determining moments in the final days and hours of a woman who has become, and deservedly, something of a modern icon, there was a calculation going on, unspoken and never finally resolved, in the head of a person who was then, and is now, of no importance in Claudia's story. I was like the torturer's horse in the poem by W.H. Auden, scratching its innocent backside against a tree while the dreadful martyrdom runs its course. Could we, I was asking myself, make love—could we *fuck*—on that bed, in full view of the maisonette window slightly higher than mine and just across the lane, where the woman who took such an interest in everything on my side was working at her kitchen bench? In the new century the answer might have been yes; but this was 1963, and I was not only 'skinny'—I was shy.

Claudia read my hesitation as unwillingness, my silence as cowardice—a fear of saying no—and her response was predictable. There was in those days (has it really changed?—again in the new century I suppose it has) a rule, or perhaps not so much a rule as an unavoidable truth in human relationships, that in such encounters, where there was an invitation to sex, a woman might say no and give no offence—indeed the refusal was often expected—but a man to whom a woman offered herself was almost obliged to accept. To say no to one who had so generously and courageously put herself beyond the pale of propriety would be deeply insulting.

Claudia was an original thinker but she was also a woman of her time and her anger was huge. It didn't express itself in shouting or breaking things. It simply expanded like a cloud, the black genie emerging from the bottle of her wrath—so dark, so pungent, so negative that, if some solution to the problem of the missing curtains had at that moment occurred to me, it would have been too late.

As she got up to go her silence was saying, 'I needed you and you failed me'—and it was true. That silence has gone on saying it ever since. She did not need the particular person who answered to my name, but she needed significant action as a release from her torment. She needed a sense that she had some power left—that she could hit back at Jack, and that she had done it. What would it have mattered whether it was a wise action or foolish? What would it have mattered if the woman across the lane had watched us, or if I, troubled and embarrassed by these circumstances, had proved a less than wonderful lover? Something should have happened—anything—to fill her mind, to make her feel relief from the accumulated pain Jack's desertion had given her, and from the depression it had caused.

I have thought about her often in the intervening decades, and what strikes me always are the ironies—that the woman who demanded brawn, and died for love of a man, should have become a hero of radical feminism; that the man who made the world aware of her genius should be represented as the thief of her fame; that the survivor, Jack, should be silenced by the death which has given her a public voice; and even (this is not something I can believe, or want to believe, but which hovers there like dark laughter) that I, who had neither power nor influence in her life, might have saved it if only my landlady had not removed my curtains.

It is not just traditional literature that asks for heroes and villains. Ideology clamours for them even more, while perhaps reality, if we can only see it clearly, permits of neither. That evening, after her visit to my flat, Claudia went back to her friends' house, then to her flat in Paddington where she ate a meal, wrote several messages and postcards, including the last of the long and brilliant letters to her sister which have since been published, and went out to post them. She drank some whisky and water, took a handful of her sleeping pills, went to bed with her little handgun under her pillow; and then, perhaps waking later in the night, or possibly as she was drifting asleep, she shot herself in the head.

There was little publicity about her death, and since my relationship with her was hardly known (she liked to keep her life in discrete compartments) no one told me of it. So when two days after her visit I received a card from her, I took it to be a sort of olive branch, mocking, but also forgiving. I was just then on the brink of a visit to the United States, so I took off thinking that perhaps when I returned we might re-establish our friendship. This time, I resolved, I would do better. I would behave more like a man of substance; a man who might be (as the New Life

Superstore's machine so recently put it) 'light' in frame but one who had bulk of *character*.

I still have the postcard, of course, along with my other few mementoes of Claudia. It reads,

M.—

One weepy tramp went for a wimp. He escaped. No regrets,
—C.

It is a long time ago, and all that is left composes itself now as in a marble frieze. Claudia shines—she has her glory in death. Jack is there—he has life, and his fame, still slightly tarnished but less so as the years pass. Those who played a part in the tragedy, loving or hating, helping or failing to help—they all have their places in the picture. And right at the edge, already turning away, there is the insignificant fellow who was once made anxious by an absence of curtains. He has his anonymity—and his story.

Last season's man

EIGHTEEN MONTHS AGO, when Mario Ivanda's obituary on the Kultura page of Zagreb's *Vjesnik* spoke of him as 'our supreme man of the theatre', there were still some who wondered whether the phrase was meant in a tone of unequivocal enthusiasm; or was it to be read as meaning he was very good at a lot of things—writing, acting, directing, movie-making—and fell just short of the best in all? Had he moved up into that category of 'supreme' just by outliving one or two of his contemporaries, and in particular Tomislav Buljan? Or was he truly one of the 'greats'?

Most however were impatient of all such equivocations. We saw them as provincial, a flashback to the bad times when we Croatians lacked belief in our own talents.

Now the last remaining equivocators seem to have fallen

silent, and today, when Mario's bronze statue was unveiled in the town woods close to Dubravkin Put, one heard nothing but good things about the man, and about his films and plays that are being shown in a week celebrating his lifetime's achievement. Springtime for Mario Ivanda!—the trees over his bronze head in full leaf, the market tables by the Zagreb railway station scarlet with strawberries. Will Judge Time confirm his place? Who knows, and why should we care? For those of us alive now in the new, liberated, self-confident Croatia, the matter is settled. Mario is 'our very own Bergman'. He is 'among the immortals'!

That, anyway, is what the Minister of Culture said to Mario's widow after she had unveiled the statue and spoken briefly, with feeling and dignity, of the man and the writer as she remembered him in the final decade of his life.

'The immortals,' she repeated, faintly amused perhaps at the extravagance, but certainly not displeased. 'Thank you, Minister. I hope so.'

IT MUST BE AT LEAST twenty years ago that Tomislav Buljan wrote his famous article, 'Last season's man', which Mario was sure was meant to end his career as a writer and kill him dead as a force in the theatre. And because it hit hard, even with a certain devilish and unarguable accuracy, it very nearly succeeded. Mario didn't respond. He knew that self-defence would only draw more attention to the article, and that it was best to behave as if he hadn't felt it, didn't care about it, was indifferent, impervious.

Tomislav was twenty-eight at the time while Mario was already in his forties—not a great difference but enough for Tomislav to feel that he and his two or three closest associates were 'the new wave' arriving to sweep away what was already 'old-fashioned' in the theatre. Tomislav was tall, well built, Byronically handsome and charming. Everyone loved him and talked about him. He was 'in fashion' and could do no wrong. You saw him at book launches and art openings, and at BP, the jazz club which had become a meeting point for Zagreb's intellectual community. He was relaxed, smiling, witty, knowledgeable. If it seemed to Tomislav that someone, either in what he wrote for the theatre, or in what he did there as a director, was (as the deadly article said) 'causing an obstruction in the fast lane', then you had to listen. In the end you might disagree; but you could take it on trust that Tomislav would have acted without malice, in the interest of what he saw as progress and the greater good. He was truly 'a nice guy'. That he was also capable, not of malice, but of a certain critical ruthlessness amounting in effect to cruelty, took everyone by surprise. There were gasps; and then praise for his courage in telling the truth as he saw it.

But that was not as it seemed to Mario Ivanda. He thought a younger man was attempting to destroy him. His confidence was shaken. He was deeply hurt and full of rage. He imagined meeting Tomislav at a party and punching him in the mouth without warning; or going to his door and doing it. And then there were dreams in which he seemed to be kicking him to death in a dark alley close to Zagreb's Gavella Drama Theatre where their two plays had been put on, one after the other, and where his rival had won superlative reviews for a work that seemed to Mario shallow and insignificant.

We are a small country with a tight intellectual community. If things go against you, as they did for Mario Ivanda, you can be left like the chicken in the enclosed yard all the other chickens turn against, your skin bleeding and your feathers plucked.

What made it worse was that this occurred right at the time when Mario was going through the break-up of his second marriage. He was sensitised, precarious, in need of a secure place of retreat and the support of a loving wife. Before the article appeared theatre people, those 'in the know', had been divided, some for Mario, others for Katarina. After it, the balance swung against Mario. It was as if he no longer had the protection, or the excuse, of his talent. He was just one more unfaithful husband ('a casting-couch director' was the common gossip), and Katarina had been right to send him on his way.

She had kept the house and their two children, and changed the locks. He was out on the street with nowhere to go but the home of friends, a couple whose welcome was genuine but troubled, affected by the climate of the moment. And with the end of that marriage Mario had lost also the financial certainty of a wife who was a middle-ranked civil servant, and whose income had given him freedom to take risks in the theatre. He needed security in his professional life and felt now there was none.

Mario had long since given up on the church, but at this time he used to go into a side chapel of the cathedral at unusual hours and light a candle, which he was always careful to pay for, in case the magic didn't work, and which he would add to the forest of lights at the foot of the painting of the Virgin. On his knees there, his brow in his hands, he would pray for the death of his enemy. 'Holy Mother, if you can make Tomislav's decline long and painful, so much the better. But if I have not earned this bonus, if it must be sudden, a heart attack, a traffic accident, at least, I beg you, give me his death. And please, before his last moment let him know that I, the rival he tried to destroy, live on, still writing. Let him go to Heaven if he has earned a place there, but let him know first, and beyond any doubt, of his earthly failure.'

It gave Mario comfort to make these appeals to the same image of the Virgin he had looked upon with awe as a child, and with a reverence bordering on lust in his teenage years. Now he was liberated from deep faith, and felt able to pray without worrying that such requests might be blasphemous. He would leave it to her to decide on the technical aspects of his petition. He could tell by the way her eyes looked down at him that she was listening, and he felt he could even joke with her, as with an old friend. 'You can do it, Mary love. I know you can. Please— just this once, for your loyal fan Mario? Give that bastard what he deserves, and make sure it hurts.'

His professional life continued, but for many months, a year, two years, he felt himself unsteady on his feet, precarious, threatened. Finally, by what all of us at today's unveiling would agree was persistence and courage, he regained a place in Zagreb's theatre world, but one that was still insecure. Reviews of his work were of the 'on the one hand, but on the other' kind; and when he met and talked to people, even good friends, there was often something unspoken hovering between them   a cloud, a reservation, a faint aura of embarrassment.

And then the news came that Tomislav Buljan had cancer. It came, as you say in English, 'from the horse's mouth'. Tomislav himself had decided to 'go public'. He wanted it known that he was 'confronting this challenge head on, and determined to beat it'. He 'hoped he might be an inspiration to other sufferers'. There was a photo of him in *Vjesnik,* and one or two magazines ran stories about his current work and his plans for the future. He was interviewed on television. His wife and twin boys were pictured clustered around him. One article offered the piece he had written about Mario Ivanda as an example of his 'fearlessness and integrity', his 'critical seriousness' and 'utter devotion to telling it as he saw it' in everything pertaining to the theatre.

Mario made another visit to the Virgin. 'Are you teasing me, Mother of God? Giving me my wish in a form that is itself a punishment?'

He asked this because he believed that Tomislav was making the most of very little, that he was exploiting his health scare by making it public, and that he would go from 'cancer sufferer' to 'cancer survivor', emerging with his halo enhanced, larger and brighter than ever.

'If this is my punishment,' Mario told the holy icon, 'I deserve it, and accept it.' But he knew she would be able to see into his black, unforgiving heart, and that she would find there, in its darkest corner, a faint hope, as uncertain and wavering as the candle he had just placed at her altar, that she was not teasing at all; that his prayer was being answered in the affirmative.

After that first flurry of attention the news stories about Tomislav tapered away. There were months of silence; and meanwhile the uncertainty promoted in Mario a rush of creativity such as he had not experienced since his first days in the theatre. In less than a year he wrote two new plays and a television script. All were accepted. One of the plays went straight into production in the Gavella; the other was 'workshopped' at the national theatre in Split, with the prospect of full production later. The television script earned him a large cheque, with more promised when it was translated into German and produced by a company that had bought it in Vienna.

It must have been some time in 1990 that the news came—confirmed, denied, then confirmed again—that Tomislav Buljan's battle was all but lost. Chemotherapy and radiation had both failed. Secondaries were spreading and his liver was affected. Death was still some way off, but inevitable.

Tomislav's dying was protracted. By now Croatia had declared its independence and we were coming under Serb attack in the Krajina. The war, as it developed, occupied almost all our waking thoughts. Wasted, pale, coughing in a way that was hard to listen to, his lovely hair all gone and his youth and good looks destroyed, Tomislav appeared on television and gave a 'final' interview. It was as if he was reluctant to leave, felt it an injustice that he should be required to, and an insult that so much attention should be paid to the war and so little to himself. He was no longer rational. Someone was to blame, someone should be made to answer for what was happening to him. He rambled, asserting that the whole medical event had been mishandled and misreported and that he intended to live many years. Then he wept. That was his last public appearance.

Meanwhile one of Mario's new plays was produced. At first the reviews were positive but cautious, concentrating on performances rather than the play itself. But then an article by Zagreb's most authoritative theatre critic appeared in *Vjesnik*. It hailed the play as something entirely new, not only for Mario Ivanda but for Croatia—'brilliantly new', it said, 'a step forward, out into the future, out into the unknown'. 'It breathes the very air of this moment in our history,' the critic went on. 'It is a work of Croatian genius.'

Ten days later Tomislav Buljan died.

The war was bitter. At its height Mario disappeared from Zagreb, and it was reported he had been involved in the fighting in Bosnia and in the Krajina; and later that he had been wounded, his arm broken, when Serb forces shelled Zadar from the hills above the town. He wrote of none of this; but there had always been an element of Croatian nationalism in his work, and now it seemed more obvious—something that should have been recognised and welcomed sooner. Steadily, as peace returned, Mario re-established himself in the theatre, and was reinstated to his old place of respect and, gradually, of dominance. It was as though Tomislav Buljan's article had never happened.

Mario lived alone now, saw his two children, a son and a daughter, regularly, was civil to, even friendly with, their mother, who, with a new, faithful and (it was said) rather boring partner, was inclined to retrospective forgiveness. In his private life Mario contrived to have a succession of women-friends, each of whom had to accept that he was not about to repeat for a third time the painful experiment of falling in love and marrying. He described himself as a serial monogamist but with a rapid turnover.

He worked industriously and with a kind of stillness that was new. He was in a state of expectation, 'waiting' (as he explained it once to close friends) 'for the blow to fall'. He had prayed to the Virgin, in whose powers he did not believe, requesting the painful death of his rival, and she had proved her powers by answering his prayer. This could not be right. It could not be the Justice of Heaven. Sooner or later Herself would have to be even-handed. Something more must come—a blow, an unexpected reversal. During his involvement in the war he had expected to die, or worse, to be maimed. It had made him fearless. Self-protection would not help. During the bombardment of Zadar, when walls had crashed around him, he had said to himself, 'Ah so here it is at last'—but had woken with only a broken arm and a headache.

He had a small apartment in Zadar, left to him by his mother. It was close to the sea, and he worked there alone, driving up to Zagreb in his little Škoda when required in the theatre. In spring and summer his day began at first light when the swallows did their sudden chattering swoops across his terrace under its shallow roof and down into the gardens of vines and olives stretching away towards the harbour. The sun came up behind the houses and seemed to touch alight the farthest reaches of the sea. After breakfast he swam, or walked several kilometres along the seafront, and then settled to a long morning's work. Lunch might be at home in his own kitchen, or in the town with friends and colleagues; then a siesta, and more work late in the afternoon. Everything in his life was productive and orderly as it had never been before. That peculiar stillness held. He did not feel safe. He worked, and he waited. Whatever form the blow was to take, he hoped he was ready for it.

One morning, taking his walk towards the town, he saw a woman he recognised as Tomislav Buljan's widow, Vesna, coming towards him. They passed within feet of one another. He was sure she knew him, and knew that he knew her. There was embarrassment on both sides. It happened again the next day. Clearly each had a routine which might put them together in this place at this time of the morning. He thought he should avoid her, but on the third day gave up a planned swim in order to see her again. He knew he should speak, tell her how sorry he was that Tomislav had been cut off so cruelly in what promised to be a brilliant career; sorry that she and the twins had sustained such a loss. But he could not say it; knew he would choke on the words—so they passed with flickers of recognition, each silent but seeming to give the other an opening to speak.

A week or two passed with no encounters, and then they found themselves in the same room at an art opening. Now Mario felt he must speak, but was prevented by something new. Each time he had passed her on those morning walks he had been struck not only by the recognition that she was a fine-looking young woman, but by the feeling, stronger each time, that he was in love with her. It hit him full force, as if he had been a very young man. His heart raced, his mouth went dry, he was breathless. He told himself this was nothing more than a fit of nerves, a panic attack, confusion brought on by the memory of what her late husband had written about him. But he didn't believe it. He believed he was in love.

So, in that room full of new fresh bright paintings, oils and watercolours, with French doors opening on to white pillars and a green garden, he looked at Vesna Buljan and looked away; looked again . . .

It was she who broke off her conversation with a friend and came towards him, blushing slightly but holding out her hand.

'Mario Ivanda.'

'Mrs Buljan. Vesna. I should have spoken first. I'm sorry. I'm sorry about . . . So sorry that he . . .'

'Thank you,' she said. 'I'm sorry too.' And he felt that perhaps she was not just saying she was sorry Tomislav had died (though no doubt she was), but sorry he had written that terrible article.

Their talk was brief, and as soon as it was over Mario left the party and walked all the way back to his apartment. He had not felt such passion since the first and unrequited love of his youth. Much of the night he lay awake inventing brilliant things he would say to her which only morning would reveal were quite inappropriate. Just before first light he fell into a deep sleep from which he failed to wake when the swallows made their noisy early-morning strafes across his terrace.

Two wretched days later he had to be in Zagreb, and there he found time to call on his friend the Virgin. He bought her a larger, more expensive candle, lit it and placed it where she could see it. 'So this is my punishment, Holy Mother? I am to be in love with the wife of the man I killed. The woman I can never touch.'

Her smile as she looked down at him was faint, enigmatic, but he believed she was answering 'Yes'. Her sense of humour was subtle, but the pain she was inflicting was real.

On an impulse (so much now was impulse) he went into the confessional. After the usual preliminaries he said, 'Father, it is a long time since my last confession. No doubt I have committed many sins, but I am here because I killed a man.'

Even through the heavy grille he felt the priest's excitement. 'How did you kill him, my son?' His voice was young.

'I prayed to the Virgin that he would die of a painful disease, and that is what happened.'

There was a sigh, perhaps of relief, more likely of dis- appointment. 'You did not kill him, my son. Only God decides who dies and how they die.'

'But I prayed to the Virgin . . .'

'That has nothing to do with it.' The priest's voice was impatient and had lost its authority. Mario felt a rush of amusement. 'Ah Father, if even you doubt her powers, who is there left to speak for them?'

In the weeks and months that followed Mario's work continued uninterrupted, but when he looked up from it, or moved away from his desk, the thought of Vesna Buljan was likely to return. He tried to avoid her, but saw her often enough to know that some other force within himself was contriving to ensure that they met.

Once they had coffee together on the seafront and, thinking it might precipitate some kind of resolution, he told her that when they were together there was always an elephant in the room. She probably knew what he meant but waited for him to explain.

'Last season's man,' he said, using the name Tomislav had given him.

'I'm sorry,' she said, putting her hand over his on the table. 'I was sorry at the time. I argued with him about it, but that was Tomislav. Once he had an idea, he carried it through. He was unstoppable. It must have been very painful.'

'I wanted him dead,' Mario said. And then in a rush that felt desperate, suicidal, 'I prayed that he would die.'

She nodded. She was disconcerted, but managed to say, 'I understand.'

It was this—not the almost twenty-year gap in their ages, but the sense that he had killed her husband—which made it impossible for him to touch Vesna; to kiss her; to invite her home to his bed. He knew that his prayers to the Virgin, in whose powers he had no faith at all, had nothing to do with Tomislav's death. But some intractable part of himself, some dark child in his psyche, believed quite the opposite. This dark child was Tomislav's killer, coldly triumphant and not yet satisfied. It was the dark child who now made him believe he was in love.

Mario was invited to London. One of his plays had been translated into English and was to be produced at the Donmar Warehouse. He was to watch and comment on rehearsals and to be present on the opening night. His English was only fair, but sufficient, and everything went well. While there he went, when he could, to the RSC, in those days at the Barbican, and to the

National Theatre. It was at the National he saw a production of *Richard III*, done in modern dress, with Richard a military dictator.

Shakespeare was difficult, the language unfamiliar. Reading the play the night before he was to see it, Mario found the scene in which Richard successfully woos the wife of the prince he has murdered unbelievable. But in the theatre it came to life. It was powerful, full of the hero-villain's wit and daring. Richard the crookback killer had the glamour of wickedness. It made Mario feel that nothing was impossible.

When he returned to Zadar he sought Vesna out and did not find her. He had no address for her and her name was not in the phone book. How strangely the Powers that ruled his life were behaving. What if, having so to speak stumbled on her by chance, he should now fail to find her by design? He pursued more than one phantom Vesna along Kalelarga, and had to make embarrassed apologies.

When at last he saw her in her usual place on her morning walk along the seafront his relief was so obvious she blinked in surprise, backing away and laughing as he rushed up to her.

'I thought I'd lost you,' he explained. 'Will you have lunch with me? Or dinner?'

Two nights later they were lying together naked on his bed holding hands and staring at the ceiling. The sliding doors were open on to the terrace. The moon was silver on the olives and gold over the sea. He dozed, and woke when she said, 'Why did it take you so long.'

'So long?'

'To ask me out. To invite me here.'

'I thought you'd think . . .' he took a deep breath '. . . you might think it was because of Tomislav's article. That it was just an act of revenge.'

She didn't reply. Was that a thought he should not have aired? But she yawned and stretched, and he saw it had made no significant impression. 'It might have been my revenge,' she said.

'On Tomislav? For what?'

'I don't know. For dying. For leaving me all alone.'

He rolled over and, propped on one elbow, looked into her fine eyes, ran fingers through her tousled hair, and kissed her.

So they settled into a life of living apart but together. Mario was happy, but still with the feeling that he was unsafe, that the story was not yet over. It was another year before they married. They spent the last decade of his life together, tranquil, orderly, fond, settled into that unfashionable but mysteriously powerful unit, a married couple.

His death was sudden, a smoker's heart attack ('Good,' he would have said. 'Over quickly and no fuss'), and today, with the Minister of Culture's tribute, and Vesna's unveiling of the monument, he was duly celebrated, his place in our literary history acknowledged.

After the crowd had dispersed from Dubravkin Put I stood looking at him, now permanent in bronze against the spring-green background of the town woods. He was not far from the statue of Miroslav Krleza, in the same style, and a good likeness. I had known Mario many years. I and my wife were the couple who had opened our doors to him when his second marriage foundered. Bronze is bronze, but the shape of the head, its slight downward and sideways turn, and the sense the sculptor had imparted to the lean torso and limbs of someone whose movements must have had a certain grace and elegance—it was Mario as I had known him. I felt I was looking into his eyes, and into his soul.

'Old friend,' his effigy said, 'you must know there is no Justice. That I am here and Tomislav is not is neither right nor wrong. The Universe is indifferent and does not love us. Everything is Chance.'

Class, race, gender: a post-colonial yarn

IT WILL PERHAPS SERVE a disarming purpose and make what I have to record seem less serious than it is, or than it ought to be, if I begin by explaining that this is a story told by Bertie to Billy, who told it to me. More recently Bertie told me the story himself, so I've heard it twice and have had the chance to fill gaps that remained after the first hearing.

I got to know Bertie and Billy a long time ago when we were all studying in England. Bertie was, and indeed is and will always be even when he's dead, an Englishman. His fuller (though not entire—there are several intermediate ones) name is Herbert Lawson-Grieve. Friends and family called him Bertie, and so, although we, Billy and I, found it absurd, adding to the general feeling that he was less a real person than a character out of P.G. Wodehouse, Bertie is what we called him.

Billy is South African. His full name is Villiers de Groot

Graaf which among our group became Billy Goat Gruff—Billy for short. Billy and Bertie were friends before I knew them. They were at Oxford together, at the same college, Merton, Billy studying ('reading', as they say in England) engineering, Bertie law. Like Bertie, Billy had money, lots of it, which came from what he called 'a family in diamonds'.

I was a graduate student on a scholarship from New Zealand, writing a thesis which I hoped might be published as a book. But it was our passion for sport that brought us together—that, and a particular kind of boyish behaviour. ('Laddish', I think it might be called these days, and with strong disapproval.) There was a lot of beer drinking, a lot of horsing about, a lot of talk about 'girls'. We loved Western movies and practised shoot-outs in the parks. I think we were quite serious students, but we were having a good time.

There was another student of that time I should mention because he has provided my title—or the first half of it: Peter Mapplethwaite from Scunthorpe. I've once or twice glanced at a map looking for Scunthorpe and not found it, but the way Pete pronounced it, and the word itself, suggested slums, coal mines, sunless skies and rickets—the part of England which those of us who were (shallow and ignorant, no doubt) visitors skirted around on our way to the lakes or the moors, to North Wales or to Scotland.

Mapplethwaite was a Marxist and a man of the people. Peoplethwaite, Bertie called him; and then Pepperpot, Maxiwank, Whistlestop, Cuttlefish—anything at all but his real name. Pete could be good company. Billy and I imitated his accent and he imitated ours. He knew me as the New Zillander who liked igg sendwiches; and Billy as the Seth Ufrican who didn't want to talk about Bleck prytest.

Pete had absolutely no sense of tune, but he sang dialect songs—I suppose they were from his region—in a flat ugly-funny voice. Some of these took the form of dialogues, one of which went, as I remember,

> *'Where's tha bin, lud?'*
> *''awkeen paypers.'*
> *''oo for?'*
> *'Me uncle Benjamin.'*
> *'Wha's 'e gin thee?'*
> *'Skinny ole 'et'ny.'*
> *'Silly ole blawk*
> *'e ought ta dee.'*

I tried to make Pete part of the group but it was no use. It didn't matter too much that he sometimes wanted to lecture Billy about the situation of the 'Blecks'. There were a few occasions when Billy hung his head in helpless shame, and then flared up in angry Boer pride; but mostly he could cope with it.

But it was the two Englishmen, Pete and Bertie, who couldn't mix. It wasn't even that there was great animosity between them. It seemed more like embarrassment.

Once I asked Bertie was it a problem for him that Mapplethwaite was a Marxist. Lord no, he said; that was no problem at all. Lots of chaps from school (he always spoke of 'school' as if the word meant to me exactly what it meant to him) had been 'of that persuasion'. When I wanted more he said, 'It's just chalk and cheese, old boy.'

So it was 'chalk and cheese'; but I've gone on seeing Pete on my visits to England, calling on him at the North London polytechnic where he lectures on what's called Culture and Gender Studies, and going for a drink with him at his local.

Over the years Pete has been a Moscow communist, then a Peking communist, his faith coming to rest finally, when Mao died and the Gang of Four were arrested, on the regime in

Albania. Later again, when the Berlin Wall came down and piece by piece the whole communist empire fell apart, I expected to find him depressed and defeated, but he wasn't. On my last visit he seemed more relaxed and confident than he'd been for years. Communism was pure now, pure theory; it hadn't yet, he explained, been put into practice—not anywhere. All those attempts at it had been corrupt and imperfect. Communism lay somewhere up ahead, the great future which all the world's peoples would enjoy when at last they came to their senses and realised the evils of capitalism. Meanwhile all serious 'analysis' (his favourite word) of anything and everything came down to three things: class, race and gender.

That's why Peter Mapplethwaite figures in my account: because if I told him this story (something I can't imagine I would want to do) he would say that it illustrates perfectly the justness of the intellectual framework which has ruled his life; whereas to me it illustrates (if it illustrates anything) just the opposite—that life is subtler and more complex than the theories humans construct to explain it.

I've also continued to see Bertie—much more of him than of Pete—and so has Billy. But Billy's visits to England and mine have never coincided; and it wasn't until he came to New Zealand, accompanying the Springboks on their first post-apartheid tour, that we were able to get together again. Our talk was of rugby, of the new South Africa (which made him proud, but nervous too), and of the old days when we'd been students at Oxford. Bertie's name came up often, and we were sorry he wasn't with us, but we knew he would be watching the test matches on television.

Bertie, of course, speaks that tortured, alternately clipped, squeezed, swallowed and diphthongised English which signals, even (and perhaps especially) to those who mock it, impeccable social credentials. He has lived most of his adult life in a fine old house with a beautiful walled garden in the town of Marlow on the

Thames. He inherited the place from a maiden great-aunt when he was still a young man; and for many years he commuted all the way in to London where he worked as a solicitor specialising in marine insurance which he liked to tell us was properly called 'bottomry'. After his first marriage ended Bertie gave up the city firm in which he'd risen to become a partner, and opened a small office of his own in his home town. He's there still, prosperous and apparently content, with a wife so young he sometimes jokingly introduces her as 'My wife and child'.

Bertie's house is full of sporting prints and cricketing photographs. Along the hallways and up the stairs you can see the rugby and cricket teams—school, university, business and local—he has played for. There's a cabinet of sporting trophies; and two painted portraits of himself, one in cricketing whites with a bat across his knees, and one in flannels and a Merton blazer with a rep pocket.

In his youth Bertie let his hair grow rather long, with sideburns, and that's the look he has tended to stick with; and as the hair has thinned and gone grey-streaked, and fashions have changed, it has left him looking less than the dashing and fashionable fellow he once was. But he's tall (six foot two or three), strongly built, still handsome, still full of charm and energy and generosity. Bertie does things in style; and to be met by him off the train with flowers and champagne, as if you were a visiting foreign dignitary, is to experience a sort of expansiveness few of us where I come from would be capable of, even if the wish and the impulse towards it should happen to stir.

It was when Billy was on one of his visits to England that Bertie told him the story about his involvement with the cockney woman whose name was Michele Button, but who was known to her work mates as Shelly, or sometimes Shell, and to her husband as Mish. During Billy's Springbok-accompanying visit to New Zealand he passed the story on to me. ('You're a writer,' he said;

'you can disguise it can't you?') And so, on my most recent visit to England, when I recognised during a late-night drinking session with Bertie that we were on the borders, so to speak, of this same narrative territory, I prompted, listened, questioned, remembered. Here is what I learned.

Bertie was, as he put it, 'between marriages at the time'—depressed, bored, restless. This was in the last of his years working for the big impersonal city firm he'd been with for almost twenty years. His wife Françoise had left him, not for another man, nor for any reason except that she'd grown to hate living in England. One day she packed her things and, with their one child, returned to Paris.

'It was a fearsome blow to the pride,' Bertie said. 'Nothing quite like it had ever happened to me before. So of course the old mind went blank for a time and I came to consciousness a few months later realising I was drinking too much, eating fast fodder, not getting any exercise, becoming fat, ratty and inefficient. It was bad. All bad. That was when I started thinking about Shell.'

She served lunches in a popular place where lawyers often went for a quick bite when they weren't entertaining clients. She was small, well-shaped, bright-eyed, pretty, good-humoured, with the broadest of London accents, and she and Bertie had hit it off right from their first encounter. She teased him; he responded. Their exchanges were always (as he put it) 'remorselessly jokey', but with an undertone of flirtation. But what really attracted him was her hair. It was shiny brown, wiry and curly, and despite her best efforts to keep it neat, it sprang out from her head as if it had a life of its own. It was the kind of hair, he said, that you want desperately to touch.

Bertie never thought about this woman except when she was there in front of him, serving him salad or cottage pie. She was a very minor character in his life, one of hundreds with walk-on parts. The idea that she might be more, or other, never occurred to him. When she disappeared from the lunch place and went to work somewhere else he didn't notice she was gone.

Then one day he met her in the street. He was used to seeing her in a white smock and apron, and if it hadn't been for that head of hair he might not have recognised her. She told him she had a new job, with hours that suited her better because she started early and was finished in time to pick up the kids (she had two, Jack and Jill) from school. Also she had every Wednesday afternoon free.

And then, taking him by surprise, she said if he was ever passing on a Wednesday afternoon he ought to drop in for a cuppa.

'It was the boldness of the thing,' Bertie said. 'You couldn't be mistaken about it. She just looked me in the eye, grinned and said it. And then she wrote her address on a piece of paper and pushed it into my hand. I must have looked flabbergasted, but that only made her laugh. She said, "Come on, Mr Lawson-Grieve. Hasn't a pretty girl ever invited you to tea before?" And she walked off and left me there.'

Shortly after that Françoise left him. There were those months of dereliction, and the realisation that he must take himself in hand, re-order his life, discipline himself. But it shouldn't be all hard work. There must be some fun, entertainments, some good times. Clearing the pockets of a jacket and trousers one day, readying things for the dry cleaner, he found the slip of paper with Michele Button's address, and remembered that invitation with its suggestion of a good deal more than tea.

So an affair (if that's the word for such an arrangement) started. Michele, or Shelly as he was soon calling her, lived in a block of flats just off Clerkenwell Road near to Gray's Inn, only twenty minutes' walk, or five by taxi, from Bertie's office which was close to the Barbican. His secretary learned to keep the hours from one to 3.30 clear on a Wednesday and he spent them in bed with Shelly; and even after however many years had gone by since what was to be their last dreadful encounter, Bertie couldn't speak of the first weeks and months of that association without a certain brightening of the eye and a lift in the voice.

The flat, on the second floor of a red-brick apartment block, was drab and cramped, but it had a balcony looking inward to a shady courtyard with a single tree. They used to make love, then lie in bed looking out into the upper branches of the tree, talking, exchanging stories, dozing, until they'd recovered sufficiently to do it again, after which they would shower together and return to their separate lives.

Their talk was full of teasing and banter, but with a rich undertone of affection. He told her about the people in his office; she talked about Jack and Jill, family, neighbours. Because he called her Shelly he told her about the poet Shelley who had once lived in his town of Marlow, writing revolutionary poems, and about his wife Mary writing *Frankenstein* after the poet had been drowned in Italy. A week or so later she had *Frankenstein* beside her bed. She'd found it in a second-hand bookshop, bought it and read it. He asked what she thought of it.

''orrible,' she said. 'Did you like it Ber'ie?'

He had to admit he'd never read it.

Once he bought her a gold chain, knowing—or thinking—that she would have to hide it from her husband. But she made him help her put it on, saying she would never take it off.

'What about Arthur?' he asked. She said she would say she'd found it in the street.

Bertie seldom asked about Arthur, preferred not to hear or think about him; but now and then she would speak of him. He was a guard at the British Museum, and though she always said he was 'harmless', that seemed to be the best she could say of him. All day he sat in a chair watching over ancient vases and statues, and in the evening he sat watching television, especially football, which didn't interest her. His back was bad. He never had much to say. 'Not like you, Ber'ie, you old gasbag.' Sometimes Shelly would tell Arthur about something she'd read or seen and he would say, 'That's very interesteen, Mish.' That's what he'd said when she told him the story of Frankenstein. 'Interesteen'. She seemed to find Arthur's pronunciation of that word unforgivable. It drove her mad. It excused her infidelity.

As Bertie explained it to me, it was some time before he began to understand what kind of a woman Michele Button was and why she'd made him this, as it had seemed, outrageously frank offer of herself. She was not at all what he'd supposed—not 'wild', desperate, a beaten wife, or even attracted to him by his patrician looks and manner. Shelly was not inexperienced; but her life had been on the whole sober and orderly, constrained by modest beginnings, low income, early marriage and two children born just a year apart.

As for Bertie's attractions: she knew perfectly well that he was of a certain 'class'; but to her such men had always seemed faintly comic ('You're a joke, Ber'ie, you know that?'). It was almost an obstacle to her liking him; just as her 'class'—the fact that she referred to her husband as 'Arfur', complained that her children came home 'filfy' from school, talked about someone having 'nuffing in 'is 'ead', or said she'd heard this or that 'on good aufori'y'—had made her seem to Bertie quite beyond the pale. No. Bertie's attractiveness to her had been something else, something she told him she didn't understand. She said his voice was nice even though his accent was posh. And also, once she got to know him better, there was his smell, which was especially nice and had nothing to do with soap or aftershave.

But almost from the first exchange between them she was falling in love with him. This was a fact which slowly became clear to him. He found it flattering, disconcerting, unintelligible, reassuring—both welcome and unwelcome. It made for great sex, and helped restore the confidence a much-loved wife's departure had undermined; but it added a burden of responsibility and of guilt. Increasingly as he got to know Michele Button, Bertie felt affection and gratitude. Her talk was lively and funny. Her generosity was boundless. Her body was lovely and her hair magical. He began to think of her as his secret garden. But to fall in love, even a little, with someone who had things 'on good aufori'y' was quite beyond him.

'Not possible,' he said when I asked him. 'Simply out of the question. Sometimes, you know, I'd try to imagine taking her to things—to dinner parties, Lords, Wimbledon, Covent Garden. It was . . .' He looked at me with an expression that appealed for understanding, for absolution.

'*Unfinkable?*' I suggested.

He laughed. 'Yes exactly. Unfinkable.'

So he'd decided he must stop seeing her. If she'd been able to take their affair as he did, as an adventure, a diversion, an unlooked-for luxury, a secret bonus that life had handed out with no strings or complications, it would have been different. But he could see that every visit made the love she felt for him, and which he couldn't think of matching, more powerful, more all-consuming.

She, of course, soon recognised that this depth of feeling troubled him, and she tried to conceal it or make light of it. But there were moments when she would say, 'I'd die for you, Ber'ie,' or even (and much worse), 'I'd let you kill me if you wanted to. I'd love you for it.' He would be struck with a sense of awe and helplessness then, and with the wish to escape. To have evoked great love could only be good for his wounded ego; on the other hand, to find himself unable to return it inevitably reduced the beneficial effect. Herbert Lawson-Grieve's secret garden had begun to have about it the feel of a cage.

But still the decision that he must end their affair wasn't translated into action. He would think of it as he left her flat, resolving that this visit would be the last. By the following Monday the resolve would be gone. By Wednesday he would hardly be able to complete his morning's work for thinking of what the afternoon was to bring. But now, because he was in two minds about Shelly, an ambiguity had begun to creep into his feelings about what he did in that bedroom. He enjoyed—and yet did not. He marvelled, and was half repelled. Sometimes he felt like a circus animal required to do ever more remarkable tricks. Shelly was the trainer and her whip was true love.

The break didn't come until he was asked to go to New York on business for the firm. He accepted the task willingly, and even made it last longer than was necessary. By the time he got back to London he felt the Shelly habit had been broken.

But now came phone calls from her; and when these were blocked off by his secretary, there was a postcard. It was of a large pink breast painted to look like a winking pig, the nipple its snout. On the back she had written, 'Here's my knocker, Bertie luv. Where's yours?'

This, coming to him in the office, giggled over by the secretaries, was outrageous—but of course she meant it to be. Bertie was angry; but he was also ashamed. It had been cowardly and wrong to try to end the thing by simply absenting himself. He was an honourable chap, wasn't he? He must go and (as he put it) 'face the music'.

The 'music', however, when it came the following Wednesday was not a simple and catchy tune. At first, when he tried to tell her they must call it off, she reproached him—something she hadn't done before. She wept, told him he was a bastard and a cunt; and then, worst of all, pleaded with him, telling him how much she loved him—adored him. He found it painful, and the pain focused especially on one fact. He had given her some kind of advance warning, a hint that he had 'something very serious to tell you'. Possibly she'd guessed what it might be because she appeared to have dressed herself up for the encounter, and the clothes seemed to him in the worst possible taste.

As Bertie explained it to me, he has no exact memory for women's clothes, often doesn't remember colours, or remembers them incorrectly, yet at the same time he always takes away a generalised, and in some ways quite precise, impression. Shelly, as he remembered her that day, was wearing a short yellow dress of some kind of stiff material, and around her head, over that rebellious but briefly tamed hair, a band of the same colour.

'There seemed to be little bows and frills everywhere,' he said. 'I may be exaggerating, but it seemed to me she only needed a tray of sweets and ices and she could have gone to a fancy-dress ball as an old-fashioned cinema usherette.'

He had never, he told me, felt so fond of her, nor so self-reproachful and so determined to protect her. He couldn't give her what she wanted—he could not; and so the only thing for it was to remove himself. That's what he tried to explain while she argued, wept, pleaded.

At last, when he was on the point of exhaustion, she changed tack. She appeared to accept that he was going, and that he wouldn't be back. Before he went, however, she would like, she said, to show him her old friend. 'You didn't know I 'ad a boyfriend before you, did you, Ber'ie?' She went to the drawer beside her bed and took something out. He was expecting a photo of some dingy local lad. In fact it was what he called 'a large phallic object'. She pressed a small switch and it began to buzz. 'My vibra'or, Ber'ie. Say 'ullo to it.'

Bertie's account of what she did next was graphic. It was the cage again and he was being drawn back into it. His mouth was dry and he found it hard to speak, but he managed to tell her he was going. She put her head back, as if she was really enjoying what she was doing to herself, and said, 'You're not going nowhere, Ber'ie.' She was right of course. He thought he was heading towards the door but he wasn't. 'She was a magnet. It was like being dragged bodily, against your will.'

He'd been looking down into his drink as he told me all this, and I remember how he looked up now, appealing for a friend's compassion. 'You have to understand, I was hungry for it. I'd been all those weeks in New York, and there'd been nothing.'

'So . . . What did you do?'

It was a silly question. 'We got on with it. I thought, Fuck it, life's too difficult. Let's just enjoy ourselves. And that's what we did. Three o'clock came around, 3.30—I didn't care. I was busy. I was happy. I was being myself for a change and I was enjoying it.'

So the afternoon passed; and it occurred to him afterwards that she must all along have counted on success, because she'd arranged for Jack and Jill to go to a friend's place after school. They fucked and they talked, and finally they slept . . .

Bertie was woken by her shaking him, staring down at him. 'Wake up,' she was saying. 'Jesus Christ, Ber'ie, wake fucking up. It's 'im! It's Arfur!'

Then she was out of bed and across the room to the hallway. He heard her snib the Yale lock. There was a conversation going on in the corridor—Arthur talking to a neighbour. In a moment he would try to open his own door with the key and find he couldn't.

Back in the bedroom Shelly was gathering up her things. She hissed at Bertie to get dressed. ''e'll go downstairs to the caretaker to report there's something wrong with the lock. Then you scarper. Go down the other stairs. I'll pretend I snibbed it by mistake.'

She vanished into the bathroom. And now from the front door came the scraping of Arthur's key as he tried to turn it in the lock. Bertie dragged on his underpants and trousers, wrestled with and tore his shirt, which he found had lost a button in the earlier, equally violent, struggle to get it off.

Arthur's voice came through the door. 'Mish? You in there?'

He rattled the door handle. 'Mish?' And then the key was withdrawn, the voice muttered to itself, footsteps receded down the corridor.

Now, Bertie thought—his chance to escape. He would get out and would never come back. He thought of setting off, running, carrying his shoes. But no, some sort of dignity had to be preserved.

He was sitting on the bed's edge dragging on his socks when he heard a new sound, a scraping and scrambling. The balcony out there was shared with the flat next door. Arthur had gone through the flat of the neighbour he'd been talking to in the corridor. Now, from the balcony, he was scrambling up over a locked window to an open fanlight.

From where Bertie sat he could see, across the hallway and through another door, a pair of long black-trousered legs pushing, sliding, hanging, dropping.

There was a thump as two feet hit the sitting-room floor. Shelly's voice quavered from the bathroom. 'That you, Arfur?'

Bertie put his head down and dragged at his shoes. He tugged at the laces. Footsteps approached. At that moment, he told me, he felt a desperate calm. The blow would come down on the back of his head, on his neck—he had no doubt of that. He wouldn't defend himself; couldn't. He would die; but it wasn't fear he felt—it was embarrassment. It was shame.

Two large black shiny guard's shoes arrived and planted themselves opposite the two brown shoes which Bertie's feet had just reoccupied. He pulled the laces tight and tied them.

'One has to do something while waiting to die,' Bertie said. 'I remember wondering would the blow hurt, or would I pass instantly and painlessly into another world of floating shapes saying things like, "Hullo, dear. I'm your mother."'

But there was no blow. Nothing was said. There was only the heavy breathing of a wronged husband who had just climbed through a fanlight.

'I raised my eyes slowly.' (Bertie was acting it out for me now—bending forward, twisting his head around to look up at the occupant of those shiny shoes.) 'There was the line of the trousers. When I got to the thighs I saw the hands, hanging at his sides. They were coffee-coloured, with paler palms. I raised my eyes further and there was a coffee face to match. My first thought was, Why the fuck had she never told me he was black?'

The dark mask looking coldly down at him did not seem on the verge of violence. That ought to have been a relief; but violence would have been simpler. It would have given him something to do. He tried to read Arthur's face. There was anxiety in the eyes; and around the mouth something like contempt.

'This is a dreadful business,' Bertie managed to say. 'I'm really most frightfully sorry.'

He stood, picking his jacket up from the floor. That uncovered the vibrator. They both, he and black Arthur, looked down at it lying there like a severed penis.

Bertie said he'd better go.

Shelly had been right—Arthur wasn't a talker.

Bertie moved out into the hall. His walk was unsteady. At the bathroom door he stopped and called to Shelly that he was going.

The bolt slid back and she appeared in a dressing gown. Behind her he could see the yellow dress trampled on the wet tiled floor. She nodded to him, glanced at Arthur.

Bertie moved to the front door—only a step or two in those cramped quarters. He unsnibbed the lock, opened the door and felt a moment of relief.

But was it right to leave without another word? He turned. Shelly had come out of the bathroom, Arthur out of the bedroom, and they were standing side by side, 'like two piano keys,' Bertie said, 'the ebony and the ivory. They made a handsome couple.'

To Arthur, Bertie said, 'You won't hurt her.' He meant it to be something midway between a question and an instruction.

Arthur said, 'Out, cunt.' That was the beginning and the end of his talk.

Shelly looked at Bertie. Her expression was anxious but not frightened. She was safe, Arthur wouldn't hurt her seemed to be the message. So he went, closing the door behind him.

Out in the street he was assailed all over again by embarrassment. He turned west, away from his office, crossed Gray's Inn Road, walked along to Southampton Row. In Kingsway there was a men's clothes shop that had always, as long as he could remember, announced that it was having a Closing Down Sale. He went in and chose himself an unpleasant business shirt that had a faint shine and a green tinge to it. It would replace the one with the tear and the hanging button. He also thought of it as a penance.

Handing over his credit card he asked the young woman did she have any with hair linings.

'So-rree?' she said, not understanding. He didn't repeat it.

It was raining now. He took a taxi back to the office. The secretaries had gone. He sat at his desk looking out at rain drifting past the ugly looming portals of the Barbican. He thought of Françoise and a few tears sprang into his eyes—a mixture of anger and regret. He thought of Arthur's shiny black shoes and winced. He heard the partner in the next office getting ready to leave. He went to her door. Her name was Coral Strand. They'd worked together for years, knew one another well.

'That's a nasty shirt, Herbert,' she said at once. 'It's not the one you had on this morning.'

He had never got used to the fact that women noticed clothing so precisely. 'The other one,' he said, 'got torn off my back by a woman desperate to have me.'

Coral smiled wearily. 'Of course.' It was a tired old joke. How odd, Bertie thought, that it should be true.

'Do I seem to you an absurd person?' he asked.

'Not especially.' She snapped her case shut. It was a signal that she had no time for talk. Deluded by her name, which still suggested to him a tropical paradise, Bertie had long ago, and very briefly, imagined he and Coral Strand might become lovers. Inwardly he now thought of her as the Head Girl.

'Not especially,' he repeated. It was hardly reassuring.

'About average,' she said, easing him into the corridor and closing her door. 'We're all a bit absurd sometimes, aren't we? See you tomorrow, Herbert.'

He didn't go back to Marlow that night but spent it at his club. He has taken me there sometimes for lunch or dinner and I can report that it seemed a dreadful place where faded lackeys served tasteless food to dead men in suits. Bertie, however, finds some kind of ancient comfort in brown leather and panelled walls, and comfort was what he needed.

Next morning he went first not to his office but to the British Museum. After a lot of aimless wandering through the halls and galleries he found Arthur dozing on a chair in a corner among ancient clay burial urns. Bertie roused him with a sharp cough and said his piece: that he was very disturbed at what had happened. That it had not been as bad as it must have seemed (this in an attempt to allow for any story Shelly might have concocted) but that he wanted to apologise sincerely. That it had been his fault entirely, not Michele's. That she should not be blamed—he took full responsibility. That it would never happen again.

Arthur didn't get up. He listened, staring with bloodshot eyes at a large broken urn. When the little speech was over he asked, 'You got fifty quid?'

Bertie was taken by surprise. For just a moment it seemed a wonderful relief, the possibility of doing something, paying something, by way of recompense, of absolution.

Yes, he said, he had fifty, certainly. Possibly more . . . All the while scrabbling to get his wallet out, to get it open . . .

He held out a fistful of notes. There was at least fifty . . .

Arthur beckoned him closer. Bertie leaned down over him, holding the money.

'Now stick it up your arse,' Arthur said, 'and fuck off outta here.'

Out in the street he seemed to have lost control of his legs. He ambled uncertainly in the direction of the city, still holding the fistful of notes, looking for a passing taxi showing a light and then, when one came along, not hailing it. He saw a florist's shop, went in and put the money down on the counter. What he wanted, he explained, was as many flowers as this would buy sent at once, this morning, to . . . And he gave her name and address.

'And for the card, sir,' the florist said.

Ah yes, the card. He took it and after a moment wrote, 'To Shelly from Keats. Love you for ever.'

For the duration of the brief moment it took to write it, Bertie said, and for perhaps thirty seconds afterwards, he felt it was true.

I didn't quite believe—or was it just that I didn't want to believe?—that that was the end of the story.

'Just for thirty seconds?' I said. 'No more?'

He met my eye for a moment, shrugged and looked down at the table between our comfortable chairs. 'Let's refill these glasses,' he said.

The name on the door is not mine

One: Quinton: 'the office of Ashtree'

ON THE BUS THIS EVENING I thought, 'Anything can look like a movie of itself—i.e. unreal.' Can I recover the buoyancy of that thought? I was leaving the Quinton campus for my apartment across the river. There was snow on the fir trees and on the steps of the Faculty Club, the lawns and gardens were buried under it, it bulged on the house-roofs. It was banked thick on everything except the brown ragged-edged strip of roadway kept clear by snow-ploughs, the tracks dug from sidewalks to doors by householders, and the city sidewalks themselves over which I and the students skittered to the bus stop.

I will call it 'my apartment' and 'my office'—I have them on loan, one, the office looking over snow-bound fir trees down to a frozen river, the other, the apartment, looking from the city down to the river and up to the university. If I could occupy them both at once I could wave to myself, and would do it to relieve the loneliness. I am 'Distinguished Visitor' for just a couple of months, introduced to everyone, forgetting all their names, avoiding them all because avoidance is my habit, and hungry for company.

A Distinguished Visitor is worth quite a lot of money—or a lot by his own modest standards. This morning an account opened in my name to receive my reward. 'Age?' the young lady asked, needing my details for future ID. Home address? Mother's maiden name? Name of my first school? My first pet? There had to be a photo taken too, for which I was asked to remove the peaked cap I was wearing in the style of the German Chancellor of some years back, Helmut Schmidt.

What was the movie I seemed to see myself cast in as I came out of the Hubert Harrison-Jones Memorial Building on to the Harriet Harrison-Jones Memorial Highway to catch my bus? It was of course a North American campus movie. A student—a young woman student, with pink fingers searching for her bus pass—ought to have accidentally spilled the contents of her bag on my lap. Apologies. She's flustered. The bus starts. She falls back half into the seat beside me, half on my lap among the books. More apologies, while her things are gathered up and returned to the bag. We talk about the weather (what else?). She discovers that I am a visitor. Not the Distinguished Visitor, Helmut Schmidt? I admit it is so. She's so pleased she tells me about her boyfriend. He was supposed to meet her this evening. Didn't show up. Unreliable. She agrees to have dinner with me. Later in the week (to condense this tedious and trivial narrative) we go skiing together and finish up in a chalet, naked in a barrel of hot water soaping each other's nipples . . .

No student fell into my lap this evening, none spoke to me

nor recognised me as the Distinguished Visitor, Helmut Schmidt. Not even as Dr Henry Bulov visiting the English Department from New Zealand. I don't complain of this or believe it ought to have been otherwise. I note only that it is these little divergences that make the reality of a movie, or, as this evening, the reality of reality, unreal.

Now it's night and out there the northern prairie weather means business. It's minus 26°F, the scraped sidewalks hard with ice, and you fight your way along inside a big old German tweed overcoat which adds kilos to that figure of 75 so lightly offered by the bathroom scales this morning, and looking like a big old German. But it's no longer the cute Helmut Schmidt cap in wapiti leather peaked over your northern blue eyes but a red, white and blue skiing toque tight down over brow and ears, your scarf over your chin, and the breath between faintly holding the chill at bay from that chiselled (or chisel) nose. Yet in empty Archibald Square you hear 'Les bicyclettes de Belsize' piped to the icy skies and a scrape-scraping to its rhythm. Surely not? But yes, two hardy teenagers in the half-light and togged to the eyebrows are skating on its flooded-and-frozen centre. The tweed is doing its winter work but the frightful chill is getting into the toque and through the shoes; your trousers at and below the knee feel as if they've gone over to the enemy; and you press desperately into the little Italian restaurant at the door of which you hesitated last evening and turned away because then as now there were no customers—not one. But the dish when it comes is tasty and cheap, with no frills, distinctly and edibly *melanzane parmigiana*.

Warm and replete, you're ready for the short battle homeward. There is, you reflect, something to be said for a climate that makes simply setting forth an adventure—never mind setting forth for what. Your apartment is on the twelfth floor and you will soon be drifting to sleep with the curtains open, looking at the lights of the city and the snow falling on your balcony. Contrarily, these past days, through all the invasions of melancholy, loneliness and disorientation, has come the old absurd ebullience, the unreasonable sense that life is its own reward.

THIS WAR BETWEEN VANITY and convenience, the cap and the toque, has led me to inspect my ears in the mirror. I conceived of them, if at all, as small and neat. In fact they appear rather large and sprout a few untoward and random hairs, but they lie flat against my head. At 8.30 this morning on Channel 4 which gives constant print-outs of the weather I watched the temperature dropping and rising between minus 29 and minus 30. Two hours later it was 'up' to minus 22. In between I had walked, capped, two blocks to the Hudson Bay Company for supplies. The ears burned and froze and stung and ached. Two flaps of flesh one has hardly acknowledged as existing in their own right are bidding to become determinants of behaviour.

This morning too I did the balcony experiment—one dish of water put out there and one into the deep-freeze. As expected, Nature won. There was a skin of ice on the balcony dish in the time it took to walk across the room and back. Minutes later the Kelvinator dish hadn't begun to freeze. So, you darlings in the South Pacific to whom I wrote that stepping out here is like stepping into a cool-store—revise it please. And remember that the air in this deeper-freeze moves. It's what they call a 'wind-chill factor' and it's why God designed you flap-eared—so you could have fair warning. When some oil-rich sheikdom invites me to its university as Distinguished Visitor and provides me with a handsome apartment I will of course fry one egg on the balcony rail and another in a pan on the stove, and again, no doubt, Nature will triumph.

But it's Sunday afternoon I've a need to record. I was taken to the home of the chairman of Quinton's Department of Comp. Lit. (my host department) to meet the chairman and his family and some members of his staff. Chairman Hyde is big, sandy-haired and slow-spoken. His wife is small, quick and pretty, still youthful, shy at first, but soon the confidence appears, and with it the pride, and the impatience. She's almost certainly smarter than her husband, and has recently completed her PhD. She tells how someone phoned recently and asked, 'Could I speak to Dr Hyde?' to which she replied, 'Which of them do you want?'

ACROSS THE STREET the neighbours are shovelling snow off the roof. Paths have been dug to the sidewalk. More members of the department arrive. There is one, Eugene Fish, who has a thin moustache and the look of a band leader of the 1920s—a sort of Scott Fitzgerald look. His wife is plump and must have once been pretty. She's still pretty, but plump. Her dress has a design of tiny shoes that run around it in circles. She's one of those faculty wives who cause embarrassment by offering perfectly ordinary and sensible domestic observations and reminiscences. She's shy and never raises her voice or moves her lips much, but it's obvious she's a compulsive talker once set in motion through a gap in the conversation, and Eugene Fish covers for her with quick loud quips, like a back-up gun in a Western movie.

There is also a big man, an American, Hank Judder, who arrives on skis, wearing mukluks and a large Indian fur-lined coat with a hood. He's a poet and lives in the woods out of town with his wife, who weaves and does Indian craft work and arrives minutes later in an SUV. Judder hasn't sat down before he's wanting me to agree that the eighteenth century is the sanest. I feel he's checking me out before deciding to stay. I say, 'The sanest might be most insane.' I'm not sure what this means, except that it's a way of evading the question, which I don't understand either.

He looks doubtful, probably disappointed, but he accepts a drink from Chairman Hyde and sits down, chewing on my aphorism.

Faculty talk goes on making considerable use of numerals. It's like that story about monks who've lived together so long they've reduced all their jokes to numbers. In faculty talk the numbers are all courses—3.307 Literature and Silence; 2.903 Comparative Semiotics; 4.747 Frontier Feminism; 3.208 the Syntax of Self in early America. So it goes 'We need to have another look at 1.425.' 'I've got to get through 2.901 before I can begin to think about that.' 'But that won't be until the next session.' 'The Chairman's setting up a committee anyway to look at all the 3s.' 'Did that student in 4.301 get hold of you?' 'Someone told me your lectures in 2.223 have been brilliant this semester.'

Out there a squirrel is rippling along a bough, and I remember I've read somewhere that the word squirrel comes from the Greek and means 'shadow tail'. The youngest Hyde describes to me the animal's regular path—over the woodshed at the back, along the fence, across the roof, down the elm bough . . . He asks about animals in New Zealand. I tell him about the possum I feed. He tells me about the skunk that got under the porch. In a minute the numbers are dropped and everyone is exchanging animal stories. A moose has been seen this year down on the frozen river. The lady with the little coloured shoes walking in circles around her dress tells how she got up in the night and saw 'a nice dog' in the moonlight on the snow. 'And then it put its head back and . . .' They all laugh and junior Hyde explains to me that the 'nice dog' was a coyote. Hank Judder explains his problem with bats which maybe ought to be killed because they're said to carry rabies but which up close have such nice faces. There's a story about bears one summer on the shores of one of the lakes . . .

Numberless, we seem more relaxed. The animals have humanised us. The drinks maybe have something to do with it as well. Outside there is the sound of shovels scraping on paths and sidewalks. I resolve inwardly, solemnly, never to write about these people. Cross my heart. Chairman Hyde asks if I'm finding Ashtree's office comfortable.

Already Ashtree has taken my fancy. There's that shelf of handbooks on writing in his office—*On Writing Better and Best, Styles and Structures, The Writer's Control of Tone, The Canadian Writers' Handbook* . . . Why should a distinguished Canadian poet keep all that stuff on his shelves? I suppose all it means is that he teaches one of those courses that aim to turn literary sows' ears into publishable silk purses. I imagine a text called *The Sow's Ear's Handbook.*

I tell Chairman Hyde that the office is comfortable, the view fine, and I thank him. It's a room of course hermetically sealed. The windows can't be opened and you must accept the weather sent you through pipes. I'm told that on one side of the building the combination of piped weather and natural sunshine turns the offices into something like a sauna. With snow drifts heaped up against the unopenable double panes, and great icicles hanging from the eaves, they sit sweating and trying to cool themselves with electric fans. I have no such problem. But does Ashtree mind my occupancy while he's on leave? Was there a problem of some kind?

My question produces what feels like a moment of awkwardness. Is Chairman Hyde embarrassed? Quick as a pretty ferret his lady, Dr Hyde II, says if the Distinguished Visitor is comfortable then there's no problem. None. And she offers to refill his glass. I'm reeling already, not used to drinking in the afternoon. Maybe that's why I persist. I mention the letter I've had from Ashtree himself. 'Dear Dr Bulov,' it began, 'I have just been informed that you, as Distinguished Visitor to Quinton campus, have been assigned to my office for your personal use throughout the duration of your tenure.' I think some of those handbooks could have been profitably brought to bear on that sentence, but Ashtree was writing under pressure. He went on to explain that there had been 'no consultation'. He'd had 'no prior warning' that someone would be 'poking about' in his office, which, he continued, like everyone's he supposed, contained papers which were 'personal and private'. In particular he would be grateful if, 'instantly upon arrival', I would turn the key in the top of his filing cabinet and hand it (I assumed he meant the key, not the cabinet) to Mrs Merrill in the department office for safekeeping. The top key, I would find, locked all four drawers at once.

I responded to this as to an electric prodder. Already when his letter reached me I had been in occupation three days. It was too late for action 'instantly upon arrival'. But in those three days I hadn't so much as looked at his filing cabinet. I don't believe I'd noticed it was there. Now I sprang into action—out of the chair in which I was reading his letter, across the room, turning the key that was sticking out the top of the cabinet, guiltily locking its contents away from my own prying gaze and taking the key at once to the imperturbable Mrs Merrill who said it would go straight into the departmental safe.

I convey something—a little—of this to the Sunday afternoon, but there's no response. If there's anything odd about Ashtree, they're covering well for him. 'I should have warned the poor guy,' Chairman Hyde admits. 'I thought I did warn him. There's so damned much to remember these days.'

After the others have gone I'm retained, along with Hank Judder and his weaving wife, for dinner with the family. There's a dispute about whether it's true that the bathwater goes down differently in the northern and southern hemispheres—clockwise in one, anti-clockwise in the other. I try to use my wine glass as a globe to show that a clockwise spin is anti-clockwise when looked at from below. I spill some wine and the point is not understood. The children insist that the difference between hemispheres bathwater behaviour is real, and they have a name for the phenomenon. Hank Judder asks me about my tastes in music.

His are classical, mine romantic, and I lumber into an admission of a passion for Wagner, which becomes in turn a defence of such a preference, and then of Wagner.

THE DAYS ARE GOING BY. I clamber into the toque (the Helmut Schmidt look has admitted defeat) scarf coat gloves and go out to buy the few things I need. I sit staring at the long green hair of the carpet in my apartment and at the snow falling in the streets, thinking of nothing. Quinton seems unreal, so does New Zealand. I'm tired, sleep too long and wake tired. I force myself out of doors into the bracing air, crunching over the ice, to wake myself. Sun shines on the snow, the huge icicles hanging at the corners of the Faculty Club glisten, the skiers glide by among the trees, the brief day is dazzling and beautiful but the cold drives me indoors again. I write letters home but there's little to report. In the afternoons I sit in Ashtree's office watching the shadow cast by this slope climb the other beyond the river towards the base of my apartment tower. Downriver there are factory chimneys casting white smoke into the icy blue, which seems edged with green at sundown. In the far distance there is a single gas-flare. It's hard to imagine the river, a quarter of a mile or more wide, is still flowing down there under its ice.

Somewhere under the faces people in the department present to me I sense warring factions. I try not to identify them, not to guess where I belong in them or for whom my invitation may have been a triumph and for whom a defeat. The long-tailed magpies dart about in the empty trees and I wonder what they find to eat. Melancholy loves me dearly and wants to hug me to her heart.

Ms Libby Valtraute, on the other hand, is probably not interested. She presents a paper on the poetry of Alban Ashtree to the Graduate Seminar on Canadian Literature. Being a feminist she takes a strong line with certain aspects of Ashtree's work. His 'Muse obsession', for example. His Snow White Goddess, she calls it. She admires him for his independence as a Canadian (lucrative offers from US campuses have been declined). She loves his sense of 'the divine in the derelict'. She approves of the way he has refocused the central image of Canadian literature on 'the cold wastes that were always there as a challenge to the imagination'. But in human relationships he is, she says, 'manly' (which she gives a negative emphasis) and 'cock eyed'.

I've always been drawn to strong, intelligent, verbal, not to say literary women, as some are drawn to rock climbing, or hang gliding, or canoeing down rapids; and Ms Valtraute is tall with a beautiful freckled nose, a perfect mouth, keen clear observing eyes and thick red-gold hair. She plans to write her thesis on sexual politics in selected Commonwealth poets and I'm wondering where in her life sexual politics, as she calls it, ceases to be political and is permitted to re-inhabit its long social and biological history.

This afternoon is Friday and the sun has failed to shine. Cloud presses down on the tall buildings across the river; snow is falling, and cars crossing the bridge have their lights on. An awful silence has descended over the department, signalling the onset of a weekend in which I have nothing to do, no one to talk to. My eye goes around and around the room, which I designate in my thoughts (because of how it sounds on the inner ear) as 'the office of Ashtree'. A student from Bangladesh knocks and asks to borrow a stapler. I find one in the desk. The student uses it, thanks me and vanishes into the silence. My last human contact until Monday? My eye going around again falls on drawer three (counting from the top) of Ashtree's cabinet. It seems to be protruding a few millimetres. I go over to it, look at it closely, pull at it gently. It opens. I slam it but it won't shut. The bolts, closing downward from the top, have left drawer three unlocked while locking the others. I rush out for Mrs Merrill so I can borrow the key and relock the whole cabinet. She's gone like everyone else. It seems I'm to spend a weekend with that naked lady, the filing cabinet in 'the office of Ashtree', baring her bosom or belly at me.

My thoughts return—I return them there—to Ms Valtraute. Libby. A few nights ago she sat three rows in front of me at Quinton's National Film Theatre. She was wearing a coat with a fur-lined collar and in the half-light it reminded me of something out of my past—or was it out of the forbidden filing cabinet? (Already I'm uncertain.) I was in Denmark in the late autumn, a little snow was falling and I was standing outside a discotheque called *Locomotion* with a woman whose name was Bodil. We had been dancing in the discotheque—God knows why. Bodil was a respectable Danish lady with a husband in banking and two delightful children. But I, or Alban, had been a visitor (Distinguished?—yes I think so) and she had been entertaining me. First dinner (teaching me how that Danish table with its apparently random offerings is to be approached in the proper order) and Danish beer, then wine because I had wanted it, and finally, by no very clear progression, *Locomotion* where Bodil feared she might be seen by some shop assistant or bank clerk.

And now we were standing in the flurries of light snow, outside the discotheque and down the road from my hotel, and Bodil was drawing the pale fur collar around her throat and declining to kiss me.

'I am very hot-blooded,' she explained, as if it was a deficiency. 'If I kiss you I get excited.' She was about to get into her car. I took hold of her—it was just a big friendly hug in the snow, my mouth somewhere between the collar and the throat, touching both. I felt her resist and then relax. She sighed. 'Goodnight, Mr Dancer,' she said. And she got into her big German Ford, waved a small gloved hand and drove away.

I ENJOY SHOPPING AND BUY more than I need. It's the standard form of stimulation isn't it, for people who live inside a protective cocoon. But I've neglected to buy soap powder. I decide to manufacture some out of the airline toilet soaps I've collected along the way. I choose UTA and it takes almost half an hour sitting at the table with the bread knife turning the little bar of soap into Lux-style flakes. I've done that and the machine's already into its second rinse when I remember that this apartment block has a shop which is open on Sunday.

Some kind of tussle goes on in me about whether I should go to 'the office of Ashtree' this afternoon. There's nothing else to do, it's true. And yesterday I proved for the first time it's possible to go there on foot. I bought one of those knitted hats concealing a mask you can pull down to your chin, with gaps for eyes and mouth. Crossing the long bridge over the river I had to pull down the mask against the wind. Inside my trousers I was wearing pyjamas and inside my shoes two pairs of socks. My heavy German tweed coat with its woollen lining was doing its heavy German work. I was cold at the extremities but I made it in three-quarters of an hour, and no frostbite. So it can be done—that's not the problem. It's only that I wonder should one go in every day, weekends included. I'm suspicious of that voluptuous filing cabinet with its see-through drawer, its keyhole opening up the Snow White Goddess. Have I ever been to Denmark? Did I ever know a bourgeois Danish lady called Bodil who danced like a demon and refused to kiss me in the snow? Was it part of something dreamed last night (when I woke and couldn't remember the geography of my apartment)—or am I right in remembering someone telling me that Ashtree's itinerary will take him to Scandinavia?

Strange things happen in strange lands. One of the movies I shared inadvertently with Ms Valtraute was by Pasolini. It was called *Theorem*. A beautiful young man comes into a middle-class household—mother father son daughter and maid. Beautiful young man is Christ—or at least I think that's the intention. Each member of the household becomes obsessed with him and they all respond to him sexually because (I'm guessing at what maestro Pasolini intended) that's the only way we, the modern decadent bourgeoisie, have of responding to anything. And isn't it true? Ms Valtraute's fur collar in the half-light of the movie house has set me thinking about Danish Bodil whom I hugged (or Ashtree hugged her) in the snow, and who might have said to Jesus Christ disguised as a beautiful young man, 'I am very hot-blooded. If I kiss you I get excited.' A boy with an angel face runs in flapping his arms and bearing a telegram calling the beautiful young man away. The BYM goes. The whole family is bereft and each goes mad in a different way. The most successful is the maid because she still has the vehicle of primitive Catholicism. She returns to the village, sits out of doors, refuses all food but boiled nettles, cures a sick boy, levitates about the rooftops (a good job here by the special effects team), and finally has herself buried alive on a muddy building site at dawn.

At the interval I watch Ms Valtraute's fur collar but it sits facing forward and doesn't move. It's possible (anything seems possible) she has vacated it. Round two is a French movie by Resnais, *Mon oncle d'Amérique*. It portrays three lives that intersect, and the narrative, documentary style is cut into by a 'scientific' account of human behaviour in terms which mix Skinnerian behaviourism and Freudian psychology. It seems to me affectionate, tolerant, with a nice 'tone', but on some point of sexual politics Resnais may well have erred. When the lights go up Ms Valtraute and her fur collar are nowhere to be seen.

Back in my apartment I'm getting ready for my big empty bed when the fire alarm sounds. I remain very calm, reading the instructions on the back of the door. I should inch the door open. If there's flame out there I should close it again and head for the

253

balcony. I'm on the twelfth floor—twelve out of thirty-four—and I remember someone saying the longest ladder would only go up ten floors. If there are no flames and not too much smoke I should proceed groundward by the stairway. Don't use the lift. I put on shoes, take my big coat and scarf, toque—but no, why not die in style? I put on the Helmut Schmidt cap and make my way to the stairs. There are no flames, no smoke, just the clanging of bells, deafening, impossible to ignore, and a lot of people, increasing in number as I work my way down. Walking to the university in daylight on a Sunday it seemed Quinton had been vacated—all but two or three of us, unwitting survivors who had missed news of the evacuation or survived the neutron bomb. But why should anyone come out on a cold Sunday? Outside working hours a North American city in winter is a lot of people watching television or reading. Here they come now, down the stairs, wearing anything from nightdress to battledress. We gather in the foyer. The firetruck arrives. Someone on the eighth has set a kitchen alight. It's soon out, but down in the foyer we're getting to know one another. Someone has a tape deck, a regular ghetto-blaster up on the railing of the mezzanine, and soon we're all drinking and dancing, the flashing red and orange lights of the firetruck turning the lobby into a disco. This is *Locomotion* again. Oh, hot-blooded Bodil! Oh, chilly Ms Valtraute! Where are your furry collars? Where are your sexual politics?

Lonely and tearful, happy to be clasped to Melancholy's incomparable bosom, the Distinguished Visitor dances solo among the beer cans in the flashing lights of Quinton's largest firetruck.

SEEN FROM OUTSIDE, the Hubert Harrison-Jones Memorial Building (in which 'the office of Ashtree' is situated) is anonymous dull brown, executing a quarter-turn to imitate a bend in the river, so all its rooms along one side look down that wooded slope to the ice. Inside, it's all white stucco, glass and open spaces, with cloth banners in orange, green and gold hanging down through two and three floors of a central opening area and catching the afternoon sunlight.

I sit at Alban Ashtree's desk reading a poem-sequence by Alban Ashtree. Maybe he sat here writing it. It's about Death and the Snow Maiden. He longs for Death. He longs for the Snow Maiden, who has red-gold hair. I keep looking up from the poem and down through the trees below the window. The shadows appear curiously blue across the clean white surface. Through the trees comes a tall shapely figure. She pauses at the top of the slope to regain breath, pulling off her toque and shaking out a shower of red-gold hemp. She looks up at this window and I wave nervously down to her. In a moment, looking up as if at me, she appears to be in tears. Is that possible, or an effect of the light? There's no return of my wave and in a moment she's skimming away out of sight, around towards the main entrance.

I turn to the poems submitted for tonight's Creative Writing session. Some contain Snow Maidens and other Divine Derelicts. The Ashtree, it seems, like the one in Wagner that sheaths the magic sword, casts a long shadow. The sun's still shining and I tog up and go out trying to find a firmly trodden trail, down to the river. In less than twenty minutes I'm on the bank, the ice stretching away upriver and down, with drifts of snow heaped on it. I want to walk on it, never having walked on water, and I'm sure it would be safe. There are ski-tracks across it, and someone has told me the ice is two feet thick. But there's no one about, I've seen the trail of thaw where warm water spills out from the upriver power station, I know my optimism where water is concerned often leads me into error (is Ms Valtraute an Aquarian?) and I can imagine how quickly the heavy German tweed would go down. One Distinguished Visitor vanished without trace! So I content myself with one long look and two photographs. By the time I've found my way back up the slope my legs feel deeply chilled and my face is burning.

My phone rings. It's Dan Dugan wanting to talk about the submissions, and warning me to go easy on blonde Megyn Kegan, who is under sedation for an unhappy affair. I promise all due caution with Ms Kegan. My eyes go around the room while we talk over the poems submitted, and I notice drawer number three with its few millimetres of overlap. I wonder about calling Mrs Merrill in to unlock and re-lock the cabinet with drawer three in place, but the nervous urgency of that Friday afternoon has gone, replaced by something else—curiosity? No I think it's more the serious scholar's sense of responsibility to an inquiry in hand: a sort of academic/forensic professionalism. So, not yet, thank you, Mrs Merrill.

IN MY APARTMENT this weekend, devising diversions and exercises for myself, I did some jogging. The apartment is large, but not large enough. I ran I think it was fifty times from the entrance to the sliding doors that open on to the balcony, then past the television set into the bedroom, around and across the double bed, back through the living room to the door again. Then I got more adventurous and extended my run out of my apartment into the vestibule, or lobby, or whatever that space out there is called. The building is circular you understand, with elevators running up the middle. When you step out of an elevator you're at the still centre, with green carpet (green on this floor—different colours for different floors) longer haired but matching the apartment in colour, and running off the floors and up the walls, I suppose for insulation against noise. Encircling this central space runs the corridor off which the apartments open. So I listened out for the bells that would warn me if the lift was stopping at my floor and included that circular corridor in my run. It made for some fine turns of speed, and a little excitement.

MY FIRST PUBLIC LECTURE as Quinton's DV is called 'What is Modernism and where did it go?' The department seems to like the title, but in the course of delivering it I stray away from my notes and begin to talk about Ashtree's poems; and I wind up with a quotation from one of his unpublished notebooks—one of many memorable remarks of his I've found and jotted down on scraps of paper and which I'm just beginning to systematise. 'To be perfectly lucid,' the quotation goes, 'is to deprive yourself of mystery and your reader of that sense of effort and discovery necessary to high art.'

Chairman Hyde is silent as we walk away from the lecture theatre. We're joined by Dan Dugan, Eugene Fish and one or two others. The talk is desultory and general. Only the most routine plaudits for my lecture. Have I caused offence? We drink coffee in the Faculty Club and Eugene Fish tells a story about a gay tourist at the Vatican watching the Pope in purple soutane officiating at some important mass, swinging a censer. 'I love his drag,' the tourist tells the woman next to him, 'but his handbag's on fire.'

Back in my/his office I take down Ashtree's poems again and read here and there, trying to remember what I said about them and to guess where in my remarks I went wrong. And then a small fist knocks at the door and it's a fur collar standing there surrounding the freckled blue-eyed face of Ms Valtraute. Has she come to say something nice about my lecture? Only indirectly. She asks could we talk some time about sexual politics in Commonwealth poets. I pretend to consult a crowded diary before suggesting tomorrow and 4 p.m. 'Let's go for a beer,' she says, 'so it will be business and pleasure.'

'I look forward to it,' I say, truthfully.

A minute later there's another knock. Bob Wilcox, who has the office next to mine, is inviting me to eat pizzas with him and his teenage daughter and his daughter's friend who is from Mexico. I throw Ashtree into my bag and follow Bob down to the carpark. At the pizza place the two girls talk in Spanish and play records while Bob and I talk about French Canada, and Margaret Trudeau having sex in a car with Jack Nicholson, and Commonwealth literature, and finally Alban Ashtree. Bob wasn't there to hear my lecture, so I explain how I drifted on to the subject of Ashtree's poetry, and then felt uncertain what people thought of the lecture. 'Well I guess,' Bob Wilcox says, 'they don't like him.'

'You mean his work? They don't admire it?'

'Oh his work's OK,' Bob says. 'It's him they don't like.'

On the way back from the pizza place Bob gives some friends a lift. Daughter Monica climbs on to my knee to make room for them, and for a few minutes I have hair in my face and my arms around a teenage daughter.

OTHER CASUAL ENTRIES in Ashtree's notebooks read: 'I am too much given to doing my duty' and 'Writing is a poor substitute for sex. But so is everything except sex.'

It seems clear that the moment Bodil refused Ashtree's request to let him kiss her in the street outside the disco, she regretted it. Next day they met by chance in the city art gallery and, being an honest and direct Scandinavian lady, she told him. He suggested he kiss her at once, behind a large piece of sculpture, but she had something more thorough-going in mind. What's not clear is why they did not use Ashtree's hotel room. Of course it may have been some sort of bizarre preference. But whatever the reason, Ashtree's record is plain enough. That night the big German Ford was parked at the edge of a ploughed field outside the town, with its windows up, its seats down, its engine running and its heater working. And while snow drifted down Ashtree discovered (his notes are graphic) what a respectable Danish bourgeois lady meant when she said, 'If I kiss you I get excited.'

ANOTHER APHORISM FROM the cabinet: 'The generation of writers before mine suffered the pain of going unread because they were Canadian. Mine lives with the indignity of being read only for the same reason.'

And a postscript: 'Most of the bastards live with it without discomfort.'

A familiar dilemma—and unfamiliar candour! And yes, I can see they would not have liked him.

THE FORECASTERS HAVE BEEN predicting that some high-level meeting of contrary streams of air over the Rockies will send temperatures '*soaring* towards zero!'—but I've seen no sign of it. The bus strike, long threatened, has begun, and I walk to Quinton University across the high-level bridge wearing pyjamas and socks under my trousers and on my head the toques, the one with the mask under the other. Where is the Helmut Schmidt look? The little cap of wapiti suede lies crushed and defeated at the bottom of my bag. Below the bridge I can see skiers on trails through the trees that cover the slopes down to the river. In a school playground children rocket down an ice-slide into a bank of snow. A hot-air balloon floats over the city. A bookshop has a display of the work of a Canadian woman poet who killed herself in Quinton three or four days ago. If they'd had the display last week, would she be still alive?

In Ashtree's office I discuss the works of Iris Murdoch with a PhD student who is writing a thesis on them. He's a Kurd from Iraq, and he won't be returning home. He calls me Professor Ashtree, and seems not to understand what I mean when I tell him the name on the door is not mine. I read poems offered me by a sessional from Bombay. They are full of fine old flourishes, as if the English language had been set aside this past century and taken up fresh out of the cooler. He too farewells me as Professor Ashtree. I take a class on 'The Waste Land' for which I receive a faint round of applause. At 4 p.m. I keep my appointment with Ms Valtraute. We drink beer under the drab rafters of the Graduate Club, and talk about Allen Curnow, and Les Murray, and (drifting off the theme) her childhood on a farm in Saskatchewan. The farmhouse had no electricity and no central heating. It was heated by a furnace in the kitchen. In Libby's bedroom upstairs icicles hung from nails in the wall, frost formed on the inside of window panes, and the water in the glass by her bed was frozen by morning. Until she was twenty she never saw a tree taller than eight feet. She was twenty-three when she first saw the sea. I don't tell her how far into my forties life has taken me before showing me my first frozen river.

As for Curnow and Murray—she may be more relaxed over her beer but she's not prepared to sign an armistice in the war of the sexes, and I can see will convict them, Curnow especially, of transgressions. We call a cab and cross the river to the town side, to a Japanese restaurant where a cook in a tall white hat prepares a meal for a dozen people grouped around a table which adjoins his large electric hot-plate. It's a curious combination of East and West, intended to be orientally occidental but better described (it's my little joke for Libby Valtraute) as accidentally disoriented. We get a lucky number with our meal and Libby wins third prize, a little Japanese vase. I am given a free set of chopsticks.

The meal has been large, enjoyable if unremarkable, and the *sake* has loosened us a little. I suggest coffee at my apartment, which is only a couple of blocks away, and I'm aware of the predictable pattern of all this, and the fact that, feminism or not, I am permitted to pay the bill. The coffee is instant—all I can offer; but we turn the lights down and look out at the city towers glittering in the icy air, and the broad white wandering ice-path of the river under starlight. I sit beside Libby on the couch and now and then our knees touch. What next? Who is to make the first move? What about feminism? Has she no principles—or is this just a big Man Trap leading to a small Saskatchewan fist in my Pacific mouth?

MY SECOND PUBLIC LECTURE, a week after the first, is called 'Modernism—an art of fragments', and it goes much better than the first because I stick to my notes and keep off the subject of Alban Ashtree. At question time an elderly academic expresses doubts. Fragments are fragments, he says, and art is art. My reply is to remind him of Eliot's 'these fragments I have shored against my ruin' (already quoted), and remind him that this is a very old battle, long ago fought and won. 'This is literary history,' I tell him, and he detects in my sighing tone the suggestion that so is he—and takes offence.

My eyes wander over the audience towards Libby Valtraute inconspicuously placed near the back door. I haven't seen her today though I've been conscious of her in bed with me during the night. She has in the past few days taken possession of the spare key to my apartment and she comes and goes according to whim, or some schedule of her own, often creeping in after I've gone to sleep and leaving early before I wake. Only her fat-free yoghurt in the refrigerator, her lemon and honey soap in the bath, and her red-gold hempen hair around the plug-hole, reassure me that she's not a figment or an invention. But though I'm certain of her reality and occasional presence in my bed, I can't be sure whether it's an accurate memory or a deluding dream that I woke in the middle of the night to find her cradling my head against her naked breasts and weeping silently into my hair, murmuring a word I can't catch but which puts into my sleep-fuddled brain the thought of breakfast.

An hour or two after the lecture I come into the Faculty Club and half a dozen of the Comp. Lit. Department are discussing it. There's an awkward silence until Eugene Fish explains to me that they've been discussing my resemblance to Alban Ashtree, and the coincidence that I should be occupying his room. It's not just appearance, he tells me, but certain gestures, body language. For some reason today it was particularly noticeable.

I'm not sure this is something I want to know; but some dark part of my brain is listening to Ashtree's forename, Alban, as they pronounce it, and hearing something quite close to 'All Bran'. Is that what I have woken to, hearing Libby whimpering it as she wept in the night?

THE HIGH-LEVEL MEETING of air-streams with its consequent thaw comes and goes too rapidly to change very much. For half a day the snow turns to slush in the streets and begins to run away into gutters, but that night it all turns to ice again and in the morning fresh snow has fallen. Bob Wilcox has the afternoon off and finds gear for me so we can go cross-country skiing. We take a trail down to the river and cross the ice to follow another trail along the river bank for an hour or more until it brings us to a lodge where there's a fire and hot drinks. It's late when we get back and in the Faculty Club there's a tense atmosphere. Eugene Fish tries to tell us something but stutters to a halt. Chairman Hyde assumes the mantle of his office and delivers it straight. The department has had a telegram this afternoon. It's about Ashtree. Not good news. Bad in fact. A grievous loss. Ashtree died in an avalanche yesterday, climbing or skiing somewhere in the Austrian Alps.

I LIE AWAKE IN my overheated apartment wondering what it would be like to die under an avalanche of snow. It seems such gentle soft stuff and I'm so unfamiliar with its ways I can't imagine it as a violent death; but then I think of the sea, and the weight of water crashing down as surf . . .

I'm drifting towards and away from sleep, asking myself could anyone be called Alban Ashtree and die so alliterative a death, in an avalanche in the Austrian Alps. Are there Alps in Austria? Or, on the other hand, if it's real and true, could it really be an accident? Has Ashtree seen himself off—designed a picturesque end for the poet of the Snow White Goddess?

Without getting out of bed I phone Libby Valtraute again but there's still no answer. I slide back both panes of the little half-window that opens from my bedroom on to the balcony, and for a few moments the cold blast is refreshing, but soon it's too cold and I close one pane, leaving the other just slightly open. Out there the moon is shining on the snow that has heaped and frozen in layers on the unused balcony. I wonder whether Libby has heard the news of Ashtree's death. I have his latest book of poems by my bed and I open it and read the lines

> *Idea of a river was harder than*
> *the river itself while the winged*
> *mercury fell through floors*
> *through ice through*
> *layers of sleep that were*
> *a kind of death.*

His reputation has been growing in recent years—everyone seems agreed on that, and Chairman Hyde has said there will be Canada Council money for whoever gets the job of editing his collected works.

I pull the sheet over me and turn off the light. From this angle the big white moon appears balanced on the balcony rail. My eyes flicker towards sleep again and the moon's face is the face of

Libby Valtraute. 'Alban,' she weeps. 'Alban Ashtree.'

His snow-maiden! His Snow White Goddess!

Two: Of angels and oystercatchers: the home campus

MONDAY: (BLOODY MONDAY). Reply from Registrar, i.e. Promotions Advisory Committee, i.e. HOD (blame him? Not altogether. But, yes) to say application for Promotion to Associate Professor declined—this in the week of turning fifty, turning the corner, going over the hill, the landscape of eternal Senior Lecturerhood ('Specialist in Commonwealth Modernisms') stretching away. Fate, you desert flower, you mercenary, you crippled smith, you fucking fairy—you are not kind. Does the Applicant's present (and pioneering) work on the poetry of Alban Ashtree count for nothing? Or was it considered by those magisterial unworthies, sheersmen, ball-breakers, punks-on-high, that Ashtree's being Canadian rendered him less significant than . . . etc., etc. Shakespeare, yes. Wordsworth, certainly. T.S. Eliot, why not? Witi Ihimaera, perhaps? But Alban Ashtree? Never heard of him!

Well, you dark darlings in your committee-corner: that is something that may change; and it may be 'the Applicant' who will bring it about. At least he doesn't propose to give up on Ashtree. Not yet.

He? Notice, please (as he has himself just noticed) that in this journal, only now taken up, not touched since his leave as 'Distinguished Visitor' to the Quinton campus, Alberta, Canada, interrupted it, the discourse is past its second, and now well into its third, paragraph—and still no I pronoun; no first person. This has not been policy; not decision or design. Does it tell something about its author, his state of mind?

'His'? Let him be 'he', then (and let there be light!). Is such possible? A diary in the third person? 'He did this, he did that . . .' 'He' short for Henry. 'Henry' long for the ninth letter (in caps) of the alphabet. Henry Bulov, otherwise (or once) known as 'the Fly', and reminded of it, as recently as this morning, by Kevin on the balcony. Kevin-in-his-socks O'Higgins—drainer, Leftist, old schoolmate: 'What's all this Bulov bullshit, Henry? You were Blow then; you're Blow now.'

No use telling him that Bulov was the family name; that Grandfather changed it during the 1914–18 War, when anti-German sentiment ran rife; that Henry went back to it long—thirty long—years ago.

Kevin knows. The change unsettles him. He wants his past undisturbed, and if Henry Blow is part of that past Henry Blow should not be erased by a stroke of the pen. Or is it just that Kevin likes to think of his old mate as the Fly?

'How many miles to Babylon? Three score miles and ten'—and Kev liked to add, 'as the Blow flies!'

3 JULY: THEY, KEVIN AND 'HE'—third-person-Henry—looked at old drainage maps this morning. Karaka Crescent: once Violet Crescent. There must have been a small stream down here, dry in summer, flash-flooding in winter. Now drains run in what was the stream bed. Kevin's team is putting in new pipes, separating sewage and stormwater; having problems because the fill is soft—trench sides collapsing, buried logs (big ones) blocking the digger, chainsaws grinding and groaning and stalling eight feet below lawn-level. Days of work lost. Kevin grumbles.

Working at home a couple of mornings each week, Henry talks to Kevin when he stops for coffee. Invites him, bootless, up on the balcony. Even Kev's socks shed mud-flakes. Their talk is what K calls 'ketchup'. Henry explains: 'Alban Ashtree was a Canadian poet killed in an avalanche in the Austrian Alps. I study his work—have written about it and will write more.'

Kevin explains: 'I left the Party years back—have a new wife.' More than that—much more; but that is what it comes down to.

Kev's first wife was the hard-and-fast Marxist, though he used to deny (still does) that she talked him into it. Says his Marxism came from the heart. 'What would you expect? Dad a wharfie locked out in '51; Mum first woman vice-president of the Labour . . .' (Something-or-Other. Henry, author of these notes, can't remember) '. . . Council.' That was in the days when Labour meant 'the socialisation of the means of production, distribution and exchange'.

Kevin left university to 'join the workers'. 'Undergrad' became 'Undegreed', as he wrote to Henry a few months later, and then 'dungareed'. Worked as a drainlayer. Became a contractor; bought equipment, diggers; 'graduated' to heavy machinery, got rich, went broke, learned to lay off workers, got rich again . . .

Now he looks around his old mate's modest house, full of books, paintings, the academic detritus of decades. Always nods thoughtfully, appreciatively. 'It's nice.' You could see it this morning—he wouldn't mind living like this rather than in the steel-and-glass palace up on the Remuera ridge he bought with Wife-2, Cheryl. She's a modern young businesswoman, something to do with the stock exchange (Futures Market?), with padded shoulders and a briefcase.

'I'm still a Marxist.' (This was Kev on the balcony.) 'In theory. It's just that in the real world theory's got no battalions. No bullets. No balls. You with me?'

And yes, Henry was 'with him', if the question meant did he understand. 'In practice,' Kev goes on, 'I just hate fucking unions, mate. I've had to deal with them. And welfare state bludgers. And Polynesian whingers. And especially I hate white liberal wankers.'

4 JULY: LAY IN BED this morning ('he' did) wondering is he still a 'white liberal wanker', and if he is how is it that he doesn't dislike Kev? No. Worse than that—likes him; likes him even when he says those unacceptable things . . . Something to do with authenticity? The plain man speaking the plain man's mind? Maybe, but Kevin's not 'the plain man'—not really.

Remembering school and Kevin. Chess. Crossword puzzles—more and more difficult ones, filled with anagrams. And swapping books—Edwin S. Ellis, James Fenimore Cooper, Rider Haggard, Robert Louis Stevenson, Charles Kingsley, John Buchan, Baroness Orczy, Conan Doyle—stories (fuckit!)—was reading ever better?

And the experiments they did together in mental telepathy: communicating colours and numbers with a success rate beyond statistical probability . . .

Thinking about overhearing Kevin's team ribbing him in the trench about 'a hard day's night' with Cheryl, twenty years younger. Remarks about 'shagger's back' and being 'saddle sore'. And then Kevin telling him discreetly, up on the balcony away from the lads, that his new sex life is 'very nice and relatively quiet. Cosy.'

Strange to have old mate Kevin and his team digging up the front lawn!

Re. Ashtree's death—paste Xerox from Mountain Safety Manual here:

> *Avalanche rescue: In most avalanche accidents rescue of trapped victim(s) depends on the action of the survivors. Organised rescue from afar usually turns into a body recovery. Fifty per cent of avalanche victims suffocate if not uncovered within 30 minutes. Survivors must not panic, but must note with respect to fixed objects—trees or rocks—first, the point on the slope where the victim was caught, and second, the point where last seen.*

Sliding snow flows like water, faster on the surface and in the centre than on the bottom and at the sides. When an avalanche follows a twisting channel the snow and the victim conform to the turns.

After an escape route has been chosen and lookouts posted to watch for further slides, the rescue party hurries down the victim's path, scuffing their feet through the snow to uncover clues—items of gear, or his avalanche cord. They look around trees or outcroppings which might have stopped him, and beneath blocks of snow on the surface.

They shout at intervals, then maintain absolute silence while listening for a muffled answer.

Henry listens to the silence. The white slope glistens in the winter sun. Ice drips from the fir trees. The echo of the survivor's call goes down the mountain slope and across the valley, and comes back from the other side. There is no 'muffled answer' out of the beautiful treacherous snow. Thirty minutes, and then suffocation. The last of the poetry is squeezed out of Alban Ashtree.

FRIDAY (EVENING): THIS MORNING over coffee, Henry talked again to Kevin about Alban Ashtree. And about crosswords. They had a shot, as in the old days, at making anagrams. Tried avalanche. The drainlayer came up with 'a leach van'. Did it in his head. The Senior Lecturer (for life?), who always suspected Kevin was smarter, used a pencil and took longer, but produced 'have a clan'.

As in, for example, 'Four down (9): Have a clan in the Highlands? Be careful.'

The advantage of this clue (they agreed) is that the experienced crossword solver, alert for an anagram, won't at first know whether 'have a clan', 'highlands', or 'be careful' contains the nine letters in which the wanted word is concealed.

Same coffee break/smoko Kev pointed out that Alban is an anagram for banal. Henry replied that Kevin is an analogue for cunt. Kev thumped him one on the upper arm. They were back in the lower sixth.

SAT: ASHTREE'S LAST POEM sequence looks very 'post-Modern'— double-margin (i.e. some lines justified left, some right); lack of ordinary punctuation; fractured grammar and syntax; forward momentum and a sense of a voice speaking straight out of the text. Yes. But when all that's set aside, what is offered the reader? Stories, really. Anecdotes. Can too much be made of the narrative element? Maybe; but much more likely to make too little, it so easily passes unnoticed. (In lit. as in life everything becomes Story.)

Henry mentioned this to Kevin yesterday. Kevin said 'The Big Bang theory never made sense to me. Why should everything start from nothing?'

End of conversation. Now, writing it down, Henry wants to give 'everything' and 'nothing' capital letters. 'Why should Everything start from Nothing?' And (he asks himself) how is it that drainlayer Kevin's remarks often seem not quite intelligible, but pertinent? He was always like that.

8 JULY: HENRY'S CALL at HOD's office. HOD had just been notified that Henry didn't get promotion. Wanted to say he'd supported him 'to the hilt'. 'Et tu, Brute!'—that sort of 'to the hilt', Henry wondered; and it may be supposed HOD saw Distrust Writ Large on these paranoid features because he said no more—went straight to his filing cabinet and pulled out the confidential memo he'd sent to the Promotions Advisory

Committee. Double embarrassment for Henry, because HOD had said such nice things, especially about the work on Alban Ashtree. He (HOD) has been on the phone this morning to find out what went wrong. Thinks Henry's case was spoiled by the English Department's own rep on the committee, the little theorist whose name eludes Henry. He is reported to have told them that Henry Bulov said 'Fuck theory' in a department meeting. This turned the woman from Sociology against. And then the Maori rep, who had been 'for' because he thought Ashtree was a Native American, changed his vote when the theorist told him it wasn't so—Ashtree was purest Anglo. It had been a near thing, but that had turned it around.

All hearsay, HOD points out; nothing of these meetings is supposed to be reported, so there's nothing to be done. But for the record (what record?) Henry Bulov did not say 'Fuck theory' in a department meeting (though he thinks it often enough). All he did was to report, by way of an amusing anecdote, the graffito he saw on the Quinton campus: 'Theoreticians are Saussure they know everything, but they know Foucault about anything.'

Late-at-night (when dark postscripts make best sense): Note that among personal belongings of Alban Ashtree, found in his Quinton office after news of his death came through from Austria, was a small squarish automatic pistol and some rounds of snub-nosed ammunition—a luggage label tied to it, the name Alban Ashtree and address printed on one side; on the other, 'DRINK ME'. It's idle to speculate, but . . .

TUESDAY: FILM SOCIETY (Anne likes to forget the law, Henry to forget literature). This week it was *Wings of Desire* by Wim Wenders, about two angels whose beat (wingbeat) is Berlin. They're benign but their world is black and white. At first you see it only as they see it. Then there are brief moments when you see the human world—in colour, which both of these angels crave. One opts out of angelhood and joins the human race. Now it's all colour, with only flashbacks to the drabness of the angel experience. The ex-angel is obsessed with a beautiful trapeze artist (cf. Picasso?). When they meet and fall in love she makes a speech about a new world, which sounds like the old one, with colour and biology, men and women, love and sex and rock music and cities and vividness and action—except that now it's to be a world without angels.

The War (the big one) belongs in black and white, like old newsreels. The burning cities, the dead laid out in rows among the rubble, the living searching among them for familiar faces, the piles of fallen bricks and smashed concrete, the swastikas, the Jews herded into gas chambers—how is it that Wenders sees all that as the world of angelicism? Because (Henry decides) it came of a belief in solutions—'final solutions'. The angelic order and the theoretical abstract were Nazism's close cousins. Germany went the whole way—burned right through to reason's non-human end. It did the unspeakable and learned there was no escape from death, only a vacation from it, taken in hell. The price of life's full colour range is acceptance that it is subject to limit, imperfection and death; that the temporal is temporary. Also (he tells himself, excited by these thoughts) that eternity is only the Other by which time defines itself.

Henry walked out into the night wondering what it would be like to feel there really was a new world beginning; that the angels had had their day; that people would learn to live in their bodies, which meant in their minds too, but minds as parts of bodies, not minds as winged instruments of escape, space vehicles, chariots of vain hope.

11.7: ANOTHER XEROX FROM the Mountain Safety Manual:

> *When something has gone wrong swift action may be less*
> *effective than correct action. On the mountains, once any*
> *person is beyond voice range, the party has lost control over*
> *his subsequent actions. So there must be no hasty separation.*
> *Everything must be planned, prearranged, including what*
> *every member is to do under every conceivable circumstance,*
> *until he has completed his part in the rescue.*

Anne, reading over his shoulder, asked, 'Aren't there any women in them thar hills?' He told her there is, or there was, something called (he thought he remembered from an age-gone-by) the generic pronoun which is, or was, genderless—as in 'He who hesitates is lost.'

Anne said, 'Thanks for that, he,' ruffling his grizzling hair.

Since then he has been sitting here imagining Ashtree looking up, pausing to watch the avalanche snow sweep and swerve and flow down the mountain slope; and then, too late, making a run for the side of the gully. 'He who hesitates . . .' Or did Ashtree stand there saying 'Come and get me, Asshole!'? Was he suicidal? Is that how the last poems, the ones about the Snow Maiden, should be read—that his Muse was Death? Why else the pistol, and the tag with 'DRINK ME' printed on it?

Also this morning came a letter from friend John E., experienced mountaineer (he once nearly died dangling at the end of a rope in a crevasse, winter-climbing on Mt McKinley in Alaska) now living in Seattle. John says he has heard nothing of the accident in which Ashtree died. Asks was Ashtree with a party or (would he have been so foolish?) climbing solo? John will ask climbing friends to check on it. He goes on, 'The mountains in Austria are lovely, on a New Zealand scale. Avalanches certainly happen there, usually in winter and spring. Warnings go out, but people still get caught. This last spring we were on Monte Rosa (Switzerland) from the Italian side. Climbed the second highest peak in Europe by a spectacular route with an Italian guide, our communication being pretty much restricted to musical terms—presto, lento, bravo, etc.'

At the bottom of the letter he has done a black-and-white sketch (is he an angel?) of a mountain landscape with dark rock faces, white snow slopes and fir trees.

THURS 12TH: LAST NIGHT'S video: *One Flew over the Cuckoo's Nest*. The world is a lunatic asylum. Every bureaucracy, every human institution, is a lunatic asylum. McMurphy (Jack Nicholson) is there in the bin because he has too much life for what's conceived to be the common good. Like an over-spiced soup he must be diluted. Those experts who sit around a table deciding his fate are his Promotions Advisory Committee. McMurphy, they say, 'may not be psychotic; but he's dangerous'.

McMurphy's breaking of the rules is pure energy, 'eternal delight'. He bounces back from shock therapy with all his old chutzpah; but that only ensures worse is in store for him. His violence, when it comes, is 'protest'—moral indignation. Oh, Henry, you have been there! Even if only as metaphor, those desperate calm corridors are known to you. You have spent half a century looking into the cold eyes of Nurse Ratched, your country's tutelary goddess. How is it that you don't carry the final scar, the spiritual lobotomy? Or (frightening thought) has it happened and you don't even know?

(EVENING) ANNE IS PREPARING for depositions in her murder case. She has brought home documents and a book of forensic photographs (in colour!). Henry takes a few quick looks and winces away. She has become (almost, she says) used to them. He reads the three separate statements made by the accused. In the first he says a strange man wearing a feather earring did the killing. In the second he says he did it himself; says, 'I was growling like an animal.' In the third he says it was done by the wife of the deceased. The Crown case is that the wife persuaded him to do it, rewarding him in bed, before and after. The accused is seventeen. Anne intends to argue for the Defence that the second statement should be set aside because at the time he made it he was asking to have his mother with him and the police refused.

Now Henry has just had a longer look at the photographs. The dead man is Polynesian, but in death the brown skin has faded to a sickly grey. He has huge wounds which have been stitched because he didn't die at once. The stitching looks rough, as if done by a maker of fishing nets.

What Henry feels is disgust. He and Anne have just had an exchange which went roughly as follows:

H: The second statement's the incriminating one.

A: It is.

H: So if you get that struck out, there's not much of a case left.

A: Not much. No.

H: And you think because he was asking for his mum . . .

A: He's only seventeen, Henry.

H: D'you think he did it?

A: That's irrelevant, darling. This is a point of law.

H: Oh sorry. I was thinking about all those knife wounds. Silly me.

A: Well, of course, yes, he did . . .

H: Did?

A: Strike the blows—probably. Most likely.

H: Ah!

A: Henry, I say 'Of course he did.' But that might be wrong. That's why it has to be due process.

H: You mean due process is never wrong?

A: No. It might sometimes produce a wrong result. But when it does, no one's to blame.

FRIDAY THE 13TH AND Kev came to the door early. The digger had broken into an old clay pipe. Kev thought it must be the existing sewer, but it wasn't where it ought to be. Henry was able to put his mind at rest. The pipe they'd broken into was an even older one, not used any more except unofficially for taking field-tile drainage from lawns and gardens.

MUST PUT DOWN HENRY'S dream before it's forgotten:

They (he and Anne) were in London, the two of them walking through streets that got narrower, more ruined, filled with debris, fallen beams, dust, wreckage. He was worried, trying to remember where they were and where they were going. They came to a dinner table and sat down. It was properly laid—cutlery, candles, flowers, wine, glasses, napkins. Well-dressed people sat around making polite and witty conversation, but all about them lay the ruins of the city. Henry began to talk to them about his research. It had to do with Austrian milk vendors.

BASTILLE DAY: 'ALLONS, ENFANTS . . .' Henry sings, celebrating two hundred years of liberty-equality-fraternity or aspiration thereto. Remember (he writes in his diary!) the story about the Chinese Communist Government official on a visit to Paris asked what, from a Chinese point of view, had been the significance of the French Revolution in world history. Chinese official replied, 'It is too soon to say.'

Kev's team is now two doors down the street. Watching them,

Henry understands something about unemployment. They dig down more than two metres, a trench wide enough for two pipes (large and larger) side by side. By hand, that would take how many men how long? The digger does it in twenty minutes. When it comes to a hedge it lifts a section out, roots and all, to be put back later. The trench runs dead straight across the fronts of four properties. Back at the last set of man-holes two laser beams are set to fire a pencil-thin beam of red light through the centre of each pipe. As long as the beams make bullseye hits on targets set further down, the drains are laid dead straight and there's no need for a surveyor to check.

The team works in pairs. Kevin and his mate dig out the trench, put in the pipes, and fill as they go. The second team comes up behind, laying top-soil over the disturbed clay, replanting grass, replacing concrete paths, hedges and gardens.

The second team also does the new drainage around the houses, separating sewage and stormwater and bringing them down to the new lines. This part of it has to be done by hand. But the narrow-gauge pipes around the houses are plastic now, where they used to be clay.

SUNDAY: HERE'S A TRUE story. Last evening Henry and Anne went to a little Italian restaurant on Karangahape Road, the *Quattro Fontane*. Just half a dozen tables, one waitress and the owner, Frederico—first-rate cook, amiable host, loud, flamboyant, banging his pans around, shouting jokes and orders over his shoulder, singing, sending flames up to the ceiling.

Henry had his back to the kitchen. Anne watched Frederico and worried. He should go more slowly. No need for all that drama. One day he'll blow up. Etc.

No more than ten customers all evening; and late, when most have gone, Anne sees Frederico go behind a curtain to a little room, or space, under the stairs. Now she has tight hold of Henry's wrist. Something's wrong. Frederico is having some kind of seizure or spasm—she can see the curtain moving violently. There's a thump as he hits the floor, a groan just audible over the Pavarotti tape. She's sure he's having a heart attack. Henry must go and help him.

Well! It can be said, it will be imagined, that Henry was not keen. He'd had a lot of red wine. He didn't want to know about heart attacks. There was a predictable exchange—How could she be sure that . . .? How could he ignore the needs of . . .?

So now Henry gets up and lumbers towards the curtain behind which, despite Pavarotti's best efforts to drown it out, there is indeed occurring some kind of heaving and groaning. Henry pulls the curtain back. Frederico is down on the floor, right enough. Face down. But the waitress is underneath him. There is a general impression of clothes pulled up, pulled down, got out of the way without being shed. Frederico is riding up and down on a gentle swell. The waitress is smiling. Her eyes drift over an ocean of content, then heavenward over Frederico's shoulder where they meet . . . Henry's! They widen, scrunch up into a frown. She begins to beat the cook's shoulders with her small fists, hissing at him, 'Get off me. Leave me alone.'

Henry lets the curtain drop and returns to his table. He tells Anne Frederico is OK. He's just lying down—so to speak.

Anne wants to know what 'so to speak' means. He tells her.

She nods. They stare at one another, hands over mouths, trying not to laugh. She apologises.

Henry shrugs and says he supposes it's one kind of heart attack.

She says she hopes he washes his hands before he goes back to cooking.

16 JULY: HENRY HAS been thinking again about Wim Wenders and his angels in *Wings of Desire*. He writes into his diary two lines

from a poem by Edgar Allan Poe which Janet Frame (who had an angel at her table) quotes in one of her novels:

> *The angels not half so happy in heaven*
> *Went envying her and me.*

This quotation sends him hunting for an essay about Poe by Allen Tate, 'The Angelic Imagination'. He finds it and copies sentences:

> *The human intellect cannot reach God as essence; only God as analogy. Analogy to what? Plainly analogy to the natural world; for there is nothing in the intellect that has not previously reached it through the senses . . . Since Poe refuses to see nature, he is doomed to see nothing. He has overleaped and cheated the condition of man . . . Man as angel becomes a demon who cannot initiate the first motion of love, and we can feel only compassion for his suffering, for it is potentially ours.*

31 JULY: ANOTHER MONTH gone. So has Kev with all his machines and men and reminders of the long-ago. Work on Alban Ashtree is suspended, maybe for ever. Bob Wilcox has written from Quinton explaining why Henry has had no formal replies to his inquiries. There is, it seems, some uncertainty about where and how the accident which killed Ashtree occurred. It is supposed to have happened in Austria, but the only accident of this kind at that time occurred in Switzerland. Meanwhile the Canada Council has said the substantial amount it has put up for posthumous editing of his works is available only to Canadian scholars; but the funds are frozen until a death certificate has been received.

Henry thinks it a nice little irony (anger management teaches him to avert his eyes from the larger one) that Canadian funds have been 'frozen'. But Switzerland? He is sure Alban Ashtree would have wanted death by alliteration: an avalanche in the Austrian Alps.

SUMMER (WHANGAMATA): HENRY HAS been glancing through this notebook which he has neglected for how many months? Its contents have faded along with the memory of Quinton and his excitement at the idea of being first to publish a full-length study of Ashtree's poetry. This morning he and Anne sat on the sand watching the oystercatchers. Parent bird flew out to the reef (waves washing over), worked a mussel free, flew back to the sand above tide-mark, broke it open, dragged fish out, flew up to higher sand where the chick was sitting in, or walking around, the 'nest' (hardly more than a hollow with maybe a few twigs or sticks). Chick, well fed by this hour, accepted the mussel with bad grace. Parent bird returned to the reef for more. When finally the tide had covered the mussel bed, the parent bird went to the empty shells and lunched off scraps still adhering.

Time to close this notebook. Henry wonders if, when the new term begins, he will take HOD's advice and turn his critical attention to the work of Hone Tuwhare. But no—that's not a serious thought, or not for him when he remembers a filing cabinet in the depths of that Canadian winter and the insights it has left him with.

He pauses to ask himself: was the work he did and the notes he took during that lonely weekend in Quinton (and the days that followed) 'theft of intellectual property' or 'research'—especially since everything was put back in place, and it later emerged that the rightful owner was already dead? What would Anne say? Are the two, theft and research, ever entirely distinct? And does it matter now? Once certain facts are known, and ideas planted, it's difficult to un-know and un-plant them. Henry's thoughts about the mysteries of the Snow Maiden are still growing and sprouting.

No, of course he will persist with Ashtree.

Three: Brightness falls from the air: the Woodlake campus

THE SNOW HAS COME back. Henry knew it this morning before getting up and looking out—'sensed' it; which means, he supposes, that his waking eyes registered the different light, its whiteness.

And Albie has gone again. That too Henry knew while he lay there, because the silence that comes with the otherworldly light of the fallen snow was undisturbed by the poet's frantic work at the typewriter in the next room.

Now, looking out through a window, Henry is watching a cat making its way through the snow, which comes up to its shoulders. It tries a high-stepping walk; then an intermittent leaping. Henry isn't sure what it's looking for, but he supposes food. It stops to shake itself, disliking the sense that its fur is becoming wet, uncertain now whether to go forward or back.

He wonders why the sight of animals going about their daily business gives such pleasure, and decides it's because what they do exactly matches, in scale, what they need to do, whereas our doings are always an excess. He imagines them taking over when we, the human race, become extinct. They must be kin, he thinks, or there would be no pleasure in that thought.

During the past couple of days, while Albie bashed away at his typewriter and raced in and out to the kitchen and to the bench press on the cold front porch, Henry has observed the squirrels. There was no sign of snow then, and they darted about the campus lawns digging for buried nuts. Though the cold out there was intense even in the sun, it was as if spring must be just around the corner. But yesterday, while the sky was blue and the sun continued to shine, the squirrels' demeanour changed. They knew something Henry didn't know. They were anxious, and not for food. They hung upside down on the boughs and trunks of trees, stripping bark and running up to repair their nests. This morning they're gone, hiding away in those newly patched interiors, and all down the Jersey Shore the snow is falling.

There is no sky, just a low grey blankness out of which the flakes sail like an invasion of paratroopers; and the brightness seems to come, not down from above, but up from below. Light has taken on substantial form. It has broken up and is tumbling out of the heavens. Still shining, it covers lawns and paths; heaps up on hedges, statues, fences, gates, on outdoor chairs and tables. It piles up along branches, and falls from them in sudden, splintering showers. Soon the ploughs will be out to clear the road, and the shovels will attack paths and sidewalks. But for now it comes thick and fast and lies undisturbed.

Henry—Professor Henry Bulov, according to the *Times Literary Supplement* 'the world's leading interpreter of the works of Alban Ashtree'—turns on Woodlake's Memory Station which plays 'the greatest music of all time', meaning 'top of the charts '40s through '60s'. He begins to make breakfast and then, feeling the need of company, changes his mind, puts on overcoat, scarf, gloves, hat, and walks to the campus dining room where the nuns will smile and urge him to eat more, to keep warm, to look after himself.

That over, he will wait for the ploughs and shovels to do their work before walking the mile or so to the supermarket. There's nothing he needs there, but it's somewhere to go. Meanwhile, there is the latest batch of poems Albie has given him to read— more of the same he has read and re-read this past fortnight. By now Henry knows what to expect. They will be sharp, pictorial, 'Japanesey', occasionally witty, now and then gritty. But where has the grand sweep gone, the larger scale? Where are the Modernist ambulations, the parodic dislocations of the post-Modern? What has become of the great Canadian epic-maker and courage-teacher, delineator of northern wastes, servant of the mythical White Queen, poet-father of the Snow Maiden? Where among all these miniaturist nail-parings is the majesty that was Alban Ashtree? Where, for fuck's sake, is Libby Valtraute?

Crunching through the dry snow, up to his ankles in it, Henry says over to himself lines from a sixteenth-century poet whose name eludes him, and wonders whether they have sprung to mind because of the snow or because of the decline of a once major poet:

> Brightness falls from the air,
> Queens have died young and fair,
> Dust hath closed Helen's eye,
> I am sick, I must die—
> Lord, have mercy upon us.

But this is a story, and we must go back two weeks to take up the thread.

HENRY BULOV, RECENTLY APPOINTED full professor by his previously reluctant university in New Zealand, arrived at JFK with his modest and battered baggage, and was met at the foot of the escalator below the American Airlines desk by a Gofar Limo driver holding up a sign with a version of his name he hadn't encountered before: PROF BELOVE. He shook hands with the driver and they joked about the mistake. Henry told him about the fax from Woodlake College saying he would be met by a representative of the Gofar Limp Company.

There was a sixty-mile drive south to Woodlake. Henry sat in the back and pretended to read papers, pretended to sleep, did sleep—but not before he had had his views of the Manhattan skyline across water in the fading light, and seen the Staten Island 'hills' that were really New York's garbage mountains. When he woke it was dark and they were somewhere in the State of New Jersey, pulling in at the doors of a restaurant built out over a river or tidal inlet.

Ashtree, now disguised and known as Albie Strong, met him at the door. It was their first encounter, and the greetings were loud and long, the smiles broad, the handshakes strong.

'We're dining alone,' Albie explained. 'There are things I have to get straight with you.'

There were indeed. The circumstances of Henry's invitation had been mysterious—not surprisingly since it was generally understood that the poet Alban Ashtree was dead, killed (though the body had never been recovered) in an avalanche in the Austrian Alps. It was a death which had always given Henry anxiety. It lacked the sense of perfect closure that ought to accompany a genuine demise. It was not like Shelley, drowned in a Ligurian storm and his body burned on the beach at Viareggio; or Byron's death in Greece, the body subsequently returned to England in a barrel of spirits. There was an air of fiction, even of contrivance, about Ashtree's. It had been too good to be true—iconologically apt (Ashtree was poet and theorist of the Snow White Goddess), and lexically perfect, the author's name piling up in alliteration with place and event. 'Alban Ashtree,' Henry's book on him began, 'died in an avalanche in the Austrian Alps.' It had been the easiest sentence to write and the hardest to believe. Even the Canada Council, afflicted by doubts, had frozen funds set aside for the posthumous editing of the collected works.

But this uncertainty had only added to the aura surrounding

Ashtree's name and his poetry. The man for so long known only in his own country was soon being talked about in New York and in London. Two years after his 'death' the work, previously published only in Canada, was available everywhere in English, and translations into several European languages were appearing or planned. And Henry Bulov, the first non-Canadian to write seriously about Ashtree, and the only person (no one knew how this had come about) to have had access to some of his private notebooks, had found the academic escalator, for so long stalled beneath his feet, all at once lurching on up to full professorial status. Bulov had helped to make Ashtree famous; Ashtree's fame had helped to make Bulov respectable. These two, it seemed, needed one another; and now, improbably ('It's like a story,' Henry said, as they gave up the handshaking and embraced) here they were meeting for dinner in a New Jersey restaurant that looked out over a coastal inlet.

Albie (as he asked to be called) was a tall, well-constructed fifty-two-year-old with a good head of grey hair tied back in a ponytail. He wore jeans, boots, a shirt of red corduroy and a leather jacket. He talked fast, ate fast, seemed impatient, but also excited to be meeting the critic who had done so much to promote his work and his reputation. The avalanche, he told Henry, had been real, though not quite in Austria, which he preferred for reasons of euphony. He had been taken up by it, swept down the mountain slope, and then, by some miracle, or quirk of the rolling snow, had been ejected—cast out on to a ridge from which he had been able to make his way down to a village on the lower slopes. He was bewildered, slightly concussed, and it was some hours before he recovered his sense of who and where he was. By that time the news was out. Seven were missing, four already confirmed dead.

With the least possible fuss he returned to his ski lodge, where he had gone unaccompanied, removed a few essentials, and departed, leaving gear by which he could be identified. Next day, from a village further down the mountain he rang two newspapers, one in Toronto, the other in Vancouver, to report the death of the poet Alban Ashtree. It was meant only to bring him a little attention, but the story ran all across Canada, from east to west, from west to east, its authenticity never seeming to be checked. Though for a time he travelled on his own passport, and drew on his own bank account, no one appeared to notice. It would have been better from a nationalist point of view had they been Canadian snows; but as far as the Canadian literary and academic community were concerned the fact was romantic enough: Alban Ashtree the poet had died in that Austrian avalanche.

During what remained of his sabbatical year Ashtree's fame spread, promoted especially by an article Henry Bulov wrote for the *Times Literary Supplement*. Unused to his work receiving the kind of attention he always believed it deserved, Albie now found the condition of being dead difficult to give up. Casually at first, and then, as time passed, purposefully, he contrived a new life for himself, one which allowed him to keep his death alive. This involved difficulties and sacrifices. Posing as a former anti-Vietnam defector-to-Canada whose previous identity had to remain undisclosed, he had been able to get a teaching post in a minor, though well-endowed, Catholic college. But he was not able to profit by, or to enjoy (except as an observer), Alban Ashtree's increasing fame. Part of him wanted to reclaim it as his own; a more cautious self recognised that to 'come back' might be to lose it.

'I'm like the lover on the Graecian urn,' he told Henry. 'He lives for ever because he's a work of art. But because he's a work of art he's not flesh and blood—he can't kiss the girl.'

But was he intending to stay dead for ever?—that was what Henry needed to know. He put the question in a way which sounded odd even as he said it: 'Will you ever come back to life?'

Ashtree smiled. 'It's a hard one, Henry. If I do, there's going to be hell to pay. A massive critical backlash, wouldn't you say? That's why there have to be new poems first, and they have to be good.'

What he impressed on Henry during that first meeting was that in the meantime his real identity must remain secret. It was not known to anyone—not to Woodlake College, which employed him; not even to the woman in his life, Joy Gates, also a teacher at the college, whose considerable private wealth, Albie hinted, was only one of her many attractions. During the past few years he had acquired a modest reputation as a poet of the Jersey Shore. Woodlake College had issued two small collections of his new work. He gave readings, poetry workshops, was interviewed on local radio and written about in the local papers.

'No one connects my work with Ashtree's,' he explained. 'The new stuff is different. Smaller in scale.' There was a look of uncertainty as he said this. 'Tighter. Closer to the knuckle.'

After a short silence, which Henry couldn't think how to plug, Albie murmured, 'Hopefully.'

Henry was to share Albie's house on the edge of the campus. He was to read the new work, comment on it, prepare for a time when it might seem right to reveal that the two poets, Alban Ashtree and Albie Strong were one; but he was to say nothing until Albie gave the word, which might be soon or might be years away. It was possible even that it might have to wait until he died—in which case Henry would be named as his literary executor. This was something they would discuss. Together they would arrive at a strategy.

'I need someone to tell me how I'm going with my work,' Albie said when the meal was eaten and they were sitting over their decafs. 'You're the critic I can trust, Henry. The only one.'

Again there was that uncertain look, but also a glimmer of courage. 'You have to give it to me straight, man.'

IN THE DAYS SINCE that first meeting Henry has begun to understand why Albie's confidence is less than perfect. With his real name and nation has gone, it seems, his real strength as a poet. Away from Canada and the northern wastes that were his inspiration, Alban Ashtree's talent has shrivelled. As poet of the Jersey Shore, he is Samson after the haircut. What remains of his former strength is a sort of sad afterglow.

He is also away from Libby Valtraute, his Muse, with her red-gold hempen hair. He misses her, still loves her. Henry gets the impression that contact has been re-established; that she knows Albie's secret and is party to his plans.

So the visit, embarked on with such enthusiasm, has turned into a trial of character for Henry. Should he be truthful, and if so when? When a poet says, 'You have to give it to me straight, man,' is he to be taken at his word? Even if he means it, that's not to say he won't react badly when he gets it. And wouldn't the truth be like a death sentence? It would be saying in effect, 'Don't come back to life if you want Alban Ashtree's reputation to continue.' Because the new work would cast a doubt over the old. It would also cast a doubt over the value of the critical essays (mostly Henry's) that had promoted it.

But there are more immediate problems for Henry. Albie is not easy to share a house with. More precisely, Albie is extremely difficult to share anything with. All day, when he's not teaching, he sits at a desk in his room, hammering away at an old-fashioned typewriter in furious bursts interspersed with long silences and occasional eruptions of swearing, or singing, or muttering, or laughing—the latter a kind of dark laughter, more sinister than the swearing and muttering. Albie, Henry writes in the journal he is keeping, is a sort of Glenn Gould of the lexical clavier.

At intervals of about half an hour the poet jumps from his chair and rushes either to the front porch or to the kitchen. On the porch he has set up his bench press and weights. The lifting is accompanied by huge orgasmic groans and sighs. When the rush is to the kitchen he fills a bowl with fat-free granola and a fat-free fruit-yoghurt drink, downs it at speed, and returns to his room and his desk. There are no regular meals, but if Henry wants them he can take them at the university dining room.

'This is better than my old regimen,' Albie explains, leaning against the door jamb of Henry's room while he spoons out the last of a bowlful. 'Before Joy I only used to eat every second day. The starvation days were hell. You wouldn't have liked living with me then.'

Albie works till late, then unfolds an ironing board and stands at it while he watches a replay of the old *Star Trek* series. He irons not only shirts and handkerchiefs but underclothes, sheets, pillowcases, towels—everything. When there's nothing left, he re-irons clothes already done. The ironing, Henry has come to recognise, is only because Albie needs something to do, can't sit still while watching.

Then he takes sleeping pills, puts a rolled towel across his bedroom door, and turns on what he calls 'radio static', a sort of white noise, to drown out all external sound. When Henry gets up in the night to go to the bathroom he hears that strange loud continuous hissing coming from Albie's bedroom. Fortunately Albie is not there all the time. There are days and nights when, as now, he is at Joy Gates's house, twenty miles away in a town called Brick. Then Henry has only to cope with the loneliness of the little suburban house at the edge of the campus, a house in which the furnishings and pictures provided by the nuns, sober, dull, proper, self-abnegating (and including by way of uplift only a golden Christ on a midnight-blue cross over the living-room door), fight a Cold War with the items Albie has introduced—a Tiffany lampshade over an art deco dining table in black glass on a red central column; a shiny red plastic wall-hanging representing an English telephone box; an Algonquin shield and spear; several big-faced 1940s electric clocks advertising dairy products, motor oil, piston rings; a white sofa with red cushions; a telephone in transparent plastic which lights up in blue when it rings; a print from the Utamaro brothel series. Slowly the sensibility of Albie is winning its interior-decor war against the pale restraining hands of the Sisters of Mercy, but there are battles yet to be fought and in the meantime no truce is in prospect. The Joseph House, as it is called, is not a house of peace.

Henry leaves it to walk to the supermarket. By now the ploughs have done their work on the roads, and the pavements are partly cleared, but patches of ice make the going on foot slow and dangerous. Up and down the street men are out with shovels. Without exception they are dressed in black with broad-brimmed hats, some with a long lock of hair trailing somewhere over face or neck. These are Hassidic Jews, and the suburb is full of them. Their wives wear wigs so their hair will not be seen by strangers, their children are innumerable, their cars are large old station-wagons with many dents, and their lawns are covered with plastic toys in bright colours sticking up like wreckage through the whiteness of the snow. The Hassidim are devoted to prayer and propagation, but also (Albie's *Random House Dictionary* informs Henry) to joy. Their responses to his morning greetings, however, are mostly grim and formal. He is not one of them.

It is almost two miles to the shops—far enough for Henry's ears to feel the cold painfully. He buys fruit and cheese and chocolate and wine. At the liquor store he checks his ticket in the New Jersey lottery. He has not won a prize; but the storekeeper tells him there is a huge jackpot coming.

By now the ears have thawed and he is ready for the long march back.

Joy Gates, the woman in Albie's life, is a glamorous, energetic divorcee, a woman in her forties who wins Henry's approval not by cleverness (though she may well be clever, and probably is) nor by charm (though he's quite sure she could charm if she chose), but simply by smiling. Joy's smile is warm, wry and self-sufficient. It seems to come from good health, self-acceptance, and an inner electrical charge. No doubt, Henry reflects, it could be defeated, but the circumstances would have to be dire—flood, famine or slaughter.

Joy seems, in her egocentric way, to love her poet and to do all she can to promote his work. She doesn't live with him, however, except overnight, or sometimes for two nights on end, and Henry understands why. No one, not even Joy Gates, could live for long with Albie and keep smiling.

Today, a Saturday, is Joy's mother's seventy-fifth birthday, and they are to take her to New York to see a matinee performance of a play by Edward Albee, *Three Tall Women*. Joy has ordered a white stretch limo as part of the birthday treat, and it arrives at the Joseph House a few minutes early. Joy's mother, Gay, is already in the car. They will drive next to the town of Brick to pick up Joy and Albie, and then on up to New York. The driver is wearing a suit and bow tie. 'Do you have boots, sir?' he asks at the door.

Henry says he doesn't need them.

The driver frowns, looking at the path deep in snow. 'I'll try to clear some of this while you're getting ready, sir.'

Henry tells him not to be silly. 'Wait in the car and keep warm.' But when he emerges the driver is waiting on the porch with a golf umbrella. His eagerness, and the size and whiteness of the stretch, which seems at one moment to vanish into the snow, at another to be materialising out of it, signal generous expense. This is something grander than the Gofar Limo Company. Joy is turning it on for her aged parent.

Inside the limo there are two pairs of leather chairs, facing one another. There is a drinks cabinet, and ice. Gay, in furs and a fur hat, has a face that must once have been pure Hollywood and is still glamorous. She introduces herself, they shake hands and he wishes her a happy birthday.

'Happy birthday?' she repeats, puzzled. And then, 'Oh yes. Sure.' She laughs, revealing a perfect bow of upper teeth, all her own.

It is Saturday and the Jews are walking to the Synagogue in family clusters, not along the sidewalks but in the middle of the suburban street where the snow ploughs have made the deepest impression. The men have shed their broad-brims and are wearing immense fur hats out of Russia or central Europe. The limo crawls behind them. When it tries to go around them there are angry shouts and gestures of protest.

When they get out of the Hassidic suburb and on to the highway Gay begins to tell stories about Joy's infancy. 'She didn't creep like other children. At eight months she just got up and walked. Her first words were, "I do it."'

'I *do* it?'

'*I* do it,' Gay says, putting the emphasis in the right place. 'She was always very independent.'

Yes. Henry can imagine that.

'From the time she was seven,' Gay goes on, 'I never had to manage money. Joy looked after it. When we went shopping, she had the purse. If I bought something, she paid. If I wanted something too expensive, she told me I couldn't have it—there wasn't enough in the purse.'

'From the age of seven,' Henry repeats, not disbelieving, but by way of showing that though his eyes are on the woods and the river and the white, transformed landscape, he is listening. He is aware that Gay must be a widow. He asks about her husband.

'He was a Sioux,' she tells him. 'A beautiful man with a fine body. He was a pilot.'

'So Joy's father was an Indian . . .' He corrects himself. 'A Native American . . .'

But Gay is shaking her head. 'Joy's father was Samuel. Walter was the Sioux.'

'He was your second husband?'

'My third,' she replies, and then appears uncertain. In any case Henry is not sure whether they are now talking about Samuel or Walter.

'What did he—Joy's father—*do* so to speak.'

Gay's eyes have gone dreamy with reminiscence. 'He was a beautiful man, a pilot, and I lost him . . .'

But wasn't it the Sioux who was the pilot? He gives it up. 'I've heard good things about this play,' he says.

She sighs, still sad at the thought of Walter. 'Is there an orange juice in there?' She is pointing to the drinks cabinet.

He opens it and finds what she wants, a bottle, up to its neck in ice. 'I won't have it now,' Gay says. 'Later.'

He pushes it back into the ice. 'Drinks can make you think you need to eat,' Gay says. 'I eat only once a day, in the morning, and it's all I need. It's how I kept slim. Of course,' she acknowledges, 'I'm not so slim now . . .'

She is not slim, it's true, and he lets this invitation to contradict her pass. There is a long, thoughtful silence. Snow has begun to drift down again, and now she is telling him what she cooks for that one meal. There are many items, and she explains in what special way each of them is nutritious.

He stops listening. And then, 'Yes,' he hears her say. 'A play. He's a talented boy isn't he?'

Henry wonders how to deal with this. 'I'm sorry,' he says. 'I drifted off for a moment. Who is talented?'

'Albie.'

'Albie, of course. His poetry . . .'

'His poetry. And now his play.'

His play? Has she confused Albie and Edward Albee? To get it clear which of them is confused, Henry asks, 'What did you say Joy's father did for a living?'

'Samuel,' she says, in a tone both firm and dismissive, 'worked for my father. He was an instructor.'

They are driving now into the town of Brick, and she makes him promise he will not let Joy know that she has told him things about her infancy. Albie and Joy are waiting at the door of Joy's townhouse.

Before they leave Brick, Albie gets the driver to stop at a shop that sells tickets in the state lottery. There's a jackpot draw coming that's to be worth at least 17 million. They each put in five dollars. That will give them twenty shots at the pick-six. Albie comes back waving the tickets. 'Seventeen million among four,' he says. 'That's four each with a million over for a party.'

He stuffs them into his bill-fold.

'I might go on a world cruise,' Gay says. 'I've never been to foreign places.' She stares out at the snow. 'Or maybe Miami.'

'Los Angeles for you, Mom,' Joy says. 'Hollywood. They'll put you straight into a movie. You'll be a star.'

Gay says, 'When I was young that's what everyone told me. Go to Hollywood, they said. You've got the looks. You'll be a star.'

'With four million,' Albie says, 'you could be a star without doing the movie. You could just buy yourself a big house in Brentwood and throw parties.'

Gay purrs. 'I'd like that.'

Albie is restless as they drive on. He keeps checking their speed, the distance covered, the time the play is due to start, and on his iPad the state of roads and weather. He takes ice from the drinks cabinet and sucks or chews it, presses it to his wrists and along the back of his neck. As they get nearer to New York Gay becomes excited. It's a long time since she has seen the city, which was once her home. She recognises landmarks—fuel depots, derelict warehouses, refineries, generators, ash heaps, wreckers' yards— greeting them as if they were things of great beauty. When they come out of the tunnel into Manhattan she lowers her window.

'Halloo, New York!' she shouts up at the skyscrapers. 'Hi there, New York! Halloo!'

She turns her face to them, at once smiling and tearful. 'Ah, New York,' she says. 'Isn't it great? And Gene Kelly had to go and die on me. That was a man I would have married.'

The Edward Albee play turns out to be about an unpleasant old woman, attended in the first half by a sadistic nurse and an angry lawyer. These are the three women of the title, and they are named in the programme as A, B and C. There is a lot about A's imperfect control of her bodily functions, and at the end of the act she suffers a stroke. In the second half A, B and C represent A's three selves, old, middle-aged and young. Her sex life is recounted—a beautiful teenage experience, unappetising marital sex, and a brief violent affair with a groom in her husband's stables. Throughout this half of the play A, the terminal stroke victim whose earlier selves these three now represent, lies unconscious in a big bed wearing an oxygen mask.

It is hardly a play to celebrate a woman's seventy-fifth birthday and Henry feels such embarrassment at what seems like a bad mistake he finds it difficult to concentrate. During the second half he's relieved to see that Gay has fallen asleep. Joy rolls her eyes at him across her mother seated between them, as if to signify that she too is embarrassed. But as they come out of the theatre Gay seems refreshed and cheerful. 'Did you write that about me?' she asks Albie.

'Write what?' he asks; and then darts forward in the crowd, looking for the white stretch.

'Of course he won't ever admit it,' Gay says in an undertone to Henry.

They get the driver to take them to a famous deli on Broadway where they order a soup of barley and beans, and then pastrami and gherkin sandwiches which are so large they must contain, each of them, a pound of meat. Gay appears to have forgotten that she eats only once a day. Albie jokes with the waitress, who comes from Costa Rica.

'I like your ponytail,' she tells him, flipping his tied-back hair with her pencil.

'Hey,' he says. 'Will you marry me?'

'I don marry no one,' she says. 'I was married once and you know what I say? I say marriage sucks.'

'I see a poem here, guys,' Albie tells them. When she returns with their orders he asks her what was the worst thing about her marriage.

'Getting married was the worst,' she says. 'I was fourteen. And best was when I leave him.'

It is already dark as they drive away from Manhattan with their brown bags of unfinished pastrami giving the heated interior of the limo a strange salty aroma.

THAT NIGHT ALBIE COMES back with Henry to the Joseph House. He doesn't work at his typewriter, is restless, seems constantly on the brink of saying something which doesn't get said. He suggests a walk around the campus and Henry, wanting to be agreeable, goes with him, slipping and skating in the dark along the icy paths.

'I used to love this place,' Albie says as they walk under trees and down towards the lake. 'I'd done that thing in Europe— killed myself off. I didn't belong anywhere. Didn't know what I was going to do. The nuns gave me work, didn't ask too many questions, made me feel at home.'

The tone in which all this is said seems to put it firmly in the past.

'Joy . . .' Henry offers.

'A wonderful woman.' Albie says that, too, with a kind of

retrospective finality.

They stand staring at floodlit statuary above the lake. It belongs to the time when the grounds and buildings were the mansion estate of a rich railroad-owner. There are classical columns and a naked Graecian youth. On the far side of the water the nuns have added a statue of the Virgin. The Virgin and the boy stare at one another across the ice. 'For ever wilt thou love and she be fair,' Albie quotes.

As they head back towards the Joseph House he says, 'It's truth time, Henry.'

Henry feels a nervous tremor. 'Truth time?'

'My new poems.'

'They're good.' He says it too fast, too brightly, conscious that if he meant it sincerely it would have sounded different. Also that Albie will have registered a lack of conviction.

'How good, Henry?'

'I think I need time . . .'

'No, you've had time.'

'To assess . . .'

'You're leaving . . . When?'

'Next week.'

'And before that there's . . .'

'Yes, my visit to Princeton.'

'So let's have it, man. How do they compare?'

'Compare?'

'Compare, for god's sake. With the earlier stuff. With echt Ashtree.'

'You wrote them, Albie. They're good. What else could they be?'

Albie doesn't press it any further. There's no need. He knows the thumb has gone down on his new work. They walk on in silence. Back at the Joseph House Albie says, 'You were supposed to give it to me straight.'

Henry has gathered himself now. He has been brought all this way, it seems at Joy's expense, and he owes it to the poet to give him what he asks for.

'OK,' he says. 'They're nice publishable poems. Well turned, sharp observation, some brilliant images. But no, they're not as good. The range is lost, or the punch, or the guts, or something, I don't know what. The life. Something's missing, Albie.' He thinks Libby Valtraute is missing, but doesn't say it—says instead, 'I guess what's gone is the Snow Maiden, the White Goddess, the inspiration.'

Albie smiles at him. 'Attaboy,' he says. 'The truth. It wasn't so bad, was it?'

There seems no bitterness. For just a moment, and it's the only time since they first greeted one another, Albie looks at ease, as if a weight—of doubt maybe, or responsibility—has been lifted. He pats Henry's arm. 'Thanks for that, friend.'

He goes to his room and shuts the door. Henry waits for the sound of the typewriter. Or will it be a gunshot? After a time he hears the hissing of Albie's white-noise machine.

HENRY IS AWAY for most of a week. He spends three days at the Princeton University library, enjoying his new status as 'Professor', studying books and manuscripts. There are a couple of days in New York, looking at libraries, visiting museums and art galleries. When he gets back to Woodlake he notices changes in the Joseph House. Albie's room, looked at from the passageway, has become more orderly. The clutter of books and papers seems reduced. The old Olivetti is down on the floor, replaced on the desk by a laptop. There is a cardboard box piled high with discarded files.

The bench press and weights are gone from the front porch. In the living room the Algonquin shield and spear are missing from the walls; so are the Utamaro print and the wall-hanging representing a phone box.

'I was getting tired of those things,' Albie says. 'Time for some changes.'

He does no work at his desk, apart from more tidying and clearing of old papers. That night he borrows two video movies and they watch them. Both are about life in prison. In one the hero is found guilty of a double murder he didn't commit and locked up for life. Most of the movie takes place in the prison where he spends more than twenty years. It's a bleak story, but at last he escapes, gets right away to start a new life for himself in some idyllic place with a long white beach, blue water and palm trees.

The other, said to be based on a true story from the old San Quentin days, is much darker. A prisoner, guilty only of stealing five dollars from a post office, tries to escape and as a consequence spends three years in solitary confinement, only taken out at intervals to be beaten and tortured by a sadistic prison superintendent. Driven mad by this treatment, he murders the inmate who gave away his escape plan. His defence lawyer reveals the nature of the torture he has undergone and the prisoner is found not guilty. He is returned to San Quentin to serve out his other sentence and three weeks later is found murdered in his cell.

After four remorseless hours of prison life the interior of the Joseph House looks strange to Henry; to Albie too, it seems, because he says, 'Prisons aren't like that any more.' And then he adds, 'They're more like this place, I guess.'

He opens a bottle of whisky and insists on a nightcap. It's not something Henry likes or wants, but he accepts one drink, then a second, to be sociable. He sleeps soundly but wakes some time after 3 a.m. and heads for the bathroom. There is a light on in Albie's room and the door is open. The bed is unmade and the room wildly untidy, as if stirred by a gigantic spoon. The rolled-up towel has been pushed back by the opening of the door. The white-noise machine is issuing its insistent hissing static.

Henry tries to think of a rational explanation—that Albie has gone out for a walk, that he has gone to his office, that he has driven over to Joy's house. But the word that springs into his half-asleep brain is 'Escape'. He looks out to the street and sees that Albie's car is still parked there.

Next morning nothing has changed. Henry calls Joy but Albie is not at her house. He is due to give classes but he doesn't turn up for them.

TWO DAYS LATER HENRY is ready to leave Woodlake, and there is still no sign of Albie. He has vanished. Everyone is worried. The nuns are saying prayers for his safety. The police have been notified. There is talk of dragging the lake.

Joy comes to say goodbye. It is early March and a Jewish festival is taking place. All the children in the neighbourhood are in fancy dress. The men wear their usual black suits and hats, but some have put on red noses, funny face-masks, Batman cloaks. The women bustle about carrying cakes in boxes and string bags. The big old bent and broken station-wagons go up and down, filled with shouting children. An ambulance decorated with balloons and streamers is driven around the streets broadcasting music.

Henry's bag is packed and he's ready to leave. He stands with Joy looking out into the street, waiting for the Gofar Limo car that will take him to JFK. Another snow storm is coming through and he's worried he will miss his flight.

'But these storms delay the flights too,' Joy tells him. 'They have to plough the runways and de-ice the wings. If you're late, they will be too.' She gives his hand a reassuring squeeze.

'I'm sorry to be leaving you right now,' he says. 'I wish I could be of use.'

She shakes her head. 'He's gone.'

'You mean . . .'

'Not passed . . .'

'Passed?'

'Passed away. Not that, no. Just gone. I figure I won't see him again.'

'Did he say . . .'

'No. Nothing. Not a thing. There was no warning. Maybe that's why I feel so sure.'

Henry thinks of Libby Valtraute, the Snow Maiden, the Muse. Is she waiting for him at some secret location? But he says only, 'He must be mad.'

Joy looks up and, recognising what he means, smiles and shakes her head. 'If you mean to flatter . . .'

'I mean to praise.'

She pats his arm. 'Well thank you. But I'm not what he needs.'

Henry resists an urge to tell her that Albie Strong is Alban Ashtree. A few minutes later the car draws up in the street. Snow is falling fast now.

He hugs her and they say their goodbyes. He has his suitcase halfway across the porch and is handing it to the driver when she asks, from the door, whether Albie checked their lottery tickets.

Henry tells her he doesn't know, hasn't given it a thought. 'He didn't tell you?'

'I forgot to ask.'

'Well, I guess we didn't . . .'

She says, 'Mom tells me she heard someone say the winning ticket was sold in Brick.'

'Really. You sure?' Henry thinks about that. 'Seventeen million?'

'She says it was eighteen.'

'Wow—that's a lot of millions.'

They stare at one another, not speaking. Anything is possible is what they don't say.

All the way to New York the snow goes on falling, the ploughs along the highways and on the turnpike working to clear it and scatter salt. For a time it freezes as it falls and the driver can't go faster than twenty. The vehicles keep a respectful distance from one another. Now and then a car up ahead goes into a graceful slow-motion skid, sliding and circling away out of the traffic into trees or bank or ditches.

Then, quite suddenly, the surface seems to thaw. The snow falls and melts. They pick up speed. 'We'll make it,' the driver calls over his shoulder, as Henry takes his last look across the water at Manhattan's alphabet on a pale page of sky.

When they reach the terminal Henry pushes twenty dollars into the driver's hand. The driver thanks him. 'And I'm to give you this, Professor Bulov.'

It is a sheet of paper with a typewritten message, in capitals and with no signature:

> DEAR HENRY:
> ASHTREE IS DEAD, AND STAYS [REPEAT: STAYS]
> DEAD UNTIL FURTHER NOTICE—OR MAYBE
> FOR EVER.
>   HE KEEPS HIS FAME AND YOU KEEP THE
> FLAME—BEST FOR US BOTH, NO?
>   REPUTATION IS AN INVENTION. WE, YOU AND
> I, HAVE THE PATENT ON THIS ONE. LET'S KEEP
> IT THAT WAY.
>   ME, I GO AWAY, A LONG WAY, FOR A LITTLE
> R & R AND A LOT OF
>   QUIET COMFORT.
>   BEST OF LUCK FOR NEW PROMOTIONS—YOUR
> OWN, AND ALBAN ASHTREE'S.

By the time Henry has absorbed this and its implications the driver has taken his bag out and put it down on the sidewalk. 'When did he give you this?' Henry asks.

'I'm sorry, sir. I'm not free to talk about it.'

'It's from Albie. Albie Strong.'

The driver is getting back into his seat and closing the door.

Henry says through the window, 'You drove him up here in the night.'

The driver looks away. 'I'm sorry. Please excuse . . .' He presses a button and the window slides up between them. He puts the car into drive and slides gently away from Henry, forward, and out into the traffic.

HENRY—PROFESSOR BULOV—international expert on the poetry of Alban Ashtree, a scholar of modest means but rising reputation who always travels Economy, or as American Airlines calls it, Coach, finds at check-in that he has been upgraded to Business.

He asks how this has happened. The young woman at the counter is unsure. 'It's on the computer,' she says.

'Well thank you. Good news. I won't argue with the computer.'

She labels his bags and prints out boarding passes. He turns away, looking at the second boarding pass for his flight on from LAX, and turns back. 'This upgrade—it's not just for one leg?'

She checks. 'All the way to New Zealand, sir.'

He nods thanks—'Even better!'—and moves on towards Security.

About the author

C.K. (Karl) Stead is a distinguished, award-winning novelist, literary critic, poet, essayist and emeritus professor of English of the University of Auckland. He is the current New Zealand Poet Laureate, has won the Prime Minister's Award for Fiction, and is a Member of the Order of New Zealand, the highest honour possible in New Zealand.